Following Kate

a novel

Cheri J. Crane

Covenant Communications, Inc.

OTHER BOOKS BY CHERI J. CRANE

The Fine Print

Kate's Turn

Kate's Return

Forever Kate

Published by Covenant Communications, Inc.
American Fork, Utah

Printed in the United States of America
First Printing: August 1998

05 04 03 02 01 00 99 98   10 9 8 7 6 5 4 3 2

ISBN 1-57734-319-0

For Delena Stronks, Ruth Blackburn, and Jean Passey, three wonderful women who taught me more than they'll ever know.

Ackowledgments

Again, I must give credit where it is due. This book would not exist without the loving support of several people. To my wonderful husband, Kennon, and our three delightful, but *independent* sons, Kris, Derek, & Devin: "Thank you!" isn't enough. You alone see the hours spent in front of the computer. You have lived with *interesting* cuisine from the freezer, piles of unwashed laundry, and moments when patience wasn't a virtue. For that I will be eternally grateful.

Gratitude must also be expressed to an extraordinary cousin of mine who has kept me going through so much this past year. Words cannot express what is in my heart. Thank you for the encouragement, the laughter, and the early morning wake-up calls. RaNae, you are an "eternal *soeur.*"

Again, my hat is off to the Burdick bunch of Bennington for your willingness to proofread text in a limited time. Je'taime, Shelley!

And a special thanks to everyone at Covenant for your continued efforts and support.

CHAPTER 1

September

After losing the most recent verbal battle with her mother, Sabrina stomped downstairs to the family room to sulk. The feisty fourteen-year-old was grounded for getting home late—again—last night. She had gone to the movies with some of her friends and had lost track of the time. What was the big deal? Thirty minutes past the curfew set by her parents. Thirty lousy minutes!

Flopping down into a comfortable recliner, Sabrina glared at the paneled wall across the room. This was so unfair! She hadn't done anything wrong! It wasn't like she was out doing horrible things—like her sister, Kate, had done at her age. Unlike Kate, Sabrina had never touched alcohol, she had never tried smoking, and despite what everyone thought, she didn't run around with a wild crowd. Her friends were the girls she had grown up with, young women from their LDS branch. Fun girls who just wanted to have a good time. But, thanks to Kate, that was getting to be impossible.

This is all Kate's fault, Sabrina angrily seethed, flipping her long blonde hair over one shoulder, a recent spiral perm making it soft and wavy. Her sapphire eyes darkened, her beautiful facial features hardening as she pictured her older sister. Lately it seemed like she was always in the middle of a contentious scene because of Kate. If it wasn't with her mother, it was with her dad, or her Young Women leaders. The message was always the same. "Learn from what Kate went through at her age. Avoid her mistakes." Glowering now at a picture of Kate, Sabrina was tempted to knock it off the wall. "What are you smiling at?" she angrily demanded, rising to her feet. "What's your problem?" the silent picture seemed to taunt, further spoiling her mood.

Turning her back to the exhibit of family pictures hanging on the wall, Sabrina focused on the rock fireplace instead. Her blue eyes settled on another disturbing picture, one of Kate and her husband, Mike Jeffries. Sabrina crossed the room, took the picture off the mantle, and glared at it. The photograph was of her sister and brother-in-law in a forest setting near their hometown of Bozeman, Montana. It was a copy of the original that had been taken two years ago for their wedding invitations. Disgusted, Sabrina studied the picture. Auburn tresses cascaded down Kate's back. Kate's eyes were the same color as their mother's, emerald green. Annoyed by the ecstatic look on her sister's face, Sabrina glanced at Mike. His thick brown hair was closely cropped, his dark brown eyes sparkling with mischief. As everyone had been quick to point out at their reception, they made a handsome couple. "They'll have such beautiful children," was the general consensus. Sabrina smirked. So far, Kate and Mike had failed to produce any offspring, a cause of concern for most of the family. Sabrina didn't care. So what if there weren't any little Mikes or Kates running around? She didn't think she could handle it if there were.

As Sabrina stared at the picture in her hands, scenes from Kate's reception came to mind. That was where most of the trouble had started. Kate had asked her to be a bridesmaid, and in the beginning, Sabrina had been delighted. It had meant a fancy new dress, a chance to be in the spotlight, and an opportunity to show everyone that she was just as pretty as her older sister. Her excitement had gradually soured as the evening had progressed. Instead of receiving the expected compliments, she had been deluged with well-meaning advice.

"Oh, Sabrina, look how happy Kate is," most had crooned. "She made it. She was married in the temple. Just like you can be someday." The night had been downhill from there as most people had continuously challenged her to learn from her older sister. One exception had been Aunt Paige. Instead of comparing her to Kate, the petite, blonde woman had made it a point to compliment Sabrina on how gorgeous she looked in her new pastel blue dress. Hoping that had meant things were turning around, Sabrina had then been inundated with more unwanted advice from neighbors, family, and members of their LDS branch as people passed through the reception line. By the end of the evening, she had been ready to scream.

Things weren't much better now. Her blue eyes glittering, Sabrina slammed the picture down hard on the mantle. "I am not you!" she exclaimed, incensed by the critical comparisons she continuously endured. "Does anyone realize that?!" she demanded, pointing an accusing finger at Kate's smiling face. Constantly fearing the worst, her parents panicked over everything Sabrina did. As a result, she had heard the Kate stories once too often. "Kate made a lot of bad choices when she was your age," their mother stated every chance she got. "She did find her way back, but she was lucky. Some people never do."

"Kate suffered so much," Sister Blanchard had added to the chorus. Kate's former Laurel leader, Lori Blanchard, was now Sabrina's Mia Maid leader in their LDS branch. "Please be careful, Sabrina. The decisions you're making now can affect the rest of your life," Sister Blanchard advised too frequently.

"Like I don't know that!" Sabrina now exclaimed. "I don't need things spelled out for me. I'm not Kate!" She hated how everything she did or said was scrutinized. The pressure to measure up seemed to increase with each passing day.

Tyler had had it easy. As the only boy in the family, there had been no set pattern for her older brother to follow or avoid. He had sailed through high school without much trouble at all. There had been an occasional argument with their parents, but for the most part, Tyler had been the golden child of the family. Elder Tyler Erickson, who was now serving a mission in California.

Not for the first time in her life, Sabrina wished she hadn't been blessed with the honor of being the youngest. "I hate you, Kate," she exclaimed, knocking the framed picture of her sister and Mike to the carpeted floor. "I hate what you've done to my life!" Throwing herself onto the sofa, she began to shed tears no one would ever see.

CHAPTER 2

October

Slowly rising from the chair behind her wooden desk, Kate stretched. It had been an extremely long day. Anticipating the holiday weekend ahead, her high school students had been restless, most of them unable to absorb the historical facts she had tried to teach them that day. It had been the same in the drama class she had been pressured by the superintendent to teach this year. She enjoyed the class most of the time, but today had been an exception. As they had rehearsed the short scenes Kate had assigned last week, the students had hammed things up, adding a ghoulish touch here and there, indicating that Kate would not get anything of a serious nature out of them that day.

Smiling as she recalled some of the witty ad-libs that had been shared that afternoon, Kate crossed the creaky wooden floor of her classroom to gaze out an open window. She was certain the unseasonably warm October day had added to the rambunctious spirit that had prevailed. If this kept up, the local spooks would be out in force tomorrow night as Halloween descended on this small Idaho town.

Still smiling, Kate returned the wave of one of her students, Bev Henderson, and briefly wondered how Bev would celebrate Halloween. Knowing what she did about the junior, Kate guessed the sixteen-year-old had planned a party. Beautiful, intelligent, and fun-loving, Bev didn't lack for friends. Most of the time she chose to hang out with another junior student, a girl named Karen Beyer, a quiet young woman who tended to keep to herself.

"I don't know about you, but I'm ready to get out of this place," a cheery voice called out.

Kate turned, grinning at Doris Kelsey. Short and slightly overweight, the English teacher was one of the most popular faculty members at Blaketown High. The students loved her quick wit and entertaining style. Her forty-nine years made her twice Kate's age, but Doris had become one of Kate's closest friends, taking it upon herself to ease what was usually the most difficult time for a new teacher—the first year out of college.

Kate had grown to appreciate the wisdom offered by this warm-hearted woman. Doris had explained several subtle traditions prevailing at Blaketown High that would spare Kate from future conflicts with their principal, Miss Cleo Partridge. Kate had been hired by an enthusiastic superintendent who had been impressed with her college record; however, his excitement hadn't been shared by the high school principal. Still smarting over her sister-in-law's rejection for the same position, Cleo had welcomed Kate with a cold smile, letting Kate know from the beginning that she already had one strike against her.

After Kate and Mike had graduated from Brigham Young University the previous spring, they had learned about an opening with the Forest Service office in Blaketown, Idaho. Mike had just completed his bachelor's degree in Wildlife and Range Resources with plans to work for the U.S. Forest Service somewhere in the Intermountain West. This southeastern corner of Idaho had beckoned. Kate and Mike had spent a few days checking out the location and were impressed by the tall mountains and thick, green forests that surrounded this small, pristine community. When Mike was hired for the job, he and Kate were thrilled, unlike their parents who had wanted them to move closer to home, near Bozeman, Montana.

"This is paradise," Mike had exclaimed the day he had first carried Kate over the threshold of their new residence. The cramped duplex was hardly the home of their dreams, but the rent fit their conservative budget. Most houses available for sale in that area were out of their price range. As a result, they had settled on renting half of a colorful duplex. They were convinced their landlord had purchased the fluorescent yellow paint that adorned the outside of their new home for a good price and tried to make the best of it. It had become a game, inventing reasons why fluorescent yellow was a *fun* color; it was so bright, sunny, and cheerful. Sunglasses helped them tolerate the glare whenever they worked in the small yard surrounding the duplex, protecting them from the sun's ultra-violet rays, and from the interesting looks cast their way when people drove by.

When Mike and Kate had first considered moving to Blaketown, they wondered if Kate would be able to find a job teaching in the same area. She had contacted the superintendent of the local school district and discovered there was an opening for a high school history teacher in the small town. Excited by the news, Kate had met with a committee for an interview. This delegation had consisted of the superintendent—a greying man with a warm sense of humor; the high school principal—Miss Cleo Partridge, a middle-aged woman Kate now referred to as "the ice queen"; the high school counselor—a man in his thirties who doubled as the football coach; and a fun-loving English teacher who had been there longer than most—Doris Kelsey. Doris and the superintendent had given Kate high marks; the counselor and principal hadn't been as kind, stressing her inexperience and *youthful* appearance, which they felt would be a distraction for some of the students.

In the end, the superintendent had made the tie-breaking decision, concluding that Kate was the best choice for teaching history to the Blaketown high school students. Pleased with her high grade point average in college, he had contacted the two teachers who had supervised Kate's student teaching. Both had given Kate enthusiastic referrals.

When the superintendent had called Kate to welcome her to the Blaketown faculty, she had asked him about the possibility of teaching a computer class.

"History was my major but I minored in computer science," she had explained.

"We already have a qualified computer teacher but we're hoping you won't mind taking the drama class instead," he had replied. "The retiring teacher taught both courses—history and drama."

Kate had admitted she didn't feel competent to teach drama. She had never been one to participate in plays or productions of that nature. But the superintendent had assured her she would be perfect for the class.

"With your enthusiasm and the creativity I saw in your portfolio, you'll do just fine," he had encouraged. Hoping she could live up to his expectations, Kate had accepted his proposal. Now here she was, two months into the first trimester, still trying to get her bearings as she coped with her chosen career.

She was convinced Mike had had it easier. Her husband had settled with relative ease into his new role as manager of the local Forest Service office. Charmed by his dark good looks and fun sense of humor, his staff eventually gave up their original intent to treat him with indifference. Resentment had circulated throughout the office the first week after Mike's appointment. Who did this young newcomer think he was, invading a well-established district, filling the vacancy a native ranger had aspired to after their former manager had transferred to Wyoming?! To their surprise, they learned Mike was well-trained and a natural at handling the pressure that went with his position. He had earned their respect by working alongside of them whenever there was a less-than-pleasant job to take care of.

Late in the summer, during the fire that had claimed several acres in the hills above Blaketown, Mike had proven to be a much-needed asset. Keeping a cool head, he had quickly organized emergency teams, synchronizing fire-fighting units with a skill that contradicted his age. He later explained that he had helped with a similar situation in Star Valley, Wyoming, when he had worked one summer for the local Forest Service in that area.

Mike was now an accepted part of the team that made up the Blaketown office. Unfortunately, Kate was still struggling with that challenge at the high school. But with the helpful guidance of people like Doris Kelsey, she felt confident she would eventually get the hang of this new phase in her life.

"Your contract may state that the teacher in-service meetings are optional, but your attendance is *vital* if you want to stay on Cleo's good side," Doris had cautioned at the beginning of the year. "Also, our principal has been known to make surprise classroom visits. She especially likes to drop in unannounced on new teachers. Don't let her shake your confidence. Your best bet is to pretend she's not there."

"How?" Kate had asked incredulously.

Doris had grinned. "It isn't easy. Even when that woman sits down, she towers over most of the students. But it can be done. Learn to block her out, or handle her the way I do."

"What do you do?"

"I make quite a production out of her appearance," Doris said, laughing. "I give her a warm welcome—ask questions like 'Is there anything I can do to make your sojourn more congenial?' Cleo gets flustered, trying to figure out what I said. It focuses unwanted attention on her—my students find themselves watching her every move." The English teacher's eyes had twinkled with mischief. "Cleo hates it if she appears less than supremely composed, which is probably why she doesn't drop in on me more often."

"That woman scares me," Kate admitted. "I don't know how I'll deal with her visits."

"You'll do just fine," Doris had encouraged her.

Kate had forced a smile. "Anything else I should know?"

"The teacher's lounge is a misnomer."

"A what?" Kate had asked, confused.

"A misnomer—it's inappropriately named," Doris had explained. "Because of our cramped office space, it houses the copy machine, the first-aid supplies, and anything else Cleo can stuff in there. You're better off to eat your lunch in your classroom or at one of the local drive-ins."

"What about the cafeteria?"

Doris cringed. "Only if you don't value your sanity, or if you happen to pull teacher duty, which I noticed Cleo assigned you this month." Amused by Cleo's shallow attempts to bully Blaketown's newest faculty member, Doris had laughed. "Don't worry, eventually Cleo will latch onto something or someone else to be all fired-up about. She's a sleeping volcano, full of hot steam, but major eruptions are very rare."

Kate had grinned, enjoying the colorful analogy. Doris had a flair for painting vivid mental images. It was one of her gifts, something her students benefitted from as she instilled in most a love for the world of literature and writing.

"How about a hot fudge sundae run?" Doris now invited, something these two women enjoyed on a regular basis at one of the local drive-ins. It was a way to unwind after a hectic day, a chance to compare notes as they continued their valiant battle to influence young lives in what they hoped was a positive way. "I think we need some bolstering before tomorrow night descends."

Nodding in agreement, Kate hurried to her desk to retrieve her purse and jacket.

"Let the games begin," Doris dramatically exclaimed.

CHAPTER 3

Miles away in Bozeman, Montana, the *games* were already beginning as Sabrina and her friends excitedly hid behind a group of parked cars near the high school, cradling the water balloons they had painstakingly filled earlier that day. Impatiently they waited until the school bell finally rang, then they plastered everyone who had the misfortune of walking in their direction. All too soon, a couple of determined-looking teachers made their way toward the group of giggling freshmen girls. Realizing they had been reported, Sabrina and her friends scattered, unaware that other teachers had moved in behind them. Three of the five girls escaped through the football field. Making a wrong turn in the excitement of the chase, the other two—Sabrina Erickson and Tracie Monroe—found themselves pinned against a brick wall.

"All right you two, that's enough!" Coach Brandt hollered, sensing these young women were tempted to bolt again. Out of breath, the burly football coach was also out of patience. Sabrina and Tracie bore the brunt of his ire as he escorted them back to the school and into the principal's office. He quickly explained what had taken place and left them to the judgment of Mr. Dryer, a man who was well-rehearsed in stifling teenage mischief at Bozeman High School. With enrollment just slightly over 1600 students, there were days when the maintenance of student discipline took more than its fair share of valuable time.

"Okay," the principal said tiredly a few minutes later when the two friends refused to answer his questions. "We know there were others involved, but you seem determined to protect them." He glanced from one girl to the other. "Does it occur to either of you that they aren't being very good friends, letting you two take the blame for this? Where are they? Probably at home, laughing at the two of you." When this failed to jar a response, he tried a different approach. "We have witnesses, and we know who the other members of your gang are. We'll call their parents and arrange a meeting."

Sabrina flinched. He was referring to her group of friends as a gang? This was ridiculous! She could imagine her mother's reaction to that phrase. Silently groaning, she wondered again why she hadn't headed through the football field.

"Were you aware that you had pelted the wife of our superintendent with one of your water-filled missiles?" Mr. Dryer continued, running a hand over his balding head. "You managed to hit her in the side of her head. And she had just had her hair done," he said, repeating what Mrs. Klepper had angrily exclaimed a few minutes earlier. It was all Mr. Dryer could do to keep a straight face. He really didn't care much for the temperamental woman, but an infraction had been committed, and he had little choice but to make an example out of these two. Respect for authority had to be emphasized. If he let this minor incident pass without retribution, it would escalate into more serious offenses.

Sabrina stole a glance at Tracie, a petite, dark-haired girl. Both were amused that at least one of their balloons had reached their intended target. Mrs. Klepper was extremely unpopular with the youth in their community. She was always harping about rules and regulations that needed to be enforced, leading the battle to promote a policy of school uniforms, a notion most of the local teenagers despised.

"Do either of you have anything to say about this matter?" Mr. Dryer pressed. He glanced at Tracie, a young woman who was from a large LDS family. He had enjoyed getting to know her two older brothers; both had been exceptional athletes. The oldest girl in her family, Tracie had impressed him with the way she helped her mother with the younger children during her brothers' games. It bothered him that Tracie wouldn't look at him. Her grades had been disappointing this term. He had been dismayed to hear an occasional obscenity spring from her lips in the hall, and had been shocked by the way she had mercilessly teased some of the shyer students. He sensed this attractive young woman was heading for trouble and wanted to do something to ease her back on the straight and narrow.

His gaze shifted to Sabrina. This young woman promised to be as lovely as her older sister, Kate. After today, he wondered if she was destined to follow in her sister's wayward footsteps.

"You girls leave me little choice," he finally sighed. "I'll have to call your parents and explain what happened today, beginning with how you five girls cut class last hour." He gave Sabrina and Tracie a meaningful look. Tracie rolled her eyes, but Sabrina turned considerably paler. Taking that as a sign of remorse, he continued, "While we're waiting for them to appear, I'll escort you two young ladies out front where you will begin cleaning up the mess you made. I don't want to see pieces of balloon anywhere on this campus. Not only is it unsightly, but I'm sure you've heard of the effect they can have on the birds that might consume them. After that, we'll see what else we can have you two do around here to atone for your misdeed this afternoon."

Sabrina silently groaned. Why had she agreed to this prank? It had all seemed like harmless fun in the beginning. A simple Halloween caper, something that would no doubt ruin the weekend ahead.

* * *

" . . . imagine my reaction when I'm then informed that my daughter hit the superintendent's wife in the head with a water balloon!" Sue Erickson fumed, glancing away from the road to glare at Sabrina. Enraged as her daughter continued to sullenly ignore her, Sue returned her focus to the traffic ahead, barely hitting her brakes in time to avoid plowing into the car ahead of her. "Why some people think it's beneath them to signal I'll never know!" she exploded.

"They did signal. You just didn't notice," Sabrina quietly muttered, still refusing to look at her mother.

Taking a deep breath, Sue angrily struggled for control. It wouldn't do to fully unleash her Irish temper on her youngest daughter. "Remember Kate," she silently reminded herself. "Yelling at Kate pushed her further away." In heavy silence, she drove them to their newly remodeled home.

This past year she and her husband, Greg, had decided to invest in vinyl siding and new doors. The grey color of the siding blended nicely with the doors they had selected, the etched glass windows in a half-moon shape adding an elegant touch to the off-grey wood. As Sue approached their house, she realized with a start that the refuge from the world she had tried so hard to establish for her family had once again become a battlefield.

Sighing heavily, Sue drove the Dodge Durango, Greg's newest toy, into the garage. He had been so excited to buy the bright blue sport utility vehicle, insisting that it was the perfect four-wheel drive outfit for their wintry climate. Shutting off the engine, Sue silently prayed for guidance concerning the volatile climate that now existed in their home. "Sabrina," she quietly began.

"Let me guess . . . ," Sabrina interrupted her. "I'm grounded! No Halloween celebrations for me . . . I might turn out just like Kate!" Sabrina angrily sputtered, exiting the Durango. She slammed the car door for emphasis and stomped inside the house.

"Why me?" Sue questioned, resting her head against the steering wheel. Slowly sitting up, she leaned against the cushioned seat, reluctant to face the battle that waited for her inside the house. It would probably be a good idea if she and Sabrina both cooled down before discussing this matter further, she decided as she released the seatbelt. Greg was right; this was the softest seat in the house. She reached for a lever and tipped the bucket seat back. Gradually she relaxed, closing her eyes as she tried to think of a way to reason with her youngest daughter.

"Why do my daughters have to be so feisty?!" she softly murmured a few minutes later.

"Because they take after you, dear."

Blinking, Sue sat up. Where had that comment come from? No one else was in the garage. Somewhat alarmed, she glanced around.

"Remember the arguments you used to have with your own sainted mother?" a decidedly Irish accent questioned.

Sue lifted an eyebrow. There was still no one in sight. Slipping out of the Durango, she nervously started toward the house.

"Susan Mahoney Erickson, I would like a word with you."

Freezing in place, Sue closed her eyes. "It's finally happened. I've snapped," she said, jumping when she felt a light tap on her shoulder.

Reluctantly turning around, she found herself face to face with her third great-grandmother, Colleen Mahoney. Sue's mouth fell open in stunned surprise as she gaped at the woman in the brilliant white gown who seemed to float above the cement floor in the garage.

"Come now, dear, there's no need for that," Colleen advised, gently pushing Sue's chin up until her mouth was closed. "There, that's better."

"But . . . ," Sue stammered.

"We don't have time for this. I've got a thing or two to say to you, and then I'll have to go. There's so much work to do. So little time," Colleen said, smiling brightly. "I'm here with you now because of your daughter."

"But Kate is doing fine," Sue countered. In the past, Colleen had taken a vested interest in her namesake, Kate, formally known as Katherine Colleen Erickson. Colleen had been part of the dream Kate had experienced while in a coma several years before. That dream had been the catalyst behind Kate's dramatic change of heart, something Sue would always be grateful for. "Sabrina is the one who—"

"I know, my dear," the smiling woman interrupted her. "Do you think Katie is the only one I care about? I love her dearly, as I do all of you. You're all part of my posterity, including that youngest daughter of yours. The fire in Sabrina's eyes reminds me of my Molly years ago."

"Molly?" Sue stammered, remembering what they had learned about Colleen's willful daughter. Molly had suffered through several harrowing trials during her life. After Kate had recovered from the coma, she had found a journal kept by this pioneer ancestor. The entire family had been captivated by Molly's story, which included her eventual return to the Church. Kate especially had been affected by what Molly had endured, which had helped Kate turn away from temptations that would have led her down a similar path.

"Molly," Colleen firmly replied. "Now, Susan, I'm here to help you, to tell you that if you aren't careful, your beloved daughter Sabrina will turn away from everything she should hold dear to her heart, including you."

"You're here because of Sabrina?" Sue repeated.

"Aye. Were you aware Sabrina has cried herself to sleep more nights than she hasn't lately?!"

Sue's eyes widened. She didn't think Sabrina was capable of tears; the hardened look on her daughter's face was too reminiscent of Kate at that same age.

"She's struggling to find her own way. Give her that chance."

"We're trying to help her . . . we want her to avoid what Kate went through."

Colleen smiled sadly. "As with most parents, you wish to pave the road your daughter will follow in this mortal life, but it must be up to her to choose. We all fought for that right before any of us ever came to this earth."

"But—"

"You've taught Sabrina the gospel. Step back now and let her learn for herself what is right. It is the hardest task required of any parent, but it's what our Father in Heaven has lovingly done with all of us." Colleen smiled warmly at her third great-granddaughter. "Lovingly guide, but never push. One thing more, if you persist in forcing Sabrina into Kate's mold, you will lose her, and the pain will be more than you can bear."

Crying out, Sue sat up. She was still inside the Durango. Realizing she must have fallen asleep, she tried to clear her head. After several minutes, she slipped out of the car. Troubled by the vivid dream, she paced around the garage. "Sabrina, I may regret this," she finally said, "but I'm going to give you some space . . . please be careful with how you use it," she tearfully pleaded. "I could never stand to lose you . . . not even for a little while." Giving herself a few minutes to regain her composure, she then made her way inside the house to fix dinner.

* * *

"Let me get this straight," Sabrina said, watching her mother's face for signs of deception. "Earlier this afternoon, I'm in more trouble than I can possibly imagine, grounded until I'm thirty, and even then you'll have to think about it if I want to go anywhere! Tonight, you want to be my friend?!"

Sue sighed. She had known this would be a difficult conversation. How could she take back the harsh things she had said? "Sabrina, I'll admit, I was furious with you. I'm not saying that's an excuse, but when your principal called—"

"I know. I was there, remember," Sabrina challenged.

Tempted to order Sabrina back to her room, Sue gathered her courage and continued with what she knew she had to do. "I'm still not very happy with what you did, but now that I've had a chance to think things over—"

"You want to ground me until I'm forty!" Sabrina interrupted, still upset over the party she wouldn't be attending tomorrow night. Everyone would be there, including all of her friends. Before dinner, Tracie had called to say she'd talked her parents into letting her go. They had agreed after Tracie had assured them she had tried very hard to talk Sabrina and those other girls out of throwing those *horrid* water balloons. What had happened wasn't *her* fault. Tracie had been *falsely* accused because of her friends' actions. As usual, Tracie's parents had believed her. Convinced that Tracie would never intentionally do anything wrong, they had instructed her to make new friends or to preach repentance to the girls she ran around with.

"Honey, you have to know that the main reason we have rules and enforce consequences is because we love you," Sue said, gazing intently at her daughter.

"Yeah, right!" Sabrina quietly muttered.

"What was that?"

"Nothing," Sabrina replied, a pained look on her face. "Is this going to take much longer?"

Certain her blood pressure was on its way up, Sue wordlessly led Sabrina down the stairs to the family room. She pointed to the wall decorated with family portraits. "When you look at these, what do you see?" she asked, trying a different approach.

"Pictures," Sabrina indifferently responded. She knew what her mother was after and wasn't about to give her that satisfaction.

"And who's in the pictures?" Sue bravely persevered.

"The *family*," Sabrina said in a mocking tone.

"Are you in any of those pictures?"

Glancing at her mother, Sabrina then focused on the pictures. "Yeah."

"Are you part of this family?"

Here we go again, Sabrina thought to herself. *Lecture number 104.*

Because I am a member of this family I must cherish certain rules and standards . . .

"Are you?" Sue pressed. "Are you a member of this family?"

"Yeah," Sabrina repeated, digging the big toe of her right foot into the plush grey carpet.

"Are you sure?"

Surprised by the question, Sabrina looked up at her mother. Just what was she getting at this time? "What do you mean?" she finally asked.

"Are you sure you're a member of this family?"

Sabrina blinked. "Yeah . . . unless . . ." Her blue eyes widened. "Are you telling me I was adopted? That would explain a lot!"

"No," Sue said, giving Sabrina a disgusted look. "I have the stretch marks to prove you weren't."

"I don't even want to go there," Sabrina said, pulling a face.

Sue smiled wistfully. "You were such a beautiful baby," she said, recalling a simpler time in her daughter's life.

"That's part of the problem. Everyone still thinks of me as the baby! You've all hovered over me my entire life," Sabrina said, defiantly folding her arms. "I'm tired of it."

"I know," Sue admitted. "And I'm sorry about that. We just wanted to protect you . . ."

"From what?"

"From harmful people, situations . . ." Sue sighed. "Maybe we went overboard, but we were trying to help you. Sabrina, you *are* an important part of this family. That's something I hope you'll always realize." It hurt to see the belligerent look on the young woman's face. Grandma Colleen had been right—they were losing this daughter. "We're all a part of an eternal family, right?"

Sabrina reluctantly nodded. This again. The *forever family* lecture. *If one person came up missing when this life was over, it would be a tragedy,* stuff like that. She'd heard it all before. Right now, she wasn't so sure she wanted to be a permanent part of this particular family.

"Before we came to this earth, we all fought for the right to have free agency. Our Father in Heaven knew that the only way we would truly learn and grow is through making our own choices. Satan wanted to force us to be righteous."

That sounds familiar, Sabrina silently accused.

"We fought against Satan and his followers for the right to choose our own way." Sue moved to the couch and motioned for Sabrina to sit beside her.

I can't take much more of this, Sabrina silently screamed as she forced herself to sit beside her mother. *If she hugs me, I'll hurl!*

Disturbed by her daughter's continued aloofness, Sue prayed to find a way to help Sabrina understand the importance of what she was saying. "Remember a few years ago, when Jace Sloan offered you a ride home."

Oh, great, this again, Sabrina mentally grumbled. "Mom, I was eight years old," she said out loud.

"Exactly, and according to what our church believes, old enough to determine right from wrong. That day you *chose* to ride in Jace's van."

"My bike tire was flat. What else was I supposed to do? It was too far to walk."

"The point I'm trying to make is, you had been warned about what kind of man he was. Kate had just told you that he was selling drugs to some of the local kids. Jace took you that day to scare us into being quiet about what he was doing."

"I know, Mom. I know *all* of this. Why do we have to keep going over it? You never let go of anything. You just keep hitting me over the head with it!" She stood up, glowering down at her mother. *I swear if you start in with one of Kate's stories, I really will hurl,* she silently fumed.

"Sit down!" Sue said firmly. "You're not going anywhere until we settle this."

Taking a deep breath, Sabrina sat down and tried to brace herself for what she thought was coming.

"Hear me out. Then if you have complaints, we'll discuss them, but only if you're ready to start acting like an adult. You claim you're growing up. Prove it!"

Aggravated by that comment, Sabrina managed to remain silent.

"That's better. Now, where were we . . . oh, yes, you had accepted a ride from Jace Sloan. Do you realize how lucky we were that you weren't hurt that day?" Sue studied her daughter's face, but could see this wasn't having the effect she had hoped. "You made a choice that placed you in danger. You'll never know what the rest of us went through because of it. I was so relieved when the police brought you safely home. I know our prayers were answered that day." Sue paused, remembering the intense emotions of that turbulent time. "We all have to be careful about the choices we make in this life. Each one can touch us in a positive or negative way—and most of our decisions also affect the people around us, especially loved ones. Always remember that."

Sabrina glared at her mother stubbornly. "Yeah, well, remember this, Jace was one of Kate's former friends. That nightmare took place because of *her!* I was eight years old, but I can remember everything about that day. I was terrified, thinking I might never get to come home again and it was all Kate's fault! Terrible things have happened in my life because of her!"

Startled by these accusations, Sue could now see the resentment that had been building. Resentment she had been unaware of until this moment. "Sabrina, you know that's not true. Kate loves you so much. She would never do anything to hurt you."

"Oh really?" Sabrina demanded, rising once again, to pace the floor in the family room. "Every time I turn around, it's 'Sabrina, don't do that, you're acting just like Kate.' 'Don't be like Kate!'" She whirled around to glare at her mother. "I am so sick of hearing about Kate I could scream!"

"Where is all of this coming from?" Sue asked.

"Serious?" Sabrina asked. "You don't know?! How about this afternoon? What was one of the first things you said to me when you came storming into the school?"

Sue stared helplessly at her hands. Sabrina was right. She had thrown Kate in her face.

"'Sabrina Erickson! How could you?! Didn't I tell you about the time Kate threw eggs at cars on the last day of school? Don't you ever hear anything I say?'" Sabrina tearfully mimicked. "It's always the same. I do one little thing wrong, then I get to hear about Kate for hours on end. Kate did this and Kate did that. I can't take it anymore!" The dam had burst. Things Sabrina had kept inside for much too long came spilling out, revealing the depth of her misery. When she finally finished, Sabrina and Sue were both in tears.

"Honey, I'm sorry. I didn't realize . . . what can I do to make this better?"

Sabrina thoughtfully considered the question.

"I know we've been a little overprotective," Sue tried to explain.

"A little?" Sabrina incredulously asked. "That's like saying the Titanic had a little hole in its side."

Sue lifted an eyebrow. Had Sabrina gone to see that movie despite what she and Greg had decreed? It was a rule in their house, absolutely no PG-13 movies. She wanted to ask Sabrina about it, but sensed this would be a bad time. They were finally attaining a fragile peace. It had to be enhanced, not undermined.

"Mom, start trusting me. Don't assume I'm always going to mess up."

"I'll try, but you need to realize that trust has to be earned."

"Give me that chance," Sabrina petitioned. "Please?"

Deciding this would be a good time for a little positive reinforcement, Sue nodded. She stood up and reached for a hug.

Sabrina endured her mother's embrace for a few seconds, then eagerly pulled back. Wiping at her eyes, she smiled for the first time that day. "Can I go to the Halloween party tomorrow night?"

Sue stared at her daughter.

"Let me prove I can make good choices," Sabrina hurried on, hoping to sway her mother.

"But—"

"I know I messed up today and I'm sorry. I'll never do anything like that again, I promise," Sabrina pleaded. "Please, Mom. Do you trust me . . . at all?"

Sue slowly nodded, suddenly feeling trapped.

"This party will be so much fun, and we won't do anything you wouldn't approve of, I promise. My friends will all be there," she hopefully added.

Choking back the response of *"The same friends who helped you get into trouble this afternoon?"* Sue reluctantly gave her consent. Praying she wouldn't regret this decision, she followed her excited teen upstairs.

CHAPTER 4

The next night, Halloween antics were rampant everywhere, including Blaketown, Idaho.

"Twick or tweat," a cute toddler witch said, glancing hopefully at Kate, who was also dressed up for the evening. "You're a big witch," the child commented.

Laughing, Kate nodded. She enjoyed seeing the sparkle of delight in the eyes of these little children as they came to collect their Halloween booty. Some of her students had also come by to show off their costumes before heading to various parties. Bev Henderson and Karen Beyer had stopped earlier, dressed as flower children from the sixties. The two girls teased Kate that she needed to dress up for Halloween, too.

"But I have," Kate had replied, confused.

"You're a witch every day," Bev had teased, laughing.

"Thanks a lot," Kate had replied. "You two had better get out of here before I take after you on my broom."

"Now we're scared," Bev had replied. The two girls had jumped down off the porch. "Happy Halloween," they had sung out, racing to their car.

"Remember I gave you each a treat. That means no tricks," Kate had hollered after them.

"We'll see," Karen had returned.

"I said, twick or tweat," the young girl repeated who was standing in front of Kate now.

Grabbing a large glass bowl of candy, Kate held it out. "Pick a treat," she said as the young girl shyly reached into the bowl. After

Kate had closed the door, Mike walked out of the bathroom, rubbing a towel over his wet head. He had felt particularly grimy that day after work and decided to shower before dressing up for the evening. He had plans to scare some of the teenagers who were up to mischief that night. Kate had tried to talk him out of it, but being a kid at heart himself, Mike was looking forward to it.

"How's it goin'?" he asked, grinning at Kate.

"Pretty good," she replied. "I'm glad I picked up that extra bag of candy this afternoon, though," she added. "At this rate, we'll need it." As if to emphasize that point, the doorbell rang. Reaching for the bowl of candy, Kate opened the door as Mike hurriedly ducked out of sight.

* * *

Grinning with excitement, Sabrina pushed the doorbell again. Finally a morbid-looking scarecrow opened the door. "Good costume, Wes," she guessed, trying to be heard above the loud music playing in the background.

"How did you know it was me?" Wes hollered in return, disappointed.

"Who else is that tall and skinny?" she teased.

Wes' eyes appreciatively took in Sabrina's costume. She had heeded her mother's advice to steer away from the revealing Elvira ensemble she had originally selected, choosing comely princess attire instead. Offering a low whistle, Wes stood back, inviting her in.

Stepping inside, Sabrina looked over the crowd that had gathered at Sindi's house. She stared as her friend Tracie approached her.

"Princess Sabrina has arrived," Tracie announced, looking pointedly at Sabrina's dress. "*Nice* costume. Did your mommy pick it out?"

"She helped," Sabrina said, slightly annoyed by Tracie's comments. She had enjoyed Wes' reaction and didn't care for Tracie's response. Seeing the low-cut, tight-fitting witch costume Tracie wore, Sabrina wondered how her friend had managed to sneak out of her house wearing it.

"Girlfriend, you need a make-over," Tracie suggested, dragging Sabrina across the crowded living room.

"Sabrina, what have you done to yourself?" Dawn Hubert exclaimed, raising her voice in order to be heard above the eerie strains blaring from a stereo across the room. "You look like something out of Disneyland!" The tall brunette stood up, stretching, well aware of the admiring glances being cast her way by some of the boys in the room. She had elected to come as Cat-Woman, from the popular *Batman* movie series, and was enjoying the attention her costume inspired.

Tracie grinned at Dawn. "Think we can help Tinkerbell adjust her costume?"

Dawn nodded gleefully as Sabrina shook her head in protest. "Let's get Marsha and Sindi to help," she said, glancing around the living room for their other friends. "Marsha, come over here," she beckoned.

A slender redhead decked out as a dance hall girl from the 1800s turned to face her friends.

"Yeah, you," Dawn hollered.

Marsha turned and whispered something to the boy who had been hovering nearby, then walked over to her friends.

Dawn continued to look around the room until she spotted a blonde pirate sporting tight shorts and a halter top. "Hey Sindi," Dawn called, "do you know where your mom keeps her good scissors?"

Adjusting her eyepatch for better vision, Sindi strutted happily across the room. So far this party had been a total success. In addition to her closest friends and a handful of other girls, several attractive boys had come to have a good time. The best part—it was unchaperoned. Sindi's parents had gone out of town for the weekend, leaving Sindi on her own. An only child, she had assured her parents she would be fine.

"I'll invite some friends over to watch videos," she had told her mother, promising to stay out of trouble. True to her word, her friends were here, and one of the Halloween movies her mother had dutifully rented was playing in the VCR. No one was watching, but everyone seemed to be enjoying themselves. Some were dancing to the loud music blasting away on her parents' new stereo. Others were devouring the pizzas she had ordered. One couple had wandered into the utility room for some privacy. As Sindi glanced around, she grinned with delight. She was convinced this party would be discussed for weeks at school.

"You need some scissors?" she asked, finally making her way to where her four friends were standing.

"You're not cutting this costume," Sabrina said, pulling away from Tracie. "We rented it. I have to return this."

"So?!" Tracie shrugged. "They'll probably thank you for the alterations. It'll become the most sought-after costume ever when we're finished with it." Giggling, Sabrina's friends pulled her out of the living room and into a bedroom down the hall.

* * *

Mike waited until he was certain one of the teenagers was carrying eggs. Then he jumped up, revved the motor of the chainsaw he had borrowed from one of his friends at the Forest Service office, and hollered at the top of his lungs. He laughed at the startled squeals as the small group of teenagers dropped everything and ran for their lives, Bev and Karen included.

"We'll be back," Bev muttered to her friend. Nodding in agreement, Karen raced her to the car they had been driving around in. There were other houses and cars to hit before the night was over. Eagerly they set off for their next destination, the house belonging to their high school principal.

"You are really sick," Kate scolded, coming out onto the front porch as Mike shut off the chainsaw. She gazed at the splattered eggs on the cement driveway. "That's attractive," she added.

"Thank you, my dear," Mike said. He lifted up the plastic hockey mask he had worn for this occasion and lowered the chainsaw.

"Not you, the driveway. Look at that mess."

"Better on the driveway than on my Chevy Blazer," Mike retorted. "Those eggs'll dissolve the paint."

Kate glanced at her husband's pride and joy, a black 1989 Chevy Blazer. The used four-wheel drive had been their first major purchase after getting settled in Blaketown although Kate still puttered around town in the car that had seen them through college, a red Dodge Neon. She had purchased it from her Aunt Paige after returning home from her mission a little over two years ago. After they'd moved to Blaketown, Mike had claimed he needed an outfit with *guts*, one that could take climbing up into the hills. When the Blazer had first shown up at Henderson's Chevrolet last September, Mike had been ecstatic, taking Kate to see it as soon as possible.

"It has four-wheel drive, a five-speed transmission—the engine was rebuilt last year. Look, the tires have most of their tread. It's exactly what I need," he had excitedly shared.

Kate had enjoyed teasing him about it, telling Mike he was acting like a little boy in a toy store. Bev Henderson had joined in on the fun, giving her father a bad time about taking advantage of Mike's excitement. Bev worked full time at her father's car lot during the summer, and three nights a week after school. She claimed it was a chance to spend quality time with her father, but her friends suspected it was another excuse she used to steer clear of her step-mother and half-brothers. Regardless, the young woman appeared to enjoy the sales world that was part of her father's life.

"Someone has to teach these kids a lesson about respecting other people's property," Mike now stated, drawing Kate back to the matter at hand.

"I don't think they meant any harm," Kate replied. "They're just out trying to have some fun. Take it easy on them, or we'll probably live to regret it."

"They won't dare come back around here tonight," Mike assured her.

"Maybe. But are you prepared to permanently stand guard?"

Mike stared at her.

"Think about it. They'll be out for revenge. I've seen these kids in action at school. Sooner or later they'll get even."

"They wouldn't dare!"

"Bet me and lose," Kate answered.

"You're ruining my fun," he complained. Then, certain he heard the pitter patter of mischievous feet, he ducked back behind the bushes and slid his mask into place.

"Promise you won't frighten anyone under the age of fourteen, or over the age of twenty," Kate pleaded.

"Deal. Now go back inside. You're scaring off the customers."

Rolling her eyes, Kate retreated inside the house.

* * *

"Well, what do you think?" Tracie asked, shoving Sabrina in front of a full-length mirror. Sabrina stared dismally at her reflection. She had succeeded in talking her friends out of cutting her costume, but knew her mother would disapprove of the way they had *enhanced* her appearance. They had ratted out Sabrina's hair to give her a wild appearance and slipped her dress off her shoulders to draw attention to her blossoming chest. Using some of her mother's makeup, Sindi had outdone herself, highlighting what she felt was Sabrina's best feature, her brilliant blue eyes.

"So . . . do you like it?" Tracie questioned again.

"I look like a slut," Sabrina finally retorted.

"All right!" her four friends giggled, giving each other a high five.

"C'mon, let's go see what everyone else is up to," Dawn suggested, opening the bedroom door.

"I can't go out there looking like this," Sabrina said, attempting to pull the dress back up onto her shoulders.

"Stop that," Tracie said, slapping Sabrina's hands away. "This is Halloween, remember. We're supposed to look bizarre—not cute."

"Tracie's right," Dawn agreed. "Now let's go have some fun." Together, the four girls led Sabrina out of the bedroom and down the hall toward the living room.

* * *

"I think that's the last of them," Kate sighed tiredly, sinking down on the gold-colored sofa they had purchased at a secondhand store during their college years.

"Really?" Mike replied, disappointed.

Kate nodded. "It's a good thing. We're almost out of candy." She glanced at her husband. "Aren't you tired yet?"

"Nope!" he said, grinning down at his wife. "In fact, I was thinking of taking my beautiful witch of a wife out for a Halloween treat."

"This time of night?" Kate asked, glancing at her watch. It was nearly eleven o'clock.

"That truck stop out by the main highway stays open all night," Mike reminded her. "How does a piece of banana cream pie sound?"

"Pretty good," Kate replied. "Give me a few minutes to change . . ."

"Change? They're offering a discount if you come in dressed up!"

"Serious?"

Mike nodded, sliding his plastic hockey mask back into place. Grinning, he reached down to pull Kate to her feet.

"And what are you going as? You're not bringing that chainsaw with us," she said firmly.

"You have a point," Mike said, glancing around the small duplex. Suddenly snapping his fingers, he ran into the bathroom. Holding out the electric toothbrush in his hand, he walked back into the living room, slipping the plastic hockey mask over his face. "I'll go as the mad brusher!"

"Why not bring the plunger?" Kate teased.

"That's even better," Mike agreed, rushing back into the bathroom.

"Mike . . . I was kidding . . . you are not taking that plunger anywhere . . . ," she said, running after him. The two of them had a tug-of-war in the tiny hallway as Kate struggled to remove the plunger in his hands. Grinning wickedly, Mike finally gave in, letting go as Kate yanked hard. Rolling, she slid into the linen closet at the end of the hall. Pushing his mask up out of the way, Mike hurried down the hallway to help her up.

"That was a dirty trick," Kate moaned, rubbing her head.

"Sorry," Mike apologized. "Where does it hurt?"

"Everywhere," Kate retorted.

Mike removed his plastic mask and moved closer. "Dr. Mike at your service," he soothed as he did his best to kiss her better.

* * *

Tearfully, Sabrina burst out of Sindi's house. She had anticipated a wonderful party with her friends, but this evening had been one of the most awful nights of her life. After her friends had transformed her from a princess to a party girl, most of the young men in attendance had been unable to keep their eyes off her. A couple of senior boys had cornered her, making lewd suggestions as they had patted and touched her inappropriately. One had backed Sabrina against the couch, refusing to let her go until she kissed him. Leaning forward, he had forced his lips on hers. Finally she had managed to pull away, only to find herself surrounded by leering boys closer to her own age. They hadn't been as suggestive as the seniors, but had made enough crude jokes about her appearance that she had tried to hide, using an afghan off the couch to cover herself.

"What's the matter with you?" Tracie had finally asked her, leaning close to be heard above the loud music. "You're over here hiding in the corner when you should be enjoying all of this attention. I wish some of those senior boys would look at me the way they're looking at you," she had added, giving Sabrina a jealous glare.

"Trust me, it's not as fun as it looks," Sabrina had replied.

"You need to loosen up," Tracie had responded. Grabbing the afghan, she had shoved an aluminum can into Sabrina's hand. "Drink some of this. You'll feel better in no time."

The dim lighting in the living room prevented Sabrina from seeing what was written on the can. "What is it?" she had asked.

"Try it," Tracie had encouraged. "It's good stuff."

Assuming it was some kind of pop, Sabrina had taken a swallow. Nearly choking, she somehow gagged down the mouthful of bitter liquid. Moving into the kitchen for a better look, she had finally realized what it was. A sick feeling had overwhelmed her as she confronted Tracie. "You're drinking beer?"

"A couple of the senior boys brought it with them."

"Why?"

"What is your problem tonight?" Tracie had retorted. "A little beer isn't going to hurt anyone . . . it might help you have a little fun."

"I don't need this kind of fun," Sabrina had returned, handing the can of beer back to Tracie.

"Keep it. It's yours now," Tracie had argued, refusing to take the can. But Sabrina had held out the can insistently, and Tracie had pushed it back at her, spilling the beer and saturating Sabrina's costume with it.

"Look what you did!" Sabrina had yelled. Furious, she had stormed out of the house and away from the party. Now, as she continued to walk away from Sindi's home, she pulled her dress back up onto her shoulders and tried to smooth her hair down into place. Walking to the nearest gas station, she went inside the restroom to clean up. She held a handful of paper towels under the faucet and attempted to remove the pungent smell of beer from her costume. Deciding it was a lost cause, she then wiped off the garish makeup her friends had applied.

Sabrina gazed at her reflection in the mirror and flinched. Why were things turning out this way? What was up with her friends? They had always had fun together, but lately, these girls were drifting too far from who they used to be. They were starting to cross boundaries she wasn't sure she wanted to explore, at least, not yet.

The five of them had attended Primary together. They had taken great delight in cheering each other on during their baptisms years ago. Excitedly they had promised that someday they would all be in attendance when they were each married in the temple. As time had passed, they had remained close, enjoying the new opportunities junior high had presented. Their seventh grade year they had tried out for cheerleader and had been thrilled when they all made it. Together, they had proudly graduated from Primary to Young Women, where as eager new Beehives, they had faithfully set and earned goals in their Personal Progress books. But gradually, things had changed as the girls discovered that popularity often hinged on being outrageous, on bending rules and ignoring standards.

Sabrina wasn't sure what she wanted out of life anymore, but she was certain she didn't want a repeat of this weekend. The water balloon fiasco had been bad enough, but this . . . how would she ever explain what had happened tonight? If her parents ever caught wind of what kind of party this had turned into, they would never trust her again.

"I never should've gone tonight," Sabrina said softly, trying not to cry. "I knew those boys would be there." She frowned at herself in the mirror. "But I didn't know it would turn out this way." A single tear slid down the side of her face. "Why did I pressure Mom into letting me go? If I'd stayed grounded, none of this would've happened. My first kiss . . . from a boy I don't even like who was so drunk he won't even remember. But I will. I don't think I'll ever forget how horrible it was." She looked at her watch. It was almost 11:00 p.m. Her mother had asked her to be home by midnight. If she showed up before then, it would look suspicious. Her parents would instantly think something had gone wrong. Sighing heavily, Sabrina decided to walk around town for a bit. Maybe it would help air out her costume. She glanced again at her reflection in the mirror, then discarded the pile of wet paper towels and headed back outside.

CHAPTER 5

November

"Looks like you survived the weekend," Doris commented, smiling at Kate as the two women walked down the crowded halls of the high school Monday morning.

"Barely," Kate said, glancing at Doris.

"Any adventures I should know about?" the older woman pressed.

"Mike insisted on scaring off a few unruly teens Saturday night."

"Uh oh," Doris replied.

"Uh oh is right. You should've seen our house the next morning. It looked like an egg factory had exploded."

Laughing, Doris followed Kate into her classroom. "Well, let's look on the bright side. At least your house was already yellow," she quipped, unable to resist.

"Not funny," Kate retorted. "Neither was the cleanup, something that turned into a major water fight. Mike nearly drowned me."

"Young love," Doris teasingly sighed as the first bell rang. Laughing, she headed out of the classroom, ignoring the indignant look on Kate's face.

* * *

In Bozeman, Kate's mother learned about Sindi's Halloween party from Lori Blanchard on Tuesday morning. "Are you sure what you heard about Sindi's party is true?" Sue questioned, as the two women sat on the couch in the Erickson's living room in front of a large picture window. "These are LDS girls . . . raised in good LDS homes," Sue continued. "Sabrina and her friends have been in a little trouble lately, but they've never done anything like this before."

The Young Women leader nodded reluctantly. "This is the largest group of Mia Maids I've ever taught," Lori sighed. "Half of them were at that party Sindi threw Halloween night."

"Sindi, Marsha, Dawn, Tracie, and my daughter?" Sue guessed.

"Yes. A few other freshmen girls attended—nonmembers—and a handful of older girls they were trying to impress. And naturally, more boys than girls were invited."

"Who told you all of this?" Sue asked, still stunned by what Lori had revealed.

"Samantha Collins." Lori gazed sadly at Sue. "Sam doesn't lie."

"No, she doesn't," Sue agreed, picturing the sweet-natured Mia Maid class president.

"Sam overheard a group of kids talking about it at school yesterday. At first, she thought it was just a bad rumor going around, but when she heard Tracie and Sindi bragging about what took place—"

"Bragging?" Sue interrupted.

"I'm afraid so," Lori replied. "What am I going to do with this group of girls? I've taught them lessons about heeding the Word of Wisdom. They know better than to drink or smoke or try drugs. Two weeks ago we combined with the Beehives and Laurels for our annual chastity chat. We used to downplay that topic for the younger girls, but now we have to be blunt with them. We've been told that morality problems are cropping up with the middle school bunch. It's scary thinking of kids that age having problems like that." Looking at Sue, Lori sighed. "Why is it some young people think the standards set by our church apply to everyone but them? Do they honestly believe they can turn their backs on the things they've been taught and repent later and everything will be all right? Repentance is a very real gift, but they need to understand that some choices lead to scarring consequences."

"I've asked myself the same thing," Sue quietly murmured.

Lori glanced around the room, focusing on a Book of Mormon that lay in front of her on the coffee table. "Would you mind if I showed you a scripture I came across the other day?" she asked.

"Go ahead," Sue encouraged.

Picking up the book of scripture, Lori thumbed through it until she found the thirteenth chapter of Second Nephi. "I'll skip around to the parts that caught my eye." Clearing her throat, she began to read: "'. . . the child shall behave himself proudly against the ancient, and the base against the honorable . . . the daughters of Zion are haughty, and walk with stretched-forth necks and wanton eyes . . .' and listen to this, Sue, it describes what these kids are wearing today: '. . . In that day, the Lord will take away the bravery of their tinkling ornaments . . . The chains and the bracelets . . . the ornaments of the legs, and the headbands . . . and the earrings; the rings, and nose jewels; the changeable suits of apparel . . .'" Lori glanced up. "Is any of this sounding familiar?"

Sue slowly nodded. "I'll tell you something that makes me sick, the way some kids are drawn to body piercing and tattoos. There aren't very many around here that have done that sort of thing yet, but it's everywhere. A couple of months ago Sabrina and I were in Pocatello, Idaho. We were on our way back from visiting with Kate and Mike and swung by the mall to look for some school clothes. There was a shop in that mall advertising discounts for body piercing. It made me sick when I saw it."

"Disfiguring the body is the current thing to do. So much for the body being a temple," Lori said, offering a tiny smile. "I've wondered how those kids eat, or brush their teeth . . . you know, the ones who pierce their tongues."

"I have a friend who works in a dental office in Salt Lake. She's says it's become very common for teenagers to show up to have their teeth worked on with chains, needles, and jewels stuck through their tongues and lips. She said that some of these same kids have an absolute fit if they need a shot of Novocain so the dentist can work on their teeth."

"It's quite a world we live in," Lori mused. "Just like it says . . . let me see if I can find it . . . here it is Second Nephi, chapter fifteen, verse 20. 'Wo unto them that call evil good, and good evil, that put darkness for light, and light for darkness, that put bitter for sweet, and sweet for bitter.'"

"We're seeing that more and more, everywhere you look. One example is TV. There are still several good movies and shows, but there's also a lot of junk on there. Talk shows that exploit every perversity in our country. Soap operas that glorify sexual immorality; some are even geared for teenagers. It's especially bad at night. Not long ago, the programs they ran during prime time targeted the family."

"They still do, only Satan is the one doing the targeting," Lori replied. "Most of the movies in the theaters aren't much better," she added. "It's no wonder some of these kids are so mixed up. Look at what they're subjected to, almost everywhere they turn."

Sue gazed at Lori. "That's why we need youth leaders like you on their side."

Lori shook her head. "It's going to take more than what I can do. Lately I feel like I'm beating my head against a brick wall. How do we get these kids to realize that they have been saved for these latter days because of their courage, faith, and talents? They've already proven themselves once, before they ever came to this earth." Lori reached into her purse, pulling out a small booklet. "All of our youth are given these booklets when they first come into Young Men and Young Women." She showed Sue the booklet entitled *For the Strength of Youth.*

"I saw a copy of that stuffed in Sabrina's scripture bag. I thumbed through it once but I've never read the entire thing," Sue admitted.

Lori opened the book. "Listen to this," she said.

> *Our beloved young men and women . . . We desire every-thing in this world for you that is right and good. You are not just ordinary young men and women. You are choice spirits who have been held in reserve to come forth in this day when the temptations, responsibilities, and opportuni-ties are the very greatest. You are at a critical time in your lives. This is a time for you not only to live righteously but also to set an example for your peers . . .*

Looking up from the book, Lori continued, "The rest of this tiny book is filled with the standards set by our church. It's all there if they'll just read it."

"I'll have to sit down with Sabrina and go through it with her."

"I hope it helps. The thing is, Sabrina and her friends are not bad girls. These kids have it rough, but they can rise above it all if they'll try."

Sue grimaced. "They'll have to try harder than they did Saturday night. Back to this party Sindi threw—did her parents know anything about it?"

Lori shook her head. "They left town thinking Sindi would spend the night with her friends."

"It sounds like she did, they just didn't realize how many and that part of them would be male," Sue retorted. "Who brought the alcohol . . ."

"Beer," Lori supplied.

"Beer," Sue repeated, "and who knows what else?"

"All I heard was beer."

"That's bad enough," Sue groaned. Rising, she shoved her hands in the pockets of her khaki-colored dress pants and paced the floor. "How wild did things get that night?"

"I don't think either one of us wants to know the answer to that question," Lori replied.

Sue shook her head. "I grounded Sabrina the day before, forbid her to go to that party. Why did I let her go?!"

"Why did you let her go?" Lori probed.

"Because I thought I was being too strict with her. We had a good talk. She promised to do better . . . I really thought we were gaining ground. She told me if I'd let her go to this party it would prove that I trusted her. Now this." Shaking her head, Sue sank down into a recliner. "Do any of the other parents know anything about what happened that night?"

"I don't think so. You're the first parent I've talked to." Lori smiled sadly at Sue. "After what we went through with Kate, I feel like there's a bond between us. I figured this was a good place to start. And to be honest, I'm not sure what to say to the others. Some of them won't believe me if I tell them what took place."

Lori was silent for a few moments, picturing the reaction Tracie's parents would have to all of this. She was certain they would think she was making it up. In Lori's opinion, Tracie had been getting away with far too much because her parents wouldn't admit their daughter was capable of making major mistakes. In their eyes, Tracie was the perfect child—and she was, around them.

"Sue, I want you to know something," Lori finally said. "I have more hope for Sabrina than the rest of those girls right now."

"Why?"

"Two reasons. The first, because she has you for a mother." Lori smiled warmly at Sue. "You know what to watch for . . . you spend time with her . . . you're talking to Sabrina. Open communication is vital."

"What's the other reason?" Sue asked, uncomfortable with Lori's vote of confidence. After hearing about Sindi's party, she wasn't sure if she had any communication with her youngest daughter. Sabrina hadn't said a word about what had taken place Saturday night.

"I don't think Sabrina has strayed as far as the others," Lori continued. "I was watching them Sunday. She was the only one out of that group who would look me in the eye. In fact, she sat by herself during class. I got the impression she was mad at the other girls."

"She's not alone," Sue angrily muttered, her green eyes flashing.

Lori looked at Sue thoughtfully. "During the time I've served in the Young Women, I've noticed something about these girls. When they're on the right track, they seem to glow. Their eyes sparkle with excitement for the future. But when they've messed up, that glow is missing. Their eyes have a dull look. It breaks my heart when I see that glow start to fade, when I see indifference instead of innocence in their faces. Sabrina hasn't lost that glow. Unfortunately, two of the others have, and the other two are fading fast."

Looking slightly relieved, Sue met Lori's concerned gaze. "How do we stop Sabrina from fading?"

"That's the golden question. I'll add another. How do we reignite those who have?"

* * *

After Lori left, Sue wandered upstairs to Sabrina's bedroom. She didn't want to intrude on her daughter's privacy, but she wanted to know for herself how involved Sabrina had been in Saturday night's activities. Sabrina was still at school. Greg was at work. This would be the only chance she would have to see if their daughter had left any tell-tale signs behind.

"Don't you trust me, Mom?" echoed silently in her heart.

"I want to, Breeny," Sue murmured, using the nickname Kate had given Sabrina years ago. Hesitating, her hand resting on the door knob, she tried to recall how Sabrina had sounded Saturday night when she had returned ten minutes before her curfew. The fourteen-year-old hadn't come into the master bedroom to share the details of the party. Instead, she had hollered from her room that she was home, she'd had a lot of fun, but was tired and wanted to go to bed. Grateful that she had arrived before midnight, Sue hadn't questioned her. The next morning, Sabrina had been quiet, but helpful. Sue had believed it was a good sign. Now, she wondered. "Why didn't you tell me what happened that night? What is it you're keeping from me?"

Her hand slowly fell away from the doorknob as she remembered the advice her third great-grandmother had recently given her. The message in that dream had been clear. If Sue violated Sabrina's trust, regardless of what she suspected, it would make things worse between them. Deciding she would wait until Sabrina was ready to talk, she turned and made her way back downstairs. Restless, she wandered into the computer room. Sitting down in the chair behind the computer desk, she swivelled around, staring at the bookcase. A book drew her attention. Rising, she pulled it out of the bookcase and returned to the chair. Opening the book she found comfort in the words of President Ezra Taft Benson.

> *Our young people are not just ordinary people. They are not just run-of-the-mill. They are choice spirits. President Wilford Woodruff said this: "The Lord has chosen a small number of choice spirits of sons and daughters out of all the creations of God, who are to inherit this earth; and this company of choice spirits have been kept in the spirit world for six thousand years to come forth in the last days to stand in the flesh in this last dispensation of the fulness of times, to organize the kingdom of God upon the earth, to build it up and to defend it and to receive the eternal and everlasting priesthood [of God]."*

For years Sue had heard that this generation had been preserved for this time. Now, there it was in black and white. Turning the page, Sue read another paragraph that seemed to jump out at her:

> *Youth is a period of timelessness when the horizons of age seem too distant to be noticed. Thus, the now generation forgets that the present will soon be the past, which one will look back upon either with sorrow and regret or joy and remembrance of cherished experiences. Satan's program is "play now and pay later." He seeks for all to be miserable like unto himself (see 2 Nephi 2:27). The Lord's program is happiness now and joy forever through gospel living.*

Her eyes misting, Sue set the book down on the desk in front of her. Rising, she knelt beside the chair and began to earnestly pray for guidance.

* * *

Sabrina wanted to scream. She hadn't done anything wrong, but she was being labeled right along with her friends. People looked at her differently now. Some with admiration, others with disgust.

"Relax," Tracie had told her earlier that day. "We're hot. We've made a name for ourselves—we've been invited to another party this weekend. Paulette Haddock is putting it together. She wouldn't come to ours, but now she wants us to come to hers. Isn't it great? A senior, inviting freshmen to something like this?!"

"It's not *great*," Sabrina had tersely replied. "What do you think'll happen at her party?"

"Well, we won't be playing 'Pin the Tail on the Donkey,'" Tracie had laughed. "We're into more exciting stuff now."

"Right," Sabrina had snorted.

"How would you know? You left before it got really good Saturday night. Sindi got so drunk, she was a riot. Those senior boys really got a kick out of her."

"Is that all they got out of her?" Sabrina asked.

"I'll never tell," Tracie had said impishly. "Besides, those guys had their eye on you that night too—and their hands—and according to Jay Kendell, much more than that."

Blushing fiercely, Sabrina had walked away. Grateful now that school was finally over for the day, she made her way down the crowded halls of the high school toward her locker.

"Hey, babe," a deep voice beckoned.

Sabrina glanced to her left, spotting the jerk who had kissed her Saturday night. She frowned as Jay Kendell eagerly approached.

"Where've you been hiding the past couple of days? I've missed you." He leaned down in an attempt to repeat what he now felt he was entitled to. She turned her face and his lips brushed Sabrina's cheek instead. "What's up with that?" Jay angrily sputtered.

"Jay, I don't know what you think you're doing but—"

"Don't you?" the senior asked. With his hands resting against the wall on either side of Sabrina, he had successfully pinned her against her locker. "You seemed to like it the other night."

"You were drunk. You don't even remember what happened that night."

"Oh, I don't know about that. One minute we were kissing and then it got really exciting . . ."

"Nothing else happened!" Sabrina thundered, pushing him away.

"That's not what I heard," one of Jay's friends said, coming forward to slap Jay on the back. "Way to go, man. You've got yourself a hot little woman here."

"I am not his hot little woman!" Sabrina yelled. For a brief instant, silence prevailed around them, then laughter as the other students glanced at Sabrina and Jay, the newest senior boy/freshman girl couple. Word had it these two had gotten *very* acquainted at Sindi's Halloween party. It was rumored that Sabrina had been ripe for the picking and Jay had been the lucky one to reap that particular harvest. It was now apparent that these two were having their first argument, which meant Sabrina might be open game for anyone else who might be interested.

Several senior boys watched in amusement as Sabrina angrily made her way out of the high school. Noisily they bragged among themselves about how much fun they would have taming the temperamental young woman.

* * *

Sabrina ran most of the way home. Slowing when she finally reached her corner, she glumly stared at her house. "Okay, fine . . . I

am *Kate, the sequel*," she angrily snapped. "Wild parties, bad reputation, a disgusting jerk slobbering over me. All that's missing is the
coma that makes everything better!" Stomping toward the house, she
entered through the garage, hoping to avoid her mother. Right now,
she didn't want to talk to anyone.

"Hi, hon," Sue said brightly, glancing up from the washing
machine in the small utility room. She had decided to keep things light,
hoping guilt would impel her daughter to confess about Sindi's party.

At least I'm consistent. My run of good luck is still holding, Sabrina
sullenly thought. Forcing a smile at her mother, she nodded, hoping
to escape to her room without a conversation.

"I'm putting in a small batch of hand washables. Need anything
washed?"

"Nope," Sabrina replied, easing her way into the kitchen.

"What about that Halloween costume? It needs to be cleaned
before we take it back."

Sabrina silently cursed. This just wasn't her day. "I don't think it
can be washed in the machine. I'll rinse it out by hand."

"This cycle is very gentle. I'm sure that costume will be fine," Sue
stressed, hoping to trigger a dialogue about Saturday night.

"I'll rinse it out right now," Sabrina responded, hurrying through
the dining room before her mother could protest. The last thing she
needed was for her to smell the beer on that dress. She should've
been smart enough to rinse it out before now. Instead, she had
stashed it on the floor of her closet, trying to decide what to do with
it. Praying it was still where she had left it, she ran upstairs,
pretending not to hear her mother's request to bring the costume
down to her.

* * *

Rubbing as hard as she dared to get out the ugly brown stain,
Sabrina began to panic. She didn't know what this fabric was, but it
refused to relinquish its hold on the discoloration. "What is it going
to take to get this thing clean?" she muttered.

A knock sounded at the bathroom door. "Sabrina, are you
through yet? You're wanted on the phone."

The phone? She hadn't even heard it ring. Shoving the princess dress into the water, she dried her hands. "I'll get it in my room," she said as she passed her mother in the hall. "I'm letting that costume soak for a minute," she added, hoping her mother would leave it alone.

"Did you get something on it?"

"I . . . uh . . . spilled . . . my drink that night. I thought it would wash right out, but I was wrong. I think it will after it soaks. Who's on the phone?" Sabrina asked, changing the subject.

"I think it's Tracie."

"Oh. She probably wants to know what today's math assignment was. She never pays attention." Hurrying into her room, she picked up the phone. "Hi, Tracie."

"Hi. Way to make a scene after school today," Tracie began.

"Just a minute," Sabrina cautioned her friend. "Mom, could you hang up the phone downstairs?" she hollered.

"On my way," Sue replied, already walking downstairs. It was tempting to listen in on this conversation, but she obediently hung up the kitchen phone. Then, deciding to see if she could get the stain out of Sabrina's costume, she walked back upstairs. She wasn't surprised to see that her daughter's bedroom door had been shut. She could hear Sabrina's muffled voice, but knew better than to hope she could hear anything that was being said. Besides, that would be eavesdropping, something she normally frowned upon.

Entering the bathroom, Sue moved to the sink. As she pulled the dress up out of the water, a pungent smell assaulted her. "What in the world did you get into?" she gasped, staring at the large brown stain on the front of the costume. It smelled like rotten yeast. Dropping the light pink dress back into the sink, Sue sank down on the edge of the tub. Beer. Her daughter had been drinking beer. Everything Lori had heard was true. No wonder Sabrina hadn't wanted her to stick this in the washing machine. She had been trying to hide it. A fragile trust dissolved, much easier than the ugly stain in the sink.

CHAPTER 6

"I'd ask how your day went, but I've already heard," Doris said, walking into Kate's classroom. Now that school was out, she had come to bolster the young woman's sagging spirits. One of Kate's students had managed to sneak out of class, something Cleo had immediately brought to Kate's attention when the young man was spotted downtown at a local drive-in.

"I didn't even see Gerald leave the room," Kate admitted, close to tears. "I was writing some historical dates on the chalkboard and he must've slipped out. What made it worse was that I didn't even notice he was missing after he was gone."

"We've all had our moments," Doris soothed. "Just remember—some of these kids like to push the boundaries. Gerald Reynolds is a prime example! A regular *chip* off the old block." Rolling her eyes at the unintended pun, Doris explained she had taught Gerald's father, Chip, several years ago. "Chip Reynolds has always believed he was above the rest of the community. Mr. Football, Mr. Perfection—he thought he was quite a lady's man, too. Unfortunately, so did half of the girls who went to school with him. He was Mr. Jerk as far as I was concerned. At least he married the girl he got into trouble, Marcy Hastings. She was one of my best students."

Doris shook her head as she continued. "I just wish Gerald had more of his mother in him. Marcy has always been a sweetheart. If only she hadn't fallen for one of Blaketown's *finest*." Still grieving over Marcy's lost potential, Doris showed her disappointment openly. "I'd always thought Marcy would go onto college someday. She wanted to be a doctor. She would've made a fine one. Instead, she's married to someone who doesn't deserve her!"

"But Chip Reynolds is on the school board," Kate protested. "I met him after we first moved here. He seemed very supportive."

Doris gave Kate a long, meaningful look. "He probably liked what he saw," she countered. Ignoring Kate's blush, Doris continued. "If I were you, I'd steer clear of Mr. Wonderful," she cautioned. "He tends to have a roving eye."

"But isn't he in the bishopric in his ward?" Kate asked, disturbed by her friend's uncharacteristic censure. Doris had never been judgmental in the past, except when it came to Cleo, an issue they both agreed on.

Doris nodded. "Second counselor in my ward to be precise. I guess they figured he'd stay out of trouble with a calling like that. Who knows? Maybe he has changed. I hope so for Marcy's sake."

In the time she had lived in Blaketown, Kate had learned there were many rumors of that caliber flying around the community. It seemed like everyone had something to say about everyone else, and usually it wasn't a compliment. There were no secrets in this small town, something she wasn't sure she liked.

Doris realized she had shocked Kate. "I guess I've never forgiven Chip for getting Marcy in trouble. Then seeing their son act up just like Chip used to . . . it makes me mad. It's almost like seeing the whole mess start over again. If Gerald ever hurts a girl—a student of mine like his father did—"

"Do you really think Marcy's pregnancy was all Chip's fault?" Kate interrupted.

"Probably not," Doris sighed. "She was young, naive, and thought she was in love with him. I suppose they were both at fault." Deciding she'd said more than enough concerning the matter, Doris examined one of Kate's bulletin boards as she attempted to calm down. "You up for a hot fudge Sunday run?" she said, changing the subject. "I think I could use a little sweetening today."

"Sure. Mike won't be home for a couple of hours and I'm too upset to read through these essays right now."

"Let's go," the older woman advised. "Don't worry. Someday we'll look back on today and laugh."

"I'll bet Cleo won't."

"I don't think she's ever laughed in her entire life," Doris replied. "She might cause grievous internal damage if she did."

"You mean that old volcano might erupt?" Kate said, failing to see the principal as she walked out of a classroom behind them. Doris caught a glimpse of Cleo out of the corner of her eye and nudged Kate before she could say anything else.

"The old volcano might erupt?" Cleo suspiciously repeated, catching up with the two teachers.

"Ah, yes, Kate was just telling me about one of those old volcanoes down in . . . Peru was it?" Doris said, trying to come to Kate's rescue.

Her face as red as the sweater in her hands, Kate nodded.

"Oh, really? I went to Peru once a few years ago. Which volcano?"

"Uh . . . let me see, which one was I talking about?" Kate stammered, exchanging a worried glance with the English teacher.

"Oh, you know, *that* one," Doris replied, being less than helpful.

"The Ubinas or the Sabancaya?" Cleo pressed. "Those are the two that have been the most active in recent years."

Figuring she had a fifty-fifty shot at this one, Kate gathered her courage. "The Ubinas," she guessed, trying to sound sure of herself.

"What makes you think it's going to erupt?"

"Just something I . . . uh . . . came across recently," Kate offered.

"I'd like to know where you read that," Cleo commented. "The Ubinas is the most active volcano in Peru, you know."

"She knows," Doris quipped, avoiding the dirty look Kate was sending her direction.

"I wonder if there have been recent phreatic outbursts?" Cleo excitedly ventured.

"I understand there was one today," Doris teasingly supplied, trying to keep a straight face. "It started spouting off earlier this afternoon," she added, unable to resist.

"This is so exciting. I'll have to watch the news tonight. Maybe it'll be in the paper."

"Maybe," Kate weakly replied as the principal hurried off down the empty hallway. As soon as she was out of earshot, Doris burst out laughing.

"Phreatic outburst?!" Kate repeated, giggling nervously.

"That was the perfect finishing touch," Doris said, holding her side.

"I just hope the woman forgets before the news comes on tonight," Kate responded.

"Oh, cheer up. Even if she doesn't, it'll give her something else to think about. She'll forget all about Gerald Reynolds."

"I'm beginning to wonder which is the lesser of the two evils."

"Quit worrying. Let's go get those sundaes," Doris said, leading Kate out of the high school.

* * *

"Hi, Mom," Kate said after her mother picked up the phone.

"Hello, Kate," Sue replied, sounding more depressed than her oldest daughter.

"I called for a little moral support," Kate sighed.

Sue's sigh echoed Kate's. "I could sure use some myself."

"What's wrong?"

"One word—Sabrina."

Kate lifted an eyebrow. "This doesn't sound good."

"It's not. I'm afraid your little sister is heading for some big time trouble."

"What's going on with her?"

"I wish I knew," Sue responded. She then told Kate what had taken place during the past week, including the dream about Grandma Colleen. When she finished, Kate was no longer feeling sorry for herself.

"I'm sorry, Mom. I wish there was something I could do. Would it help if I talked to her?"

Frowning, Sue sat down in a kitchen chair. She had purposely left out Sabrina's comments about Kate, knowing how hurt her oldest daughter would be. "Let's see how things go," she finally said. "I'm not giving up on her yet," she added. "I just hope she'll level with me eventually. Now, before we run your phone bill up too high, tell me what's going on down your way," she encouraged, changing the subject.

Settling back against the couch, Kate began sharing her sad story of the day, beginning with her runaway student.

* * *

Later that night as Sue finished typing a letter to her missionary son, Tyler, Sabrina entered the computer room.

"Mom, can we talk?"

Surprised by the question, Sue turned away from the computer screen to face her youngest daughter. "Sure," she replied, gesturing to a folding chair that was leaning against the wall. Part of her wanted to rejoice; the other part dreaded what she thought she might hear.

Sabrina closed the door behind her. Reaching for the metal folding chair, she opened it up and sat down.

"First, I want you to know that I had no idea Sindi's party would turn out the way it did. If I had, I wouldn't have gone," Sabrina started. Hesitantly, she revealed everything that had taken place that night. When she finished, she stared miserably down at the floor.

Breathing a sigh of relief that her daughter had had enough sense to leave Sindi's party before it had gotten too wild, Sue smiled at Sabrina. "Thank you for being honest with me."

Sabrina glanced up at her mother. "Aren't you even going to say 'I told you so?'"

"Only if you want me to." Sue forced a stiff smile. "Now I'll be honest with you. I'd already heard about Sindi's party."

"What?" Sabrina exclaimed, stunned by this news. "Why haven't you said anything?"

"I was hoping you would. I was trying to trust you."

Stung by a twinge of guilt, Sabrina focused on the floor again. "Who told you?"

"Rumors are flying everywhere," Sue said in an effort to protect Lori, not wanting to jeopardize Lori's relationship with Sabrina.

"Tell me about it," Sabrina glumly replied. "People all over school are talking about it . . . about my friends and what they supposedly did . . . and that guy who kissed me that night . . ."

Sue's knuckles turned white as she clenched her fists. Her baby wasn't even sixteen yet; it infuriated her to know that a drunken senior had robbed Sabrina of something that should've been special.

"He's telling everyone that we . . . that . . . that it was more than a kiss. Much more," Sabrina stammered, blushing.

"You're kidding?" Sue replied, tempted to turn Greg loose on this jerk. It would serve him right! Greg didn't handle it well when he thought someone was taking advantage of his daughters.

"I wish I was. He was so drunk that night, he doesn't remember anything. He's making it all up. I don't know who he's trying to impress. We never . . . you know . . . but everyone seems to believe him."

"Your friends know the truth. Get them to stick up for you."

"My friends are still mad because I walked out on them that night—they think it's funny that I'm the one getting a bad reputation. You should've heard Tracie this afternoon when she called. I finally hung up on her."

"She doesn't sound much like a friend," Sue commented.

"Right now, she isn't," Sabrina agreed. "Mom, what am I going to do? Jay tried to kiss me again after school today."

Sue's eyes widened. That did it. This guy was dead! At least, he would wish he was when she and Greg were finished with him.

"He thinks I'm his own personal property. I don't even like him. And I hate what everyone is saying about me . . . it's awful . . . I hate what my friends are doing . . . they're changing."

"I've noticed," Sue said, giving her daughter a pointed look. "Why do you think I've been so worried about you?"

"I wish I'd listened," Sabrina moaned. Her head was pounding. She pressed her fingers against her temples, trying to make it stop. "Now what do I do?"

"You'll have to make some changes yourself."

Staring at her mother, Sabrina quit massaging her head.

"It's part of growing up," Sue informed her.

"But . . . this is so hard. Does it have to be this way?"

"Sometimes. It was for your sister." Sue mentally kicked herself for mentioning Kate. It had become such a habit, she hadn't been able to stop herself.

Bristling, Sabrina choked back the anger she felt. This had all started as a way to prove she was nothing like her older sister. Now people would say she had become just that.

"My advice to you is to steer clear of Sindi, Tracie, Marsha, and Dawn for a while," Sue hurried on. "You're being lumped in with them. People hear stories of what those girls did that night, and they assume that because you're all close friends, you were involved, too. It won't be easy, but you need to make new friends with girls who have higher standards. You'll always be judged by whom you associate with. And like the scriptures tell us, we're to avoid the appearance of evil. If your friends persist in participating in these wild parties, they're asking for trouble, something you definitely don't need right now."

Nodding, Sabrina quietly absorbed what her mother was telling her. She knew it was true, but she was scared. She'd always hung around with those four girls. Now what? She didn't know how to make new friends and wasn't sure she could. "How do I make new friends, especially after what happened Saturday night?"

"Actions speak louder than words. If you aren't hanging around with those four girls anymore . . . if you aren't seen at any more of these parties, what's going around right now will die down."

"Promise?"

"I think so," Sue replied. "Maybe if you started running around with someone like Samantha Collins—"

"Sam?!" Sabrina exclaimed, scowling as she thought about the president of her Mia Maid class.

"What's wrong with Sam?"

"Mom, she's . . . we have nothing in common! She likes choir, band, and she's a member of the Honor Society."

"This makes her a bad person?" Sue asked.

"You're not getting it. She's not . . . the kids at school think she's kind of weird."

"She's not popular enough for you?"

"Well, yeah."

"Sabrina!"

"There's always been two groups . . . even when we were younger . . . in Primary. Our group and Sam's."

"Why?"

Sabrina shrugged. "We never got along very well with Sam and her friends. They're . . . they're weird, like I said. They think they're better than everybody else because they're so good."

Sue gave her daughter a long, hard stare. In her opinion, Samantha Collins was a well-behaved, polite young woman.

"And you should see what they wear to school," Sabrina continued, trying to defend her precarious position. "They're just not cool."

"Who would you rather be seen with right now, Sam's group, or Tracie's?"

"Neither!"

"Is there anyone else at school you could run around with?" Sue asked, exasperated. "There has to be someone you could get along with . . . someone who doesn't thrive on getting into trouble."

Sabrina glumly considered this suggestion. "I don't know," she finally said. "I mean . . . what am I supposed to do . . . walk up to someone and tell them I want to be their friend? That is so lame!"

"Get involved in some of the clubs at school. You could meet people . . . make new friends . . ."

"Mom, those things are for losers."

"Says who?" Sue probed.

"Tracie," Sabrina mumbled.

"I rest my case!" Sue gazed steadily at her daughter. "Honey, before you and your friends became so set on becoming popular, there were a lot of things you used to enjoy. Because of Tracie, you dropped out of band. It was *uncool* to play the clarinet. Because of Dawn, you all turned up your noses at getting involved in drama. Because of what Sindi said, you gave up running for student council."

"But—"

"You've let these other girls run your life for so long, you don't know what you like anymore. Why is it things are so turned around today? It used to be that the kids who were out partying were considered low-lifes. The popular kids were the ones who got involved, who served on the student council, who joined the different clubs. Now if you have a high grade point average, everyone thinks you're scum."

"We don't think they're scum, and I get pretty good grades," Sabrina pointed out.

"I know," Sue responded. "But the way you make Samantha Collins sound—"

"She likes being the teacher's pet. I don't want to be like her. Everyone makes fun of her."

Deciding she was getting nowhere fast when it came to Samantha, Sue let Sabrina's comment pass unchallenged. "Just remember, you need to be careful about who or what you get involved with. Carefully consider where it will take you. And before you decide someone or something is beneath you, give it or them a chance first. Don't automatically assume that everything Tracie has told you for years is the gospel truth."

"No worries there," Sabrina responded. "I've pretty well had it with that woman."

Silently cheering, Sue smiled at her daughter. This was going better than she'd ever thought possible.

CHAPTER 7

December

It had been another in a series of trying days for Kate. Deciding some of the students in her drama class were very talented and more adept at directing than she might be, she had selected three of her most gifted students to direct three one-act plays: Bev Henderson, Nate Winegar, and Leslie Snow. Kate had carefully chosen comedies she thought would be enjoyed by the students performing, and by those who would later have to watch. Her class had seemed excited over the prospect of trying something new. There had been one exception, a sophomore student named Terri Jeppson.

Upset that she had been passed over for a directing job, Terri had informed her mother of the unfairness of it all. That afternoon, Margo Jeppson had confronted her with Terri's accusations. Kate had tactfully explained that she had selected three students who were mature and talented enough to handle directing the other students. She had also assured Margo that her fifteen-year-old daughter was extremely gifted too, stretching the truth for the woman's benefit. Kate may not have dabbled much in the creative arts, but she knew poor acting when she saw it. Terri tended to over-dramatize her lines. She could also make an exciting sentence sound monotone, and possessed a tendency to whine if things didn't go her way. After talking to Margo, Kate understood where Terri had inherited that trait from.

"So, what you're saying is, my daughter isn't as talented as Beverly Henderson?!" Margo had reproachfully stated. "Beverly isn't even a member of the Church!"

Biting back the question of why that should matter, Kate had tried another approach. "I want *all* of my students to grow, to develop their talents. They have different abilities."

"And you feel that casting my daughter in a minor role will help her discover her talents?"

Kate had prayed for guidance at this point in the conversation. "But Terri fits that role so well—"

"And was it your idea to give her a part with only five lines?"

"I allowed the student directors to assemble their own casts," Kate had responded.

Margo had smiled, jubilant. "That explains it. Beverly has always hated my daughter because of Terri's high standards. This is her way of getting even!"

Kate had stared at Margo. Beverly, or Bev, as she preferred to be called, had made it very clear that she was not a Mormon, and had no intentions of ever becoming one. That didn't make her a bad person. Quite the contrary. Bev possessed several personality traits Kate wished more of her students would display—respect for the teachers, a strong sense of who she was, and a willingness to learn. Bev was an honor student and well-liked by most of the other students, unlike Terri whose habitual complaints and fault finding had driven most of her friends away. At the beginning of the year, Kate had felt sorry for the young woman. Pity had ultimately been replaced with frustration.

"The student directors have tried to cast their plays as fairly as possible," Kate had calmly said to Terri's mother. "Those who have minor roles this time will have a major role in the next set of plays."

"I assume that means Terri will get a chance to direct one of *those* plays," Margo had sniffed.

"We'll see," Kate had replied, refusing to allow a parent to dictate the rules for her classroom. Hurrying off to another appointment, Margo had finally left, convinced she had straightened Kate out on this matter. After her departure, Kate had headed home, unwilling to subject herself to any more humiliation.

"Hi, honey, I'm home," Mike teasingly sang out later that afternoon as he walked into the small living room of the duplex. "Where's my pipe and slippers?"

Kate stepped out of the kitchen where she had been checking on the hamburger casserole she had fixed for dinner. "Your bubble pipe is in the bathroom on the side of the tub where you left it after your bath last night, *Mikey*. Your slippers are under the bed," she said.

Mike grinned. "Hard day at the office?"

Nodding, Kate slipped into his waiting arms. "It was horrible. I spaced an in-service meeting yesterday afternoon. Doris usually reminds me, but she's out of town this week. I can't believe I forgot about it. As a result, Cleo wasn't too happy with me today. Then I had to face an irate parent after school this afternoon. She felt I had overlooked her daughter's *obvious* talent in drama."

"Where did Doris go?" Mike asked, leading Kate to the sofa. He had been grateful for the friendship Kate had developed with the English teacher. Doris had a way of defusing Kate, of helping her see the humor in most situations.

"She's off chaperoning the debate team."

"So, because of Doris' thoughtlessness, you missed a *lip-service* meeting?" he joked, pulling her down onto his lap. He wrapped his arms around her, giving her an intense squeeze.

"That's basically what they are. Everyone sits around and tells Cleo how wonderful she is. What a good job she's doing."

"And what was this month's topic? The evils of hiring such a beautiful, young history teacher?"

"You're awful, do you know that?" Kate retorted, jabbing him in the ribs with her finger.

"Gotta love me," he replied, pulling her close for a lengthy kiss. "There, that should make it better."

"Oh, really?" Kate challenged.

"I must be losing my touch," he quipped. "We'd better try that again." This time they were both so distracted, they failed to hear the hesitant knock at the door.

"Uh, I guess you forgot we were coming," a gruff voice interrupted. "We tried the doorbell—it doesn't work. Must be a short in it."

Kate jumped up off the couch, nearly knocking over the lamp sitting on an end table. Mike rose up quickly behind her, smoothing his hair back into place. Both were mortified by the sudden appearance of their home teachers, Ryan Shaft and George Rogers.

"Ryan here glanced in the window and thought you two were home. I guess you didn't hear us knock," fifty-two-year-old George stammered. He avoided looking at Mike and Kate, embarrassed by what he had seen.

"Perfect end to a perfect day," Kate breathed just loud enough so Mike could hear.

"Sorry for the interruption," thirty-four-year-old Ryan said, grinning. "I keep forgetting you two are still pretty much newlyweds."

Kate's face turned an even deeper shade of red.

"No problem. Kate was just welcoming me home," Mike said, grunting slightly when her elbow connected with his rib cage. "Won't you please come in?" he added, trying to catch his breath. He motioned to the couch, but both men elected to sit on the plastic chairs in front of the living room window. Reaching for Kate's hand, Mike led her back to the couch. This time they sat apart from each other.

"Well, I'd ask how things are going, but I think we already know the answer to that question," Ryan said, still grinning.

Normally, Kate enjoyed Ryan's sense of humor. Today, she wasn't in the mood. Taking a deep breath, she prayed these men wouldn't stay long.

"Sorry for the intrusion," George added, finally glancing at Kate. "If we'd known . . . what I mean is . . ."

"No harm done," Mike assured the older man. "So, how are things going at the garage?"

George beamed. "Lately, we can't seem to keep up with the work that comes our way."

"A sign of a good mechanic," Mike replied.

Kate smiled at her husband. Mike had a gift for putting people at ease, especially in awkward situations.

"How about you, Ryan? How's the restaurant business these days?" Mike asked.

"Things always slow down in the winter," Ryan replied. "But we're doing all right. It'd help if some of you tightwads would take your wives out to dinner once in a while." He glanced at George.

"Dinner!" Kate exclaimed, rising to her feet. She'd completely forgotten the casserole. The three men watched as she ran into the kitchen.

"I wasn't going to say anything, but I thought something smelled like it was burning," George said quietly.

Mike grinned. "That's how supper always smells around here."

"Not funny, Mike!" Kate called out, staring with dismay at the charcoal mess in the casserole dish. She had meant to turn the temperature gauge down, but must have accidentally turned it up instead. What else could go wrong today? Grumbling under her breath, she sorted through the casserole to see if there was anything worth salvaging.

"Why don't you take your sweet young thing of a wife out to dinner tonight?" Ryan said with a smile.

"Let me guess, to the Shaft Cottage?" Mike asked, referring to Ryan's restaurant.

"Is there anyplace else?" Ryan proudly asked.

"Well, now that you mention it, there is that little café out on the main highway, Ettie's Place. Then there's that drive-in across town, Sandler's . . . and . . . ," George helpfully supplied.

"Thanks for the support, George." Ryan playfully glared at his partner. Reaching into his jacket, he pulled out a slip of paper and handed it to Mike.

"What's this?"

"A complimentary gift certificate for dinner at the Shaft Cottage. I like to hand these out to my home teaching families around Christmas. The wife doesn't put plates of candy together anymore. Says it takes up too much time."

"Thank you," Mike said, returning Ryan's grin as he accepted the gift certificate. "I think we could use this tonight."

"Got any more of those certificates?" George asked, nudging Ryan.

Rolling his eyes, Ryan pulled out another slip of paper, handing it to George.

"Hey, thanks. It's Clarice's bowling night and I was informed it was my night to cook. This'll take care of it," George grinned.

Deciding the casserole was a lost cause, Kate slipped back into the living room to sit beside her husband. George smiled at her, an idea popping into his head. "Say, how would you like to join my wife's bowling team?"

"I don't know. I'm usually so tired when I come home from school . . . then I have papers to read and correct—"

"Dinner to burn," Mike teased, this time deflecting his wife's elbow.

"Think about it," George suggested. "They're losing a member of their team in a couple of weeks."

"Oh? Why?" Kate asked.

"Sarah's about to produce another Yates," he replied.

"What?" Kate asked, confused.

"It's George's way of saying she's about to have another baby," Ryan explained.

"Oh," Kate said, forcing a smile. She avoided Mike's concerned gaze. They had been trying to have a baby of their own for several months with little success. For now, they had decided not to worry about it, to let nature take its course, but there were times when Kate ached to hold a child of their own. To ease her heart, she reminded herself they were just getting established. They were trying to pay off student loans and could barely afford to support themselves, let alone a family.

An uncomfortable silence enveloped the room for several seconds. Finally George spoke, deciding it was time to share the message of the month. "Ryan here was in such a hurry to leave my place, I forgot to grab the *Ensign*, so this month's message will have to be unprompted."

"Impromptu?" Ryan suggested.

"That's what I said," George replied. Sometimes this younger fellow got on his nerves something fierce, but Ryan *had* given him a complimentary gift certificate. The man couldn't be all bad. "We don't want to keep you from dinner," George said out of habit. Then realizing his mistake, he plunged ahead. "This month's message had something to do with being more Christ-like. We should follow our Savior's example and be full of good warts." George ignored his companion's laughter as he rubbed the wart on his hand. "I meant works. We should be anxiously engaged . . . ," he paused, fighting the urge to sneeze.

"And then get married?" Ryan offered, unable to resist the temptation.

"Yeah. No. That isn't what I was gettin' at, although marriage is a wonderful thing and you two seem to have a good one of those." George blushed again, recalling what they had interrupted earlier.

Kate tried very hard to keep a straight face. She didn't dare look at Mike, but could feel his choked laughter as the couch vibrated.

George glanced at his watch. "Dang how the times flies by. We better be going, Ryan. We don't want to overstay our welcome." He quickly rose to his feet, heading for the door.

"It was good to see you again," Ryan said, grinning first at Kate, then at Mike as he shook their hands. "Carry on," he added as he headed out the front door. "Only this time, close your drapes."

"I hate that man," Kate moaned when their home teachers were out of earshot.

"You don't either," Mike chided. "Besides, he's providing dinner tonight. He's a wonderful human being." Reaching for Kate, he pulled her up beside him. "And so are you." As they began to kiss, they heard the storm door creak open.

"Sorry to interrupt again," Ryan laughed. "George thinks he left his keys in here." Walking over to the chair George had vacated, he knelt down and felt around under the chair. With the keys at last in hand, he stood, patted Mike on the back, and headed out the door.

"Don't people ever knock in this town?" Kate asked, storming into the kitchen.

Mike was laughing too hard to respond.

CHAPTER 8

As Kate hurried around, getting ready for the day ahead, she glanced briefly at the scrawny, artificial Christmas tree she and Mike had decorated last night. They had purchased the tree for their first Christmas together two years ago. This year she had hoped for a real tree, one that would fill their small home with the smell of fresh pine, but there wasn't enough room in the duplex. They had barely been able to make room for the stiff replica by taking out one of the plastic chairs near the front room window. After Mike and Kate had decorated the room with the handmade ornaments Mike's mother had given them last year, it didn't look too bad. Mike had promised it would be their best Christmas yet.

Kate hoped it would be, smiling as she thought of the special gift she had laid away for Mike—a pair of used cross-country skis at the sporting goods store downtown. They were in excellent condition, something Mike had pointed out to her during one of their frequent tours of the store. He had been so disappointed when the skis were gone the last time the two of them had wandered in to look around. Kate had shared a secretive smile with the store owner, grateful that the older man had been willing to let her pay on them as she could. She figured she would be able to pay them off in a couple of weeks, and could hardly wait to see the look on Mike's face when he saw them Christmas Day.

Christmas Day. Kate sighed in anticipation. By then they would be in Bozeman. Mike had saved up a week's worth of vacation days, and she looked forward to a wonderful break for both of them. They had already worked out the details of the visit in a way that would satisfy his family, and hers. They would stay with her family through Christmas Eve, then spend Christmas Day with his. After that, they would continue to rotate between the two families, making sure quality time was spent with both. Kate had grown to love Mike's family almost as much as her own. It would be good to return home to Bozeman.

Home. Something that didn't come to mind yet whenever she thought of Blaketown. Kate glanced at her watch and frowned. Grabbing her purse and the black satchel that contained school papers and tests, she hurried out the front door.

* * *

"With a little more practice, I think we'll have this play ready by next week," Bev Henderson said brightly. The sixteen-year-old tucked a strand of black hair behind one ear as she leaned against Kate's desk.

Kate smiled back at Bev. "If anyone can pull this off, you can," she encouraged the striking young woman. Bev's medium-length, black hair and large, blue eyes were a stunning combination. She also possessed a delightful personality. In Kate's opinion, Bev was a well-rounded young lady with tremendous potential.

An amused look appeared on the tall girl's face. "Oh, yeah, I can work wonders," she replied. "Just ask Terri Jeppson."

Trying not to smile, Kate played with the pen in her hand. "I think next time we'll see to it that you two are in different productions."

"That would be greatly appreciated," Bev said with a grin. "I don't know how you put up with her. I'm about ready to strangle that girl myself. *'Wait, I can't say my line. I have a hangnail. Bev, we have a problem. You've placed me too far back on the stage. My parents won't get a good picture of me for my scrapbook,'*" Bev mimicked.

"We all have our little quirks," Kate pointed out to the young woman.

"Some of us more than others," Bev murmured as Terri entered the room.

"I can't find my script," Terri mournfully complained, moving to the front of the classroom. She shook her head from side to side, her brown hair bobbing under her chin.

"You had it in your hot little hands a few minutes ago," Bev said accusingly. "Remember, we just went through it on stage in the auditorium?!"

Glancing from one girl to the other, Kate sensed an eruption was close at hand. "Terri, did you leave your script in the auditorium?"

The younger girl glared sullenly at Kate, then at Bev. "No! I had it when I left rehearsal. Someone must've stolen it!" she said dramatically. "Now, I don't know what to do."

Kate shot Bev a warning look, sensing the sixteen-year-old was fast approaching the fringe of her tolerance level.

"I'll tell you exactly what you can do—" Bev began.

Loudly clearing her throat, Kate continued to stare at Bev. Finally taking the hint, the angered teen backed down. Turning, Kate concentrated on Terri, a young woman who could be as attractive as Bev, if she could get past a few flaws in her nature. "Terri, where did you go after class?" Kate asked. "Did you set it down somewhere— maybe in another classroom?"

"Of course not! I always know where everything is!" Terri exclaimed.

Bev pulled a face, but restrained herself.

"I can't possibly be in this play now," the younger girl whined.

An expression of hope appeared on Bev's face. Kate shook her head slightly. Sighing with exasperation, Bev glanced at Terri. "You don't really need your script," she suggested. "You already have your lines memorized."

"It's not hard to do when there are only five of them," Terri sniffed.

To avoid exploding, Bev examined one of Kate's bulletin boards, pretending to study a large map of the United States while she silently fumed. "You *are* a gifted actress," Kate silently thought to herself, admiring Bev's self-control. Kate forced a smile as she spoke to Terri. "Why don't you check with the office? Maybe somebody found your script and turned it in."

Before Terri could reply, a slender blonde walked into the room. "BEV?! You in here?"

"Right here," Bev answered, grateful for the diversion. "What's up?"

"We need to talk," Karen replied.

Bev studied her friend's face, sensing she was upset. "Let's go," she said, leading Karen out of the classroom.

"Those two deserve each other!" Terri indignantly exclaimed.

"Why would you say something like that?" Kate asked, irritated by the comment.

"Well, it's true! They're both troublemakers! They do whatever they want and they don't care what anyone thinks!" Terri complained. "Bev treats me horribly. You've seen that in class. Karen's just mean. She's in my ward, but she never comes to church."

"That doesn't make her a bad person," Kate said with a strained smile. She already knew a great deal about Karen's troubled background. Doris had explained why the young woman sometimes seemed so angry with life.

"Karen's mother, Edie, married at a young age," Doris had told Kate a few weeks ago. "It wasn't a very pleasant marriage. In my opinion, the only good thing that came out of it was Karen. After a painful divorce, Edie turned to alcohol for relief.

"Most of the time, little Karen was left with Edie's mother while Edie worked as a waitress at a local restaurant. After work, Edie usually got together with some of her friends for a few drinks. Getting drunk became a way of life. Eventually, Edie was arrested twice for driving under the influence. No one was ever hurt, but both times her car was banged up. The last time it happened, she spent a few days in the county jail. Not long after that, she became involved with a man named Mark Wray.

"Mark was new in town," Doris had sighed. "He and Edie met in a bar, hit it off, and started living together. Mark got Edie hooked on mixing alcohol and drugs. Neither of them could hold down a job, so they were always short of money. Late one night, Mark robbed a local convenience store. He wounded the store clerk when the man reached for a gun he kept under the counter."

Shaking her head, Doris had continued, "I don't think Edie had any idea what Mark was up to when he went into that store. To save his own hide, he later claimed in court that she had planned the entire thing. I still don't believe it! Edie might've had a problem with alcohol and men, but she wasn't a thief!"

"You mentioned they went to court. What happened to Edie?" Kate had prodded.

"When Mark came running out of the store that night waving a gun, he climbed into Edie's car and hollered for her to drive off. She panicked and did exactly that. Unfortunately, she'd had a little too much to drink earlier. She plowed her car into the side of a flower shop. It didn't take long for the police to pick them up after that.

"That's how one of my former students ended up in prison," Doris had concluded. "Edie was charged with her third DUI, and with being an accessory to armed robbery. The judge gave both of them a stiff sentence. Mark was awarded a ten-year fixed sentence because of the violent nature of the crime. Edie was given two sentences that were to be served consecutively. Five years for the DUI—two years fixed if she agreed to participate in a state-sponsored rehabilitation program for substance abuse—and another five years for being an accessory to armed robbery. That was three years ago— three years of misery for Edie, Karen, and Adele, Edie's mother.

"Edie Beyer has a good heart," Doris had concluded, sadly. "She's a mixed-up girl who started hanging around with the wrong crowd in high school years ago. She would never purposely hurt anyone. But this town has permanently labeled her. Not only is Edie considered a tramp for living with a *druggie*, but now she'll be branded as a convict the rest of her life. Poor Karen has to live with that stigma. It's eating her up inside."

" . . . my mom says Karen'll grow up to be just like her mother!" Terri snapped, drawing Kate back to the present conversation.

Anger flashed from Kate's green eyes. Taking a deep breath, she gripped the top of her desk for support. "Terri, you haven't had to deal with the challenges Karen has! I don't think any of us are qualified to judge her!"

Looking like she'd just been slapped across the face, Terri whirled around and ran out of the room crying.

"Nice!" Kate groaned, running a hand through her hair. Terri was Cleo's personal monitor of the infractions taking place in the high school. Kate knew she hadn't heard the end of this conversation. She knew she was in for a confrontation with either Cleo, or Margo, Terri's mother. Neither prospect filled her with joy.

* * *

"Let's get out of here," Bev said to Karen as the two juniors ran down the cement steps of the high school. "My stepmother gave me the keys to her new car today. We'll find a place where we can talk—away from all of these *sensitive* ears."

"You mean, Terri," Karen said as she followed Bev to the luxurious blue Pontiac Grand Prix. She knew Bev didn't care much for her stepmother, Gina, but letting Bev use her car was one thing the woman could do to win points with her stepdaughter. This car had everything. A super-charged V6 engine, traction control, anti-lock brakes, power windows, and most important, a CD stereo.

Bev's own mother had died ten years ago from ovarian cancer, and her father had remarried six years ago, against Bev's wishes. Bev tolerated the woman her father had presented as her *new* mother, but consistently rejected Gina Henderson's attempts to establish a bond between them. The ultimate insult had been the announcement three years after her father and Gina's marriage that her stepmother would be supplying Bev with a half-brother or sister. As fate would have it, Gina had given birth to twins, boys that seemed bent on making Bev's life more miserable than she imagined it could be. Twins that Bev despised. Brothers who reminded her she had to share her father with someone else. Three-year-olds who were nothing but a royal pain as far as Bev was concerned. Ignoring Gina's pleas for help with her small sons, Bev had willingly shouldered several household duties instead. She had wanted nothing to do with the wailing infants she considered intruders. Her opinion hadn't changed in three years. As far as Bev was concerned, Jake and Drake, or Jerk and Dork as she called them, were Gina's responsibility—not hers.

"Are you sure you want to do this? You'll be in trouble with *Cleo* again," Karen asked, leaning against the car door on her side.

Bev shrugged. "My dad's on the school board, remember. I don't think Cleo will complain too much about this."

Karen looked across the car at the other girl. "I thought your dad told her he wanted to be kept informed if you skipped any more school," she reminded her friend.

"I'll let *Cleo* worry about it," Bev responded, slipping inside of the car.

Karen followed Bev's example, unwilling to stick around school without her best friend.

"Where should we go?" Bev asked as they drove down Main Street.

"How about Sandler's drive-in? We could get some hot chocolate, maybe a sandwich. I'm starved. I didn't eat breakfast."

Nodding, Bev glanced around for the local police, then flipped a quick U-turn.

"You're really set on getting yourself into trouble today," Karen muttered.

"Let's just say I've had my fill of some people," she replied, still steaming over Terri's complaints.

Hurt, Karen silently glanced out of the window.

"I didn't mean you," Bev said. "Give me a break. I hate having to watch everything I say and do. I shouldn't have to do that around you." Reaching over, she nudged Karen with her hand. "Okay?!"

"Okay," Karen quietly replied. "Sorry. This has been a rotten day."

"I can tell. Wanna talk about it?"

Karen glanced at Bev. "Let's wait until after we eat. If I tell you now, I may lose my appetite."

Several minutes later, both girls were seated in a booth in the deserted drive-in, finishing the hamburgers they had ordered.

"So, what's up?" Bev tried again.

Karen stared down at the empty Styrofoam cup in front of her.

"C'mon. It can't be that bad."

Still staring at her cup, Karen silently disagreed. "Edie's getting out of prison just before Christmas," she finally revealed.

"Your mother is up for parole?" Bev asked, amazed by this news.

"*Edie,*" Karen said, stressing her mother's name, refusing to call that woman 'mother.' "*Edie* is being rewarded because of her *model* behavior. Someone from the prison called my grandma last night. They approved Edie's release." Karen's eyes filled with tears. "Some holiday vacation that's going to be."

Bev solemnly gazed at her friend. "Karen, I'm sorry."

"Me too. I don't suppose I could live with you for a while?"

"You just say the word."

"Yeah, right. Like my grandmother will go for that. She's convinced everything will work out fine. You should hear her, singing around the house. She thinks this is wonderful news."

Bev played with the plastic spoon she had used to stir her hot cocoa. "Could it be?" she finally ventured. She'd give anything to have a second chance with her own mother.

The look of depression on Karen's face answered that question.

* * *

"It isn't bad enough you sent one girl to the office crying, but you allowed two others to leave the school grounds without acceptable authorization," Cleo informed Kate. She had insisted that the young teacher sit in front of her while she remained standing, her tall frame giving her what she assumed was a domineering edge. Folding her arms, Cleo scowled her displeasure while Kate silently seethed. "Now, I have to call Bev's father. I don't need to remind you he's a member of the school board."

"This is a misunderstanding . . . ," Kate attempted.

"You're right! You don't understand our school policy at all! I don't know what our superintendent was thinking, hiring someone without any experience."

"I'm very qualified for this position and you know it!" Kate replied, revealing the temper she normally worked very hard to control.

"That may be. I have yet to see it." Cleo's grey eyes narrowed to give Kate a disdainful glare. "Consider this a warning. It will appear on your record. I've overlooked other things the past few months . . ."

The high school secretary interrupted the heated discussion, knocking at the office door. Without waiting for a response, the rotund, pleasant woman opened the door to Cleo's office. "I thought you'd want to know—Bev Henderson's father is on line one." The secretary glanced at Kate, sending her a sympathetic look. Kate returned a small smile.

"I'll take it in here," Cleo muttered, waving the secretary out of the room. Then, looking at Kate, her frown deepened. "I don't know how I'll explain this to him. Beverly's father is one of our biggest supporters. Every year during homecoming, he allows us to use new cars and trucks from his car lot for our parade. That wonderful man is always doing something to help us out. He donated the money we used to purchase two new computers last year." She glared at Kate.

"The education of our students is important to him, which is why the man serves on our school board. If Beverly doesn't quit skipping school, her grade point average will suffer. That is a terrible reflection on this school."

On you, you mean, Kate thought to herself. Aloud she replied, "Bev is an excellent student. If she left with Karen today, they must've had a good reason." Rising, she moved to leave the office.

"An unexcused reason. Terri says they probably didn't want to go to their math class."

Kate returned the icy glare. "Terri says a lot of things that aren't necessarily true." Then, before Cleo could reply, she walked out of the office.

* * *

"I'm sorry," Mike said, holding Kate against him on the couch.

"No wonder the students despise that woman!" Kate fumed. "Cleo doesn't give an inch! She's always right—everyone else is wrong! It's always someone else's fault!"

"I'm sure Cleo would appreciate that assessment."

"Just like I'll cherish the *glowing* report she's going to send the school board." Kate grimaced. "I'm sure that will go over big."

Mike smiled warmly at his wife. "You're too good of a teacher for them to take these petty comments seriously."

"I hope they think so." Sitting back against the couch, Kate grabbed a sofa pillow and hugged it. "I wish Doris would hurry up and get back. I didn't realize how much I've grown to depend on her. She keeps me sane in that asylum."

"When will she return from the debate trip?"

"Sometime late tomorrow," Kate sighed. "She'll be at school on Monday."

"Today's Friday. You've survived till now." He grinned, hopping up from the couch. "I know, we'll go do something fun tomorrow! Maybe rent a couple of snowmobiles. I've been dying to take you up to see Harper Canyon. It's beautiful!" He leaned over Kate, bending down for a kiss. "You up for a jaunt into the local winter wonderland tomorrow afternoon?"

Kate nodded. "Anywhere away from this town."

"You don't mean that."

"Today isn't the day to ask," Kate assured her husband.

* * *

Beckoning to Sabrina, Marsha led the way down the sidewalk toward her house, noting that her mother's car wasn't in the driveway. She tried the front door and found that it was locked—another good sign. Marsha reached into her backpack, retrieved a key, and unlocked the door. She walked in and motioned for Sabrina to step inside, then firmly closed the door behind them. "Mom?" Marsha called out. "Brian?" When there was no answer, the slender redhead breathed a sigh of relief. "Good, no one's here," she said quietly to Sabrina. "I think my brother had a dentist appointment after school—that's probably where they're at," Marsha explained. "We could use the privacy," she added, removing her coat.

Sabrina silently agreed, watching as Marsha carefully hung her coat in a nearby closet. When Marsha reached for Sabrina's coat, Sabrina shook her head. "You're sure?" Marsha pressed.

"Yeah," Sabrina replied. "I don't think I'll ever get warm today."

"Okay then—just thought I'd ask." Marsha moved to the living room. As the two girls entered the large, beautifully decorated room, a car drove by. Glancing out the bay window, Marsha relaxed when she saw that it was the neighbors. "Sabrina, to be safe, let's go downstairs to my bedroom," she suggested. "That way if Mom and Brian show up, they won't hear what we're saying."

"Why does it matter—everyone's talking about me anyway!"

Marsha smiled sadly at Sabrina. "Not everyone," she tried to console her friend. When there was no response, Marsha pointed to the stairs and headed for her room. As she surveyed the clutter in her bedroom, she wished she had taken the time to straighten it earlier that morning. Embarrassed, she hoped Sabrina wouldn't mind the mess. The look on Sabrina's face indicated that she didn't care where she was as long as it was away from the critical stares that had followed her that day at school. "Let's see if we can find a place to sit down," Marsha invited, walking into her room.

Sabrina numbly followed. Still struggling with what Tracie, Sindi, and Dawn had been spreading around earlier that afternoon, shock was giving way to anger. She was grateful for Marsha's insistence that they come here after school, realizing her own home was the last place she wanted to be right now.

Marsha quickly moved clothes, a blow dryer, and a pile of CDs to clear a spot on her bed, gesturing to Sabrina to have a seat. Turning, Marsha brushed a pile of dirty clothes off a nearby chair and sat down.

Sabrina sank down on the bed, convinced her life was ruined. She glanced at Marsha, in her estimation, the only friend she had left in this town. In a surprising twist, she and Marsha had become very close the past couple of weeks. Marsha had finally had her fill of their former friends, deciding the parties *were* getting out of hand. She also didn't approve of the way Tracie had treated some of their classmates, including Sabrina. Marsha's conscience had plagued her until she had finally sided with Sabrina. In retaliation, Tracie, Sindi, and Dawn had started several vicious rumors, most about Sabrina; all were untrue. Today's insinuation had opened a permanent rift between the five girls, wounding Sabrina deeply.

"Why would they say that I'm pregnant?" Sabrina now asked, still tortured by what had been going around school that day.

"Because they're morons!" Marsha replied. "They think they're getting even with us by spreading these stories."

"Getting even for what?"

To avoid the hurt look on Sabrina's face, Marsha concentrated on her hands—on the ring Tracie had given her for her birthday several months ago. Scowling, she pulled it off, throwing it across the room. She glanced up, meeting Sabrina's searching gaze. "Tracie gave that to me—" she began to explain.

"I know," Sabrina responded. "I wish it was that easy to get rid of this mess. How did it get so bad?"

"It's crazy!" Marsha agreed. "When you stopped hanging around with us, you know, after Halloween—everyone was really mad," she revealed. "Tracie said you thought you were *too good* for us. Then she said you weren't *good enough* to run around with us. She convinced us that you were the one being a jerk. I suppose we wanted to believe her because it made us feel better about what we were doing." Tears came to her eyes. "But I knew you were the only one in our group who was trying to do the right thing. I wish I'd been brave enough to walk away when you did." She paused, remembering the long talk she'd had with their branch president last week. It had been difficult, admitting to the things she had done. Her one consolation was the knowledge that she had finally drawn the line, that she hadn't lost control of herself as some of the other girls had done at these parties. It was amazing what people would do if they were drunk enough, something that had scared Marsha into turning her life around. "Sabrina, I am so sorry for what we . . . I . . . put you through."

"We've already settled that," Sabrina reminded her.

"I know, but sometimes I still feel so bad," Marsha tearfully admitted.

"What really makes me mad—Tracie and her *friends* are the ones out having such a *good time* and I'm the one everyone is talking about."

Marsha nodded. "I'm sure it was Tracie's idea. She probably thinks it's funny."

"Just so everyone gets a good laugh. That's the important thing!" Sabrina tried not to cry, but hot tears defiantly slid down her face. Marsha stood and drew her into a hug. A few minutes later, Sabrina pulled away.

"This time Tracie's gone too far! I don't care who she thinks she is— she can't get away with this!" Sabrina threatened, wiping at her eyes.

"What are you going to do?"

"First, I'm going to let my mother know how I really feel about things. Between her and Kate, I don't have a life anymore! They were the ones who told me to ignore Tracie. Look where that's gotten me!"

"I'm sure they were just trying to help," Marsha suggested.

"I don't need this kind of help. From now on, I'll handle things my own way, without their interference."

"What are you going to do about Tracie?"

"I don't know, but she's not going to run over the top of me—or you—anymore!" Sabrina promised.

CHAPTER 9

Edie Beyer took a final look at the place she had called home for three years. Cinder block walls decorated by a solitary calendar. The pictures of her daughter, Karen, had already been carefully packed inside of the worn suitcase that held her worldly possessions. Shifting her gaze, Edie stared at the steel bars that had concealed her from the rest of the world. It was a time to step beyond their confining protection. Edie grimaced, feeling certain she wouldn't emerge from this cloistered cocoon as a delicate and lovely butterfly; but rather, more like an ungainly caterpillar. Edie felt ugly although physically she had been graced with features most would call beautiful—long blonde hair that shimmered in the sunlight, soft brown eyes, and fair, unblemished skin. But Edie saw herself as ugly on the inside, where it mattered most of all.

"Well, Edie, today's the day," a gruff voice called out. "I'm glad the parole board finally came to their senses. You don't belong here."

Edie glanced at the guard, a large woman with a heart to match. She had been Edie's only friend during her incarceration. Madge Holmes—known among the inmates as Sergeant Homely. Madge rarely smiled, but when she did, it lit up her entire face. Madge had taken a liking to the thin, quiet inmate, and had offered protection to Edie during the first weeks of her sentence. When three female prisoners had cornered Edie in the exercise yard, pinching, slapping, hitting, Edie had been terrified. "We got ourselves a Barbie doll," one of the women had gloated. If Madge hadn't walked out to see what all of the commotion was about, Edie shuddered to think what might have happened. Instead, Madge had intervened and had seen to it that Edie was moved to a different cellblock.

"They'd probably kill you next time, or maim you for life," Madge had said, explaining that she had gone to the prison officials to request the transfer that had placed Edie in a minimum security pod. "I see no reason why you should be mixed in with a bunch of animals," Madge had later told Edie. "You can serve your time just as well in one piece."

Edie had been too numb to fully appreciate what Madge had done. It hadn't registered until later how lucky she had been.

"All packed?"

Madge's question jarred Edie back to the present.

"Yes," she softly answered.

"Okay then," Madge said, grinning as she unlocked Edie's cell. "Let's get you out of here."

Edie silently picked up her small suitcase and followed the guard out of the cellblock. She tried to ignore the jeers and insults that followed her departure.

"Pay them no mind," Madge soothed. "They're jealous. They'd all give their right arm to trade you places today."

When they reached the final door, Madge paused, turning to smile encouragingly at Edie. "Now, I want you to promise me something."

Edie remained silent, waiting.

"You made a mistake, but you've served your time. Put the past behind you. Try to find some happiness in life now."

Edie slowly nodded.

Madge smiled again at the fragile woman who was about to be released. "This is a chance for a brand new start." Turning, she unlocked the door and escorted Edie to the parole officer who was waiting to meet her. "Be happy, Edie."

* * *

Karen Beyer slumped down against the faded couch with the flowery design. No one would ever know how much she was dreading this reunion. It had been horrible enough, enduring the visits, seeing her mother in that awful place. Now, Edie Beyer was finally free.

When her mother had first been arrested, Karen thought her world had come to an end; she knew it had when Edie was led from the courtroom in handcuffs that final day. Sobbing uncontrollably, the thirteen-year-old had fled, ignoring her grandmother's cries to come back. Karen had run out of the brick building and down the sidewalk, bumping into strangers who stared after the grieving girl.

Three years later, Karen was still trying to put the pieces of her life together in a pattern that made sense. Some fragments wouldn't fit, no matter how hard she tried. One piece in particular had frayed her heart; her father didn't want anything to do with her. That hadn't changed even after Edie had been hauled off to prison.

"It's not my fault Edie messed up," Roger Beyer had told his former mother-in-law when Edie's trial was over. "I can't look after a kid. Karen belongs with you." Then he had walked away from his daughter a second time, causing even more pain than he had after the divorce.

As a result, Karen didn't trust anyone. She didn't believe in myths that weak people hung onto, like Santa Claus or God. She didn't need any of it and she didn't need anyone, her mother least of all.

* * *

Adele Hadley quietly wept by the side of her bed. Her daughter was coming home today. Begging for strength, she poured her heart out to her Father in Heaven. *"Soften Karen's heart. Help her to know how much Edie loves her,"* Adele silently pleaded. *"Help Karen to know how much Edie needs her now."* Burying her face in the comforter, Adele continued to cry.

She had wanted to be the one waiting outside the Idaho State women's prison in Pocatello for her daughter, Eden—Edie, as she preferred to be called. Instead, she had heeded the advice of both their bishop and the church-approved counselor Karen had been seeing. Both had agreed this reunion would be better at home, away from the harsh image of the prison.

The probation officer had offered to drive Edie from Pocatello. She felt it would give her a chance to get better acquainted with her new charge, and to see for herself the conditions Edie would be living under in Blaketown. Adele had agreed to this arrangement, although it made her nervous to think Edie's probation officer would be evaluating them. But at least her daughter would be home.

It tore at Adele's heart whenever she thought of her beautiful daughter, locked up in prison. It had been three dreadful years, two years shorter than Edie's lawyer had predicted. That had been a blessing. Time off for good behavior. As Adele wiped the tears from her eyes, she couldn't help but ask why Edie hadn't been a model of good behavior years ago, when all of this could've been avoided.

Shaking her head, Adele knew dredging up the past wouldn't help. Edie had already paid a horrible price.

* * *

Edie hesitantly reached to ring the doorbell.

"Go on," the parole officer encouraged. Concerned by Edie's silence during the two-hour drive from Pocatello, Robin Sheridan had tried to start a conversation several times, finally giving up when she realized it would remain one-sided. As they drove into Blaketown, Robin noticed Edie had nervously clenched and unclenched her fists at least a dozen times. Smiling reassurance, Robin silently prayed Edie's reception would be amiable.

Summoning her courage, Edie pressed the round, lighted button. When the door opened, Adele and Edie gazed at each other for several long seconds. Then, Adele tearfully reached for her daughter, holding her close. Edie kept her emotions tightly reined, a skill she had polished during her incarceration. She remained stiff as her mother continued to cling to her, crying. Finally, sensing Edie's aloofness, Adele pulled away, inviting both women into the house.

Robin chewed her bottom lip. She had hoped Edie would loosen up, that Adele's warm welcome would help her daughter to relax. Instead, Edie seemed more nervous than before. Robin glanced around at the modestly furnished house. Compact but clean, it seemed cheerful enough. Christmas decorations added a festive touch. Robin followed Adele and Edie into the living room. Looking up, she gazed at a beautiful painting of Jesus Christ. A good sign. If Adele was as religiously inclined as that painting indicated, it would make this transition easier. Robin had found that most people with a religious background tended to be compassionate. From Adele's emotional greeting, Robin was convinced Edie would receive adequate support from her mother. Even then, it would be a difficult adjustment.

An attractive young woman slowly rose up from the couch. Robin glanced at Edie, then at the girl, assuming this was the daughter that had been mentioned; the resemblance was quite pronounced. Edie's stiff resolve appeared to weaken at the sight of her daughter. Sensing this would be a good time to fade from view, Robin motioned for Adele to follow her from the room. There were things she needed to discuss with Adele in private. Quietly the two women slipped out of sight.

Unaware that her mother and probation officer had left the room, Edie stared at Karen. It had only been two months since she had last seen her daughter, but she was amazed at the changes that had taken place during that time. Changes she had been too numb to observe before. Her daughter was growing up. As a myriad of emotions overwhelmed her, Edie struggled for something to say, a familiar ache filling her heart.

Karen returned the stare, then focused on the floor. She would not cry—she would not give this woman the satisfaction of knowing how much she had missed her.

Timidly, Edie touched Karen's face, then brushed back a strand of her daughter's long, blonde hair. Her fingers conveyed what she couldn't say. *I love you. I'm sorry for the pain I've caused. Please forgive me.*

Closing her eyes, Karen struggled. Plaguing her were memories of betrayal, pain, and sleepless nights. As her mother suddenly gripped her in a stifling hug, Karen panicked, pulling away to bolt from the room.

* * *

Adele eased down on the bed beside Edie. Her daughter was lying quietly on her stomach, crying, as she had often done when she was small and afraid. Placing a hand on Edie's trembling back, Adele gently rubbed, trying to massage in the comfort she longed to give.

Closing her eyes, Edie gradually relaxed, allowing her mother to take them both back to a time when life had been simpler, before everything had gone terribly wrong.

* * *

"Do you know how hurt your mother was this afternoon when you ran out of the house?" Adele softly chided as Karen changed into a nightgown.

"It doesn't come close to how I've felt," was the sullen reply.

"She cried herself to sleep," Adele tried again.

"Does she know how many nights I have?!"

"Karen, it isn't good to be this angry—"

"It's how I've learned to survive!"

Adele gazed at her granddaughter, a young woman who was becoming more like Edie had been every day. Full of angry resentment. Full of bitter pain. And, like her mother, Karen steadfastly refused to listen.

Edie's father had died years ago in a farm accident, but Edie had never come to terms with his death. When the tractor Hyrum Hadley was driving had stalled going uphill, he had jumped down to take a look at the engine. The tractor had slipped out of gear, rolling down the hill, pinning Hyrum underneath.

Thirteen years old at the time, Edie had turned her back to the comfort offered by family and friends. Worst of all, Edie hadn't wanted anything to do with the Church. "Why pray to someone who doesn't care?" she had asked, blaming God for what had happened. Adele could see that same haunted look in Karen's eyes now.

"Grandma, I know we have to share a bedroom—now that *she's* back—but no more lectures, okay?! I'll deal with this my own way." Turning, Karen headed down the hall to the bathroom.

"That's what frightens me most of all," Adele murmured.

CHAPTER 10

"It's good to finally be home," Kate exclaimed as her mother gathered her up in a hug.

"I've missed you both so much," Sue Erickson said, releasing her oldest daughter to reach for her son-in-law. She gave Mike a quick embrace, then motioned for her husband, Greg, to take over.

"Hi, Dad," Kate said, wincing slightly when her father grabbed her in a tight bear hug.

Greg Erickson grinned, thrilled to see Mike and Kate. Due to bad weather, the young couple hadn't been able to make the trip up to Montana for Thanksgiving. It had been nearly four months since their last visit. Giving Kate another squeeze for good measure, he let go of her to shake Mike's hand.

"Where's Sabrina?" Kate asked her mother.

"With Marsha," Sue replied. "Those two are inseparable right now."

"Is this a good thing?"

"I hope so," Sue replied, leading Kate into the dining room to show her the new centerpiece she had made for Christmas.

"How's it goin'?" Greg asked his son-in-law.

"Fine," Mike replied.

"You still content to dwell in Idaho?" Greg asked, walking with Mike into the living room.

"It grows on you. Why?"

"We heard there was an opening in the Forest Service office up this way."

Mike lifted an eyebrow. "Oh?"

"Your dad was telling me about it. He wanted to discuss it with you after Christmas. I just thought I'd put my two cents worth in now. You know we'd love to have you two close by. Sue misses Kate—she's always telling me how much fun they'd have together, shopping, decorating each other's houses—you know, women stuff," he said, grinning at Mike.

Mike nodded in agreement.

"Confidentially, Sue can hardly wait to be a grandma. It kills her to think you two would be so far away when that time finally comes." Greg sat down, pointing to the other recliner for Mike. He waited until his son-in-law sat in the chair, then continued to share his good news. "From what your dad tells me, this position wouldn't put you under as much pressure as the job you have now—you'd be the new fire management officer. You'd be in charge of controlled burns—that sort of thing. You might take a slight cut in pay, but think of the advantages this opportunity would offer."

Mike glanced back at Kate to see if she had heard this new bit of information. His wife was still laughing with her mother near the dining room. He breathed a sigh of relief. As much as he loved Bozeman, Mike was hesitant to give up what he and Kate were slowly building in Blaketown—a firm foundation for the rest of their lives.

He had reveled in the scenic discoveries he'd made in the rugged Idaho mountains and forests surrounding the valley where they now lived. He also enjoyed working with the staff in the Blaketown office. There had been a few struggles in the beginning, as there had been with Kate and her job, but he was content to remain where they were, for now. He had seen the impact Kate was starting to have on several teenagers. He knew his wife was capable of making a difference in the lives of these young people and hated for her to give up that chance.

The place they were renting was small, but it was home. Someday they could look into buying a bigger place. In the meantime, they were slowly paying off their student loans, setting aside a portion of their earnings in a savings account for a future day.

Their relationship continued to be strengthened by the amount of time they were able to spend together. They relied on each other, just as they had done in college. He was sure that aspect would never change—even if they moved nearer to their families. But moving back to Bozeman wasn't as appealing as it might have been a year ago.

Leaning forward, Mike motioned for his father-in-law to do the same. "Dad, I appreciate you telling me this, and I will talk it over with Kate, but let's keep it between ourselves for now. Kate could really use a break from making major decisions—"

"Is she all right?" Greg interrupted. Slowly, a light seemed to dawn. "Wait a minute, are you trying to tell me something?" he excitedly asked.

Mike sighed. He and Kate had been expecting this question. He might as well get it over with now, then Kate wouldn't have to deal with it later. "She's not pregnant, if that's what you're asking," Mike answered in a low voice.

Disappointment radiated from Greg's eyes.

"We keep hoping, but so far it's just not meant to be."

"Have you two thought about seeing a doctor?" Greg asked.

Mike shook his head. They had already decided if Kate wasn't pregnant by next fall, they would take further steps. Until then, they would patiently wait. He knew that was easier for him than for Kate. Each month when a certain day rolled around, she quietly grieved. Mike was convinced the time wasn't right yet. Deciding to leave it in the Lord's hands, he tried not to worry about it. Things had a way of working out for the best. He smiled at his father-in-law, hoping he could convince Greg Erickson of that theory.

* * *

As she walked into the living room of her parents' home, Kate couldn't believe it was already Christmas Eve. Kneeling down beside the Christmas tree, she fluffed up the smashed ribbon on the long box her husband would finally open tomorrow morning. It had been difficult, ignoring Mike's excited questions as he had struggled to attach it to the top of their car for the trip to Bozeman. He had joked, claiming the box was longer than their full-size Chevy Blazer.

"Still admiring Mike's gift?"

Startled, Kate glanced back at her mother. Grinning, she stood. "I don't know who's more excited—Mike or me. I can hardly wait for him to open it."

Sue laughed, smoothing back her short, red hair. "I know the feeling. I haven't told you what I got your dad yet." She glanced around, making sure Greg couldn't hear. The last she had seen, Greg and Mike were engaged in a fierce battle of Space Invaders on Tyler's Super Nintendo entertainment system downstairs in the family room.

"What did you get him?" Kate asked, moving closer to her mother.

"Let's put it this way—it's too big to fit under the Christmas tree," Sue said, her green eyes sparkling with excitement. "I had it delivered the day before you and Mike arrived," she added mysteriously.

"What is it?"

Motioning for Kate to follow, Sue led her through the kitchen and out into the garage. She flipped on a light, then pointed to a large item covered with a green canvas tarp.

Kate glanced at the tarp, then at her mother. "I give up. Just tell me."

Sue walked over to the tarp, lifting it up to reveal a huge, gift-wrapped box. "Guess how many rolls of paper it took to wrap this thing," Sue laughed. "And I didn't bother to wrap the bottom. I can't begin to lift this by myself," she added.

"What is it?" Kate pressed.

"A weight bench," Sue proudly revealed.

"What?"

"It has all kinds of features. A bar-bell bench press, leg curl, a pulley setup for push-downs, weights— "

"You got him a weight bench?" Kate asked again, mildly shocked.

"Yes. He's always wanted one. Remember how he loves working out on your Uncle Stan's in Salt Lake when we visit?"

Kate nodded.

"Your father doesn't have time to go to the health club anymore. I figured he'd take time out to exercise here at home if I got him one of these. Think he'll like it?"

"Yeah . . . I think so," Kate said, trying to sound positive. She knew her father detested any form of diet or exercise. Her mother had been fighting an uphill battle for years, trying to get him to take care of himself. His blood pressure had steadily increased with his age, a cause of concern for both his doctor and his wife.

"Do you think we can get this into the living room later tonight?"

Kate glanced at the large box, then at her mother. "Probably, if Mike and Sabrina help us."

"I think you and I and Mike can handle this."

"What about Sabrina?" Kate ventured.

"Only if she volunteers."

"What?" Kate asked, confused.

"I'm trying to give your sister some space. Currently, she resents anything I ask her to do."

Kate had already noticed the friction between her younger sister and their parents the past couple of days. It also seemed like Sabrina had been avoiding her and Mike since their arrival. "I thought things were better between you two."

"They were, for about a month. It's been tough for Sabrina. She went through quite a bit breaking away from those other girls . . ."

"Sindi, Tracie, and Dawn?"

"Those are the ones. Marsha wasn't very happy with the way things were going either. She and Sabrina splintered off together, and it looked like everything was going to settle down."

"What happened?"

"The other girls have been making life pretty miserable for them. They've started spreading rumors that aren't exactly nice."

"Like what?" Kate asked, remembering how awful it had been for her in high school when false rumors had been spread about her own behavior, some by people she had considered to be friends.

Sue gazed somberly at her oldest daughter. "Little things like your sister is pregnant. Tracie started that one a couple of weeks ago."

Kate stared at her mother. "No wonder Sabrina seems so upset."

"She is, and I don't know what to do for her. The harder she tries to do the right thing, the worse it gets for her."

"People will start to see Tracie for what she is," Kate suggested.

"I don't know about that. Tracie's gained several 'popular' friends this year. Unlike Sabrina, she's gliding up that particular ladder of success."

Sitting down on the small cement steps in front of the door that led into the house, Kate looked up at her mother. "We've got to do something to help Sabrina," she said.

"We're trying," Sue replied. "But I'm not sure how to make this one better."

"What if she started fresh somewhere else?"

Sue returned Kate's intense gaze. "Like in Blaketown?"

Kate nodded.

It was something Sue had already considered. The only thing holding her back was the bitter feelings Sabrina still possessed toward her older sister.

"I could steer Sabrina toward some good kids. It's a smaller school . . . it might be easier for her . . ."

"I know, Kate, I've thought about all of this before, but remember when you were ready to leave Bozeman your senior year?"

"Yeah," Kate replied, thoughtfully. In high school, when she had tried to change her life around, people hadn't been very receptive to the new version of herself.

"You were ready to give up and move to Salt Lake to live with your Aunt Paige and Uncle Stan."

"But we finally decided I couldn't run away from my problems."

Sue sadly smiled. "And eventually, things turned around. You made new friends, wonderful friends, including Mike."

"True."

"I think for now, we'll see how things go. If it gets any worse, I'll bring her to Blaketown myself."

"Okay," Kate agreed.

"In the meantime, let's try to keep things light and fun the next few days—I want Sabrina to realize who's really in her corner."

Nodding, Kate followed her mother inside the house.

* * *

"Here, I think you'll enjoy reading this," Sue said, handing Kate the most recent letter from Tyler.

"I haven't heard anything from the brat in nearly two months."

Sue smiled. "I'm lucky to get something from your brother every two or three weeks. And then it's usually a short note. I guess he decided since it was Christmas, he'd send a real letter this time."

Kate eagerly drew out the letter, quickly scanning its contents. "Two more baptisms? He's doing great!"

"He is," Sue agreed, glancing at the kitchen clock, surprised that it was already five o'clock. "I hope Sabrina hurries." The traditional family seafood dinner would start at 6:30 p.m. She had hoped Sabrina would heed the instructions she had given her earlier that day. "Please be home by 5:30. Kate and I could use your help with dinner," she had told her youngest daughter. Sue wanted to avoid a contentious scene tonight, hoping an atmosphere of love and peace would prevail. It was the best gift her youngest daughter could give her for Christmas. Sabrina had sullenly replied that she and Marsha had a lot of things to discuss and she'd be home eventually.

Sue hated the wedge that had been driven between herself and Sabrina the past few weeks. She sensed that Sabrina was blaming her for the way things had turned out. Sabrina probably would've walked away from those other girls on her own, but because Sue had encouraged her to do so, the way Sabrina was being treated at school was now her mother's fault. That was teenage logic for you, Sue sighed. Convinced it would all die down eventually, Sue was patiently biding her time until Sabrina could see that it was all worth it. In the meantime, knowing how important Marsha had become to Sabrina, Sue was willing to do anything to make this transition easier for the two girls.

But it was Christmas Eve. She wanted the family to be together tonight and was hoping to patch things up between Sabrina and Kate, something that would be impossible if Sabrina continued to stay away.

* * *

"She'll be here anytime now," Greg assured his wife, glancing again at his watch, noting it was 6:45 p.m.

"Let's just start," Sue replied. She was tempted to take back the special gift she and Greg were giving their youngest daughter this year; a new CD player with three of the CDs Sabrina had requested—Wallflower, Savage Garden, and a group called Chumbawamba. It had cost a small fortune, but it was the only thing Sabrina wanted. Convinced their daughter had earned it for the way she had stood up to her former friends, Greg and Sue had taken great pains to get the best CD player they could find for the money set aside for Sabrina for Christmas.

Deciding this evening was not going according to plan, Sue gathered the rest of the family around the dining room table to begin the dinner. Mike, Kate, Greg, and Sue bowed their heads for the blessing. Halfway through Greg's prayer, Sabrina burst into the house.

"Hey, all. How's it goin'?"

When Kate opened her eyes to glance at her mother, the expression on Sue's face was one of livid rage. But, unlike the mother Kate had known years ago, Sue controlled herself. Waiting until Greg finished blessing the dinner, Sue then stood, facing her youngest child. "Weren't you wearing your watch?" she asked, trying to remain calm.

Sabrina shrugged, playing with a long strand of permed, blonde hair. "I lost track of the time."

"I see," Sue said dryly. "Without your help, dinner is ready. Go wash up and come eat."

Kate's eyes widened. Her mother had mellowed so much. Years ago this scene would've turned into a shouting match, with their mother doing most of the shouting.

"I'm not hungry. Marsha and I got a pizza about an hour ago," Sabrina responded. Turning, she ran upstairs to her bedroom.

"Sabrina!" Greg started. Sue reached across the table to touch his hand, giving him a warning look. "Sue, I will not have her treat you like this!"

"Greg, it doesn't do any good to yell at her. She tunes us out."

"So, we just let her run over the top of us?!" Greg retorted.

"No. She'll know she blew it tonight."

Greg rolled his eyes as Kate and Mike exchanged a look of concern.

"She'll clean up the mess Kate and I made out of the kitchen," Sue informed her husband.

"And how do you propose to accomplish that miracle?" Greg asked.

Sue knew exactly how. Much to everyone's surprise, several minutes later, Sabrina quietly did up the dishes after the delicious seafood dinner. Sue didn't tell them about the short conversation she'd had with Sabrina when everyone was through eating. Going up to Sabrina's room, Sue let her youngest daughter know there would be no gift from Santa under the tree the next morning if she didn't start behaving.

"I know you're going through a tough time, but that is no reason to take it out on the rest of us. All we've ever tried to do is help you. Now, you march yourself downstairs and clean up every one of those dishes!" Sue hated to resort to threats, but Sabrina had to learn there were limits, even if she thought her life was ruined.

A few minutes later, Sabrina had appeared in the dining room and began stacking the plates. After the dishwasher was nearly loaded, Kate walked into the kitchen. "Why would you rather clean up the kitchen by yourself than help fix dinner and eat a wonderful meal with your family?" she asked.

Sabrina gave her sister an extremely dirty look, then rinsed off another dish to add to the dishwasher. *Don't push it, Kate,* she silently threatened.

"What is with you tonight?" Kate asked, irritated by the silent treatment.

"You don't want to know," Sabrina replied turning her back to Kate.

Kate studied her younger sister. Sabrina was becoming a beautiful young woman. But her scowl and the cold look radiating from her sapphire eyes indicated trouble. Shuddering, Kate looked away. It was like seeing a reflection of herself at that age. Defiant, angry, bitter. Glancing toward the dining room at her mother, Kate saw a pained expression she had been responsible for too many times. *No, Sabrina,* she inwardly moaned. *Learn from my mistakes—don't repeat them.*

CHAPTER 11

Early the next morning, the Ericksons and Jeffries gathered in the living room to see what Santa had brought. As Kate had anticipated, Mike was thrilled with the cross-country skis. Eager to try them, he called one of his brothers to see if they could work something out that afternoon. His older brother, Scott, was an avid cross-country skier. He assured Mike they would give his new skis a good work-out later that day.

For the first time since Kate and Mike's arrival, Sabrina smiled and meant it when she saw the CD player her parents had picked out. It was the model she had requested, similar to the one Marsha had bought a couple of months ago. She thanked her parents for the gift, then disappeared with it upstairs, anxious to listen to the CDs she had found in her stocking.

Mike had given Kate a video collection of the Civil War epic she had secretly coveted, as well as a new dress. Delighted, she hugged her thoughtful husband. Kate had noticed the forest-green dress in one of the local shops in Blaketown and had been drawn to the classic design. Decorated with elegant lace around the neck, it would be perfect for the school district banquets they sometimes had the opportunity to attend.

Greg had given Sue a new dress coat, one she had pointed out to him a few weeks ago. He had taken the hint, including a little surprise. Telling her to look in one of the pockets after she tried it on, he watched happily as Sue pulled out a small velvet box. When she opened it, she was stunned by the beautiful mother's ring. Three colorful jewels—one of each of her children's birthstones—adorned the golden band. Sliding it onto her finger, she found it was a perfect fit.

Now it was Greg's turn. They had forced him to wait until last, making jokes about the huge box in the center of the living room. Calling Sabrina back down to witness this event, Sue finally gave Greg permission to open his gift. Acting like a young boy, Greg eagerly tore into the paper although he couldn't begin to open the box until Mike finally went to the kitchen for a steak knife. Then, quickly cutting through the strapping tape, Greg opened the lid of the box. He stared at the contents, then at his wife.

"It's a little something you and Mike can put together while Kate and I fix breakfast," Sue said, smiling.

"This may sound a bit silly, but what is it?" Greg asked.

"It's a weight bench," Sue revealed, giving him a hug.

"Oh. How nice," he said, trying to act enthused. "All for me. How thoughtful."

"I know how much you enjoy Stan's. I figured it was time you had one of your own," Sue said, failing to notice the disappointed look on her husband's face.

"Hey, this is a nice one," Mike said, trying to salvage the moment. "You're a lucky guy."

"Oh, yeah," Greg replied. "I feel very blessed."

Kate stifled the urge to giggle. "Mike would be happy to help you put it together," she offered, knowing that Mike would now be as amused as his father-in-law. He hated assembling things. Even as a young boy, he had ignored the Lego brick and erector sets he had been given. He loved sports and the outdoors, exciting things like that.

"Well, Mike," Greg said, rubbing his hands together. "Looks like we're going to have a fun-filled morning of Christmas bliss."

"Yep," Mike said, giving Kate a look that indicated he would be getting even in the very near future.

* * *

After two hours of less than enthusiastic effort and concentration, Mike and Greg tightened the final bolt of the weight machine.

"Not bad," Greg sighed, looking it over. "I guess I'll get used to having it around." He glanced at his son-in-law. "Between you and me, I hate these kind of things."

"But Mom said you loved working out on Uncle Stan's machine."

"Mike, let me clue you in. There's always been a little friendly competition between me and Sue's older brother. Stan challenges me to lift weights—I fight to protect the family honor. It's as simple as that." Glancing at the machine Sue had given him, Greg pulled a face.

Mike laughed. "You know Mom's just worried about you," he said.

"I know and I wish she'd quit it! First it was the diet, now this. Next thing she'll be signing me up to jog in marathons."

Grinning, Mike shook his head. Moving to the weight bench, he decided to try it out.

"Let's see if this thing really works," he suggested. Lying back on the padded bench, he lifted up the weighted barbell.

"Show-off," Greg accused. "I hope you pull a muscle."

Laughing, Mike continued to lift the barbell up into the air. "Hey, this is kind of fun," he said a few seconds later.

"My idea of fun is sitting in a recliner, munching on buttered popcorn while I flip through the channels of a big screen TV." Then, turning his back to his son-in-law, Greg marched into the family room and proceeded to do just that.

* * *

"Sabrina?" Kate called out, knocking at her sister's bedroom door. She wanted a chance to visit with Sabrina before she and Mike drove over to his parents' house. She waited for a response, but heard only the thumping rhythm of Sabrina's new CD player. Taking a deep breath, she turned the knob and entered the room. She glanced around at the jumble of clothes, magazines, and CDs and experienced a sense of déjà vu. It resembled her room years ago.

"What do you want?" Sabrina asked, looking up from the bed. She continued to lean back against a fluffy pillow as she listened to one of her new CDs.

"Do you mind if I turn this down?" Kate asked, pointing to the stereo. Sabrina nodded.

"We need to talk," Kate replied, crossing the room to shut off the stereo.

Sabrina's blue eyes narrowed. Sitting up, she glared at Kate. "What did you do that for?"

"Because we need to talk," Kate repeated.

Pulling a face, Sabrina continued to glare. This was the last thing she needed.

Kate walked over to the bed, setting aside the pile of magazines Sabrina had been thumbing through to make a place to sit down. "You're getting quite a collection of teen magazines," she said, glancing at the stack of colorful publications.

"Yeah," Sabrina agreed. "Does that make me a bad person?" she challenged.

"No." Kate forced a smile. "Sabrina, why are you acting this way . . . ," she began.

"Who's acting?"

Kate met Sabrina's accusing glare with a solemn look. "Mom told me about what a tough time you've been having at school this year," she said quietly. She waited for a response, but when Sabrina refused to speak, she continued, "It's devastating to be accused of things you haven't done, especially by the kids your age. Those rumors can get so ugly. I know exactly how you're—"

"I've heard all of this before," Sabrina interrupted. "I don't need an instant replay . . . and especially not from you!"

"Why are you treating me like the enemy?"

Sabrina glowered at her older sister. She didn't want to discuss this now, if ever. Besides, it was Christmas. She had promised their mother last night that she would try to get along with everyone, that she wouldn't cause any major scenes. It was the only gift her mother had requested, and despite what everyone thought, Sabrina always attempted to keep her word.

"We all love you so much," Kate tried again. "We would do anything to help you."

"Trust me, you and Mom have done enough to help me already," Sabrina muttered under her breath.

"Don't do this to Mom, please," Kate pleaded.

"Do what?"

"You know what I'm talking about. Don't judge Mom so harshly. Our parents aren't perfect, but they care about us. They've tried very hard to teach us what this life is all about."

"Some of us didn't listen very well, did we?" Sabrina threw back at her.

Kate studied her sister's face. Sabrina had always been so sweet, and Kate hated to see this metamorphosis take place. Her sister's angry sorrow was changing to a defiant bitterness, something she had observed with some of her students in Blaketown. "Mom loves you. Don't hurt her like this," Kate said softly.

Sabrina tried very hard not to roll her eyes. Did anyone care how hurt she had been the past few months?

Rising from the bed, Kate looked down at her younger sister. "When I was your age, no one could tell me what to do either. I've learned to regret that, and what I put Mom through. I want to spare you from— "

"*I am not you!*" Sabrina angrily exclaimed. "I wish people would understand that and leave me alone!" She stood up, moved to the CD player, and turned it up louder than before.

Sighing heavily, Kate left the room, firmly closing the door behind her.

* * *

Bev opened the gift her stepmother had handed her. Gina was now anxiously waiting for her reaction. Purposely keeping the pleasure she felt out of her voice, Bev murmured a quiet "thank you." Setting aside the gorgeous new ski coat—something Gina must've seen her admire a few weeks ago—Bev reached for the gift her father had given her, something she really didn't care for, a set of what he called "writer's tools": a thesaurus, a rhyming dictionary, and a huge Webster's dictionary. Bev pretended to be thrilled with the books, to drive home the point that it didn't matter how hard her stepmother tried, she would never measure up to Bev's *real* parents.

Stung by Bev's reaction, Gina ignored the ache in her heart and watched as her two small sons played with their new toys.

After reloading his camera, James Henderson stepped back into the family room, wading through the sea of wrapping paper that covered the floor. The tall man smiled down at his sons, enjoying their boisterous pleasure. He then glanced at his daughter, pleased that she was still examining the books he had given her. Aware of his daughter's desire to write, he had thought they were the perfect gift. Gina had argued with him, explaining that teenage girls wanted clothes, CDs, perfume—the items she had purchased for Bev. His gaze shifted to the gifts Gina had selected, which Bev seemed to be ignoring—the clothes, CDs, and perfume. It was obvious to him who really understood Bev. Smiling at his wife, he wondered if she would ever figure out his daughter. He decided not to worry about it and snapped a few more pictures to record this delightful holiday morning.

* * *

"Edie, go ahead," Adele quietly encouraged.

Edie stared at the colorfully wrapped box in her lap, a gift her mother claimed was from her and Karen. Edie knew better. Karen wanted no part of this Christmas celebration. Edie had overheard her daughter complaining to a friend on the phone last night. "I suppose she expects me to buy her a gift," Karen had angrily exclaimed to Bev. "A gift to show how much I appreciate everything she's done for me!" Edie now glanced at her daughter. Karen was in a far corner of the room, selecting a chocolate from the large box of candy Santa had brought them.

Edie wasn't in the mood for Christmas either, but her mother had gone to a lot of work to pull all of this together. The least she could do was pretend to enjoy it. Smiling at Adele, Edie opened the gift. Moving aside the delicate tissue paper, she gasped. It was the most beautiful sweater she had ever seen, soft pink with scalloped embroidery around the neck and sleeves. As she recognized her mother's handiwork, tears filled Edie's eyes. Edie knew her mother's arthritis had worsened in the time she had been gone, and that it must've taken Adele weeks to knit this.

Wordlessly, Edie reached for a hug. Once again, her mother had suffered to give her a gift of love. Feeling as though her heart would burst, Edie clung to the woman who continued to give her life.

CHAPTER 12

January

Kate thumbed through the grade book on her desk. She wasn't sure she liked this new idea of Cleo's—a special back-to-school night for the parents. The students wouldn't return to school until the next day when Christmas vacation officially ended. Kate didn't mind meeting with most of the parents, but she didn't have much to show them. The school had started a new trimester in December, but because of Christmas vacation and all of the class parties and activities held before school had let out, most classes hadn't done much in the way of serious work.

"This way we start the new year on a positive note. You can tell the parents what your plans are for the coming weeks," Cleo had enthused at their last in-service meeting. "And we can alert them to any problems that may be developing," she had added, giving Kate a meaningful look.

"So are you excited for tonight, or what?" Doris now asked, walking into Kate's classroom.

"Oh, yeah," Kate replied. "And you?"

Doris shuddered.

"I agree," Kate laughed. "Cleo must have a good reason for this, although I thought we were planning a parent-teacher conference for February."

"Who knows? That was the original plan. Maybe Cleo wants both. It makes perfect sense to me. Take tonight, for instance. '*How is your little Johnny doing? Well, I don't know yet, because we haven't done much this term. But I'm sure he'll be adorable,*'" Doris hammed.

"I don't even know some of these students very well yet. What do I tell their parents?"

Doris shrugged. "Not one to question authority, I will do as bidden." Kate pulled a face.

"Now, none of that." Doris smiled as a bewildered parent wandered into the classroom. "Here we go," she said under her breath, saluting Kate as she left the room.

* * *

"I appreciate your comments," James Henderson said, beaming at his wife, then at Kate. "I've always said that daughter of mine will go places. Bev's a bit headstrong like me, but I agree, she is a natural-born leader!"

"I've enjoyed having her in my classes," Kate responded. She gazed at Bev's stepmother, an attractive brunette. This woman hadn't said a word during the past ten minutes. Kate wondered if she was always this quiet.

"Mr. Henderson," Cleo Partridge sang out, marching into Kate's classroom. "I heard you were here. I'd like a private word with you, if you don't mind."

"Official business, eh?" Bev's father asked, his blue eyes twinkling. He smiled at Kate. "Serving on the school board is anything but dull." Turning to his wife, he gave her a peck on the cheek. "Guess I'll have to leave this up to you for a bit." He stood and followed the principal out of the room.

Kate watched them leave, then smiled warmly at Gina Henderson. "It must be a challenge to have him so busy all of the time."

Gina nodded. "It is," she said quietly.

"He seems like a wonderful man, though," Kate added.

Gina nodded again.

"Do you have any questions about how Bev's doing, or what I'm planning on covering this term in history or drama?"

"Actually, I do have a question for you," Gina replied. "How did you do it?"

"Do what?" Kate asked, confused.

"How did you break the ice with Bev?"

"I'm not sure what you're getting at," she said cautiously.

"Bev is always talking about you at home. She admires you—she thinks you're wonderful."

"Thank you for telling me," Kate responded, pleased by this news. Her smile drooped into a frown when she saw the look of pain on Gina's face, catching on that the observation wasn't meant to be a compliment.

"I've tried to reach that girl for years. You knew her mother died of cancer when she was young?"

Kate nodded. Doris had told her about it at the beginning of the year.

"I swear that girl hates me," Gina revealed. "I don't know what I've done to upset her . . . I've just tried to be her friend . . . I've never tried to replace her mother."

"I've never heard Bev say anything negative about you," Kate said, trying to console her.

Gina forced a stiff smile. "Spend more time with her. You will."

"Can I do anything to help?" The offer was out of her mouth before Kate could think it through.

Gina looked up at Kate. "I honestly don't know. It doesn't matter what I do, it's the wrong thing."

"That sounds like a typical mother-daughter relationship to me," Kate tried to joke. When Gina failed to smile, she quickly sobered. "Mrs. Henderson—"

"Gina," the other woman invited.

"Gina," Kate repeated, "without going into a lot of details, I didn't always get along with my mother while I was growing up either. In fact, there was a time when I think we actually hated each other."

"Really?" Gina asked, surprised.

"Yes. I'm ashamed to admit it, but I caused my mother many sleepless nights."

"Why?"

Taking a deep breath, Kate struggled for an answer. "That's a difficult question. I was young. There were a lot of things I didn't understand. I thought my friends were always right, and she was always wrong. She didn't agree with the choices I was making . . . they weren't very good choices, but I couldn't see that."

"Did it ever get better?" Gina probed.

"Yes, it did."

"What changed?"

"It's complicated, but I finally realized how much I had hurt her. How much I loved her. For a while, I didn't think I'd ever see her again . . . I was in an accident. I wasn't in very good shape for a while," Kate explained. "That's what did it for me. When I recovered, I wanted to make it up to her." She smiled at Gina. "When I finally started to grow up, I began realizing what was important. Now my mother is one of my best friends. So there is hope."

Gina reached for a piece of tissue out of her purse, dabbing at her eyes. "It would kill me if anything happened to Bev. I'd rather have her treat me this way than see her hurt."

"Do you want me to talk to her about this?"

Gina shook her head. "She'd resent it. She'd know I said something to you."

Kate silently agreed. Still, there had to be something she could do. Deciding to give this situation some prayerful thought, she watched sadly as Gina moved out of the room.

* * *

Doris was surprised to see one of her former students walk into her classroom that night. She had heard Edie Beyer was out of prison, but she hadn't anticipated meeting up with her this soon. Rising, Doris smiled warmly at the younger woman, motioning to a chair in front of her desk. "Edie, it's so good to see you."

Edie flushed slightly, knowing Doris was one of the few who actually meant that phrase when she said it. Most people had been polite since her release, but hushed whispers followed her everywhere she went.

"How are you?" Doris asked, her eyes soft with concern.

"Fine," Edie replied, knowing that was the answer most people wanted to hear. She shyly moved forward, sitting in the chair Doris had offered.

"You look wonderful," Doris commented, continuing to smile. "And what a gorgeous sweater. I don't think I've ever seen a prettier one."

Edie flushed at the compliments. She had worn the sweater her mother had given her for Christmas, hoping it would give her the courage to face tonight. "My mother made it," she quietly acknowledged.

Doris nodded. "Adele has always had a special talent with that kind of thing. Me, I'm a total klutz when it comes to sewing, knitting . . . anything like that."

"You're a wonderful teacher," Edie pointed out. "One of the best I ever had."

"Thank you. I guess we all have our weaknesses and strengths," Doris said, gazing intently at Edie.

Embarrassed by the double meaning, Edie looked down at the wooden floor.

"Edie, you were always such a gifted artist. Do you paint anymore?" Doris asked, trying a different approach.

Edie shook her head.

"That's a real shame. You have such talent—"

"How's Karen doing in this class?" Edie interrupted, directing the conversation toward a more comfortable topic.

Picking up the hint, Doris changed the subject to Karen. She pulled out Karen's file. Sifting through it, she handed Edie the best of what her daughter had composed in the creative writing class the past few weeks.

* * *

"Did you survive the evening?" Doris inquired, walking back into Kate's classroom.

"Barely," Kate replied.

"That bad?"

Kate stood, stretching her arms above her head. "Let's just say I ended on a sour note."

"Margo Jeppson?"

Kate nodded.

"I saw her head for your room after she left mine. I figured you were going to have your hands full."

Walking to a darkened window, Kate stared outside. "It doesn't help that she's in my ward. She keeps trying to bring the Church into this. '*My daughter's eternal salvation depends on whether or not Terri gets to direct the next play.*'"

"She didn't say that?" Doris asked, moving beside Kate.

"Pretty close. I wish Margo could understand—Terri doesn't belong in drama, although that girl can put on quite a performance when she wants to."

"Agreed," Doris sympathized. "What will you do with her?"

"Talk her into transferring. Don't you have room for her in creative writing?"

Doris pulled a face. "Oh, no, you're not brushing Terri off onto me. I already endure her in one English class as it is."

"Only one? I have her in world history and drama."

"Key point," Doris laughed. "You have her—you keep her."

"I had an interesting conversation with Bev Henderson's step-mother tonight," Kate said, changing the subject. She stepped away from the window to sit at one of the student desks.

Doris followed her example, sitting in the aisle across from Kate. "Gina Henderson actually spoke to you?"

"Yes. But only because Cleo dragged James out of the room."

"I see. The poor man," Doris said. "What did Gina have to say about your star pupil?"

Kate gave Doris a curious look. "Why doesn't Bev get along with her stepmother? Gina seems like a nice person."

"She is," Doris replied. "Too quiet, if you ask me, but nice. I think that's part of the problem—Gina needs to be firmer with Bev, but that's my own opinion. Bev has no respect for her stepmother. From what I've seen, that girl enjoys antagonizing Gina every chance she gets."

"I can't see Bev acting that way," Kate said in defense of the young woman.

"You don't have to live with her. You're merely her favorite teacher."

Kate blushed.

"It's true. Word gets around." Doris leaned over to pat Kate on the back. "If you can impress Bev Henderson, you can handle the Terri Jeppsons that come your way."

"Thanks for reminding me," Kate groaned.

"I had an interesting conversation myself," Doris continued. "Remember me telling you about Karen Beyer's mother?"

Kate nodded. "The one in prison?"

"She's home now," Doris informed her. "They released Edie just before Christmas."

"That's wonderful! How's Karen handling it?"

"Not very well if what I picked up from Edie is any indication." Doris frowned. "She wouldn't come right out and say it, but I think Karen's making her life pretty miserable right now. I don't envy either one of them."

Kate sighed. "Sometimes there are no easy answers," she commented, thinking of her younger sister.

"No, unfortunately, there aren't." Doris stood, gesturing toward the door. "Come read something I didn't let Edie see tonight."

Kate followed Doris across the hall into the brightly decorated English classroom. Colorful pictures and inspiring quotes adorned the bulletin boards. Kate glanced at one quotation before walking up to the desk at the front of the room.

> *Reach high, for stars are hidden in your soul;*
> *Dream deep, for every dream precedes a goal!*

Kate smiled. She knew these were words Doris lived by.

"Take a look at this," Doris said, handing Kate a piece of notebook paper.

Kate glanced at the paper, noting it was an untitled poem Karen had written.

> *Sinking*
> *Into empty blackness*
> *No*
> *sight*
> *sound*
> *or*
> *sorrow*
> *But*
> *freedom*
> *and*
> *peace*
> *are*
> *one.*

Kate lifted an eyebrow, reading the poem again.

"This girl is a talented writer," Doris said. "She's written other things that are very impressive. She wrote this poem before she went home for Christmas. It scares me."

"It's not exactly cheerful," Kate replied, handing the paper back to Doris. "What do you think she's trying to say?"

Doris gazed sadly at Kate. "I hope I'm wrong, but I'm afraid we're dealing with a young woman who's reached the end of her rope."

"What will you do?"

"I'll tell you what I won't do. I won't stand idly by and watch another young life be ruined." She walked to her desk and replaced the poem in Karen's file. "You and I have been given a unique opportunity to touch lives. Every day we deal with teenagers from all walks of life. We see kids from wealthy families, and kids from families who are living on the edge of poverty. We work with some students whose biggest concern is what color of fingernail polish they're going to wear. Then there are the others who are dealing with challenging trials that would overwhelm most adults. It breaks your heart, seeing the unfairness that sometimes seems to exist in this life. You and I both know we're all here on this earth to be tested. Some of our students have no idea why they're here. And all they see is what's right in front of them. They can't see beyond high school. They don't realize that every choice leads to a consequence—good or bad." She smiled. "I've given this a lot of thought over the holidays. I think I've come up with a plan that might help some of our troubled students. Are you with me?"

Silently nodding, Kate knew she would help with whatever Doris had in mind. Teaching *was* more than a job, it was a calling—one she had been preparing for most of her life.

CHAPTER 13

"Cool CD player," Marsha commented, glancing at Sabrina's Christmas gift. "It's a lot like mine."

Sabrina nodded, adjusting the volume of her new stereo. Soon they were enjoying the newest CD released by the Backstreet Boys, a gift Marsha had given her for Christmas. The two girls sat on the floor, leaning back against Sabrina's bed to listen.

"So, are you excited for school to start tomorrow?" Marsha asked a few minutes later.

"What do you think?" Sabrina replied, frowning.

"Same here," Marsha sighed. "Thanks to Tracie, Sindi, and Dawn."

"At least they're not spreading rumors around about you," Sabrina responded.

"Oh, yeah?" Marsha challenged. "I just didn't tell you."

Sabrina stared at the slender redhead. "What are they saying now?"

"That the reason they dumped me is the boys all think I'm ugly."

"They didn't dump you . . . you dumped them, the jerks!" Sabrina raged. "And you are not ugly," she hurriedly added.

"Right," Marsha sarcastically replied. "Red hair and freckles. Legs like toothpicks. I'm a winning combination."

"My mom has red hair and everyone thinks she's beautiful," Sabrina retorted. "Your hair is fine. You're just as pretty as any of them."

"Pretty disgusting, according to our former *friends*. They're telling people that I was dragging them down—that I have no personality. That the boys stayed away because of me."

"The boys aren't staying away from them now!" Sabrina exclaimed. "It's sickening to see the way they hang all over those three. And they don't care who's watching, or where they're at."

"I know," Marsha agreed. "That last home basketball game, I couldn't believe how Tracie just sat there and let Rick Brown run his hands all over her body. It made me sick."

"Me too," Sabrina agreed. "But, according to Tracie, I'm the one who's out getting pregnant."

"Well, at least we both know what's really true," Marsha sighed. "I don't know what I'd do if we didn't have each other to lean on right now."

Sabrina nodded in agreement.

"How did things go between you and Kate over Christmas?" Marsha asked, remembering how worried Sabrina had been about her sister's visit.

Shrugging, Sabrina pretended to study the CD on top of the small pile beside her on the floor.

"Did you talk to her?"

"Not much," Sabrina finally replied. "I really don't have anything to say to her—anything she'd like to hear. Mom is always stressing that line from *Bambi*, you know, 'If you can't say something nice, then don't say anything at all.'"

"I thought you were through listening to your mother."

"It depends on my mood. I know she means well, but she just doesn't understand what I'm going through. I try not to argue with her, but Kate thinks I'm being a monster. Over Christmas, she tried to lecture me about not hurting Mom." She glanced at her friend. "Right. She's the one who used to break Mom's heart every time she turned around."

"Maybe she's trying to help you—"

"I don't need her help. She's done enough damage!"

Marsha sighed. "There've been times when I've wished I had an older sister, someone I could talk to . . . especially now."

"You can have Kate!"

"Why do you hate her so much?" Marsha asked, curious. She knew how much Sabrina resented Kate, but had never asked why until now.

"Where do I start?" Sabrina snarled, rising to her feet. Moving to a bright purple bean bag chair, she sat down in the middle of it and faced Marsha. "I'm sick of everyone comparing me to her. Because Kate messed up, my parents, our Young Women leaders, and some of the teachers at school think I'm going to be just like her. It drives me crazy!"

"What did Kate do that was so bad?"

"Everything. She hung out with the wrong crowd. Wore strange things. Went to wild parties . . . ," she stopped, uncomfortable with Marsha's searching gaze. "What?"

"Kate went through some of the same things you're going through now. Maybe she *could* help you."

"That'll be the day! Look, you're not getting it. Because of everything Kate put my parents through, they're twice as strict with me. They question everything I do and say because they think I'll make the same mistakes."

"Haven't you?" Marsha asked.

"What happened at Sindi's Halloween party was not my fault! I didn't plan it . . . I didn't go there to get drunk or to make out with some guy. I left when I could see what it was turning into. Kate never did until it was almost too late."

"But she did get her act together," Marsha continued.

"Yeah, not that it's any help to me."

"I think you're being too hard on her. It's not her fault that we're fighting with our friends. She didn't have a thing to do with the rumors that are going around about us."

"Maybe not, but you can bet there are people in this town convinced I'm turning out just like Kate because of those rumors. They won't even give me the benefit of the doubt. They look at me and think, 'She had a wild sister. She's acting just like her. It must run in their family.'"

Giving up, Marsha reached for one of Sabrina's teen magazines and started thumbing through it. "Maybe what we both need is a total make-over. Then no one will recognize us. We can start over," she pointed to a model on the page in front of her. "I want to look just like her."

"Not me," Sabrina said, moving to sit beside Marsha. Picking up another magazine, she scanned through it until she found a picture of a different model. "That's who I'll look like."

Giggling, the two girls continued to search for the perfect face and body, something they were sure they would never possess.

* * *

"Tracie, is it true you were seen kissing a boy in the hallway at school yesterday?"

Alarmed, Tracie glanced at her mother. Who had talked to her?

Celia Monroe gazed at her daughter compassionately. "Now, I know you've had a rough year because of Sabrina and Marsha. What we heard was probably a result of the rumors they've been spreading around about you."

"I'm sure it was," Tracie agreed, trying to look indignant. "It makes me sick, seeing what those two girls are doing." Forcing tears, she looked up into her mother's eyes. "They'll never make it to the temple doing those kinds of things."

"I just can't believe those two girls would change so much," Celia replied, shaking her head sorrowfully. "We were all hoping Sabrina would learn from what Kate went through, but I guess she'll have to find out for herself. Some people take a hard road in life."

"I've tried to talk to her," Tracie said, starting to relax. If she could keep the focus on Sabrina, it would distract her mother from whatever she had heard concerning her own behavior.

"That's probably why she's out spreading rumors about you," Celia angrily responded. "It makes me so mad! I'm tempted to march over to the Erickson house and let Sue know just what I think about that daughter of hers!"

Panicking, Tracie tried to think of a way to calm her mother down. "It won't do any good, Mom. Sue doesn't believe Sabrina is out doing any of those things I told you about."

"You're probably right," Celia sighed. "Still, she needs to know what's going on. I would want to know if my kids were in trouble."

Pricked by guilt, Tracie glanced away from her mother. The uncomfortable feeling quickly passed. As time went on, things that had bothered her in the past didn't seem to matter anymore. She was having fun, and the best part was, she was becoming very popular. Someday she'd settle down and aim for a temple wedding—in the meantime, she wanted to enjoy life. She had plenty of time to worry about that kind of thing. Besides, everyone around her seemed to be doing what she was doing. It was fun to have boys pay attention to her, especially the senior boys. It made her feel important, special. It wasn't like she would ever go all the way with any of them. After all, she had her standards. She knew where to draw the line.

As for the stories going around about Sabrina and Marsha, they deserved it. They were the ones who were acting like they were so much better than everyone else—they were the ones who had started this by walking away. Hurt by their rejection, Tracie had merely dropped a few hints, knowing others would jump to the wrong conclusions. Those people were the ones spreading the stories. It would be on their heads, not hers. She had done nothing wrong, she assured herself every time a bad feeling crept inside of her heart.

CHAPTER 14

February

"This is so cool!" Bev exclaimed to Karen. "*The Blaketown Buzz*—we finally get our own school newspaper!"

Karen shrugged, sitting down at a desk beside her friend.

"C'mon, you have to admit, this sounds fun."

"It gives me another reason to avoid going home, that's what matters," Karen replied.

"Same here, but it still sounds fun. I can't believe Doris and Kate talked Cleo into this."

"Don't you mean *Mrs. Kelsey* and *Mrs. Jeffries*," Karen snidely commented.

"Lighten up. Kate and Doris have both given me permission to use their first names."

"Isn't that nice?!"

"Karen, chill out. I'm your friend, remember?"

Karen stood and walked across the room. Turning, she glanced back at Bev. "Sorry," she said quietly.

"It's okay," Bev responded, forcing a smile. She was so worried about Karen. Her friend was growing more moody and despondent by the day. Something she wasn't sure how to handle. Glancing at her watch, she saw that it was nearly 3:30 p.m. Kate had said to meet in her classroom right around then. Two more students walked in—a senior, Kim Johnson, and a junior named Gerald Reynolds. Bev scowled at Gerald, then shared a look of disgust with Karen. Gerald was a conceited jock who thought he owned the school. Bev couldn't stand the guy.

"What are you two doing in here?" she asked, her question more for Gerald than for Kim.

Kim smiled at Bev. "Doris Kelsey asked me to meet her here. She said something about putting a journalism class together. I guess you're here for the same reason?"

Bev nodded, crossing the room to stand beside Karen. She didn't like the way Gerald was staring at her friend. She moved until her back was to him, successfully blocking his view. By then a handful of other students had arrived, excitedly visiting about this newest endeavor their favorite teachers were undertaking.

"I heard they're doing this on their own time. That was the only way Cleo would let them try it," one sixteen-year-old boy said.

"I heard they really went the rounds with Cleo, then finally went over her head to the superintendent," a sophomore girl added.

"Hey, Gerald, your dad's on the school board. Did he say anything about it?" a junior girl asked.

Gerald grinned, pleased to have everyone's attention. "My dad tells me everything," he boasted.

"Did he tell you why the nurse ran screaming out of the room the day you were born?" Bev asked. "Something about she'd never seen anything that ugly in her life." Several students chuckled. It was a well-known fact that Gerald was fond of his good looks.

Irritated, Gerald chose to ignore Bev. He shifted his gaze once again to Karen, liking the way his stare made her uncomfortable.

"Hey, you gonna let Bev get away with that?" a younger boy challenged Gerald. Before he could reply, Doris and Kate walked into the room.

"A pretty good turnout," Doris murmured.

Kate nodded, relieved to see that Bev and Karen had both shown up. Nearly half of the students they had handpicked for this project were here because they needed a new focus. The others had been selected because of their talent. It would be an interesting combination. Kate was glad she didn't have to tackle this challenge alone. Together, she and Doris had formed a team that had successfully forged past Cleo's objections and concerns. The principal had initially turned them down, telling them there wasn't room for a journalism class in what she considered to be an already crowded curriculum.

Cleo had also protested the added expense she felt this class would generate. Refusing to give up, Doris and Kate had then approached the superintendent.

"We have several talented students and others who need positive feedback in their lives," they had stressed. "Putting a school newspaper together would give them all a boost they really need right now." The superintendent had been receptive to their idea, but had agreed with Cleo that funds were extremely limited. Kate and Doris had agreed to teach this class on their own time, using few school resources.

It had been a satisfying compromise for everyone involved, with the exception of Cleo. Convinced these two *renegades* were taking on more than they could handle, she had silently vowed to keep track of the entire enterprise. When she had tried to insist that all articles be cleared through her, she had been annoyed to learn that the superintendent had already decreed that Doris and Kate were capable of judging what was appropriate material to submit before the eyes of the student body.

Cleo planned to watch this process very closely. One mistake and she would take control of a situation she was certain would soon be out of hand.

* * *

"That was my dad again," Mike revealed, walking into the kitchen where Kate was preparing dinner.

"He wants to know what we've decided about the job in Bozeman," Kate guessed, carefully cutting up the chicken in front of her.

"Yep."

"And what have *we* decided?"

Moving next to the sink, Mike winced as Kate cut through a chicken thigh. "Easy, woman, that's a delicate surgery."

Ignoring her husband, Kate continued to carve through the chicken, cutting it into several pieces.

Mike grabbed a nearby stool and sat down, selecting a potato out of the sink. He reached for a peeler and began to relieve the potato of its skin. "I think I'll give you my answer after you put that knife down," he finally said, as Kate sliced the fat and skin from the chicken.

Kate turned, smiling at Mike. "Do I really make you that nervous?"

Nodding, he ducked when she threw a wet dishrag at him. "Hey, you mussed my hair."

"Good!"

"Before I tell you how I feel about the job in Bozeman, let's hear your opinion," he prompted.

Kate washed and dried her hands, then turned to her husband. "At Christmas time, this opportunity sounded very tempting. I'd love to be closer to our families. Especially now that Sabrina is having all of this trouble."

"But . . . ," Mike coaxed, sensing where this conversation was heading. Relieved, he grinned at his wife. As much as he loved Bozeman, he really didn't want to move right now.

"But I've taken on some new responsibilities . . ."

"The journalism class," he supplied.

Kate nodded. "Mike, I can't turn my back on these kids right now. Some of them are really struggling. Maybe I can help them. Bev has just started to open up to me about her stepmother. Karen actually smiled yesterday and meant it. And I'm finally getting a feel for this school. This term, my classes are going much better. I'm even making headway with Cleo . . . at least, I'm learning how to deal with her." She returned her husband's smile. "I never thought I'd hear myself say this, but this town is starting to grow on me. Most of the people around here are all right."

Pretending to topple from the stool in shock, Mike stretched out on the floor. His eyes flew open when Kate dumped a few drops of water on him. "Now you've done it," he threatened, chasing her, finally cornering her in the living room. Holding her down on the couch, he tickled Kate without mercy. A quiet knock went unobserved as the two of them kissed.

"Uh . . . I thought Ryan here made arrangements with you last night," George Rogers stammered, moving aside so his home teaching companion could get a better look.

"I forgot they were coming tonight," Mike mouthed to Kate. He let go of Kate, pulling himself up to greet the home teachers.

"You are so dead," Kate promised in a hushed voice as she slowly sat up, choosing to ignore the grin on Ryan's face.

* * *

The handful of students who had originally been selected to participate in the experimental journalism class blossomed into nearly twenty students. After a couple of weeks, others had wandered in, begging for a chance to help with a newspaper that was gaining recognition and popularity. The town newspaper had offered to print up the school paper, giving it a professional finish. The only thing asked in exchange was that some of the students involved make the rounds of the local businesses to drum up ad sales. The enthusiasm of the students rubbed off onto the businesses, making this a profitable venture for all concerned. Much to Cleo's dismay, *The Blaketown Buzz* appeared to be a permanent high school fixture, giving the students a community forum for their concerns.

"This article is brilliant!" Doris exclaimed one afternoon, smiling at Karen.

"Really?" the young woman asked.

"Oh, yes. This will definitely make a few heads turn. That's what we want. To stir things up a bit." She handed Karen's paper to Kate. "Take a look at that. I think it should be our editorial this week."

Kate quickly scanned the well-written article. Its theme: Blaketown's tendency to label people, a subject Karen had researched with her life. "This is very good," Kate agreed. "Let's run it as the editorial."

"But . . . ," Karen stammered.

"What is it?" Doris asked.

"Can I talk to you . . . alone?" Karen asked.

Nodding, Doris led the sixteen-year-old out of Kate's crowded classroom into her own room, closing the door behind Karen. "Okay, what's wrong?"

Karen nervously played with the pencil sharpener. "First, I appreciate this chance you've given me . . . you know . . . to write."

Doris patiently nodded.

"But . . . this is a mistake. I can't let you publish that article."

Mildly surprised, Doris waited for an explanation.

"It just hit me. Do you know what people would say—how they would treat me if they read that article, knowing I wrote it?"

Unfortunately, Doris had a good idea of how people would react. Initially, she had relished the idea of making people reconsider how they treated each other. Now, she wasn't so sure about running the article. It would cast a lot of unwanted speculation toward Karen.

"People have enough to say about my life right now. This would just make it worse."

Doris motioned to a nearby desk. She waited until the young woman sat down, then sat beside her. "Karen, I know it hasn't been easy for you . . . or for your mother."

"This is not about Edie," Karen angrily stated.

"I think it has everything in the world to do with your mother," Doris said as gently as she knew how. "Karen, I taught your mother in school when she was your age. I know she made some mistakes, but she *is* a good person," Doris pointed to her heart, "in here, where it counts, like your article says."

"Edie has no clue what she's done to me!" Karen said bitterly.

"Karen, you're judging her, just like you're accusing others of judging you."

Rising, Karen glared at the teacher. "I don't need another lecture. That's all I've heard from my grandmother since Edie came home!"

"I'm sorry," Doris said, standing. "But I hate to see someone with your talent this consumed by anger." She frowned when Karen reached for the door. "Karen, that's the last you'll hear from me on this subject. Just know I care, and I'm here for you if you ever need to talk."

Karen stiffly nodded.

"Also, I have an idea. What if we ran your article without using your name?"

Releasing the door knob, Karen turned to stare at Doris.

"Your article will remain intact and no one will know who wrote it."

"Really?"

Doris nodded. "You have my word. Kate and I are the only ones who will know. We'll keep that secret for as long as you want us to."

"Promise?" Karen asked, calming down.

"I promise. What do you think?"

Karen offered a tiny smile. "I think you have an editorial for this week."

* * *

Assigned lunch duty again, Kate slowly walked around the cafeteria quietly alerting the students to her presence to thwart mischievous notions. She wandered by the table where Terri Jeppson had elected to sit with some other sophomore girls.

" . . . I think it's terrible—the way that editorial points fingers at everybody. I've never said anything about anybody unless they deserved it!" Terri indignantly complained.

"Who wrote it?" a girl sitting across the table asked.

"I don't know, but I'm going to find out," Terri said smugly. "I'm friends with some of the newspaper staff." She smiled at the other girls. "I took a copy of the paper to Miss Partridge."

"You mean *Cleo?*"

Terri vigorously nodded. "She hated that article! She said it makes our school sound disreputable. She's going to look into who wrote it, too."

Walking away, Kate rubbed at the temples on each side of her head, feeling a tremendous headache coming on.

* * *

"Are you serious about taking drama next term?"

Sabrina smiled at Marsha. "I think so. It sounds like fun. And it's a sure bet Tracie, Dawn, and Sindi won't be taking it." The two friends looked over the changes they wanted to make in their schedules, changes that would further separate them from those three girls. Last year the five of them had all planned their schedules together and were in many of the same classes. Now deciding that had to change, Sabrina and Marsha were trying to figure out a schedule that would work.

"All right, let's go talk to the counselor and see if we can get into that class," Marsha said enthusiastically.

"Deal," Sabrina agreed, picking up the notes she had been making. The more space they could put between themselves and their former friends, the better. It was time to move on, to focus on more positive ventures, beginning with the changes in their schedules. Together, they would survive the ordeal this year had become.

CHAPTER 15

Adele breathed a sigh of relief when she finally heard Edie enter the house. She didn't have to glance at the glowing alarm clock to know it was late. She had lain awake for a couple of hours, praying Edie would come to her senses and return home. Across the bedroom in an identical twin bed, Karen softly snored, unaware of the crisis they were facing. Silently climbing out of bed, Adele reached for the robe she had set out earlier and opened her bedroom door.

Things had seemed a little better lately between Karen and Edie. At least Karen wasn't alienating her mother at every turn. Adele had hoped for more, but it was a start. If only Edie and Karen would let go of the past. Adele frowned. But even if those two were willing, this town would never let them. Maybe it was time to think about moving somewhere else for a fresh start. As it was, Edie couldn't find a job in this valley. The three of them couldn't live forever on the social security check Adele received once a month. Something had to change before Edie reached her breaking point. Adele hoped that hadn't already happened. Edie had done so well, passing every interview with her probation officer with flying colors. But her daughter was only so strong—she could only take so much.

"Please, Father, grant Edie the strength she needs to get through this," Adele now prayed, wrapping the warm robe around herself as she began to walk down the hall.

* * *

Edie quietly crept down the hallway to her bedroom, eased inside, and shut the door. She had waited until she was certain her mother and daughter would be sound asleep before coming home. It was too hard to face them day after day with the news, "I couldn't find a job."

She had tried. She had filled out applications and had taken resumes around until she'd lost track of how many had been distributed. What she couldn't forget were the rejections, the excuses that were mumbled whenever she checked back: *"Sorry, we just filled that position"* or *"We're looking for someone with a few more qualifications."* It was the same story everywhere she went. What they wouldn't tell her was the truth. *"Sorry, we don't hire ex-convicts"* or *"We're looking for someone we don't have to watch around the clock."*

Why couldn't they give her a chance to prove she had changed? Would they always treat her as a social leper? Some of the women treated her like a common trollop while several of the men had given her leering looks, making Edie extremely uncomfortable. She had tried to avoid them, but stinging comments were flung at her back, hushed insults that sliced through her heart. Remarks she would never want her mother and daughter to overhear. She prayed they never would and feared they already had.

Edie had spent tonight feeling sorry for herself. She knew she had no one else to blame for how her life had turned out, but this was unbearable. Her own daughter hated her. The only person she could really talk to in this town was her mother, and she tried to protect Adele from the criticism she quietly absorbed every day.

Earlier tonight, she had driven to the edge of town, heading up an icy hill. As she had looked down over Blaketown, Edie had contemplated her future. This place had never held anything but heartache for her. It had been a mistake to return. She should've gone somewhere else, away from the accusing eyes. She should've stayed out of her daughter's life. Adele had done a wonderful job raising Karen. From what Edie understood, Karen hadn't become a handful until she had learned of Edie's release from prison. The twinkling lights of the town did little to ease the misery that burden generated. Deciding there wasn't a simple solution to this dilemma, Edie had finally driven back into town, seeking a comforting friend from the past.

Now at home, sitting on her bed, Edie stared at the brown paper bag in her hand. "My own daughter can't stand the sight of me," she murmured, pulling out a bottle of vodka. She twisted off the cap, anticipating the warming sensation that would make her numb. As she brought the bottle to her lips, she glanced at the window, seeing a hazy reflection of herself. "Is this who I want to become again?" Edie wasn't sure why the unbidden question surfaced, but suddenly felt repulsed by the bottle in her hand. This is what started all of the trouble in the first place. Replacing the cap, she set the bottle back inside of the paper bag and hid it in the bottom drawer of the small nightstand that served as her dresser. She promised herself she would throw it away first thing in the morning.

Falling onto her bed, Edie sobbed, eventually crying herself to sleep. She hadn't noticed the crack that had appeared in her door when her mother had walked down the hall to check on her. Adele had quietly watched her daughter's bitter struggle. Tearfully, Adele had closed the door when she saw who had won this battle. Grateful for the victory, she sensed the war was still ahead.

* * *

Edie smoothed down the grey skirt she had chosen to wear for the day. Once again, she had selected the pink sweater her mother had knitted. Her current wardrobe was extremely limited and would be until she could find a job. She had already decided that if she didn't find one today, she would talk to her mother about moving. It might even be best if she left town by herself. Karen had friends here. Her mother still lived in the house her father had purchased years ago. Unlike herself, they had roots in Blaketown. Convinced there was nothing left in this town for her, she would make one last attempt before moving on.

She had heard there were openings for a couple of nurses' aides at the local hospital. Grateful she hadn't given in to the temptation to get drunk last night, Edie was clear-headed and extremely sober. Walking into the large brick building, Edie headed for the office. From there she was directed to the hospital administrator. She hesitantly knocked at his office door, then waited for a response.

* * *

Gary Tucker glanced up from the high school newspaper he had been reading. Chip Reynolds, a member of the school board, and a good friend of his, had handed him this copy, asking him to read an editorial he had considered quite impressive.

"Whoever wrote this has a real understanding for human nature. They use an analogy, comparing us to a flock of chickens. If someone is different, we pick away at them until we draw blood. That is so true," Chip had said. "Take me for instance. I made mistakes years ago, but I'm not the same person I was then. It doesn't matter how hard I try, people still dwell on the past. I'll always have a reputation for being a philanderer. Do you know what that does to my wife—to have people infer how unworthy I am to serve in a bishopric?"

Gary looked up from the article that had stirred Chip into voicing an extremely personal concern. Whoever had written it had touched on a sensitive topic with a fiery passion. Gary was disturbed by the insinuations that had been printed about this close-knit community.

The knock sounded a second time. "Come in," Gary called out, rising when an attractive woman entered his office.

"Gary Tucker?" Edie asked.

Gary smiled. "Yes. And you are?" He noticed immediately the strain behind this beautiful woman's smile.

"I'm . . . Edie Beyer," she reluctantly conceded. Usually that's all it took for a prospective employer to determine her ineligibility for the job.

Gary held out his hand, reaching to shake hers, then motioned to a chair. "Have a seat," he encouraged.

Blinking with surprise, Edie sat down.

"What can I help you with?"

Edie pulled a piece of newspaper out of her purse. Her mother had cut out the want-ad earlier that morning. "I came to apply for a job," she said, showing him the ad.

Glancing at the ad, Gary shifted his gaze to Edie. "I was hoping to see some applicants this week. We've been extremely short-handed lately. Our patient load increases during the winter months, and I doubt we'll have a flurry of LPNs or RNs move into the valley. So we've decided to hire two or three nurses' aides to tide us over." He smiled at Edie. "Have you ever worked in a hospital before?"

Edie shook her head. "I'm a quick learner . . . and a hard worker."

Gary noted the hidden appeal in that phrase. This woman needed a job. In his experience, applicants of this nature usually became the best employees. Anxious to please, they often went above and beyond the call of duty. "Did you happen to bring a resume?"

Edie nodded and reached into her purse once again, handing the administrator a folded paper. She hadn't wanted to fold it, but it had been snowing hard that morning. Putting it inside of her purse was the only thing she could think of to protect it from getting wet. Instead of having her mother drive her all over town, she had elected to walk. The hospital wasn't that far from their house, and the walk had given her a chance to clear her head.

Gary quietly unfolded the paper and glanced at the information she had recorded. He studied the dates of her last employment, then smiled at her. "I see you haven't worked anywhere for the past three years," he said, making conversation. It surprised him when she stood, reaching to reclaim the resume.

"I'll save us both a lot of time. I spent the last three years in prison. I was charged with being an accessory to armed robbery. I'm currently out on parole. I'm trying to piece my life back together but this town . . . ," she couldn't finish the sentence. Picking up her purse, she stuffed the resume inside and started for the door.

"Wait just a minute," Gary said indignantly.

"Believe me, I've heard it all several times," Edie said, unwilling to face more degradation. Opening the door, she hurried through it.

"For someone who claims to be discriminated against, you sure haven't given me a chance," Gary called out to her.

Stung by this accusation, Edie stepped back into the room.

"That's better," Gary said, smiling. "Let's start over." He held out his hand to shake hers. "Hi, I'm Gary Tucker. And you are?"

* * *

Adele hugged Edie again. "I'm so proud of you," she murmured over and over, holding her daughter tight. "A job! You got a job!"

When Edie was finally able to pull away from her mother, she smiled at her excitement.

"When do you start?"

"Tomorrow," Edie replied.

"Tomorrow! This is wonderful!"

Edie nodded. "There is one problem."

"Oh? What?"

"I need to come up with a pair of white knit pants, a suitable top, and a pair of comfortable white shoes." Edie glanced down at her hands. She knew they couldn't afford any of those things. She wasn't sure how she would work this out. It had been too embarrassing to admit her lack of funds to the hospital administrator who had been good enough to hire her.

"Edie, we'll go shopping this afternoon. If we can't find what you need here in Blaketown, we'll head over the hills. We'll drive to Pocatello if we have to, but you'll be ready for tomorrow."

"Mom, we can't afford this right now. Maybe after I get my first check, but I don't—"

"Edie, we can," Adele said, moving a chair in front of a kitchen counter. She climbed up onto the chair and reached into the cupboard, pulling down a heavy metal container.

"Mom!" Edie exclaimed, recognizing the can. Her mother had kept rare coins in that can for years. It was the family treasure, something she hadn't even told Mark about when they had been together three years ago.

"This money doesn't do us any good sitting in that dark cupboard," Adele responded, pulling out a handful of bills, revealing another secret. This can contained more than rare coins; Adele had squirreled away a small fortune for a rainy day. This day hardly seemed like a storm, but the need was great. Her daughter had a job! They could stay together in Blaketown. Things were definitely looking up!

* * *

"Why won't you tell me who wrote this?" Cleo asked, exasperated with the two women who were sitting in front of her desk.

"You've heard of freedom of the press," Doris challenged, her brown eyes glittering.

"This is nothing but a high school paper. I'd hardly call it—"

"Miss Partridge," a voice interrupted.

Irritated, Cleo glared at her secretary.

"Chip Reynolds is on line three," the cheerful woman announced. "He says it's important."

Nodding, Cleo waited until the bubbly woman had closed the office door. "No doubt this call concerns your editorial. I've been anticipating this." She glowered at Kate and Doris. "You two have no idea how much trouble we're all in." Picking up the phone, she pushed a button and held it to her ear. "Hello," she said with as much dignity as she could muster.

"Cleo," Chip began, "I've just finished reading this latest edition of *The Blaketown Buzz*—"

"Oh. Yes. I'm very sorry about that—"

"Sorry about what?" Chip cut her off.

"The editorial."

Chip was surprised to hear the frustration in Cleo's voice. "That editorial is why I called."

Cleo gave Doris and Kate a disgusted look.

"It's one of the best articles I've ever read in my life!"

"Again, I'm sorry. I'm talking to Doris and Kate about it right now . . . What?"

"I said, that's one of the best articles I've ever read! I want you to pass that on to Doris and Kate," he added, imagining the lecture those two wonderful teachers had been enduring.

"You liked it?" Cleo asked, stunned.

Doris and Kate exchanged an amused look.

"You bet I liked it. I want to see more of that kind of thing. It makes you stop and think. That's what we need in this valley. I wanted to call and congratulate you on it. That article is being discussed all over town. Your journalism staff is to be commended."

"Commended?" Cleo repeated, certain she hadn't heard right.

"Yes. I've been talking to some of the other members of the school board. We want the students involved in this project to know they're doing a remarkable thing!"

"I see," Cleo said, avoiding the jubilant expressions in front of her.

"Yessiree—we've got ourselves a winner! This newspaper is the best idea that's come out of that school in a long time."

Silently disagreeing, Cleo was relieved when she could finally hang up the phone.

* * *

"Cleo wouldn't tell us everything Chip Reynolds said, but we could tell it was killing her. I think she was looking forward to shutting us down."

Mike smiled at Kate. "From the sound of things, *The Blaketown Buzz* will be with us for a long time."

"I hope so," Kate replied, handing him the clean socks she had just folded. "You should've seen the look on Karen's face when Doris told her what Chip had said about her article. That's the biggest smile I've ever seen. That girl is so happy."

"She deserves it."

"She does. Too bad we have to keep her identity and talent a secret. But we have to honor her wishes." Kate shook her head. "It's a shame, really. There's nothing but truth in that editorial. If people are offended, it's their own fault."

Mike nodded, then headed down the hall to put his socks away.

* * *

"This is an outrage!" Margo Jeppson exclaimed to her daughter, handing Terri the objectionable paper. "Why do people in this town permit this kind of garbage to circulate?!"

Terri set the paper on the dining room table, certain they'd get to the bottom of this now. The past couple of days she had endured numerous taunts at school as several students had teasingly suggested she was the inspiration behind the editorial. Unfortunately, Terri would never realize she had brought their badgering on herself. Taking umbrage at what had been printed, she had gone around the school, badmouthing whoever had written it. Most people had sided with the phantom writer, giving Terri an extremely bad time. The final straw had been Bev's stinging comment.

"What's the matter, Terri? You don't like your reflection?"

After that retort, Terri had gone to Cleo. For once, the principal had had little patience with her, ushering the young woman out of the office with a firm admonition to cease her complaints. "I don't agree with what was printed, but for now we have to live with it."

Furious, Terri had pleaded her case before a higher court, her mother. She waited now for the expected verdict.

"How can Kate and Doris consider themselves good Latter-day Saints when they permit something like this to be written about our wonderful community?! People in Blaketown aren't like this at all! Why, I've never met a group of more Christlike people in my life." Picking up the phone, she began to dial. "We'll put a stop to this kind of thing right now!" Margo impatiently waited for Kate to pick up the phone to arrange a meeting.

* * *

"Are you sure you don't want to stay for the coming festivities?" Kate pleaded.

Doris shook her head. "Margo asked to speak to you. You get to handle this."

"Thanks," Kate dryly replied.

"I'll be across the hall, waiting to put you back together when it's all over," Doris said, walking out of the room. She met Margo in the hall.

"Doris," Margo said, forcing a tight-lipped smiled. "What a coincidence. I was on my way to talk to Kate about a matter that also concerns you. Will you join us?"

Grumbling under her breath, Doris followed Margo back inside of Kate's classroom.

"Look who I bumped into," Margo said, gesturing to the disgruntled English teacher.

Trying not to laugh, Kate stood, pointing to the chairs near her desk. Enjoying the disgusted look on Doris' face, Kate sank down into the padded chair behind her desk.

"I know you two are busy, so I'll get right to the point." Reaching into her purse, Margo pulled out the issue of *The Blaketown Buzz* Terri had shown her.

Doris met Kate's searching gaze. Now what?

"You certainly don't seem afraid of controversy," Margo said, glancing at Kate.

"Why would you say that?" Doris asked.

Margo pointed to the editorial, holding it up so both teachers could see. "Why did you allow this to be printed?"

"Because it was well written," Doris replied.

"The student who composed it is very gifted—" Kate tried to explain.

"It *was* written by a student then," Margo said triumphantly.

"Yes. That's what this paper is all about. Encouraging our students to develop their talents," Kate said.

Margo gazed intently at Kate. "That seems to be an important issue with you."

"It is."

"Even if your *creative* ideas exclude or demean other students?"

Doris rolled her eyes. Kate hid her reaction. She had little choice in the matter. Margo was staring right at her.

"We have never intentionally left out or *demeaned* anyone," Doris said firmly.

Margo reached into her purse for a handful of tissue, dabbing at her eyes. "Then how do you explain the horrible week my daughter has had at school?"

"What do you mean?" Kate asked, perplexed. What did the newspaper have to do with the way Terri was being treated at school?

"You weren't aware that the entire student body has accused my daughter of being the motivation behind that editorial?!"

Doris tried very hard to keep a straight face, as did Kate.

"Do you think it's right for one girl to suffer just so another student can get something published in the paper?" Margo glanced from Kate to Doris, who immediately sobered. "Terri is home crying right now, feeling like her life has been destroyed."

"Margo, I'm sure—" Doris began.

"And think of the reflection that article has on our town! What if a visitor or a potential new resident reads it? What kind of impression will this give them about Blaketown? There are a lot of good people who live here. This editorial makes it sound like we're all horrible."

"This editorial only applies to a few people—" Kate attempted to say.

"It talks about how harmful it is to point fingers. Whoever wrote it has done just that!" Margo angrily exclaimed.

It took several minutes, but Doris and Kate were eventually able to reason with Margo, calming her down with the assurance that future editorials would be carefully screened, and the promise that Terri could be part of the newspaper staff.

"I can hardly wait to tell Terri. She'll be so thrilled!" Margo said, leaving the room.

Doris shared a pained look with Kate. "You wanted to transfer Terri out of drama."

"I didn't mean into something else I teach," Kate groaned. "I can't believe what we've been put through this afternoon."

"Get used to it. Something tells me this adventure is far from over."

Nodding, Kate thought of Bev's impending reaction to the news that Terri would now be part of her newspaper staff. They had assigned Bev Henderson and John Packer to be the managing editors several weeks ago. The junior and senior were doing a wonderful job together, organizing the layout of the paper and assigning stories. Kate knew this information about their newest staff member would cause a fiery rebellion.

"I'd say a hot fudge sundae is in order," Doris suggested.

"With extra fudge," Kate replied, reaching for her coat.

CHAPTER 16

Bev reacted as Kate had expected when the news was broken to her about their newest reporter. "I will not work with that woman!" she exclaimed, giving Kate a betrayed look.

"I'll take personal responsibility for her," Kate volunteered.

"Why Terri?"

This would be difficult. Doris and Kate had decided to keep their meeting with Margo Jeppson quiet, knowing it would inflame an already volatile situation. Kate managed a weak smile. "Bev, I know you two don't get along—"

"Understatement of the year!" Bev snorted.

"Terri needs to be a part of this staff."

"You still haven't said why," Bev accused.

"Trust me, I have my reasons," Kate replied.

"You'll regret this—it's a terrible mistake!"

"Maybe. But sometimes you have to give people a chance," Kate said. "Even if you think they don't deserve it." She gave Bev a meaningful look.

Bev had grown to resent Kate's subtle hints about how she treated her stepmother. That was nobody's business but her own. Shrugging off the double meaning, the young woman chose to ignore Kate and the newest member of her newspaper staff.

* * *

Terri loved being part of *The Blaketown Buzz*. She immediately wrote up several questionable stories—most based on unsavory rumors going around the school. Finally Kate asked the excitable young woman to write a column depicting the latest fashions and fads. Enthralled by the idea, Terri began interviewing several different students, this assignment giving her an excuse to talk to those who normally ignored her existence. She began with a group of cheerleaders, then switched to the boys' basketball team, thoroughly enjoying this chance to rub shoulders with the elite of Blaketown High.

* * *

"Get me another gauze pad," Dr. Davis requested.

Edie removed another pad from its sterile shield and handed it to the doctor.

"This wound is pretty deep," the doctor commented, glancing at the ashen face of the man they were treating in ER.

Brett Randall nodded, trying not to look at the gash in his arm. The sight of blood had always made him feel squeamish.

"How did you manage to cut yourself up like this?"

Brett flinched as more pressure was applied to his arm. "A report came into the Forest Service office that someone was running an illegal trap-line up the canyon. Mike Jeffries asked me to check it out. I was heading up a hillside of the canyon on one of our snowmobiles when a deer jumped out in front of me. I swerved to miss it and caught my arm on the branch of a tree."

"How fast were you going?" the doctor asked, taking another gauze pad from Edie.

"Fast enough to do this," Brett grinned. "Ow!"

"Serves you right," the sixty-two-year-old physician muttered. "I guess I don't need to tell you this will take several stitches."

"I figured."

"Why did you drive yourself in? You could've radioed for help. I don't suppose it ever occurred to you that you might've gone into shock. That you might've passed out?!"

Ignoring the good doctor's intended lecture, Brett shyly glanced at Edie. He hadn't seen a woman this pretty in a long time. Not that he had ever had much luck with women. Self-conscious of a birth defect that had left one leg shorter than the other, he had allowed the noticeable limp to hamper him socially. Sports had been out of the question; others had mocked him concerning his lack of coordination. Keeping to himself as he grew up, he had developed a love for nature. More comfortable with animals and plants than humans, he had eventually eased into a career where he could work with both. He loved his job with the Forest Service; it was his entire life. Outside of the office staff, he didn't know many people in this valley. He liked it that way, enjoying the peaceful solitude. As the years had passed, he had steadfastly avoided the blind dates his relatives and friends tried to arrange. Still single, he was convinced it would always be that way.

"Let's get this arm numbed up," the doctor said, noting that the wound was starting to clot.

"I'm a nurse's aide," Edie reminded him. "I don't have access to the drug cart. Do you want me to round up Mabel?"

The doctor shook his head. He hated working with the bossy RN. "Tell you what—you hold this gauze pad in place as tight as you can and I'll fix the shot."

"Shot?" Brett nervously asked as Edie applied pressure to his arm.

"Shot!" Dr. Davis said with a grin. He turned to Edie. "Have you ever helped stitch anyone up before?"

Edie shook her head. Most of her tasks had been menial patient care. Bed-making, carrying trays of food, bed baths. Assisting patients who had trouble getting around. She had enjoyed every minute of it. It was difficult to describe the natural high she experienced each time she helped someone else.

"Then I'd say it's about time. Blood doesn't seem to bother you. I think you'll do," he said, hurrying out of the room.

"So, you work for the Forest Service," Edie observed, glancing at Brett's uniform. She had found that casual conversation often eased anxiety for most patients.

"Yeah," Brett said.

Edie smiled at the man who appeared to be about her age. He had warm blue eyes, a bad haircut, and a nice face. She sensed he was a good man, although she wondered at the bashful way he kept turning his head away from her. "Your name is Brett?" she asked, remembering what he had written on the insurance form.

He nodded. "And you're Edie," he said, blushing when she followed his gaze to the name tag pinned to her uniform.

"Yes. Edie Beyer."

"Brett Randall," he said, nodding at her. "You must be new in town," he guessed.

Laughing, Edie shook her head. "I've . . . been gone for a few years," she said.

"You're a native then?"

Edie nodded. "How about you?"

"I grew up in northern Idaho. I transferred here a couple of years ago."

"Do you like the area?" she asked, curious.

"Yeah, it's nice. Coeur d'Alene is pretty tough to beat though."

"That's where you're from?"

"Uh, huh," Brett replied. "You ever been there?"

"No, just here . . . and Pocatello," she guardedly revealed. "What's Coeur d'Alene like?" she asked, unwilling to discuss her past.

"It's the biggest city in Idaho's panhandle. But the forests and mountains surrounding it are what I like!" Brett replied, his face lighting up. "Dark green pines so thick you can't fit a needle between them. Then there's Lake Coeur d'Alene—it's huge. My parents live close to the lake. I used to enjoy walking down to the shore to watch the sunset." He sighed at the memory.

"It sounds like a wonderful place to live," Edie said wistfully.

"It is. But so is Blaketown."

"What about Blaketown?" Dr. Davis asked, entering the brightly lit room with a syringe.

"You're going to stick me with that?" Brett countered, his eyes widening.

"Yep. Maybe next time you'll slow things down a bit," the doctor scolded.

* * *

"I love this job! Every day I learn something new," Edie excitedly told her mother later that afternoon.

Adele quietly smiled, enjoying her daughter's enthusiasm as she continued to stir the beef stew she was making for dinner.

"Dr. Davis says I'm a natural. He wants me to take advantage of the LPN course the hospital is sponsoring in a month. It would mean traveling back and forth between here and Pocatello for a while, but I think I might try it. He said three other women have already signed up. I could probably ride with them."

"The snow would be gone by then, so the roads wouldn't be too bad," Adele commented, glancing out of the window. She would be so glad to see winter finally fade from sight. The numerous storms plaguing their valley had wreaked havoc with the arthritis in her joints. Another couple of weeks and spring should be making a welcome appearance.

Turning from the window, Adele smiled at her daughter. "I think this is a wonderful opportunity. What will it cost?"

"Dr. Davis said that they're so desperate for licensed nurses, the hospital will pay for the schooling, if we promise to return and work for them when we're through."

Adele's smile widened. "You know what that means," she commented, relieved that Edie was considering staying in the valley.

"I know." Edie smiled, thinking of the new friend she had made today. Brett Randall. She had felt comfortable around him; he was even-tempered and easy to talk to. After he had left the hospital, one of the other nurses had informed her that Brett Randall was considered to be a bit eccentric.

"He lives by himself—doesn't have much to do with anybody. A regular hermit."

Edie didn't think Brett was eccentric. He had been polite, cooperative—maybe a little shy. But when he had smiled at her, he had meant it. She frowned. Maybe he wouldn't have been so nice if he had known about her past. Shaking off the depression that went with that thought, she walked down the hall to change out of her uniform.

* * *

"You've done it again," Doris assured Karen.

Karen smiled. "You think it's all right?"

"This is better than all right. It's wonderful!" the teacher exclaimed, reading through the new article again. This time the young woman had targeted the tendency of today's youth to take material things for granted. "Have you considered a career in journalism?"

"Not really," Karen replied.

"I'd give it some thought if I were you," Doris responded. "Every week you churn out an article like this. You are very prolific!"

"What?" Karen asked, confused by the term Doris had used to describe her.

"Very productive. Talented. You have a rare gift for writing!"

Terri crept unnoticed into Doris' classroom. She had seen Doris and Karen leave Kate's room. Curious, she had followed. Disappointed when Doris shut the door, Terri had strained to hear their conversation through the varnished wood. Failing at this, she had decided to try a direct approach. Quietly opening the door, she had slipped into the classroom just as Doris had told Karen she had a rare gift for writing. Terri's eyes narrowed. No one had complimented her articles. In fact, she'd overheard Doris telling Kate that her writing was trite.

Glowering now at Karen and Doris, Terri failed to notice the pencil on the floor. When it snapped under her foot, Doris and Karen whirled around, staring at her.

"I knocked, but I guess you didn't hear me," Terri lied. "I needed to ask you a question, Mrs. Kelsey."

Doris exchanged an alarmed look with Karen. They were still keeping her identity a secret, printing editorials that had stimulated discussions all over town. How much had Terri overheard?

"Oh?" Doris asked.

"Uh, yeah. Could I talk to you in private?"

Leaning closer to Karen, Doris whispered a soothing reassurance. "I'm sure we're okay. If not, I'll find out now," she promised.

Karen nodded, giving Terri an irritated look before leaving the room.

"Okay, what's up?" Doris asked, flipping over the paper Karen had handed her. She didn't want Terri's curiosity to ruin what had become an extraordinary chance to touch numerous lives, including Karen's.

Terri moved to the front of the room, trying to come up with a logical explanation for what she had done. As an idea formed, she smiled. "Kate . . . I mean, Mrs. Jeffries, doesn't think I can handle anything more than the fashion column," she complained.

Doris gripped the chalkboard tray behind her for support. This would be an unpleasant conversation.

"How can I grow as a writer if I never get a chance to write anything serious?"

"Sharing fashion tips is . . . important," Doris replied.

"What if I came up with a story on my own? Something everyone would want to read?"

Releasing the small metal tray, Doris sank into the chair behind her desk. Kate had shown her the poorly phrased rumors Terri had typed up weeks ago. It had made her sick, thinking of the damage that would've been done if they had been printed. Most of the rumors were just that. There hadn't been a word of truth to most of what Terri had written.

"You know, something like Bev or Karen get to write all the time," Terri continued. "Why does everyone think they're so special?" she added, indignantly.

"Those two girls are naturals. Like some people excel at math or sports. They're born writers."

Insulted by the inference that she was not, Terri frowned. "So, if you're like *me*," she grumbled, "and you don't *have* any talent—"

"That isn't what I said," Doris replied. "I think you have potential—"

"Then give me a chance to prove it," Terri challenged.

"Let's do this. You come up with an idea for a story, then show it to either Mrs. Jeffries or me. If we approve, you can write it up."

Beaming at this victory, Terri thanked Doris and left the room.

After her departure, Doris reached for her purse and the bottle of Tylenol she had learned to keep handy.

* * *

"I hear you're taking drama next semester," Tracie said, smirking at Sabrina. "Drama's the perfect place for you and Marsha. Now you can hang out with the rest of the clods in that class. You'll fit right in!"

"Why are you acting like this? I can't believe we were ever friends!" Sabrina exclaimed, glaring at Tracie.

"You brought this on yourself!" Tracie shot back, returning Sabrina's glare. The two girls had bumped into each other in the hall during lunch. Sabrina had tried to ignore Tracie, but after enduring several taunting insults, Sabrina had begun firing back. Convinced this could turn into an entertaining battle, a small crowd had gathered around them, lending courage and venom to Tracie's comments.

"We don't want to be seen with someone who has your kind of reputation," Tracie stressed, glancing around at the other students. She smiled at a cute boy who was standing near the far wall. "Still suffering from morning sickness?" she added for a dramatic touch.

"I am not pregnant! You are such a liar! How do you sleep at night?" Sabrina angrily demanded.

"More chastely than you do!" Tracie wittily responded.

Several students hooted over this remark as Sabrina's cheeks turned crimson. "You have a lot of room to talk!" Sabrina accused.

"What do you mean by that?"

"Just what I said," Sabrina replied. She gazed knowingly at Tracie, her blue eyes revealing the disgust she felt for her former friend.

Stung by that insinuation, Tracie reacted without thinking and slapped Sabrina across the face. Sabrina was startled, then enraged. She lunged at Tracie and knocked her to the floor, both girls scratching and pulling hair as those around them cheered. Reluctantly the crowd parted to allow a teacher through.

Anticipating a brawl between a couple of hot-headed young men, Coach Brandt froze when he saw who was fighting. "Sabrina, Tracie! Stop it! Stop it right now!" he finally said, moving in to try to separate the two girls. It was all the football coach could do to pull the two apart. Finally, some of the students tried to assist. Dawn and Sindi grabbed hold of Tracie, while Marsha and Samantha reached for Sabrina.

"This is over. Do you hear me?!" the coach wheezed, out of breath. He smoothed his hair back into place, then firmly escorted the two young women to the principal's office.

* * *

Sue Erickson arrived at the high school at the same time Celia Monroe did. As the two women climbed out of their respective cars, they eyed each other, thinking similar thoughts.

"Sue," Celia finally called out.

Sue glanced at Celia, certain she didn't want to talk to this woman right now.

"Before we go inside, there's something I'd like to say to you," Celia continued, moving closer.

Sue stood her ground as the slender brunette approached. She had always liked Celia, but had lost respect for her during the past few months. How could Celia be so blind to her own daughter?

"I'm not sure what took place between our daughters today, but I want you to know how sorry I am for all of the trouble they've been having," Celia began. "I also want you to know that we . . . Tracie and I . . . we'll do anything we can to help Sabrina through this difficult time."

Invisible steam shooting out of her ears, Sue struggled for control. *Celia has no clue about what's going on,* she reminded herself. *She doesn't know Tracie has caused most of Sabrina's problems.*

"I was talking to Tracie a while back. I told her that if my kids were in trouble, I'd want to know. That's why I feel like I should tell you what Sabrina has been doing. I don't think you realize—"

"Celia, I know Sabrina isn't perfect. She has made her fair share of mistakes, but she has been very open with me about what is going on—unlike some of the other girls."

Celia blinked. Just what was Sue saying?

"Instead of being so concerned about my daughter, you ought to open your eyes and see what's really going on with *yours.*" Deciding enough had been said, Sue hurried up onto the sidewalk and moved toward the building.

"Well!" Celia exclaimed. "With an attitude like that, poor Sabrina doesn't stand a chance!" Following behind Sue, she angrily made her way inside of the high school, certain she had tried to perform a Christlike act of service. If Sue Erickson chose to ignore it, that was her fault—the sin would be on her head!

CHAPTER 17

"Ow!" Sabrina exclaimed as Sue continued to scrub the dried blood off her face. "That hurts."

"It should," Sue replied, rinsing the washrag in the bathroom sink. "Just how long are Tracie's fingernails?" she asked, turning to gaze at Sabrina.

Sabrina shifted around on the toilet seat. "Long enough." She looked dismally at her own short nails. "Why did I cut mine?"

"Because they kept breaking off," Sue reminded her daughter, gently wiping away at the scratches on Sabrina's face. "And, considering what took place today, I'm glad you did."

"Why?"

Sue slid her hand under Sabrina's chin. "You did enough damage to that girl without them."

"So I removed a little bit of hair—"

"Tracie has a bald spot this big on the side of her head," Sue pointed out, releasing Sabrina's chin to show her daughter how big the bald spot was.

"Cool!"

"Not cool. Did you see the look on her mother's face?" Sue chided.

"Yours was worse," Sabrina said.

"Well, the last thing I expected to hear today was that my daughter was involved in a fistfight at the high school."

"Tracie had it coming."

"Maybe. Maybe not. I'm just glad you two didn't kill each other."

"Mom, you didn't hear what she said about me."

"Is it any worse than what she's been saying since October?" Sue asked, setting the washrag in the sink. Opening the medicine cabinet, she reached for a tube of Neosporin. "Well? Was it?"

"No," Sabrina murmured. "She just makes me so mad!"

"I see. And that makes it okay to fight?" Removing the lid, Sue squeezed out a dab of ointment and began applying it to the deeper scratches on Sabrina's face.

"I don't know. She started it."

"That's what she said about you, which is why you were both suspended from school for two days. Mr. Dryer decided you two needed some time to cool off."

"Mom, Tracie hinted that I've been sleeping around, and when I told her the same thing could be said about her, she slapped me."

Chewing the inside of her cheek, Sue finished smoothing on the ointment. "She actually said that about you?" she finally asked.

Sabrina nodded.

"What were her exact words?"

"I don't know . . . why?"

"Because I think Tracie's mother and I need to finish our little chat, as much as it pains me to even think about it."

"That'll do a lot of good! Didn't you see Tracie in action this afternoon? '*Oh, Mommy, look what that horrid Sabrina did to me! She's out of control. I don't know why she hurt me like this,*'" Sabrina angrily mimicked.

"I know, I heard the entire thing. So, once again, what exactly did Tracie say to you to make you this angry?"

"First, she started dissing Marsha and me, you know, calling us 'spazzes,' stuff like that. She said that because we're taking drama next term, we're a couple of weirdos." Sabrina sighed. "I don't know how much more of this Marsha can take."

"Marsha wasn't the one duking it out with Tracie."

"No, she was crying in the corner because Tracie keeps telling her how ugly she is."

"What?"

Sabrina nodded. "Sindi and Dawn aren't much better. They don't say as much as Tracie, but they back her up."

Sue began examining Sabrina's hands. Deciding they weren't scratched up as badly as her daughter's face, she settled for gently dabbing at the scratches with the washrag. Only one scrape continued to ooze blood. Finally reaching for a Band-Aid, she encouraged Sabrina to finish her story. "What else did Tracie say?"

Sabrina leaned back against the toilet tank, wincing slightly when her mother attached the Band-Aid to the back of her hand. "After she said all of those rude things, I asked her how she could sleep at night—because of all the lies she keeps spreading."

"And Tracie made the most out of that comment," Sue guessed, discarding the Band-Aid wrapper.

"Oh, yeah. I walked right into that one. She said something like she slept . . . I don't know . . . purer . . . that's not right." Sabrina concentrated. "What else means . . . you know . . . not having sex?" she asked, flushing with embarrassment.

"Being virtuous?"

"No that's not it."

Sue sat down on the edge of the tub. "Never mind. I think I get the picture," she said, shaking her head. "You said she slapped you first?"

Sabrina nodded. "I told her she had room to talk . . . I mean, we're not blind. She has a different boyfriend every time we turn around. We've all seen what she lets some of those guys do in public . . . she lets them wrap themselves around her . . . she doesn't care who sees her. I've even seen her kiss some of those guys in the hallway at school. Who knows what she does with them when no one's watching? But according to her, *I'm* the one who's being a bad influence. I'm sick of it. She spreads lies and I'm supposed to quietly take it. But when I point out what she's doing, she slaps me, like I've said something horrible."

"It sounds like neither of you were being very nice today," Sue responded tiredly. "But I can understand how upset you were," she added before Sabrina could argue with her. "You have put up with a lot."

"Slightly!"

"Okay, so after Tracie slapped you . . . ," Sue prodded.

"I exploded. I flew into her and we both fell on the floor and started scratching and pulling hair. I think I hit her once."

"You think?"

Sabrina nodded. "Just once."

"Where?"

"In the stomach. I knocked the wind out of her. She didn't have much to say after that."

"I see," Sue dryly replied. "Anything else I should know about?"

Sabrina shook her head. "That's it. The fight didn't last very long. Coach Brandt broke it up and hauled us down to Dryer's office."

"Mr. Dryer," Sue quietly rebuked.

"Mr. Dryer," Sabrina obediently complied. "Now what?"

"Well, first I need to call your father and let him know what's going on. Then I think the time has come for Celia, Lori, and I to talk."

"Oh, great!" Sabrina exclaimed. "Tracie's mother, my Mia Maid leader, and my mom. This ought to be good."

"It won't be good, but it will be the truth, something Celia needs to hear." Rising, Sue led Sabrina out of the bathroom and turned out the light.

* * *

Later that night, Celia and Sue met again at Lori's house. Sue and Lori had decided earlier that day to meet with Celia on neutral territory. As Sue drove up, she saw Celia getting out of her car and purposely held back, allowing Celia to move onto Lori's porch ahead of her. Sue waited until Lori had let Celia in, and then, with a swift prayer for strength, she stepped out of the Durango. Gritting her teeth as she rang the doorbell, she hoped the meeting would go better than this afternoon had.

"Sue," Lori greeted her warmly, relieved by her appearance. In the moments since Celia's arrival, the Young Women leader had been inundated with Celia's complaints about Sabrina's *outrageous* behavior. Earlier, when they had first arranged this meeting, Sue had filled Lori in on what had really taken place. There were major discrepancies between the two versions, but Lori knew which one was closer to the truth.

"How are you?" Sue asked, glancing at Celia as Lori beckoned her into the house.

"Fine," Lori said, trying to make polite conversation. They had agreed it would be best if Celia knew nothing about their earlier discussion.

Celia looked suspiciously at Sue, then at Lori. When Lori had called to say they needed to talk about Tracie, there had been no mention that Sue would be here as well. "So, what exactly is this about?" Celia asked.

"We need to discuss the welfare of your daughters," Lori replied. She had been anticipating that question all afternoon and hoped she had answered it in a way that would avoid contention. She was grateful her husband had volunteered to take their children out for ice cream tonight. Their normal noisy exuberance would have been a distraction. Lori knew the only way to get through to Celia was to have a setting that would invite the Spirit; otherwise, Celia wouldn't believe what they had to tell her. "Before we start, would either of you mind if I offered a word of prayer?"

Celia shook her head, selecting to sit in a padded, wooden rocker. She was convinced that the Young Women leader had heard about what had taken place at school that day. In a way, she was relieved. She didn't want hard feelings to exist between herself and Sue. Maybe if Sue heard the truth from Lori, she would finally come to realize how troubled Sabrina was.

After offering a humble prayer, Lori sat beside Sue on the couch. Courageously, she smiled at Celia and began. "Sometimes young people don't realize how important it is to adhere to the standards set by our church," she said.

Nodding, Celia glanced at Sue, hoping Sabrina's mother was listening.

"And good kids, from good LDS homes . . . make mistakes."

"I know," Celia murmured, glancing again at Sue.

"Celia, what I have to say isn't easy, but you need to know what's been going on. This involves Sue too, which is why I've asked her to come tonight." Turning, Lori smiled at Sue. Sue returned her smile, choosing to ignore the knowing look on Celia's face. "I'm going to tell you both what I've heard and what I've seen, and what I know is true," Lori continued. "I look at it this way—we're all in this battle together. We want the same thing, for these girls to eventually realize that they are special daughters of our Heavenly Father."

Celia vigorously nodded, relieved that Lori had taken on this responsibility. Finally Sue would know what Sabrina had been up to.

"I'll start by telling you what took place at Sindi's Halloween party." Lori gazed steadily at Celia. "Celia, I know this isn't what you want to hear, but you need to know the truth about Tracie before this gets any worse."

Her eyes widening in surprise, Celia stared at the Mia Maid leader. What was Lori talking about?

* * *

For a long time, Celia stayed in the car in her driveway, crying. The insinuations about Tracie had hurt. Sue and Lori had tearfully pleaded with her to listen, to pray about what they had told her. Enraged, she had finally left Lori's house, driving around until she'd found herself in their branch president's driveway. She had decided to tell him what she had been subjected to and to demand that Lori be released from the Young Women presidency. Losing her nerve, she had started to back out when he had pulled in beside her. Stepping out of his car, he had invited her inside the house where she had tearfully shared everything that had happened that day. Patiently he had waited for her to finish, then had given her a special priesthood blessing, one that had promised she would come to know the truth concerning this matter. Now here she was at home, afraid to find out. What if it was true, all of it? How could she ever face anyone in this town again?

Finally wiping at her eyes, she left the security of the car and entered the house. She had already decided not to tell her husband until she knew for sure. There was no need to upset him if none of this was true. Determined to find out, she slowly walked upstairs to confront their oldest daughter.

* * *

"Why would they say such horrible things about me?!" Tracie stammered, trying to force tears. This was a conversation she had thought would never happen. Her mother was demanding to know in no uncertain terms what was going on. She had been stunned by all her mother had heard. There was nothing left to tell; her mother knew it all.

"Tracie, look at me and tell me it's all a lie," Celia tearfully pleaded.

Tracie made a valiant effort, but found she couldn't tolerate her mother's searching gaze. Lowering her head, she refused to answer.

"Oh, Tracie, why?" Celia agonized, finally seeing through her daughter's thinly veiled facade. "I've taught you . . . you know better . . . why?"

Still unable to answer, real tears finally made an appearance as Tracie began to realize the enormity of what this meant. Her life was now ruined, thanks to Sabrina's big mouth!

CHAPTER 18

March

"What do you think of *The Blaketown Buzz* now?" Cleo asked Terri. She had been surprised by this girl's involvement with the high school paper she had claimed to despise.

"It's okay," Terri responded as she glanced around the principal's office. "Especially now that they're giving me a chance to write a real story. Reporting fashion news isn't very exciting."

"I don't imagine," Cleo sympathetically replied. "What kind of story are you thinking of writing?"

Terri shrugged. "I'm still trying to come up with a good idea."

"How would you like to do some undercover reporting?" Cleo asked, experiencing a sudden burst of inspiration. For weeks she had tolerated the phantom editorials that in her opinion had overstepped acceptable bounds. She didn't like the inferred criticism of this school or the community and considered it a negative reflection on herself.

"What do you mean?" Terri asked.

"How would you like to break one of the biggest stories of this term?"

Terri excitedly nodded.

"Find out who is responsible for the editorials that appear in the paper every week."

"But . . ."

"It won't be easy. You can't tell anyone what you're working on. If they ask, just say you're still coming up with a story. It's the truth." Cleo smiled. Terri would be an unwitting pawn in this game of wills. Once everyone knew who the editorial culprit was, it would take away the anonymous advantage this writer had gained. The inflaming articles would stop. Cleo was convinced no one would write critical commentaries like this if they had to affix their name to them.

Terri thought about this suggestion for several seconds. Then she smiled. This *would* be the biggest story of the year. It would give her a chance to prove she was a true investigative reporter—she would earn everyone's respect.

"I'll do it!" she told the principal.

Nodding her approval, Cleo silently rejoiced, convinced this newspaper travesty was nearly at an end.

* * *

Terri hesitated until she was certain Kate and Doris had left the school building. She had waited several days for this chance. When she was certain no one else was around, Terri used a bobby pin she had borrowed from her mother to pick the lock. Her conscience pricked a little, but she blanketed that uncomfortable sensation with the rationalization that the principal had asked her to do this. Cleo hadn't instructed her to break into Kate's classroom, but she had requested the information Terri knew she would find inside. This defiant act was for a good cause.

She twisted the bobby pin around until she heard a small click. It worked! Just like in the movies. Opening the door to Kate's classroom, Terri slipped inside. This was so exciting! She felt just like Julia Roberts in the movie *I Love Trouble*. She had seen the edited version on TV last week. In the movie, Julia had played the role of a Chicago newspaper reporter, set on out-scooping a veteran reporter, played by Nick Nolte. The two competing reporters eventually united to unravel a mysterious train derailment.

"I wonder if John Packer would like to join forces with me," Terri sighed, picturing the handsome senior. He shared editing responsibilities with Bev on this paper. With romantic thoughts filling her head, Terri almost didn't notice the footsteps echoing down the hall. Quickly locking the door, she shut it, hurried to the front of the room, and climbed underneath Kate's desk to hide.

"I can't believe I left it on my desk," Kate said to Doris as she tried to unlock her door. She wondered at the way the lock seemed to resist her key. Finally giving it a jerk, it cooperated.

"No harm done," Doris replied, following Kate inside of the room. "You can't leave something like that lying around in plain sight. It wouldn't be good if it fell into the wrong hands."

"Agreed," Kate responded. The two women walked to the front of the room, stopping by Kate's desk. Neither of them noticed the trembling figure underneath. "There it is," Kate said, picking up a piece of paper. She looked over the test she had prepared for one of her history classes, a midterm quiz that would have an impact on several grade standings.

"Okay, let's go," Doris said, turning around. "There's something I'd like to show you. It's out in my car."

Nodding, Kate followed the older woman out of her classroom, carefully locking the door behind them.

"Why did they have to come back?" Terri whispered, pulling herself out of the cramped space. Disgusted at this missed opportunity, she hurried to the window to look outside. There's no way she would be able to see what Doris wanted to show Kate, the parking lot was too far away. She pulled out a small notebook and scribbled the following:

Kate took next week's editorial off her desk, right under my nose. Then they arranged to meet at Doris' car, where they'll conspire something dastardly, I'm sure.

She glanced around the room, wondering if she could find another piece of important evidence. Walking to the large, metal file cabinet in the far corner, she tried to open the top drawer. It was locked. She pulled out her bobby pin and tried to squeeze it into the lock. It was too big. Frowning her displeasure, Terri wandered back to Kate's desk to see if she could locate anything else that would work. She sat down behind the desk and opened the top wooden drawer. It was filled with chalk, pencils, pens, and paper clips.

Terri pulled out one of the paper clips and straightened the small, metal clasp. Standing, she moved back to the file cabinet. This time, she had better success. The thin wire fit inside, but wouldn't unlock the drawer. Frustrated, Terri pushed on the paper clip, breaking it off inside of the lock.

Her eyes widened. As she studied the lock, she convinced herself
that no one could tell there was anything inside of it. Deciding to
leave it alone, she tried the drawer beneath the one that was locked. It
opened easily, revealing several stuffed files. Grinning, Terri began
rifling through, discovering that it was filled with personal files Kate
had been keeping on her history students. Curious, Terri pulled hers
out. She smiled at the tests she had done well on, glancing at some of
the essays Kate had required them to write.

"I really do have talent when it comes to writing," Terri told
herself, pleased with most of the scores she had received. Then, she
came across a note written by Kate.

*This student possesses a lot of potential. If only we could get her
nervous energy channeled in a positive direction. She has a tendency to
look at the negative side of life, something I hope we can change. Her poor
attitude is a detriment to herself, and those around her.*

"I do not have a poor attitude!" Terri exclaimed. Shoving the
papers back inside of the file, she slammed the drawer shut.
Thoroughly disgusted, she then marched out of the room.

* * *

"You must've spent weeks on this baby afghan," Kate observed,
admiring the soft, blue and white blanket.

"Actually, I didn't," Doris revealed. "Adele, Karen's grandmother,
made this for me. I wanted something nice to give my son and his
wife for their baby, my newest grandson." She smiled, thinking of the
cute baby boy she had held for the first time last week. "I don't have
the patience to crochet. I called Adele after I saw the sweater she had
knitted for Edie this Christmas. It was beautiful. I figured Adele
could put something like this together better than I ever could. She
helped me pick out the right yarn, and then I paid her to crochet it. I
had to practically force the money on her for doing this, but I had no
intention of letting her do all this work for free."

"She did a beautiful job," Kate said, handing the afghan back to Doris.

Nodding, Doris stuck it back inside of the white plastic bag she
was keeping it in for protection. As she set it back in the car, Terri
walked toward them, straining to see what they had been looking at.

Before the young woman approached the two teachers, she made another note to herself:

Suspects are now concealing something in Doris' car. I will attempt to find out what it is.

"Well, I'd better get home," Doris said, shutting the car door.

"Uh . . . wait," Terri yelled, hurrying forward.

Surprised by the girl's sudden appearance, Kate and Doris both stared at her. "Why are you still here?" Doris asked.

"I was . . . finishing up a special assignment," Terri said, proud of her artful deception. It was the truth—she was working on a special assignment.

"I see," Doris replied. "Did you need something?"

"I was wondering . . . ," she glanced around, trying to come up with a reason to look inside of the English teacher's car. She suddenly smiled, hitting on a plan she was sure would work. "Could I get a ride home?"

Kate gave Doris an amused look.

"You know, I'd love to help you out, but I'm in a hurry to get to the post office right now. Besides, Kate lives closer to you anyway," Doris said, grinning at Kate.

The expression on Kate's face changed to dread.

"But . . . ," Terri stammered as Doris hurriedly climbed behind the wheel of her Honda Civic.

"I'll see you two at school on Monday," Doris said jubilantly, waving as she drove off.

Terri frowned. This afternoon wasn't working out like she had hoped.

"Come on, Terri," Kate reluctantly encouraged, unlocking the car door for the teenager.

Still seething over the comments Kate had made in her file, the last thing Terri wanted to do was to ride home with this woman. Then it occurred to her that Kate might have the paper she had taken from her desk a few minutes ago. Brightening at the thought, Terri quickly climbed into the car.

"Would you mind if I stopped by the grocery store on our way?" Kate asked. "I need to pick up a couple of things for dinner tonight."

"That's fine," Terri said, thrilled with this stroke of luck. "Would it be all right if I stayed in the car?" she asked, pointing to her backpack. "I have a ton of homework tonight. I'd like to get started. I could work on it while you're in the store."

"Sure," Kate replied, parking near the store. "I won't be long."

"Take your time," Terri encouraged, smiling.

Lifting an eyebrow at Terri's surprising cooperation, Kate grabbed her purse, opened the door and hurried toward the small store.

Terri waited until Kate had disappeared inside the store, then began a frantic search of the Dodge Neon. She found what she thought she was looking for on the back seat. Pulling a paper out of Kate's black satchel, she grinned, pleased with her ingenuity. Then she read through the midterm test. "This is what she was hiding?!" she angrily exclaimed. Glancing up, she saw that Kate was on her way back to the car. Terri quickly stuffed the paper back inside of the satchel, then threw the black bag onto the back seat. Opening her backpack, she pulled out the book Doris had assigned them to read for English literature. She turned to the middle of the book and pretended to read, watching Kate out of the corner of her eye.

Kate opened the car on her side, bent the seat forward and set a plastic bag of groceries and a gallon of milk on the floor behind the front seat. Pushing the seat back into place, she climbed into the car. She glanced at Terri, impressed that the young woman was studying so intently. Then her gaze shifted to the book the teenager was reading. Frowning, Kate pulled the book from Terri's hand, turning it right-side up. "I think you'll find books are easier to read this way," she said, wondering what this girl had been up to.

"Oh . . . yeah. I like to read upside down, it's more of a challenge," Terri said nervously, wondering how Julia Roberts would explain her way out of this one.

Giving the girl a dubious look, Kate started the car and drove her home.

* * *

Adele handed the phone to Edie.

"Who is it?" Edie mouthed.

Her mother shrugged.

"Hello?" Edie said into the phone.

"Edie, this is Mabel," the curt RN revealed. "We're running short-handed again tonight. I know you worked a shift this morning. Could we talk you into coming again tonight for a few hours, at least until we get everyone tucked in for the night?"

Sighing, Edie gripped the phone. She had hoped to corner her daughter tonight. Karen was acting strange again. She wanted to find out what was going on.

"Edie?"

"I'll be there in a few minutes," Edie replied. She'd have to talk to Karen later. She didn't want to do anything that might jeopardize her new job. Hanging up the phone, she smiled at her mother, then walked down the hall to change.

* * *

"It's getting late," Karen said, looking at her watch. "I'd better head home. My grandmother will be upset."

"Want me to drive you?" Bev asked.

Karen shook her head. "I'll walk. It's not that far."

"Are you sure?" Bev pressed. "I know Gina wouldn't mind if I *borrowed* her car again." Lately, Bev had been taking the Grand Prix whenever she wanted, with or without her stepmother's approval.

Karen shook her head. "Don't worry about it. It'll give me time to clear my head before I get home." She sighed heavily. "I don't know what to think about that mother of mine."

Bev gazed thoughtfully at her friend. "I thought things were getting better between you and your mom."

"She's putting on this big act for everyone, but I know the truth. She hasn't changed," Karen said bitterly.

"Why would you say that?"

"I went into her room—my old room—a couple of nights ago. I was looking for some of my makeup. I opened up a drawer in the nightstand." She grimaced. "Guess what I found?!"

Bev could tell by the expression on Karen's face that it hadn't been a good discovery. "What?" she prompted.

"A bottle of vodka." She scowled, still repulsed by what that bottle represented.

"She's drinking again?"

"She must be."

"Couldn't you smell it on her if she was?" Bev asked.

"I try not to get that close to her," Karen said tersely. "Besides, vodka doesn't smell as strong as other liquors. It's easier to hide. I know because she did this before."

Bev touched Karen's arm. "I'm sorry. I really thought she'd make it this time."

"Yeah, well, now I know that's just another fairytale."

"I can't believe you've kept this to yourself the past couple of days."

Karen shrugged. "It's too embarrassing to talk about. 'Hey, guess what, my mother is still a drunkard!'" she exclaimed, rising to her feet.

"Are you sure you don't want me to drive you home?" Bev offered again. She glanced out her bedroom window at the dark night.

"I'll be fine. The walk will do me some good. Who knows, maybe I can come up with another editorial. Maybe a stinging commentary on alcohol abuse. I've already gathered quite a bit of research for it."

Bev stared at Karen. Her friend had already confided that she was the one writing the editorials. Bev had suspected, knowing Karen's talent for writing. "Alcohol abuse, huh?"

Karen nodded. "Several kids in this town have a problem with it. They have a party and get drunk, and their parents have no idea what they're up to."

Bev forced a wan smile, certain she didn't like this idea.

"I'll think about it on the way home," Karen continued. "Who knows, maybe I'll feel inspired by the time I get there." Turning, she picked up her jacket and left the room.

* * *

"Let me see your key," Doris said, reaching for the key in Kate's hand.

Stepping back from the file cabinet, Kate handed the small key to Doris.

"You're right, it won't go in at all," Doris said, pursing her lips together as she tried again. "Something's jammed inside of it."

"That's what I'm starting to think," Kate replied. "It worked fine this afternoon."

"My guess is someone has tried to open it since then."

Kate stared at Doris. "You're kidding."

Doris shrugged, handing the key back to Kate. "Every year we end up with random acts of vandalism here at good old Blaketown High. Looks like you've just become a statistic."

"What were they looking for?" Kate asked, glancing around her room.

"It's hard to say," Doris sighed. "Is anything missing?"

"I don't think so. I already looked through the other drawers in this file cabinet. My desk doesn't look like it's been touched."

"When I asked you to meet me here tonight I didn't think we would be facing this kind of challenge," Doris said. "I just wanted to look over Karen's latest editorial again. There was a phrase she used that keeps bothering me. It's probably the English teacher in me coming out. I live to edit!"

Kate smiled at her friend. "Something keeps nagging at me too," she said.

"What?"

"Terri Jeppson."

Doris grinned. "Before you let me have it for making you drive her home this afternoon, keep in mind—"

"It's not that," Kate replied. "She did something very strange . . . even for Terri."

"Oh? What?"

Kate sat down in one of the student desks and waited until Doris had seated herself nearby. "When we were on our way home, I stopped at the grocery store to pick up a few things. Terri told me that would be fine, she'd work on her homework in the car while I was in the store. I was only gone a few minutes. When I returned, she was reading."

"What's so strange about that?"

"Her book was upside down."

"That is interesting," Doris agreed. "What do you think she was up to?"

Kate frowned. "I hope I'm wrong about this, but I noticed my satchel had been moved. It was facing right side up when I set it in the back. When I returned from the grocery store, it was just the opposite."

"What was in it?"

"A test I'm giving on Monday."

Doris stared at Kate. "Terri wouldn't do something like that—would she?"

"I wouldn't think so. She gets pretty good grades on her own. What would she gain by trying to cheat?"

"This would absolutely kill her mother," Doris stated. "Not to mention Cleo. Terri's her gifted pet."

"I know," Kate said. "That's why I was glad when you called about Karen's editorial. I wanted to discuss this with you before I decide what to do."

"I'll tell you what I'd do," Doris suggested. "I'd make up a different test."

"But I spent nearly a week putting this one together."

"I'd still change it over the weekend. That way you'll know if Terri looked at the first one. If she bombs it big time, then she's probably guilty. If she passes, then she must've been doing something else in your car."

"Like what?"

"With that girl, who knows?!"

"What do I do about this file cabinet?" Kate asked.

"You'll have to nab our *friendly* custodian Monday morning," Doris advised.

Kate pictured the ornery older man who tried to keep Blaketown High looking as polished as the aging building could appear. "Do I have to?" she moaned.

"Let's go look in my room. I might have some tools stashed in there somewhere." Rising, she led Kate across the hall.

CHAPTER 19

Karen shivered. The light jacket she had selected to wear had been perfect earlier that day. It was the end of March and spring was finally here, but evenings were still quite cool. Tonight, the temperature had plummeted, a stiff breeze making it uncomfortable. Deciding to jog to warm herself, she turned down the street that led to the high school. A few years ago, she had discovered a shortcut from Bev's house to hers. If she ran through the football field, it saved nearly ten minutes. Knowing her grandmother would be having a fit as it was, Karen hurried onto the school grounds.

Keeping a brisk pace, she headed toward the bleachers. It wasn't until she had nearly passed them that she realized she wasn't alone. A group of teenage boys were huddled together behind the bleachers, enjoying the beer one of them had brought from home.

"Another toast to your father," one young man sang out.

"He'll never know this stuff is missing," came the retort. "He keeps our fridge well-stopped—stocked," he slurred.

"He's a wunnerful human being," another boy called out.

"Hey, shhhhhh," another one said, "someone's onto us."

The boys started to scramble, then one teen recognized Karen. "It's just Karen, Karen Beyer," he announced.

"Karen?" Gerald Reynolds asked, coming closer for a better look.

Karen tried to run off, but was grabbed from behind by a large, athletically inclined young man.

"Let me go!" she cried out.

"Now why would we want to do something that stupid, you cute little reporter you?" Gerald asked, sliding a finger along the side of her face. He had felt an attraction toward this young woman for quite some time.

Repulsed, Karen managed to kick him in the leg.

"Hey, that wasn't very nice," one of Gerald's comrades said as Gerald hopped around, holding his wounded leg. "Boys, I think we should teach this young lady a lesson."

"That ain't no lady," another teen pointed out. "Her mother's a convict!"

"That's right!" Gerald agreed, enraged by what she had done. "Hold her still for a minute," he demanded. Three more boys stepped forward, holding Karen so she couldn't move. "I just want a little kiss. That's all." Before Karen had a chance to react, Gerald forced his lips on hers, bruising her with his drunken intensity. "There, now you can let her go," Gerald said, deciding they were even.

"You pig!" Karen angrily sputtered.

Gerald laughed. "Let her go," he repeated.

"Nah," one of the boys argued. "I've got a better idea. Let's show this lady a good time," he suggested. The other boys who were holding her agreed, shoving her to the ground.

"Guys, let her go," Gerald said, alarmed. This wasn't what he had had in mind.

"If you got what you wanted, then leave," a large teen said, shoving Gerald out of the way.

Sickened by what he now felt responsible for, Gerald took a swing at the other boy. He connected with his stomach, but it didn't seem to make much of an impression. The other boy roared his displeasure and slammed Gerald in the mouth. He then caught Gerald in the nose, knocking him off his feet.

Stunned, Gerald lay there for a few seconds, then got up and ran for help. He didn't have to go too far. From Doris' classroom, Kate and Doris had overheard the commotion and had come running out to see what was going on.

"Gerald, what are you boys doing?" Doris asked, noticing the blood dripping from the teenager's nose and mouth.

"You've got to stop them. They're hurting Karen," he stammered.

Doris and Kate ran forward, sick at heart when they heard Karen's muffled scream. Gripping the pepper spray she had brought with her,

Doris lavished it on the nearest offending teen. When he yelped in misery, the others spun around for a look. Seeing the teachers, they scattered, running for all they were worth across the field, two young men half-carrying, half-dragging the boy who had been sprayed.

Handing her purse to Kate, Doris told her to grab the cell phone out of it and call the police. She then hurried to Karen's side. "Oh, honey," she said, kneeling down to gather the hysterical girl into her arms. "It's okay. It's okay, we're here."

Clinging to Doris, Karen began to sob.

* * *

"Does anybody realize I'm living at this facility night and day," Dr. Davis muttered, replacing his glasses. As luck would have it, he was the doctor on call that night. After delivering a baby, casting a broken leg, and helping with an emergency appendectomy earlier that afternoon, he was exhausted. He had decided to crash in the doctor's lounge tonight instead of traveling twenty minutes away to his country home. Grumbling his displeasure at being awakened, he followed Edie down the hall into the emergency room.

"What exactly do we have coming in?" he sleepily asked.

Mabel looked up from the chart in her hands. "We're not sure. The dispatch said the police were bringing in two teens who had been injured in some kind of confrontation."

"Teenagers!" the doctor complained, running a hand through his thinning hair. In his opinion, the young people of today didn't have enough to do, thanks to modern conveniences. They always seemed to be in trouble, out looking for excitement. "How serious are the injuries?"

Mabel shook her head. "We don't know yet. It must not be too bad or they would've called the ambulance."

"It was bad enough to interrupt my beauty sleep," he continued to complain.

"Do you want me to stay here, or keep an eye on the nurses' station?" Edie asked.

"Until we know what we're dealing with, you'd better stick around," Dr. Davis quickly said. He appreciated Mabel's efficiency, but hated her tendency to boss him around. The fifty-three-year-old nurse thrived on being in charge. Edie was a refreshing change, someone who actually treated him with the respect he felt he deserved.

"Here they come," Mabel announced as the doors leading to ER flew open. The first casualty to come through the door was a teenage boy, bleeding from the mouth and nose. As the police officer led him into the brightly lit room, two women helped a teenage girl limp in.

Edie dropped the tray she had started to set up, staring with horror at her daughter. "Karen?!"

"Keep her away from me," Karen moaned, burying her face against Doris. "This is her fault!"

Doris exchanged a concerned look with Kate. This was going to be worse than they had imagined.

* * *

"All right, young lady, I looked over the x-rays," Dr. Davis said, walking back into ER.

Karen gazed dully at the doctor. Seated on the narrow examining table, she continued to lean against Doris for support. Doris had slipped an arm around Karen's slender shoulders, trying to keep her subdued.

"There were no broken bones," the doctor continued. "Your wrist is badly sprained. We'll wrap it—you'll have to use a sling for a few days." Dr. Davis glanced at Mabel who was opening a fresh ace bandage for Karen's swollen wrist. He shifted his gaze back to the traumatized teen. It had been a relief to discover that Edie's daughter hadn't been raped. She had been severely mauled, bruised, and humiliated, but otherwise, was physically intact. Emotionally, she was a wreck. For some reason, the young woman had gone berserk at the sight of her mother. Edie had finally fled the room and was now out in the hall, sitting between her mother and Kate on a cushioned bench.

"Mabel, if you would do the honors, I'll check on our other patient." Leaving the nurse to take care of Karen's wrist, the doctor quietly left ER. To keep Karen calm, they had moved Gerald into the recovery room down the hall. Closing the door behind him, Dr. Davis smiled encouragingly at Edie, then walked down to the room where Gerald Reynolds and his father were waiting. When the doctor entered the room, Gerald looked up, still dabbing at a small trickle of blood from his nose.

"His nose is broken," he said to Chip, Gerald's father. "It's a clean break, but it'll heal just fine. We'll set it, then tape it in place. It won't feel too bad after we're finished."

Chip solemnly nodded, still in shock. He was proud of his son for trying to help Karen, but sickened by the knowledge that Gerald had been drinking. The police had let him know Gerald's foolhardiness had triggered the attack on Karen.

"According to Karen, Gerald initiated the assault by kissing her against her will," the large officer had informed Chip. "Your son is considered a minor, but charges may be filed. If he decides to cooperate and gives us a list of the other boys involved tonight, it'll make things easier on him."

Gerald had been mortified by that news. "But, Dad, they're my friends. They were drunk. None of us were thinking straight," he had said, pleading for understanding. "We didn't mean for this to happen."

Chip knew that was true, just as he knew Gerald and his friends would now have to face serious repercussions for their actions that night.

* * *

"Karen's finally asleep," Adele announced, walking into the living room.

Edie glanced up from the arm chair. For nearly an hour she had been contemplating everything her daughter had been through.

Sighing heavily, Adele sank down on the couch, facing her daughter. "Are you all right?"

Slowly nodding, Edie gazed at her mother. "Karen's right, you know. This is my fault."

"Edie—"

"My daughter is paying for my mistakes."

"Your daughter had no business walking home in the dark," Adele replied. "She said Bev had offered to drive her home . . . if she wasn't so stubborn, none of this would've happened!" Conflicting emotions rampaged inside of her—anger at a situation that had been out of her control, disgust at what her granddaughter had been subjected to, and indignation at Karen's reaction to Edie tonight.

"I've decided I will sign up for that LPN program."

Confused by the topic change, Adele stared at Edie.

"I'll move to Pocatello and stay there until I've finished the schooling. If I have to work at this hospital during that time, I'll travel back and forth with the other nurses' aides."

"Edie, running away isn't the answer. Karen needs you right now, even if she doesn't realize it yet."

"I'll have to come back to Blaketown when the course is finished," Edie continued, as if her mother had never spoken. "It's part of the agreement—to work at this hospital. But I'll find an apartment. Karen won't even have to know I'm around. I'll stay out of her life."

Rising, Adele crossed the room, staring down at her daughter. "Edie, this isn't a solution."

Edie stood. "It is for me." She walked down the hall to her room and shut the door. Sitting on her bed, she leaned down to open the bottom drawer of the nightstand. She picked up the bottle of vodka and stared at it for several minutes. Rising, she moved to her bedroom window and opened it. She slid the screen out of the way, then opened the vodka. For several seconds, she held it upside down, watching as the contents slowly seeped into the ground.

CHAPTER 20

Edie lay staring at the darkened ceiling. How had she let her mother talk her into this? It would only make things worse. Karen didn't want anything to do with her.

"Give this one more chance before you do anything drastic," her mother had pleaded, coming into Edie's bedroom to argue her point. "Karen was hurt and frightened when they brought her into the hospital. She lashed out at you . . . she shouldn't have, but she did. What she needs right now is her mother. This is your chance to show her that's who you are!"

It wasn't Adele's nature to be very forceful, but she had been adamant about this one thing. All but dragging Edie to the bedroom where Karen was sleeping, Adele had shoved her daughter into the room and shut the door. Now, here Edie was, unable to sleep, fearing Karen's reaction when she realized who was in the twin bed across from her own.

Nearly an hour later when Edie had started to doze off, she heard a deep moan from the other side of the room.

"NO!" Karen hollered, thrashing around in her bed.

Without thinking, Edie jumped out of bed and hurried across the room. Sitting down on Karen's bed, she roused her daughter out of the nightmare that had provoked this outburst.

"Karen, it's all right . . . it's just a nightmare," Edie softly said as she pulled her trembling daughter close.

Reliving the attack behind the football bleachers, Karen sobbed against the woman holding her. As she continued to cry, that embrace tightened; salty tears mixing with her own. Leaning into the warming comfort that felt so right, Karen didn't realize who was with her until she recognized the subtle perfume her mother always wore. Her initial waves of repulsion were silenced by a need that refused to be denied. Gradually the emotional tide settled into a calming peace as mother and daughter began to renew a severed bond.

* * *

Quietly, Adele opened the bedroom door. She blinked until her eyes adjusted to the darkness, seeing the empty bed she normally slept in. Shifting her gaze to Karen's bed, she smiled. Karen was nestled against her mother, her sprained wrist carefully propped up on a pillow. Tearfully, Adele offered a silent prayer of gratitude, then softly closed the door.

* * *

"I can't do it," Karen grumbled, glaring at her shoes. It was amazing how many things took two hands to accomplish. Embarrassed, she had to rely on those around her for assistance. Her mother had helped with the bath she had taken earlier, then had helped her get dressed. Karen had attempted to tie her own shoes, but was finding it an impossible task with her right hand in a sling.

"I'll get them," Edie said, kneeling in front of Karen. She was still overwhelmed by this turn of events. When they had finally wakened, the sun had been high in the sky. Loving tenderness had given way to disconcerting awkwardness. Staring at each other, Edie and Karen had pulled apart, unsure of this new twist in their relationship.

An added concern was the panic Edie felt over missing a day of work. It had been a relief to learn that Adele had already called the hospital, requesting a day off for Edie. "Mabel said not to worry about it, especially since you pulled a double shift yesterday. You're scheduled to have Sunday—tomorrow—off, so you won't have to report back until Monday at 6:30 a.m.," Adele had calmly revealed.

Edie had relaxed, grateful for her mother's intervention. Still in shock over last night, she wanted time to contemplate this budding connection she now felt with Karen. Adele had purposely kept herself busy and aloof, leaving Karen to Edie's care. When Karen had realized the limitations she would have to live with for a few days, she had grudgingly allowed Edie to help her, something Edie had enjoyed. For the first time in years Edie actually felt like a parent. Now, as she quickly tied Karen's shoes, Edie experienced an emotional flashback, remembering when she had done simple things like this for Karen years ago. "There you go," she said brightly, smiling up at her daughter.

"Thanks," Karen managed to say. She wasn't sure how to act or what to call this woman who now stood before her. Somehow, it didn't seem right to keep referring to her as "Edie," something she had been doing since Christmas to convey her disapproval.

"How's your wrist?"

"It's sore," Karen admitted, glancing down at the dark blue sling. She closed her eyes, trying to block out what had happened at the football field.

"Are you all right?" Edie asked, sitting on the couch beside Karen.

Karen nodded. "I just can't believe . . . last night . . . Will I always feel like this?"

"Like what?" Edie softly asked.

Karen shrugged, then winced as her wrist continued to throb. "Humiliated. Angry. Like I want to scream."

"I've had a few of those days," her mother replied.

Karen looked down at her feet.

"Sorry. You don't need to hear about any of that," Edie mused.

Lifting her head, Karen gazed steadily at her mother. "Was it awful . . . being in prison?"

Edie nodded.

"Why . . . why did all of that have to happen?"

"Last night . . . or the things I did?"

"Both," Karen replied, needing answers.

"Last night happened because a group of teenage boys got drunk. When you're drinking, you'll say and do things you wouldn't normally, because you're not in control." Edie returned her daughter's searching gaze. "What took place last night wasn't your fault, although I don't ever want you out walking alone at night again," she said firmly.

Karen blinked. It was the first rule she'd received from her mother in years. She could tell Edie meant it, by the stern look on her face. "Don't worry, I won't," she murmured.

Edie nodded. "As for me . . . I made a lot of stupid mistakes. Some because of the alcohol, others because I was angry at life."

Karen waited for an explanation. She'd heard the story from her grandmother several times. This was the first time she would hear it from her mother.

"Your grandfather passed away when I was a teenager. That part you already know."

Karen nodded.

"I didn't deal with his death very well. I didn't understand why it happened. Mom tried to talk to me about it, so did some of my Church leaders, teachers, and friends. I didn't want to hear what any of them had to say." She frowned. "I wish now Mom would've kept me locked in my room until I came to my senses, but that isn't your grandmother's way, and it probably wouldn't have worked. I would've found a way out of that room, just like I thought I had found a way to quit hurting. That's when I started drinking."

Karen stared at her mother. "In high school?! Grandma didn't tell me . . ."

"Your grandmother didn't know," Edie explained. "I hid it so well, she thought I started drinking after your father and I married. I was hooked on that poison long before then."

"How did you get it . . . the alcohol . . . when you were in high school?"

"The same way those boys did last night. From a so-called *friend* who either bummed it from a parent, or from someone older who was willing to buy it for us. It's not hard to get when you want it bad enough."

"I've never tried it," Karen confessed, "drinking, I mean."

Relieved, Edie smiled. "I'm glad. I'll tell you something I wish I'd known when I was your age. Alcoholism runs in our family. My grandfather was an alcoholic—Mom's father."

"What?" Karen asked, surprised.

"It's true. Mom told me about it after I started the substance and abuse treatment three years ago."

"Are you an alcoholic?" Karen asked, voicing a suspicion she had kept to herself for a very long time.

Edie reluctantly nodded, admitting a fact she had been faced with in prison.

"Could that happen to me?"

"It's a possibility . . . that tendency runs in our family," her mother replied. "Don't ever try it, Karen," Edie pleaded. "Not even one drink . . . it's not worth it. In that rehab program I learned that scientists have discovered a gene abnormality they think is responsible for triggering alcoholism. It proves this condition can be inherited." She nervously flipped her hair over one shoulder. "This is the best advice I can give you—don't drink, then you won't become an alcoholic."

Karen silently agreed. She had been researching this very subject in preparation for that editorial she had wanted to write and had learned that alcoholism is a disease that can cripple, ravage, and even kill. She frowned, remembering what she had seen in her mother's drawer earlier that week. "Mom, I have to ask you something."

Edie's eyes glistened with joyful tears. Karen had finally called her "Mom"!

"The other day I was looking for some of my makeup . . . I haven't been able to find it since I moved in with Grandma."

Nodding, Edie wondered at the heartsick look on her daughter's face.

"I went into your room—my old room, to see if I'd left it in there. I opened the bottom drawer of the nightstand—"

Edie flinched. No wonder Karen had been so upset all week.

"Mom, are you drinking again?" Karen tearfully ventured. She had experienced a brief taste of what it could be like between them; it was something she wanted to continue. She knew the alcohol would prevent that from happening—again.

Edie forced herself to face Karen's accusation. Adele was right. She couldn't keep running. Painful situations had to be confronted and dealt with. "Karen, I bought that bottle of vodka and I intended to drink it . . . everything seemed so awful . . . sometimes you'd do almost anything to make the pain go away. And there are times when that urge to drink is so strong for me . . . it's something I fight every day."

Karen crumpled, burying her face in her one good hand.

"But I've learned something—alcohol isn't a cure. It's a plague. It doesn't heal, it destroys. Karen, I didn't touch one drop of that vodka," Edie said, lifting her daughter's chin until their eyes met. "I dumped it out last night. I don't ever want to become who I was before. I can't lose you again. You mean more to me than anything in this world. I haven't had a drink in a little over three years, and I promise, no matter what it takes, I will never drink again." Edie sealed that pledge with an intense hug, grateful for this new chance she had been given.

CHAPTER 21

Bev looked up from the editorial Karen had written. It made her extremely uncomfortable, but she wasn't about to render a negative review. Not after what Karen had been through. "It's good, Karen."

"Serious?"

"Yeah," Bev replied, handing back the paper Karen had painstakingly typed with her left hand. It was an editorial depicting the evils of underage alcohol consumption. "You'll shake up this community with that one."

Karen nodded, setting the paper on her dresser for safekeeping. The two girls were visiting in the bedroom Karen now shared with her mother.

Bev still couldn't get over the changes that had taken place in her friend's life. She was almost jealous of the closeness that now existed between Karen and Edie. So much had happened during the past two days. Friday night, her best friend had been attacked, something she hadn't known about until the next day when Kate Jeffries had called to tell her. Bev had waited until today to make an appearance, unsure of how Karen would respond. She felt responsible for what had happened, certain the attack would've been avoided if she had insisted on driving her willful friend home.

Karen had assured Bev that she didn't blame her friend for anything. Karen accepted the blame for choosing to walk alone in the dark, although she understood that a handful of drunken teenagers were responsible for what had taken place.

"I hope those jerks read that editorial and squirm," Bev angrily said. "They deserve it!"

"I just hope they read it and learn something," Karen sighed. "So many lives can be ruined by alcohol."

"You're probably right," Bev said slowly. Personally, Bev didn't think an occasional drink was that terrible, something she would never admit to Karen. Her father considered himself a social drinker, indulging in an infrequent drink with friends and associates, but Bev didn't feel it had ruined his life. She'd never seen Gina drink at all, not that it mattered. Eager to switch the subject, Bev said, "So tell me, how does it feel to finally have a mother?"

"Pretty great," Karen smiled. "I never thought I'd say this, but my mother is an awesome lady. She's been through so much, and she didn't give up."

"You're right—I never thought I'd ever hear you say anything like that," Bev agreed.

"Who knows—maybe you'll discover something neat about Gina."

Bev grimaced. "That'll be the day," she countered. Then, before Karen could argue, she stood up and began sorting through some of her friend's cassette tapes, looking for one that would keep the mood light and entertaining.

* * *

Gerald stared down at his shoes, finding it difficult to face Karen or her mother, who were both sitting on the couch in front of him. "I came to say I'm sorry . . . for . . . Friday night," he mumbled. "What I did was wrong. If I hadn't . . . if I hadn't kissed you, none of this would've happened," he agonized, sincerely regretting the incident that had taken place two nights ago.

"Maybe your *friends* still would've tried something—even if you hadn't been around," Karen replied. Looking at Gerald's face made her own hurt. He had taken a couple of nasty hits on her behalf. After the weekend she had spent with her mother, Karen was in a forgiving mood. Maybe Gerald wasn't as bad as she had originally thought. "So, what happens now?" she asked.

"We all have to appear before the judge in a few days. My dad's lawyer said that because this is a first offense, we'll probably get off with a light sentence, like doing several hours of community service," Gerald answered. "If we cooperate. I've heard some of the guys are going to claim they weren't there . . . that I was too drunk to know who was around that night. It'll make everything more complicated if we don't all enter a guilty plea for underage consumption . . . and assault."

"Do you think they'll contest the charges?" Karen asked worriedly. She didn't want to testify in court, something that would be forced upon her if these boys maintained their innocence.

Gerald shrugged. "I hope not. I'd like to get it over with." Almost shyly, he glanced up at Karen. "I probably won't have any friends left when this is done."

Edie looked at him with compassion. "Sometimes we pay a high price for the choices we make," she said quietly.

As Gerald's focus shifted from Karen to her mother, he blushed. How many times had he teased Karen over her mother's imprisonment? Now he was facing charges concerning his own conduct. He'd had hopes of getting an athletic scholarship to college next year. This might change everything drastically. His father had pointed out that Gerald was still considered a juvenile; the misdemeanor charges wouldn't transfer to his adult record. But they might be a determining factor when it came to a scholarship. Mumbling another apology, Gerald finally left the house, walking back to the car where his father was waiting.

"We've certainly had our share of visitors today," Adele commented.

Karen agreed. First Bev had come by. Then Doris and Kate had dropped in to check on her. Their bishop had just left when Gerald had rung the doorbell.

"Why don't I throw a package of popcorn in the microwave and we'll find a good movie to watch?" Adele encouraged, pleased by the new closeness between her daughter and granddaughter. A relaxing evening together would help strengthen the fragile bond that was developing.

"That sounds like a wonderful idea," Edie replied.

Karen nodded in agreement, certain she could live like this forever—safe and secure with the people she loved best. If this was nothing more than a dream, she prayed she would never wake up.

* * *

Lying on her bed in the darkness, Tracie stared at the ceiling of her bedroom. This had to be the most miserable weekend of her life. First her mother had lectured her steadily from Thursday night on. Her father had picked up where her mother had left off when he had returned home Saturday night. Both had made it clear she would be grounded indefinitely until this entire mess was resolved. Then today, to top off the humiliation she had already been subjected to, her parents had insisted that she make an appointment with the branch president. He had arranged to meet with her today right after church. That meant she had to stew over the whole mess all during the meetings that were another in a series of agonies she'd had to endure. Seeing Sabrina and Marsha together, laughing and talking, had rubbed more salt in her wounded pride. Her parents had prevented her from fleeing to Sindi and Dawn when they had appeared together before sacrament meeting, assuring their daughter that they would be talking to their parents as well. Would this nightmare never end?!

During Young Women, Lori had presented a lesson Tracie was convinced had been for her benefit, one on the importance of repentance. She had ignored most of it, finally able to share conspiring whispers with Sindi and Dawn. They had exchanged hateful glares with Marsha and Sabrina whenever Lori's back had been turned. This wasn't over yet! Paybacks were in order and in their opinion would be well-deserved.

After Young Women, Tracie's parents had firmly escorted her toward the small room that served as the branch president's office. Once again she had been subjected to embarrassing questions and a probing stare. Caving in, she had confessed to everything. The parties, the lies, the drinking, even the necking and petting. As she had sobbed through it all, the branch president had seemed impressed with her remorseful act, believing her to be sincere when she said she wanted to change. He had carefully outlined a plan of restitution, including a way to make things up to Sabrina and Marsha. Promising that she would make things right between herself and those two girls, Tracie rationalized that she hadn't lied. She *would* make things right, beginning Tuesday when she was finally allowed back in school. Sabrina and Marsha would definitely get what was coming to them!

CHAPTER 22

April

"You're moving to Utah?!" Sabrina stammered, staring at Marsha. Marsha shifted uncomfortably on the wooden picnic table where they were sitting across from each other.

"Why?"

Marsha shrugged. "Dad had a chance at a promotion. We'll head down in a couple of weeks." She avoided the hurt look in Sabrina's eyes. "We used to live in Utah, you know, before we came here. We know a lot of people there."

"You were six years old when your family moved here," Sabrina reminded her. "You probably don't even remember anyone down there. I don't suppose this has anything to do with what's going on between us and Tracie's crowd lately?"

"Maybe," Marsha admitted. "Look, Sabrina, I can't deal with it anymore . . . it was bad before, but now, it's unbearable. The nasty notes stuffed in my locker. The prank calls at night. The way everyone treats us at school . . . they act like we're the biggest jerks around . . ."

"Not everyone feels that way," Sabrina protested. "Some people are getting pretty sick of Tracie and her friends. It'll get better."

"Will it, Sabrina? I don't think so. When Dad said he had a chance to move, I didn't argue. I want out of here—I don't want to face this anymore!"

"I'm going through the same thing," Sabrina pointed out.

"You're stronger than I am. You keep trying to stand up to Tracie. I can't." Laying her head down on her arms, Marsha began to cry.

"You're letting them win."

"So, they've won. I lost. I just want to go somewhere where it's not so hard."

Sabrina wondered if such a place existed. "Good luck," she muttered.

Lifting her head, Marsha tearfully glanced at Sabrina. "Please don't hate me."

Frustrated, Sabrina shook her head. Rising, she walked around the wooden table and reached for a hug. "I could never hate you," she murmured.

"I just can't do it anymore," Marsha sobbed, clinging to Sabrina.

Nodding in silent agreement, Sabrina wished she could leave with her. Anywhere had to be better than here.

* * *

As Bev had predicted, Karen's latest editorial triggered an impassioned response. Dealing with a topic that had become extremely sensitive to her, she had vividly described the consequences of alcoholism, stressing that teenagers were at high risk for this disease. Once again, *The Blaketown Buzz* was responsible for several heated discussions all over town.

After reading her copy of the paper, Cleo threw it on her desk. This was preposterous! Outrageous! Students at Blaketown High did not get drunk! There were rules—policies that were rigidly adhered to! What had happened to Karen was an unfortunate incident that had the ill fortune of taking place on school property. Karen was to blame for that. The way that young woman sometimes dressed! The way she flaunted herself about. Then, walking alone at that time of night—she had been asking for trouble, and had found it.

Cleo's eyes narrowed, despising what *The Blaketown Buzz* had become. She wondered if Chip Reynolds would be as supportive now that his son had been branded in that incident with Karen. Would Chip still extol the virtues of a newspaper that subtly pointed fingers at Gerald and his friends? Hardly! Maybe now the school board would realize the inflammatory nature of a paper that was getting out of hand and take her side. Picking up a phone book, she found the number of the insurance company Chip worked for and quickly dialed.

"Hello, Chip?"

"Yes?"

"Cleo Partridge here."

Picking up a dart, Chip aimed at the dartboard attached to the door of his office and hit a direct bull's-eye. "How are you?" he forced himself to say politely.

"Good. I was wondering, have you had a chance to read this week's editorial—the one in the high school newspaper?"

"As a matter of fact, I just finished it."

"I think it's time we shut this operation down, don't you?" she sympathized.

"Are you kidding?! I wish this article would've come out a couple of weeks ago! It might've saved my son and his friends from a lot of trouble!" He sighed, remembering the stricken looks on the faces of those young men when the judge had handed down their sentence. At least they had all come forward, admitting to their guilt. The eight boys had been assigned thirty hours of community service; they'd also had to watch a video portraying several tragic accidents that were the direct result of alcohol consumption. Chip wasn't sure about the other boys involved, but he felt certain Gerald would never drink again. That decision had been apparent in his son's face the night he had apologized to Karen.

"You liked that editorial?" Cleo's cold smile drooped into a frown. This couldn't be happening, not again.

"I did," Chip repeated, picturing the look on Cleo's face. He smiled for the first time in days. "You tell Kate and Doris to keep up the good work. They've done a heck of a job with that paper," Chip advised before hanging up.

Replacing the phone in its base, Cleo continued to scowl her displeasure. Then, deciding to take matters into her own hands, she buzzed her secretary.

"Yes?" the bubbly woman asked, poking her head around the door.

"I'd like to talk to Terri Jeppson," Cleo replied.

"I'll find her," the secretary promised. Turning around, she bustled out into the front office to heed her newest command.

* * *

Terri reluctantly walked down to the office. She knew what the principal wanted. The problem was, she couldn't give it to Miss Partridge yet. She still didn't know who was responsible for the editorials. She had a few suspects in mind, but couldn't prove anything. She needed a little more time to solve this mystery.

"I've been very patient with you," Cleo reminded the teenager as they visited in the privacy of her office. "You've been given a wonderful opportunity to prove your worth as an investigative reporter. I'll let you have a few more days to pull this off. If you can come up with the name, I'll see to it that you become the managing editor of the new version of *The Blaketown Buzz*, a paper I will personally take charge of when this editorial disaster is cleared up."

Terri flushed under the criticism of her mentor, and at the promise that had been dangled in front of her. Managing editor—it meant she would take over for Bev—one of her suspects. "What about John Packer?" she asked. "He works with Bev on the paper."

"If he isn't responsible for writing those editorials, he'll stay," Cleo decided, certain Terri's thinly veiled crush on the senior boy might work in her favor. She smiled when Terri happily skipped out of her office. Now they'd get somewhere. Sinking back into her chair, Cleo began looking over the budget report that had been handed to her earlier that day. Sighing, she went over the figures, then began to calculate a few of her own.

* * *

"Have you decided what Terri is up to yet?" Doris asked, munching on a glazed doughnut. Kate had ordered doughnuts from a nearby bakery to reward their newspaper staff for producing another excellent edition. Copies of their newspaper had sold out all over town. They had dismissed their staff early today, instructing them to come tomorrow afternoon prepared to work.

Sitting down behind her desk, Kate held up the history test Terri had recently taken. "She received a solid 'B' on this test, so I don't think she was cheating. I made sure this test was very different from the first one."

"So, what is she doing, creeping around, making notes in that little book of hers?"

"You were the one who told her to come up with a story for the paper," Kate reminded her friend.

"Guilty as charged," Doris admitted before taking another bite out of her doughnut. "You've seen that girl in action. She brings on the tears, whines that we think she has no talent. Makes you feel lower than dirt."

"I know," Kate laughed. "Maybe she'll surprise us and come up with a good idea."

Doris cringed.

"It can happen."

"True. I didn't think Edie and Karen would ever get along, but we've seen a miracle take place between those two. This is the happiest I've ever seen Karen."

Kate silently agreed, reflecting on what she had observed. The sixteen-year-old had softened, her dark eyes radiating an excited joy. Adele no longer attended their ward alone. She had been accompanied by Edie and Karen the past couple of weeks. It had been a wonderful change. Now if they could just do something about Bev and her stepmother. That situation seemed to be worsening. Tiring of her stepdaughter's disrespectful behavior, Gina had finally grounded Bev.

"She thinks she can punish me for taking her car without permission!" Bev had angrily sputtered to Kate the next day.

"Bev, she *is* your stepmother," Kate had pointed out.

"My dad gave her that car. I should be able to use it whenever I want!"

Kate had been surprised by the childish outburst. "Don't you think you're being a little unreasonable?" she had asked. Bev still wasn't speaking to her. Kate was glad the weekend was nearly here, she could use a break from all of this. She was also looking forward to the visit her parents and Sabrina would be making. They were coming down to Idaho for a cousin's wedding reception in Pocatello on Friday. Since they would only be two hours away from Blaketown, they'd spend the rest of the weekend with Kate and Mike. Her mother had mentioned that they might consider leaving Sabrina in Blaketown for the remainder of the school year. There had been more trouble, and now Sabrina's best friend was moving from the area. They weren't sure what was the best plan of action, but they wanted Sabrina to see that there was another option.

All week, Kate and Mike had been preparing for their visit, cleaning the duplex with excited energy. They had decided to let her parents have their bedroom and would put Sabrina in the tiny guest room. She and Mike would sleep on the hide-a-bed couch in the living room. It would be crowded, but fun. There were so many things they hoped to do while her family was there. Mike wanted to take her father up one of the canyons, eager to show off some of the local scenery. Kate was looking forward to spending some time with her mother and sister. Blaketown wasn't perfect, but maybe Sabrina would be impressed enough to want to stay. After Marsha's announcement that she was moving, Sabrina was ready to leave Bozeman as well. Kate and their mother had already discussed this matter several times on the phone. Whatever happened, Kate was anxious to repair their strained relationship, hoping to dissolve the mysterious wall that now existed between them.

"Maybe I can help her figure out how to deal with what's been taking place in Bozeman," she had said to Mike a couple of nights ago. "I do understand what she's going through."

"True," Mike had agreed, putting a protective arm around his wife. "You went through a horrible time during high school. If anyone can help Sabrina, you can."

"I just wish she felt that way," Kate had replied.

"She will," Mike had assured.

Staring now at her hands, Kate wondered again if that was possible.

* * *

That night, Terri studied the notes she had been keeping. A pattern was starting to emerge. Doris and Karen would disappear into her classroom for a private talk. Then, a couple of days later, an editorial would mysteriously appear. She had heard Doris compliment Karen on her writing skills several times. Terri had read through other articles in the school paper that bore Karen's name. In her opinion, they weren't that exceptional, but they all possessed a similar style. Karen had to be writing those editorials.

Terri thumbed through her notebook, glancing at some sentences she had underlined that supported a theory she had developed:

Karen's mother gets out of prison.
Karen writes an editorial about people labeling each other.
Karen gets herself attacked by a group of drunken boys.
She writes an editorial about alcoholism.

It made sense. She wouldn't be surprised to learn that Bev was part of this, too. Bev was always in the middle of everything. It was common knowledge that Bev and Karen were favored students of Kate Jeffries and Doris Kelsey. Terri was certain these teachers would entrust them with writing the editorials. Making a few more notes to herself, she renewed her determination to shadow Karen and Bev. Wherever they went, she would go, until she learned the truth.

Reaching for last year's yearbook, Terri opened it to the page John Packer was on. She caressed his picture. "Soon, John," she promised. "We'll be the best news team ever!" Closing the book, she laid back on her bed and hugged it against her, dreaming of the time she would work hand in hand with John on the paper.

CHAPTER 23

Adele handed the phone to Edie, her eyes twinkling. "It's Brett Randall," she revealed in a hushed voice.

Avoiding the expectant look on her mother's face, Edie picked up the phone. "Hello?"

"Uh . . . hi," Brett nervously stammered. This was the third time he had called to talk to Edie since they had met in the emergency room at the hospital. After their conversation that day, he couldn't stop thinking about her. Telling himself he had about as much chance dating someone like her as he did running in the Olympics, he couldn't deny the attraction he felt for her. "This is Brett," he said, struggling to make conversation. Somehow, it was easier to talk to this woman in person, like that day at the hospital. Talking to her then had seemed natural, not stiff, or forced like it was now.

"How are you doing?" Edie politely asked. Secretly, she was pleased that he kept calling, but she wouldn't allow herself to get her hopes up. She was convinced that if this reserved man ever learned her past history, he wouldn't have anything to do with her.

"Fine. My arm has healed very nicely. I'll have a scar, but that's okay."

Edie sighed. If he only knew the scars she carried inside.

"So, do you have any plans for Saturday?" he quickly asked, before he lost his nerve again. Last time he had called, he had wanted to ask her out. Somehow, he hadn't been able to convey that desire. After he had hung up, he had thumped himself on the head with his fist, frustrated. This time he was determined to succeed.

"Saturday?"

"Uh . . . yeah," Brett said hopefully.

"I'm sorry, I have to work . . . ," Edie began.

"Oh, well, some other time then," Brett said, the disappointment he felt evident in the tone of his voice. He wouldn't bother her again. What he had felt that day at the hospital was probably what Edie shared with all of her patients. The concern, the warmth . . . it was just part of her nature.

"But I'll be off around three-thirty p.m.," she continued, his dejected reply troubling her. Even if it meant eventually telling him everything, she didn't have the heart to say no.

"Would you like to get together . . . maybe get a bite of dinner . . . and see a movie?" he asked, his excitement rising.

"Sure," Edie answered, trying to ignore her mother's animated dance around the kitchen. When she finally got off the phone, Adele gave her a quick squeeze.

"Oh, Edie, things are working out so well! Brett Randall is such a nice man. He's in our ward, you know," Adele said breathlessly. "He doesn't come out much, but that could change."

"Mom, it's just a date."

"Now, you can't tell me your face didn't light up when you were talking to him. It does every time he calls." Adele grinned. "I know I'm getting the cart before the horse, but it makes me so happy to see you enjoying life. First the job, then Karen, now Brett . . ."

"Karen," Edie said, suddenly panicking. What would her daughter think of Brett? "Mom, will Karen be okay about this?"

Adele smiled warmly at her daughter. "Why wouldn't she be?"

"Things are going really well between us right now. I don't want to do anything that would upset her," Edie replied, worried.

"You leave Karen to me," Adele reassured. "She'll be fine about this."

Hoping her mother was right, Edie helped Adele clean up the dinner dishes. A few minutes later, she walked into the living room to break the news to Karen. She had decided it would be best coming from her. She and Karen had promised there would be no more secrets from each other. Karen had leveled with her concerning the editorials she had been writing. After reading through the collection of newspapers Karen had amassed, Edie had been impressed by the obvious talent her daughter possessed. The first editorial, the one concerning misguided labeling, had been especially revealing, giving her an insight into what Karen's life had been like for the past few years. More determined than ever to make things up to her, Edie knew she had to be honest with Karen concerning Brett. She did feel an attraction for this quiet man, not that anything would ever happen between them. He would most likely be repelled by her past. Still, it would be fun to go out to dinner and maybe a movie once in a while. To have an adult friend she could spend some time with.

Stepping into the living room, Edie smiled. Her daughter was reading—again. She was learning that Karen was quite a bookworm, something she didn't mind in the least. "Karen, we need to talk," she said, hating to interrupt.

* * *

"Your mother has a date?" Bev asked, amazed by this news.

"Yep," Karen replied, walking down the high school hall with her friend.

"With who?"

"Some guy who works for the Forest Service. She met him at the hospital a few weeks ago. He had to have his arm stitched up."

"How romantic," Bev teased.

"I know," Karen agreed. "Mom says he's about the shyest person she's ever met."

"What's his name?"

"Brett . . . something. I can't remember."

"And you call yourself a newspaper reporter! Facts, woman! We need facts!"

Karen smiled. "I'm sure I'll hear more facts than I want when Mom gets home from her date Saturday night."

"How do you feel about her dating?" Bev glanced at her friend, concerned. All kidding aside, she had enjoyed seeing Karen happy and hated for anything to bring her down.

"It's okay. Mom explained it's not serious between them."

"What if it turns out to be?"

Shrugging, Karen slipped off the light jacket she had worn. A new jacket her mother had bought to replace the one that had been ruined during the frenzied assault a few weeks ago. "I guess we'll see what happens."

"Where's he taking her?" Bev asked, stopping in front of her locker. School started in five minutes and she didn't want to be late for their first class, creative writing, taught by Doris Kelsey.

"To dinner and a movie," Karen responded, opening her own locker.

"That sounds pretty safe," Bev observed.

Nodding, Karen grabbed a notebook and pencil, then shut her locker. She didn't notice Terri who had positioned herself nearby, scribbling down everything she had overheard.

" . . . and Karen's mother will be going out to dinner and a movie. Keep an eye on Karen Saturday night. With her mother out of the house, who knows what she'll do? Maybe write another editorial!"

* * *

Saturday morning dawned bright and clear. Anxious to begin the day's adventures, Mike roused Kate out of bed to help cook an early breakfast. By 8:00 a.m., he and his father-in-law, Greg, were ready to leave.

"When will you two return?" Kate asked, as Mike helped her push the hide-a-bed mattress back inside the couch frame.

"Sometime this afternoon," Mike answered, pulling her close for a quick kiss good-bye.

"So if you're not home by four o'clock we should send out the search and rescue?" Sue teased, leaning against the kitchen doorway. The commotion in the kitchen had brought her out of a deep sleep. It had been late when Kate's family had arrived last night, past 1:00 a.m. Stifling a yawn, she now glanced at her son-in-law.

Mike grinned. "I *am* the search and rescue," he shot back, zipping the jacket he had selected for the day. It was predicted to be warmer today than it had been all week, with a high near sixty-five, but the morning air was still quite cool.

"Have fun, but be careful," Kate cautioned as she replaced the couch cushions. She often worried about her dare-devil husband. His love of the outdoors was surpassed only by his sense of adventure. That combination often led to interesting predicaments—like the time he had walked into a cave to explore and had disturbed its original occupant, an irritated mountain lion. Barely outrunning the outraged cougar, Mike had jumped into a nearby river to escape. Hanging onto a floating branch, he had floated down a couple of miles before he dared climb out of the water. Kate hated it when he came home from work, assuring her he had a wonderful new bedtime story to tell her. She never knew what to expect, and continuously prayed that he would be watched over.

"Yes, dear," Mike retorted, emphasizing a nasal twang. He laughed when Kate grabbed a sofa pillow and threw it at him. "Later, woman," he added, tossing the pillow on the couch before following his father-in-law out the front door.

"Later, woman?" Greg asked, giving Mike a pained look.

"Yep. It's how we men folk talk down this a way," Mike drawled.

"Now I'm worried," Greg teased, as they walked to Mike's black Chevy Blazer.

"Think those two will come back in one piece?" Sue asked, watching out the front room window.

"Sure," Kate responded, trying to sound convincing. "What can happen?"

A shiver ran up Sue's spine. Whirling around, she gazed at her oldest daughter. "Don't ever ask a question like that," she cautioned, forcing a smile. "It brings bad luck."

"You're not serious?"

Laughing, Sue shook her head. "Well, what will we *womenfolk* do to entertain ourselves today?"

"How about we lounge around the house until Sleeping Beauty wakes up? Then we can tackle an adventure of our own—shopping!"

"I like how you think," Sue replied, settling down on the couch. "I'm still recovering from spending most of yesterday in the car." She glanced at her watch. "But we could spend all day waiting for Sleeping Beauty to wake up by herself. Let's give Sabrina a couple of hours, then we'll revive her." She leaned back against the couch, stretching out in a comfortable position.

Kate sat down in one of the hard plastic chairs. "Sabrina was half-asleep last night when you guys arrived. I really didn't get much of a chance to talk to her. Are things going any better?"

Sue shook her head. "I thought it would after we talked to Tracie's mother. The woman really tried. But now Tracie's acting like Sabrina and Marsha are responsible for the trouble she's in."

"Like she had nothing to do with it," Kate commented. "What a little twerp."

"I can think of other names that fit better," Sue retorted. "But I'm too much of a lady to use them."

"Good," Kate grinned. "I'd hate to have to call you to repentance."

"I wish someone would call Tracie."

"Didn't you tell me that you saw Tracie go in to talk to the branch president?" Kate asked.

Sue nodded. "But who knows what she told him, or what she's now telling her parents? I've about decided there's no hope for that girl."

"There's always hope," Kate chided. "Look at me."

"True," Sue said, throwing a sofa pillow at her oldest daughter. "Any suggestions, oh wise one?"

Kate shrugged. "Every kid is unique. Doris Kelsey and I were discussing this a few months ago—before we started the high school newspaper. So many kids are carrying around burdens we know nothing about. Some we understand, but usually we can't fix the problem. We can't overstep parents, we can't change home environments. We can't control how the students treat those who seem different. Cruel things happen when we're not around to see. It's hard." She drew up her knees, using the other plastic chair as a footstool.

"Thanks for the pep talk," Sue muttered. "You've been a big help."

"Has Sabrina ever said why she seems so angry with me?" Kate asked, curious.

Sue glanced at Kate. If her daughters were going to spend time together, Kate had to know what she would be dealing with. "She resents being compared to you."

"Who's been doing that?"

Offering a wistful smile, Sue pointed to herself. "And I'm not the only one. There are others in our fair community who have been guilty of the same offense."

"Nice," Kate responded. "No wonder that girl hates me."

"She doesn't hate you," Sue disputed. "She just resents you a little."

"That cheers me up," Kate responded.

"Why don't we discuss something else?" Sue suggested, trying to shake off the depression this discussion had triggered. "Where are we going shopping?"

Smiling, Kate began describing several of the local stores to her mother.

* * *

Saturday afternoon, Edie nervously searched for an outfit to wear for her date with Brett. As she stared into her closet, she was grateful there were a few more choices now. Her paychecks weren't huge, but they had been large enough to provide a few extras. Clothes for Karen and some for herself, plus enough to give her mother a little every two weeks to go toward household expenses.

Finally deciding on a pair of dark blue dress pants with a cream-colored blouse, she quickly dressed. Brett would be coming by in about twenty minutes and she still had to do something with her makeup and hair.

In the bathroom, she stared in the mirror. "Do you realize how long it's been since I went on a date?" she questioned her reflection. "I hope I can do this." Picking up a brush, she began to run it through her long, blonde hair. She usually kept it pinned up while working. This afternoon, she would leave it down. With a skill that hadn't been forgotten, she applied a thin layer of makeup, smiling at the results.

"Edie, Brett's here," Adele sang out.

"Here we go," Edie said again to her reflection. Giving herself a thumbs-up sign, she flipped off the light and headed toward the living room.

* * *

"You didn't want to be around to meet the Brett dude?" Bev inquired, glancing at Karen. The two girls had spent most of the day together, finishing up homework, listening to music, and watching videos. Sitting now in Bev's bedroom, they had been trying to come up with ideas for a new editorial.

Karen glanced at her watch, then at Bev. "I thought Mom would be less nervous if I wasn't around when he came by."

"Your mother is nervous?"

"Yeah. She hasn't had anything to do with men since . . ." Karen's face darkened. "Anyway, this will be good for her. Grandma and I were talking about it yesterday." Karen grinned. "I think Grandma is more excited than my mom about this date."

"Isn't it every mother's dream to have their daughter meet a nice guy?!" Bev teased.

"From what everyone tells me, Brett is very nice. He'd better be!" Karen warned. "I don't ever want anyone to treat my mom like those other imbeciles did."

"Was it bad?" Bev softly prompted.

Frowning, Karen nodded. She had never talked about this with Bev before. It had always been too hard. Now, it seemed easier to open up. The long talks she and her mother had been having had helped her more than any counseling session ever had. It was almost a relief to share some of her innermost thoughts and feelings. "My dad used to get real mean when he drank. Mom never let him touch me, but I always heard what he did to her. It was awful."

"Is that why they finally divorced?" Bev guessed.

"That and Dad never could hold down a job for very long." A wistful expression settled on her face. "There were times, though, when we were almost a family. That's why it hurt so bad when he told Mom . . . he told her he didn't want anything to do with me. He said I probably wasn't his anyway." Karen stood, moving to the computer in Bev's room. She brushed a thin layer of dust from the top of the monitor, then glanced back at Bev. "He yelled that in the courtroom when they were getting divorced. He said it in front of everyone. I was outside in the hall with Grandma, but I still heard it."

Bev gazed sadly at Karen. Her friend had been through more than she had imagined.

"Grandma told Mom I'd overheard. I must've been about eight or nine. I remember Mom holding me, telling me that Roger was my father. She tried to explain that he had been upset, that he hadn't meant what he said in court. It didn't make me feel any better." Karen sank down into the padded computer chair. "A few days ago, Mom and I were talking about it again. She said part of Dad's problem was he was always so jealous. He had accused her of some horrible things,

convinced that if a guy even smiled at her, something was going on."
She sighed. "It's too bad Mom always attracted the wrong guy."

"That man your mother hooked up with later on, was he any
better than your dad?" Bev asked, curious.

"You mean Mark?"

Bev nodded.

"In a lot of ways, he was worse. He didn't like me at all. He wasn't
as mean to my mother, but they still yelled at each other a lot.
Especially when they were stoned out of their minds." Karen stared
down at the floor, as painful images surfaced. "I'll never forgive Mark
for lying about my mother. She didn't know anything about the
robbery he had planned."

Bev shook her head. "How did you survive all of that?"

"Grandma," Karen replied. "I owe her a lot. I always knew I
would be safe with her. When I was younger, if things got really bad,
I'd walk down to her house. After a while, it became a permanent
arrangement." She frowned, thinking of the time she had lost with
her mother.

Sensing Karen was slipping into a state of depression, Bev stood
up, grabbing her jacket off the bed. "Let's go get something to eat,"
she suggested, glancing at her watch. It was past four-thirty and they
hadn't really eaten anything that could be considered a meal since
breakfast. They'd each taken a small bag of chips out of the pantry in
"Gina's kitchen," as Bev called it, but that had been it.

"Okay," Karen responded. "I'd better call my grandma first so
she'll know where I am."

Bev lifted an eyebrow. She was still getting used to the changes
Karen was making in her life. A few weeks ago, they would've headed
out, not caring if anyone knew where they were. Since Karen's scare near
the football field, she let her mother and grandmother know exactly
where she was and when she would return. Pointing to the phone on the
computer desk, Bev smiled. "There's the phone, have at it."

Nodding, Karen began to dial. Neither girl noticed the young
woman peeking into the bedroom window, furiously scribbling notes
to herself.

CHAPTER 24

"That was one of the cutest antique shops I've ever been in," Sue chirped happily, examining the pale pink Depression glass candy dish she had purchased for a very reasonable price. She had been collecting Depression glass pieces for quite some time, storing them in the china cabinet Greg had given her for Christmas several years ago.

"I thought you'd like it," Kate replied. "Sabrina, what did you think?"

"It was nice," Sabrina quietly answered.

"The store or the candy dish?" Sue asked, wishing her youngest daughter would cheer up.

"Uh . . . both," Sabrina replied. Too depressed to enjoy anything around her, she hadn't been paying much attention to her mother or Kate. She didn't know which was worse, what was waiting for her in Bozeman or remaining here in Blaketown with a sister that drove her crazy. Neither prospect was very appealing. Another week and Marsha would be gone. She would have to face Tracie's taunts alone. Was it worth it to put up with Kate's shadow to stay here in Blaketown? She just didn't know.

Sue exchanged a concerned look with Kate. Kate glanced around, trying to figure out something that would interest her younger sister. Then she spotted two young women across the street, Karen Beyer and Bev Henderson.

"Hey, Bev—Karen," Kate called, beckoning to the juniors. This might just be the answer they were looking for.

Turning, Bev and Karen recognized Kate. Curious, they crossed the street to see what their teacher wanted.

"Sabrina, Mom, I'd like you to meet Bev Henderson and Karen Beyer, two very talented young women from Blaketown High," Kate said, introducing her students to her mother and sister.

Sabrina glanced at the two older girls, unsure how to react.

"Bev, Karen, this is my sister, Sabrina."

"No way," Bev teased, smiling at Sabrina. "You two are sisters?"

"Yeah," Kate replied. "There's a few years between us."

"A few?!" Bev said, laughing. "I'm sorry. It's just, I didn't picture you with a family. I mean . . ."

"Why don't you quit while you're ahead?" Karen suggested, nodding politely at Kate's mother and sister. "You'll have to forgive my friend. She's a native. They don't get many visitors here in Blaketown."

"Like you're not a native. You were born here, too."

"And your point is?" Karen asked.

Sabrina smiled briefly at the good-natured banter. It reminded her how it used to be between herself and her friends before all of the craziness started.

"What are you two up to this afternoon?" Kate asked Bev, glancing quickly toward Sabrina. Catching on, Sue smiled. This might be just the thing to snap Sabrina out of wallowing in self-pity. If these girls hit it off, it might tip the scales toward Sabrina staying in Blaketown after this weekend.

"We were going to get a bite to eat," Bev responded. She glanced at Kate, then at Sabrina, suddenly picking up the hint. "Would your sister . . . uh . . ."

"Sabrina," Karen supplied, remembering her name.

"Sabrina, would you like to join us?" Bev asked, redirecting her of question. This might be interesting, spending some time with Kate's younger sister.

"I don't know," Sabrina murmured, still unsure of this situation. She didn't need Kate to pick her friends. She had no idea who these girls were. What if they turned out to be like Samantha Collins? Teacher's pets, the type of kids who drove other kids crazy. On the other hand, she wasn't doing so hot in the popularity department herself lately.

"Go on, Sabrina, have some fun," Kate encouraged.

Sabrina glanced at their mother. Smiling, Sue nodded her approval.

"Okay," Sabrina agreed.

"Do you need some change?" Sue asked, reaching for her purse.

"I've got some money," Sabrina said.

"How late do you think . . . ," Sue started to ask.

"We're just going down to the arcade," Karen supplied. "After that, I don't know. Maybe we'll hit a movie or something."

"Call and we'll come pick you up when you're ready, " Sue offered.

"I can use one of my dad's cars to bring her home," Bev responded. "Are you staying with Kate?"

"Yes," Sue replied.

"Okay. I happen to know where this woman lives," Bev smiled at Kate.

"That's not too hard to figure out in a town this size," Karen teased. She grinned when Bev nudged her in the ribs with her elbow.

"C'mon, let's go," Bev encouraged, leading the way. Karen and Sabrina followed behind, hurrying down the sidewalk.

"Well, that was a stroke of good luck," Sue said, watching as Sabrina disappeared inside of a brick building with the other two girls.

"It was," Kate responded. "Sabrina is in very good hands. If those two can't cheer her up, I don't know what will." Turning, she led her mother toward a new craft shop she was certain they would both enjoy exploring.

* * *

"How long are you staying in Blaketown?" Bev asked as the three girls continued to munch on the hamburgers and fries they had ordered.

"I'm not sure," Sabrina said, glancing around at the crowded arcade. From the number of kids in here, she decided this must be a major hangout in this town. Most of the tables were filled and several teenagers were huddled around the video games in the far corner.

"You're not sure?" Karen repeated.

Sabrina shook her head, slowly sipping at her Sprite.

"How come?" Bev asked, sensing there was a story here. It was the journalist coming out in her. She was getting pretty good at reading people. She sensed Sabrina was keeping something pretty awful inside.

"I don't know . . . ," Sabrina murmured, reluctant to reveal the events of the past year.

"Hey, you know what, both of us are really good listeners," Bev invited.

Sabrina was silent for a moment. She didn't know what to think about these two girls. They seemed friendly enough, but she wasn't sure she trusted them yet.

"If you want, start by telling us a little bit about Kate," Bev encouraged, eager to learn more about this teacher. Kate had hinted at a troubled past but had never divulged much information.

Taking another drink, Sabrina glanced at Bev. "What do you want to know?"

Bev shrugged. "Anything you'd like to share."

Sabrina frowned. Would it always be this way? Would it always come down to Kate?

Karen studied Sabrina's face. Picking up a fry, she dabbed it into the fry sauce. "It's okay, Sabrina, we can talk about something else," she said, recognizing the look in the younger girl's eye. Angry resentment. She was just as curious as Bev, but didn't want to force Sabrina into opening up.

"Let's see, you must be about our age—sixteen?" Bev continued.

Sabrina shook her head. "I turned fifteen last month."

Bev smiled at the younger girl. "You look older. So, you're a freshman?" she guessed.

"Yeah."

A sudden movement captured Karen's attention. She watched as the girl sitting behind Bev jotted something down in a small notebook. Leaning to the side, she recognized Terri Jeppson. Karen glanced back at Bev, who was giving her a concerned look, and held her finger to her lips. Then she pointed over Bev's shoulder.

Bev slowly turned, seeing immediately who was sitting behind her. Turning back to Karen, she mouthed, "Terri?"

Karen nodded, pantomiming what Terri was doing.

Catching on, Bev looked at Sabrina, who seemed amused by their behavior. "The girl sitting behind me is a royal pain," Bev explained quietly. "Just follow our lead. Trust me, this girl has it coming. She's been nothing but trouble all year."

Unsure of the situation, Sabrina decided to keep quiet. In this town, she didn't know the boundaries, she didn't know who people were, and she didn't need anymore contention in her life right now. That was one disadvantage to being new to an area. At least in Bozeman, she knew who to avoid.

"Karen, do you realize how late it is?" Bev said, loud enough for Terri to overhear. "We'd better hurry."

"I know. We have important things to do, right, Sabrina?" Karen prompted.

"I guess," Sabrina responded.

"Let's see—tonight we were going to get drunk, and then let several boys have their way with us," Bev threw out. She enjoyed the shocked expressions on Karen's and Sabrina's faces. She could just imagine what Terri looked like. "Let's go!" Rising, Bev headed for the door before she burst out laughing.

She was followed by two rather indignant girls. "Get drunk?!" Karen demanded. That was still a very tender topic for her.

"Let several boys have their way with us?" Sabrina chimed in. She didn't need this after what she'd already been through.

Bev roared with laughter. "I'll bet Terri has a stroke," she assured the two girls. "Look at her writing things down! You're right, Karen. She's keeping track of everything we do and say. I wonder why."

Karen scowled through the window at the sophomore girl. "We're probably the big story she promised Doris and Kate."

"Then let's make it a good one," Bev challenged.

"What story?" Sabrina asked, very confused.

"C'mon, let's lead Terri on a little goose chase. I'll explain everything on the way," Bev replied, running down the street.

Karen smiled brightly at Sabrina. "It'll be all right," she promised. "Most people in this town don't pay any attention to Terri. She likes to be in the center of everything and usually just stirs up trouble for herself." Turning, she began to walk down the sidewalk.

Feeling a little better, Sabrina decided to follow along. After all, if Kate had handpicked these two girls for her to spend some time with, they must be pretty safe. Picking up speed, she hurried after Bev and Karen.

CHAPTER 25

Completely stuffed, Edie ate another small bite before pushing her plate away. Dinner had been wonderful. Brett had insisted on bringing her to the Shaft Cottage, where prime rib had been the special that night. It was tender and moistened with a tasty broth, and Edie savored every bite. The dinner had also included dinner rolls, a baked potato, mixed vegetables, and a green salad. It was the biggest meal Edie had eaten in a very long time.

"Would you like some dessert?" Brett asked.

"No, thanks," Edie politely refused. "I'm full."

"Me too," Brett agreed. "I'm not sure I can even tackle popcorn during the movie, but it sure was a good dinner."

"It was. Thank you for bringing me here." She glanced around the busy restaurant, recognizing several people who had taken advantage of tonight's dinner special. In the dim lighting, it was difficult to see everyone's face, but she had a pretty good idea who most of them were. When they had first arrived at the restaurant, Brett had taken a few minutes to introduce her to Mike Jeffries and his wife, Kate. Kate, she knew through Karen. She was told that Mike was Brett's boss.

"He's the guy who keeps me in line," Brett had quietly joked, clapping Mike on the shoulder.

Mike and Kate were sitting with her parents and had introduced Brett and Edie.

"Mom," Kate had said, gesturing to Edie, "Edie is Karen's mother."

Sue had smiled at Edie. "Our daughters have spent quite a bit of time together today."

Puzzled, Edie had glanced at Kate for an explanation.

"My younger sister, Sabrina, met Bev and Karen this afternoon. They're off somewhere together tonight."

"Oh," Edie replied, wondering where the three girls were. Since her daughter's attack, she was easily alarmed if she didn't know exactly where Karen was. After moving away from Mike's table, Edie had made a quick call home.

"Mom, do you know where Karen is?"

"Not exactly, but she's with Bev. She promised she wouldn't be out too late. She'll probably beat you home," Adele guessed.

Edie now glanced at her watch. It was nearly six-thirty. The time was flying by too fast. Earlier, Brett had taken her to see the cabin he was building near the mouth of Howard's Canyon. Surrounded by trees and a small creek, it was an ideal location. He had started this project last spring, doing most of the work himself. The outer walls and roof had been finished before winter had officially settled in. During the winter months, Brett had kept himself busy finishing the interior. He figured the two-bedroom cabin would be completely done by early summer. Edie had been impressed with the way he had varnished the wood throughout the cabin. Polished knotty pine formed the ceiling in most of the rooms. The living room had a vaulted ceiling and a small bay window, already filled with green, leafy plants. The bathroom was small but cozy. Surprisingly, the kitchen was quite large.

"I like to cook," Brett had hesitantly admitted.

"This place is wonderful," Edie had enthused. She'd never seen anything like it, amazed that he had built this beautiful home with his hands. In the short time she had known Brett, she had discovered several admirable things about him. It depressed her to think there was so much about her own life she wished he didn't have to learn if this relationship continued to blossom.

"Should we go catch that movie?" Brett suggested, pushing back from the table. "It starts at seven."

Edie nodded. They started to walk away from the table when a tall, slender man approached.

"Have a seat, you two love birds," the man said, facing Edie and Brett. "We need to talk."

Edie felt sick at the sight of her ex-husband. What was Roger doing here? The last she had heard, he was somewhere in California.

Brett noticed how pale his date had become. Sensing this wasn't a welcome intrusion, he remained standing. "We were just leaving," he said firmly.

Roger shook his head. "Not yet," he advised. "Have a seat and we can settle this quietly, so we don't embarrass the *lady* here." Roger gave Edie a leering look, surprised that she was as attractive as before—maybe even more beautiful. There was a new maturity about her that gave her a sophisticated air. He wasn't sure he liked that, or the attentive way her date had guided her back to the table.

"Brett, maybe you'd better go," Edie said, unwilling to subject this new friend of hers to whatever Roger had up his sleeve. Her ex-husband looked rougher than the last time she had seen him, older than he really was. She felt a mixture of pity and loathing as she glanced at him and wondered what he wanted.

"Do you really want me to leave?" Brett asked, searching her face. Seeing the answer in her pained expression, he stubbornly sat down and motioned for her to do the same.

"Edie, I like this new man of yours. He seems quite reasonable."

"Unlike you," Edie muttered.

"What was that?" Roger asked, pulling a chair away from a nearby table to sit between his ex-wife and Brett.

"I said, 'How are you?'" Edie replied. She avoided the questioning look Brett was giving her. She didn't want to be alone with Roger, but she didn't want Brett to hear anything Roger might have to say either.

"Fine. And you?" Roger asked, enjoying her discomfort. "My folks said you'd gotten out a while back."

Edie gazed steadily at Roger, her eyes pleading with him.

"Out?" Brett asked, confused.

"Oh. This is awkward. Edie, didn't you tell this nice young man where you've been the past three years?"

"Roger, please," Edie begged.

"Your name's Roger?" Brett asked, rising to his feet.

Roger nodded, delighted by Edie's embarrassment.

"Well, Roger, I don't think Edie wants to talk to you. Now, I suggest—"

"I suggest you sit down and shut up," Roger angrily advised. "I'll say what I've come to say, then I'll leave."

"Brett, I'll be all right. Why don't you go home . . . or to the movie? Call me later . . . I'll explain all of this," Edie tried again.

Brett looked at her, then back at Roger. He didn't like the feeling this rough-looking man inspired.

"What's the matter? Are you afraid I'll say something that might shed a little light on who you really are?" Roger snarled.

That did it! No matter what Edie said, Brett would not leave her alone with this creature. Sitting down, he waited for Roger's next move.

"What's your name?" Roger asked, glaring at Brett.

"Brett. Brett Randall."

"Well, Mr. Brett Randall, I'm Roger Beyer. Edie's ex-husband."

Brett glanced at Roger, then at Edie to see if this was true. Edie slowly nodded.

"Edie and I had something good going once. We even had a daughter." He grinned at Edie. "What's her name again?"

"You know what her name is, and if you don't, you don't deserve to know," Edie said, sparks shooting from her eyes.

"Feisty little thing, ain't she," Roger commented, leaning closer to Brett. Smelling the liquor on this man's breath, Brett drew back.

"It's our daughter I've come to discuss. My parents and I feel you haven't set the proper example for her to follow," Roger said, sneering at his ex-wife. "I think we're going to renegotiate the custody arrangements."

Brett had thought Edie looked pale when Roger first arrived. Now her face drained of all color and he worried that she might pass out.

"Roger, you can't mean this," Edie stammered.

"I mean it all right. I've even got a lawyer."

"Why? You've never wanted anything to do with Karen before. Why now?"

"I think it's time my daughter and I got acquainted."

Rage began building inside of Brett. He didn't like this man or the way he kept looking at Edie. Barely maintaining self-control, he stood up again. "Roger, was it?" he said. "You've said enough. Tell Edie good-bye and leave before I throw you out," he threatened.

"Think again—Hop-Along," Roger jeered, referring to Brett's limp. He stood, breathing hard against Brett. The odor was so potent, Brett nearly sat back down.

Then Edie stood. "Roger, this is neither the time or the place. Leave now, and I'll talk to you later."

"You bet you will, little Miss Convict!" He stared at her, enjoying the way his accusation had cut through her. "I'll give you thirty minutes to meet me at Larry's Bar. If you don't show up, I'll come looking for you and my daughter." Whirling around, he swaggered out of the restaurant.

Edie begged for the floor to swallow her. She knew numerous eyes were staring at her. The eyes she wanted most to avoid were directly in front of her. Sinking into her chair, she hid her face in her hands.

Mike walked to their table. "Is everything all right over here?" he asked.

Brett glanced up at him and nodded. They exchanged a concerned look, then Mike walked away.

"Edie?" Brett softly called. He felt so helpless. He wanted to hold her, to tell her it was going to be all right, but couldn't find the words.

"I'll understand if you never want to speak to me again," Edie finally said, forcing herself to look at him.

"Why wouldn't I want to speak to you?" he asked, reaching for one of her trembling hands. He held it in his own, giving it an intense squeeze.

"Didn't you hear what Roger said . . . that bit about me being a convict?"

Brett slowly nodded.

"I am . . . you know. I was released from prison before Christmas," she managed to say. She waited for Brett to release her hand, but his grip tightened.

"I already know that," he quietly admitted.

"So I'll understand if— You already know?"

Brett nodded again. "After we met in ER, I mentioned something to Mike Jeffries about you. I guess his wife had filled him in on . . . all of that," he said, flushing slightly.

"You know everything?"

"Yes," Brett replied.

"And you still wanted to go out with me?" she asked, stunned.

"Yes, because I know who you are now . . . I also know how it is when people look down on you because you're different." He smiled warmly at Edie. "I would never do that to you." Bringing her hand to his lips, he softly kissed it.

Unable to speak, Edie tearfully smiled at the gentleman who had just won her heart.

* * *

"Are you sure you don't want me to come inside with you?" Brett asked as he shut off the engine of his car.

Edie shook her head. "I'll hear what Roger has to say, then I'll leave. I'm afraid if he sees you again, it'll make this worse." She nervously chewed her bottom lip. "He can't be serious about taking Karen away from me."

"No judge in his right mind would even think about giving Roger custody of your daughter. She's had a stable home environment for years with your mother. Now you're with her. You have a good job . . . me," he quietly teased, searching her face for the desired response. When she returned his smile, he relaxed. "I think Roger's bluffing, and talking to him right now would be a mistake. He was drunk enough when he barged into the restaurant. He'll be in worse shape now. Why don't you talk to an attorney of your own before meeting with Roger again?" he suggested.

"I promised Roger I'd meet him in five minutes. You don't know him like I do. He threatened to come after me and Karen if I didn't cooperate." Gathering her courage, she climbed out of his Suzuki Samurai. "I can't take any chances with my daughter. He's crazy enough, he'd take her in a minute if he thought it would hurt me. Take her and disappear. Do you know what that would do to me?"

Brett nodded as Edie closed the car door, reluctantly watching as she crossed the road heading toward the bar. He wondered if he should contact the police. He was friends with a couple of the officers. It wouldn't take much effort on their part to set Roger straight. Making a decision, he started his car and pulled away from the curb to search for the nearest officer on patrol.

* * *

Bev stared, telling herself they hadn't seen Edie walk into that bar. Beside her Karen groaned. "Karen, I'm sure there's a logical explanation for this," Bev muttered, unable to think of one.

Pulling away from her friend, Karen turned in the opposite direction and ran. Her mother had promised. She had promised! "I believed her," Karen wheezed, finally slowing down. Her breath came in gasping sobs. "I believed her."

As Bev and Sabrina ran after their friend, Bev had quickly explained why Karen was so upset. Catching up with her, Bev had taken her arm consolingly. "Karen," she said, "it's going to be all right."

"I believed her," Karen repeated, nearly hysterical.

"Karen, you're scaring me," Bev said, shaking the other girl. "Snap out of it!" She tried to give her a hug, but Karen pushed her away.

"Are you sure your mother went inside of that bar to drink?" Sabrina asked.

Karen and Bev both glared at Sabrina.

"Sorry. Just thought I'd ask."

Bev suddenly smiled at Sabrina, taking the life preserver that had been extended. "Sabrina's right. We don't know your mom went in there to get drunk."

"Why else would she go into a bar?!" Karen demanded, allowing anger to seal the wound in her heart. "Gee, what do they serve in bars? Salted peanuts. I don't know, crackers, maybe. Yeah, I'll bet that's why my mother had to go in there," she raged. "I want to scream!"

"Then do it and get it over with," Bev encouraged.

"Sure. That'll bring Terri running," Karen lamented. "She probably saw exactly what we did. It'll be all over school by Monday." Sinking down onto a wooden bench in front of a darkened store, Karen's resolve to be tough dissolved into tears.

Bev moved behind the bench, draping her arms around her friend. "It's okay," she soothed, giving Karen a squeeze. "I know something we can do to make this better. It might even hit home with your mother." Coming up with a plan, she walked around to the front of the bench and sat down beside her friend.

* * *

" . . . *and now Bev is trying to make Karen feel better. They've quit running, which is good. I'm tired, it's getting late, and my mother's probably having a coronary. I told her I'd be home around seven.*" Terri leaned against the brick building a few yards away from where the three young women had finally halted. Bev was still holding Karen tightly. Shaking her head, Terri almost felt sorry for Karen.

After following these three girls all over town, she had decided they were onto her, then Karen's mom had gone into a bar. Stunned, all four young women had watched, their mouths hanging open. Each had had a different reaction. Bev had been shocked. Sabrina had been confused. Terri had been appalled. Only Karen had been heartbroken.

Staring now at the darkened shapes she knew were Bev, Sabrina, and Karen, Terri debated with herself. Was it worth it to keep following them around? She was no closer to proving they had anything to do with those stupid editorials and was very likely facing her first grounding for being gone this long. Terri closed her eyes and imagined Julia Roberts in *I Love Trouble.* What would she do?

"She *wouldn't* give up," Terri muttered under her breath. She watched as Bev led Karen down the street, Sabrina following close behind. "Here we go again," Terri grumbled, fastening her jacket. The warmth of the day had disintegrated, much like her mood. Shivering, she picked up the trail once again.

* * *

Glancing around in the darkened interior, Edie ignored the coarse comments and suggestions from some of the patrons and spotted Roger who was sitting at a small table by himself.

"It's about time you showed up," Roger growled as she approached. "I was getting ready to come find you." He chugged the whiskey in his glass, grimacing as it burned its way down to his stomach.

"Roger, what is this nonsense about Karen?" Edie asked, getting to the point.

"Sit down, woman," he demanded, kicking out a chair.

Edie obediently sat, wondering why she had ever gotten involved with a man like this. *Because you thought he was exciting. You thought he was a way out of this town, and a few years ago, he was good-looking*, something inside reminded her. It was true. A few years ago, she never would have looked at a man like Brett. It filled her with shame to realize how shallow she had been. The lessons she had learned had been difficult, but there were things she would never take for granted again.

"That's better," Roger said, squinting at her. "You mind pretty good. Prison must've softened you." He grinned. "It's been a long time, Edie." He stared at her, still attracted to this woman who had caused him so much trouble in the past. "You know something, you're almost cute enough to kiss." Sitting up, he leaned across the table.

Repulsed, Edie drew away.

"I'm not good enough for you anymore—is that it?" Roger angrily accused, banging his fist on the table.

"Why are you back in Blaketown?" Edie calmly asked.

"Who do you think you are?! I'm asking the questions!" he challenged. "My mother called. Said you were out of prison, looking high and mighty. It made me mad. You ruined my life . . . you ruined Karen's. Now you act like everything's fine. Well, it isn't!"

"Is it money you're after?"

Roger glared at his ex-wife. "I'm the one who got nailed for child-support."

"And you're the one who has never paid a dime! I thought that was why you were in California. You didn't want anything to do with Karen or me, remember?"

"I wasn't certain that brat was even mine," Roger said, angered by her boldness. "I'm still not."

"Then leave us alone," Edie pleaded.

"I'll leave when I'm good and ready," he replied, rising to glower down at her. "And we haven't settled anything yet!"

"What is it you're after?"

"This," he said, suddenly gripping the back of her head. He pulled her close for a kiss. She struggled, but he held her fast. When he finally released her, she shoved him away. Enraged by her reaction, he slapped her hard across the face, knocking her to the floor. He reached back to strike her again, and was stunned by a blow to the face that flattened him.

"Leave her alone," Brett exclaimed, rubbing his fist. He'd never hit anyone before, but hadn't been able to control himself when Roger struck Edie. Brett knelt down, examining Edie's face. Holding her against him, he gently rocked her in his arms.

Outraged, Roger struggled to his feet. He stomped to where Brett and Edie were huddled together on the floor, but before he could take action, he was apprehended by the police officer Brett had brought with him.

"Let go of me!" Roger snarled as the bar crowd continued to clap and holler. "He's the one who hit me!"

"Are you resisting arrest?" the officer asked, quickly locking handcuffs around Roger's wrists. He had silently cheered when Brett had struck Roger. He felt Roger had it coming after what this man had done tonight. "We'll add it to the list after I read you your rights."

"What list?"

"The list of charges against you. Two counts of assault . . . ," he began, leading the man from the room.

"Two counts?" Edie asked, as Brett helped her to her feet.

Brett solemnly nodded. "You weren't the only one he attacked tonight."

Her eyes widened in alarm. "Not Karen?"

"No," he reassured her. What he had to tell her would be just as difficult. "Edie, first let me stress that your mother's all right."

"Mom?!" Edie felt numb as Brett led her out of the bar. "What happened?"

"Roger stopped there first, to see if you were home. When you weren't, he forced your mother to tell him where you were. That's how he knew to look for us at the restaurant."

"What did he do to her?" Edie asked, nauseated by this news.

"After Roger got the information he was after, he shoved her into the stove. She fell and hit her head pretty hard."

Edie put a hand over her mouth to stop from screaming. Once again, Brett held her close to calm her down.

"She's okay. After she regained consciousness—"

"He knocked her out?"

Brett nodded, gently leading Edie to his car and helping her inside. "Where is she now?"

"The hospital. The dispatcher had just put out word to find you when I ran into that officer. He filled me in on what had taken place." Brett closed the door on her side and hurried around to his own.

"Mom's in the hospital?"

"Yes. She's all right, but worried sick about you and Karen."

"Why is she in the hospital? You keep saying she's all right . . . if she's all right, why—"

"She has a mild concussion and had to have a few stitches in her forehead."

Edie closed her eyes. They flew open at the thought of her daughter. "Where's Karen?" she asked, sensing something was very wrong.

"We don't know," Brett replied, starting the engine. "The police are looking for her right now. They know we're on our way to the hospital to see your mother; they'll contact us there when they find Karen." Putting an arm around her trembling shoulders, Brett pulled out into the street and drove toward the hospital.

CHAPTER 26

Dazed, Karen allowed herself to be led through the towering pine trees toward a spot Bev had assured no one would ever find.

"Mom showed me this place once when we were up here camping a long time ago," Bev quietly explained. "Sometimes I still come up here . . . when I want to be alone."

Karen blinked. Bev had tried so hard to console her. Instead of comfort, she felt alienated and chilled despite the heavy parka Bev insisted she had to wear for this adventure. Bev had a closet filled with jackets, coats, and clothes she never wore—unlike Karen who had been living by her grandmother's rule of make do or do without.

"Are you sure you can find this place in the dark?" Sabrina asked, carefully following behind. The coat Bev had loaned her was a little big, but warm. The sleeves were too long, but she had managed to push them up a bit.

"I've been up here enough. It shouldn't be a problem," Bev responded. "Besides, we brought flashlights. We'll find it if it takes all night."

Sabrina looked around nervously. She should've had Bev drop her off at Kate's house. Instead, she had promised Bev she would help cheer up Karen. Now here they were, out wandering in the forest. She had tried to call her mom from Bev's house, but no one had answered. She'd finally left a message on Kate's answering machine, hoping her parents would be okay about this. Continuing forward, she heard a strange noise. "What was that?"

"What was what?" Bev asked.

"That noise. Listen."

All three girls stopped, waiting several seconds. Bev glanced back at Sabrina. "It was probably a squirrel."

"I hope that's all it was," Sabrina retorted, certain she had heard something bigger than a squirrel.

A few yards behind Sabrina, Terri started to breathe again. That had been too close. She kept still for several more seconds just to be safe. Terri was also worried about what her parents would think. But, she reminded herself, she didn't have a choice. There was a story here, one that would earn everyone's respect.

She had followed these three young women to Bev's house. Peering in the windows, she had seen them gather coats, flashlights, matches, and had watched as Bev had tucked a bottle of James Henderson's best wine inside of a small backpack along with a package of paper cups. Her eyes had widened at the sight of the violet-colored bottle in Bev's hands, convinced that what she had overheard earlier was now taking place. These girls were out to get drunk. Maybe boys would be involved. If not, maybe these girls would get drunk enough to reveal a few interesting facts, like who had been writing those editorials.

Before the three girls had slipped out of the house, Terri had made a hurried decision. She had seen Bev reach for a set of car keys. Bev's parents had taken one car for the evening. That left one in the garage, and the Jeep Cherokee parked in the driveway. Quickly climbing inside of the Jeep, Terri had scrambled over the backseat, into the storage space in the back. Luck had gone her way; it was the car Bev selected to drive. Huddled down as she was, Terri hadn't realized they were heading up one of the local canyons until their arrival at the mouth of the canyon. By then, it was too late to do anything about it.

"This story had better be worth what I'll be facing when I get home," Terri now muttered, wrapping the blanket she had found in the Jeep around herself for extra warmth. Praying the three girls wouldn't go too far, she was pleased to see them finally use the flashlights. That would make it easier to keep track of where they were. Taking a deep breath, she stepped out from behind the tree and hurried forward.

* * *

"Mom, I am so sorry," Edie tearfully said again, standing next to her mother's hospital bed. It seemed like that was all she said anymore: "I'm sorry." Simple words that couldn't fix or change anything.

Adele forced a smile. She had never experienced a headache this severe in her life, but it wouldn't do to have Edie this upset. "I'll be fine," she claimed, reaching to give Edie's hand a firm squeeze. "You know Dr. Davis—he likes to make as much money off his patients as possible."

"Did I hear someone take my name in vain?" the aging physician good-naturedly asked as he stepped inside the hospital room. He had always liked Adele Hadley, convinced she was one of the most pleasant women he knew, next to his own sweet wife.

"Every word of that is true and you know it," Adele retorted, anxious to keep things lighthearted. From the look on Edie's face, she knew her daughter couldn't take much more.

"Have they found Karen yet?" Edie hopefully asked.

The doctor slowly shook his head. "That young man of yours is still making phone calls down at the nurses' station, though," he said, enjoying Edie's blush, sensing she did have feelings for the forest ranger. He was glad. Edie needed a good man in her life. Brett Randall was definitely one of those. "I'm sure they'll find Karen soon."

"Karen's with Bev," Adele reminded her daughter. "She'll be fine."

Edie didn't think she could bear it if she lost her daughter again. "Please, Father, let her be all right," she silently pleaded.

Brett limped into the small room and nervously cleared his throat. "I've called all over town . . . everyone I could think of . . . everyone you said to try." He frowned. "Either they're not home, or they haven't seen those girls for several hours."

Edie sank down into a chair near her mother's bed. "Where are they?" she anguished. "Where could they have gone?"

"Bev's parents aren't home yet. Maybe they'll know. I left a message on their answering machine to call us here at the hospital," Brett said, crossing in front of the doctor to reach Edie's side. Slipping an arm around her shoulders, he wished he could protect Edie from the fear in her heart.

* * *

"Play that message again," Sue requested, moving closer to Kate's answering machine.

Kate obediently rewound the tape and played it again.

"Hi, Mom, Dad, it's about eight-fifteen. I'm calling from Bev's house. We're trying to cheer Karen up. It's a long story. It'll probably be late when I get to Kate's. I'll explain everything when I come. Don't worry, and don't wait up for me. I know you guys will all be tired. Sorry I missed you."

"Tell us more about these two girls she's with," Greg requested, looking at his watch. It was nearly 9:30 p.m.

Sighing, Kate accepted Mike's hand as the two of them sat down at the small kitchen table. They waited for her parents to sit down across from them. "Bev Henderson and Karen Beyer are two of my best students," she began. "They're good girls."

"I know both of these girls too," Mike added supportively. "They're characters, but I don't think they would get Sabrina involved in anything that was unwholesome."

"Well, that daughter of mine has come home late before," Sue mused. "At least this time she tried to contact us. I just wish we'd been here when she called. I wonder where they went?"

"Maybe she'll call again," Kate offered.

"One thing about it, it sounds like she's made some new friends," Greg said, stifling a yawn. He was exhausted after his day of hiking in the woods with his son-in-law. "Maybe she'll want to stay here."

"Maybe," Sue replied. She didn't want to miss out on Sabrina's last few years at home. But, if it meant her daughter would be happy, it would be worth it. She had tried to be patient but it wasn't getting any better in Bozeman for Sabrina. It might in time, but Sue was worried about the continued struggle. Would Sabrina eventually decide it was easier to join in than to resist? Maybe a clean start was exactly what her youngest daughter needed.

* * *

Margo Jeppson continued to pace the floor. Where was Terri? Her oldest daughter had been gone for hours. She glanced at the kitchen clock. It was just past nine-thirty, long past seven o'clock. The attack the Beyer girl had suffered a few weeks ago had made most parents in Blaketown nervous. Margo wished again that her husband was home, not off on a business trip this weekend. If he'd been here, she would've sent him driving around town to find their daughter. As it was, she didn't dare leave the house in case Terri called.

Passing by the phone, Margo remembered what Terri had said—something about working on a special assignment for the paper. Margo scowled. Picking up the phone, she glanced at the ward phone list and quickly located Kate's number. She pushed in the number on her touch-tone phone, then impatiently waited for someone to answer.

"Hello," Mike said.

"Hi, Mike," Margo responded, "this is Margo Jeppson. Is your wife there?"

"Yes, just a minute."

Margo drummed her fingers on the counter until Kate spoke into the phone.

"Hello?"

"Kate?" Margo asked.

"Yes?" Kate answered, trying to place this familiar-sounding voice.

"This is Margo Jeppson."

Kate frowned. Now what? Margo didn't call unless it was to complain about something.

"Do you have any idea where Terri is?"

Recognizing the fear in this woman's voice, Kate glanced at her mother. That certainly seemed to be a popular question tonight. "No, I don't," she answered.

"She called earlier around six o'clock. She said she was working on a special assignment for the school paper, and that she would be home around seven."

"What special assignment?" Kate asked, puzzled.

"I figured it must've been a story you or Doris had given her to work on."

"Margo, I don't know anything about this . . . unless . . ."

"Unless what?" Margo angrily asked.

"Terri came to Doris one afternoon . . . she wanted to write an important story for the paper. She felt like we were giving her assignments that weren't challenging enough."

"What did you assign her that would require her to be gone this long?" Margo indignantly asked.

"We didn't give her an assignment. Terri was supposed to come up with a storyline, and let Doris and I okay the idea."

"You don't know what she's working on, then?!" Margo concluded.

"Margo, let me call Doris. Maybe she knows something I don't. I'll get right back to you," Kate promised, hanging up the phone. She hurriedly dialed Doris' number, relieved when the English teacher answered the phone.

"Kate?" Doris correctly guessed.

"Doris, we have a problem."

"Tell me something new," Doris joked.

"I'm serious. Terri's mom just called me. Terri's missing."

"What?"

"Oh, yes. Terri called her mother earlier tonight around six, and told her she was working on a special assignment for the newspaper. She was supposed to be home by seven."

Doris glanced at her watch. This wasn't good news. "What special assignment?"

"I was hoping you would know," Kate sighed.

"Sorry, I don't know anything about it. What is that girl up to?"

"I don't know," Kate answered.

"I think if I was Margo, I'd get hold of the police. It's almost ten o'clock. Terri should've been home long before now."

"I know another young lady who should've been home before now," Kate commented.

"Who?"

"My sister. She's out somewhere with Bev and Karen. We're not sure where they're at either."

Doris thought for a minute. Was this all a coincidence? "Kate, didn't Bev complain Friday about how Terri had been following her around?"

"Yes," Kate replied, catching her train of thought. "Do you think those girls have something to do with Terri's disappearance?"

"I wouldn't put it past them," Doris said. "I wonder what they're up to?"

"I don't know. The only clue we have is something Sabrina left on my answering machine."

"What was that?"

"She said something about trying to help Bev cheer up Karen."

"What's wrong with Karen?" Doris asked.

"Good question. She seemed fine earlier this afternoon."

"Knowing those girls, I would dare say they're out having fun at Terri's expense."

"Probably. In the meantime, what do I tell Terri's mother?"

"Tell her to sit tight. I'll go for a drive around town and see what I can come up with."

"Want some help?"

"Sure," Doris replied. "Meet me in front of the high school in ten minutes."

"Okay."

"Oh, and don't tell Margo what we suspect. She'll blow a gasket."

"I wasn't planning on it," Kate assured her friend. "I'll see you in a few minutes." Hanging up the phone, she quickly dialed Margo's number.

"Hi, Margo, Kate again."

"Does Doris know where Terri is?" Margo frantically asked.

"No, and neither of us have any idea what this story is that Terri claims to be working on. She's doing it on her own."

Margo was frantic. This wasn't like Terri. Something was wrong— her daughter had never stayed out this late before without permission.

"Doris and I will drive around and see if we can find her," Kate continued. "We'll call you as soon as we do."

"Oh, thank you," Margo responded, relieved. "I was thinking of doing that myself, but I don't want to be gone if she tries to call. And my youngest daughter has been so sick today, I hate to leave her for very long."

"Sit tight," Kate advised, quoting Doris. "We'll do the legwork on this one."

"Legwork?"

"It's a newspaper term—it means we'll go out and get the job done. We'll find Terri."

"I hope so," Margo said before hanging up the phone. She paced the kitchen, still upset. Even if Kate and Doris hadn't assigned a specific story to Terri, they were responsible for that paper. It was their fault her daughter was missing. Grabbing the phone book, she decided to express her opinion to a higher authority. A few minutes later, she called Cleo Partridge.

* * *

Deeply disturbed, Cleo hung up the phone. She didn't know what to do about this disaster. What had that silly girl gotten herself into? Realizing now that it had been a mistake to turn Terri lose with an assignment like this, she wondered how she could rectify the situation. For the moment, she had let Margo heap the blame on Kate and Doris. But if Terri ever revealed who had put her up to this—Cleo cringed. What had she been thinking? That paper was nothing compared to the safety of her students. She hadn't meant for Terri to spend night and day on this assignment. What if something had happened to her? She'd never forgive herself. Deciding to take action, she quickly changed out of her nightgown and hurried out of her house.

* * *

Tiredly Gina Henderson hung up the jacket she had worn for the evening. After her husband had taken her out to dinner, he had wanted to stop by his office at the car lot and wrap up some paper-work. He had promised not to be long, assuring her they would catch the late show after he finished his bookkeeping. But by the time he had finally closed his books, it was nine-thirty and the show had already started. Instead of seeing the movie, the couple had picked up their two small sons, who had spent the evening with James' sister, and come straight home.

Sensing he had blown their plans for the evening, James tried to make things up to Gina by helping their twins get ready for bed. While he chased the giggling boys upstairs, Gina wandered into the living room. She glanced at her watch and wondered where Bev was. Earlier her stepdaughter and Karen had said they planned to get a bite to eat and catch the early show. The movie would have been over by 9:00 p.m., but that didn't mean Bev would find her way home until much later. Sighing, Gina wished again that she had more influence with Bev. In Gina's opinion, James was too lenient with the sixteen-year-old girl, giving her freedom instead of what she really needed—structure, guidance, and love.

Sometimes Gina's heart ached for her stepdaughter; she knew Bev's pain over losing her mother was simply vented as anger. Gina had tried to be understanding and patient, but Bev often went beyond the limits of normal tolerance. Gina's attempts to discipline Bev were always undermined by James, a man who had handled his first wife's death by blocking everything out, including what his grieving daughter was going through. James was a wonderful man, but he had tunnel vision when it came to Bev, something Gina wasn't sure would ever change.

Preoccupied by these thoughts, Gina paused beside the small wooden stand where the telephone and answering machine were kept. A blinking red light alerted her that someone had called. Hoping it was Bev, she pushed the replay button and waited while the small cassette rewound. Then, picking up a pencil and a small pad of paper, she began taking notes.

* * *

"Brett Randall?" James repeated, looking at his wife. "Who's that?"

"I don't know him," Gina replied, "but maybe Bev does. His message on the answering machine said he needed to talk to us about Bev."

James dialed the number Gina had written on the message pad for him. He impatiently waited as his call was transferred to the correct hospital room. "Mr. Randall?" he finally said when a man answered the phone.

"Yes," Brett replied.

"We got your message. Is Bev all right?"

"We hope so," Brett replied, gripping the phone in his hand. "Have you seen her or Karen lately?"

"No, not since this afternoon. Why? And how do you know Karen and Bev?" he added, confused.

"I'm with Karen's mother, Edie," Brett said. He quickly explained all that had taken place that night. "So you can understand why we're so concerned," Brett said when he had finished.

"Yes. And you think Karen and Bev are still together?" James asked. He didn't like the sound of this at all.

"We don't know. That's why we called. We were hoping you knew where they were."

James gave his wife a worried look. "Gina's been all over this house and the girls aren't here. But my Jeep Cherokee is gone. They're probably off somewhere in it."

"What color is it?" Brett asked.

"Dark green."

"I'll let the police know."

"What do we do in the meantime?"

"I guess sit and wait," Brett replied. "Unless you have a better idea."

"I think I'll start looking around town," James informed him. "There's something else I should mention. There were a couple of messages on our answering machine from one of Bev's high school teachers, Kate Jeffries. She said her younger sister is with Bev and Karen—"

On the other end of the line, Brett rubbed his forehead. "Kate Jeffries?" he repeated, thinking of Mike's wife. This was an added problem.

"Kate is one of Karen's teachers," Edie said quietly. "Maybe she knows something."

Brett nodded as he continued to listen to James Henderson.

"Kate called to see if we'd seen her younger sister. Evidently, she's with Bev and Karen and no one knows where they are."

"Hang on a minute," Brett said as he turned to Edie. "He says Kate's sister is with Karen and Bev."

Edie smacked her forehead suddenly. "I knew that. Remember, we talked to her mother at the restaurant."

"That's right," Brett agreed. "James, are you still there?"

"I'm here," James replied. "Gina and I were just discussing how to handle this. She'll stay here to answer the phone if Bev or anyone else calls. In the meantime, I'll drive around and see what I can come up with."

"Okay," Brett agreed. "Call us here if you find them."

"Will do," James replied, hanging up the phone.

"Where could those girls be?" Gina exclaimed, feeling sick inside.

"I don't know, but I'm going to find out," James promised, heading out the front door.

CHAPTER 27

Karen and Sabrina began to panic as they wandered deeper into the forest. Bev had laughed at their fears. "I know this place like the back of my hand," she had assured them. She now smiled at her friends. She had given them the honor of being the first visitors to her sanctuary, hoping it would bring Karen the peace she needed. Excitedly she led them into a secluded thicket, the destination she'd had in mind. The three girls shivered as they worked together to build a fire in a pit Bev had dug years ago. Ringed with large, smooth rocks, the fire now merrily beckoned. Almost reverently, Bev revealed how this place had become a comforting haven.

"We used to come up here camping when I was younger, before Mom got sick. It was great. Mom loved being in the forest. She was the one who showed me this place." Bev's eyes misted as she described that special time in her life.

As Bev continued to talk, Karen and Sabrina understood why she had brought them here. Here Bev had spent hours grieving for her mother. Here she had written some of her best poetry. Here she had often found the strength to keep trying.

Tonight was the first time Bev had ever brought anyone else to this location. It was an ideal hiding place. Thick patches of trees had intertwined, forming a natural shelter from the world. Pine needles and grass made a soft carpet in their shadow.

"Well, I spilled my guts," Bev finally exclaimed. "Your turn," she said to Sabrina. "It's obvious something is bothering you."

Even though Sabrina realized that Bev was trying to help Karen work through tonight by opening up about their own problems,

Sabrina was still reluctant to share her challenges of the past several months. Bev had lost her mother. Karen's mother was an alcoholic who had served time in prison. Their trials made hers seem insignificant.

"Tell us what's eating you up inside," Bev pressed.

Sabrina was quiet for a few moments, before deciding to tell these two girls what had been happening in her life the past year. When she was finished, Bev grinned.

"No wonder you want to relocate," Bev responded. "What do you think about all of that?" she added, glancing at Karen.

Still numb, Karen shrugged. She didn't have too much sympathy for anyone but herself right now.

"C'mon, Karen, tell us what's goin' on inside of you," Bev encouraged. She paused, hoping Karen would cooperate. Finally Bev reached for her backpack. "Okay, I didn't know if we would need this tonight, but I brought it along anyway. I've got to do something to liven you two up!"

Karen and Sabrina both stared as Bev revealed what she had hidden in her small backpack.

"We have a nice fire, a cozy, private place, and now something to make us all feel better," Bev announced as she set the bottle of wine down on the ground. Reaching into her backpack, she pulled out a corkscrew and began to expertly remove the cork out of the bottle.

"Obviously this isn't the first time you've done that," Karen exclaimed, looking at her friend in surprise.

Bev shrugged. As a matter of fact, she had done this several times, not that she would ever admit it. So far, no one had caught on. No one knew how many times she had managed to sneak one of her father's liquor bottles up to this location. Those bottles lay forever hidden at the bottom of a nearby creek. Bev rationalized that she only drank enough to feel better, not enough to give her secret away.

Stunned, Karen continued to stare at someone she thought she knew. Bev had a drinking problem?!

"This is the good stuff. You'll like it," Bev promised. She quickly filled three paper cups, handing one to each of the other girls.

Sabrina could tell that Karen was as upset about this as she was. "Bev, I don't think—" she began.

"You don't need to think after you try this," Bev interrupted. "Have you ever tried wine before?"

Shaking her head, Sabrina remembered Sindi's Halloween party. Would things have been different if she'd given in that night? She wondered if it had been worth it to make what she'd thought then was the right decision. After all, look how things had turned out.

"Take a sip and see if you like it," Bev coaxed. "You can dump out the rest if you don't."

Sabrina looked at the liquid in the cup. She had tried a sip of beer at Sindi's party and had hated it. This would probably be the same.

"How about you, Karen?"

Refusing to answer, Karen was carrying on her own private debate. This went against everything she had ever stood for. She had promised herself since she was tiny that she would never drink. She would never be like her mother. After the episode at the football field, she had renewed that vow with vigor.

"No one will ever know," Bev assured them, drinking from her cup. "And I promise, it will make both of you feel better about things."

Sabrina attempted to hand her cup back to Bev, but the older girl refused to take it.

"You haven't even tried it yet," Bev chided. "How can you decide if you like something without trying it first?"

"But it's wrong to drink," Sabrina started to argue.

"Says who?! You Mormons are pathetic! You let someone else tell you how to live. Show me in the scriptures where it says a person can't drink wine!" Bev challenged.

"I think it says something about it in the Doctrine and Covenants," Sabrina said bravely.

"The *what?!*" Bev laughed. "Let me guess, one of your Mormon books?!"

Sabrina slowly nodded.

"That isn't real scripture. Show me a scripture from the Bible that says it's wrong, and then I'll believe you. Look," Bev grinned at Sabrina, "it's not like we're drinking whiskey, or beer—or even vodka," she added for Karen's benefit. "Wine isn't bad for you. In fact, they've proven it's good for the heart. It helps people relax—something we could all use tonight."

Still hesitating, Sabrina peered into the cup in her hand.

"Just one little swallow. Try it—decide for yourself—learn to think for yourself, like me," Bev said, drinking from her own cup.

Sabrina *was* tired of everyone telling her what to do. Maybe it *was* time to form her own opinions; her life couldn't get any worse than it already was. She made a quick decision and followed Bev's example. Wincing after the first sip, Sabrina forced it down. It wasn't as bad as the beer, but still had a bitter, pungent flavor she didn't care for.

"You didn't give it a good try. Drink a little more," Bev said, egging Sabrina on. "Nectar of the gods!" she exclaimed, gulping down what was left in her cup.

Glancing at Bev, Sabrina tried it again. This time she was better prepared for the taste and decided it wasn't as bad as she had first thought.

Karen continued to stare at the contents of the cup in her hand. Over and over she saw her mother walk into that bar. Her mother's promise echoed inside her head. *"No matter what it takes, I will never drink again!"*

"C'mon, try it," Bev encouraged. "It'll make you feel better." She stood, adding another piece of wood to the fire they had built.

Gazing into the fire, Karen wished it could warm her heart. Maybe Bev was right, maybe this was the best way to get past the pain.

"Are you going to drink it or save it for your scrapbook?" Bev scolded. Karen had had a severe shock, and Bev was convinced she needed something to snap her out of it. Certain that this was the answer, Bev continued to encourage Karen to try the wine. "I promise we won't get drunk. Just one cup each, that's all. Just enough to take the edge off."

"It kind of burns going down," Sabrina commented, after drinking a little more. Like Bev said, it was just one cup of wine. No one would ever know. These two girls wouldn't tell Kate. It would be all right.

* * *

As Sabrina continued to rationalize, Terri looked longingly at the fire from a nearby group of bushes. Shivering, she pulled the blanket close around her body. The thin jacket and blanket offered some warmth, but not what she imagined the other girls were enjoying. It had been a challenge, keeping up with them. If they hadn't used flashlights, she would've lost them, and probably herself. She'd never find her way out of here, and now had to wait until these three were ready to head back home.

As she thought about what waited for her at home, Terri silently groaned. What had she been thinking? Her mother was probably on the verge of a nervous breakdown by now. Pulling out the little notebook, she could hardly see to write. Quickly, she recorded what had taken place since they had left Bev's house. Then, tucking the notebook and pen away, she snuggled down in the blanket, trying to keep warm.

* * *

"Where could those girls be?!" Doris exclaimed as she and Kate pulled into a convenience store parking lot.

Kate shook her head. They had driven all over town. No one had seen them. They had even stopped by the local movie theater, but the girls hadn't been there either. They had run into James Henderson on their way out of the theater. He had relayed the information he had learned from Brett about Edie's ex-husband and the threats Roger had made against Karen earlier. Kate now shared a worried look with Doris. "You don't think Roger Beyer did something to those four girls?"

"Let's not panic," Doris advised. "They have to be around here someplace."

"Doris," Kate suddenly said, feeling sick inside, "those boys who attacked Karen before have been giving her a bad time at school. You don't suppose . . ."

"I don't like that thought either," Doris answered.

"It is a possibility," Kate pointed out.

"I know, but I don't want to think about it."

"I know something else I don't want to think about," Kate moaned.

"What?"

"The phone call I have to make to my mother."

"Don't forget Margo," Doris reminded.

"I'll let you talk to her," Kate said, pulling Doris toward the small store.

"What do we tell them?"

"What James told us. The police are out looking for all four girls. We don't know where they are yet, but we'll keep looking."

Muttering under her breath, Doris reluctantly allowed Kate to drag her to the pay phone.

* * *

"I will ask this nicely one last time," the young officer said, his eyes narrowing as he waited for Roger Beyer to speak. "Did you see your daughter tonight?"

Roger kept his mouth clamped shut. He'd just about had his fill of this arrogant deputy. First, he had been booked for assault and thrown into a small cell in the basement of City Hall. Then, just as he had started to sleep off the booze in his system, he had been hauled upstairs into this tiny room where he had been hit with a barrage of questions.

"I don't need to remind you how serious this is," Deputy Walter Horton continued.

"I didn't touch that girl," Roger finally spat out.

"What girl?" Walter probed. He knew four girls were missing. Which one was Roger referring to?

"My daughter," Roger snapped.

"What about her friends?"

Roger grinned. "My daughter has friends?" he snidely asked.

Walter itched to physically wipe the grin off Roger's face. Instead, he took a deep breath and struggled for control. Turning his back to Roger, he tried to think of a way to trick this man into revealing the information they needed.

Glancing at the short, stocky officer, Roger had a sudden thought. Before the deputy knew what had hit him, Roger had jumped him, completely cutting off his air as he wrapped a wiry arm around the struggling man's neck. He pulled Walter's gun out of the holster and shoved the man to the floor. Walter lay there for several seconds, gasping for air.

"Now, you can start answering some of my questions," Roger crowed, aiming the gun at the officer's head. "Where's everyone else who works here? Are you alone?"

Walter silently cursed. He *was* alone. Everyone else was out looking for the girls. Except for the dispatcher down the hall. Slowly rising to his knees, he glared at Roger.

"Where's your backup?" Roger sneered.

"Out in the hall," Walter replied, trying to bluff his way out of this. He'd be a deputy the rest of his life if he didn't regain control of this situation. "All I have to do is give the word, and they'll rush in this room with guns a-blazin'!"

"Right," Roger sarcastically replied. "You've seen a few too many bad westerns." He kept the gun aimed at Walter and walked across the room to examine the window. Iron bars lined the exterior. He couldn't get out that way. Figuring he was already in serious trouble, he decided to round things out. "C'mon," he said, waving the gun toward the door. "Let's go for a little walk."

"You'll regret this," Walter warned, praying he could convince Roger he was outnumbered. "You think those officers out there are going to let you walk out of here?"

"They will if they think I'm going to shoot you," Roger retorted, shoving the deputy forward. "Open that door nice and slow," he commanded, sticking the gun in Walter's back.

Walter slowly opened the door. There was no way he could wrestle that gun away as long as Roger had it pressed against his back.

Roger glanced over Walter's head, surveying the area. No one was in sight. "Where's your friends, Walter?" he asked, pushing the officer out into the hall. They walked down the hall together, Roger prodding Walter along with the gun. "You mean to tell me you're the only one here?" he asked, thoroughly disgusted.

Walter refused to answer. Another few feet and they'd be within hailing distance of the dispatcher, Lucille Nalder. He wanted to keep Roger away from her, unless—he had a sudden flash of inspiration. "Roger, I'm going to warn you one more time," he hollered. "Put that gun down now, or you'll regret it."

Lucille's ears perked up. Turning down the volume of the small TV set she had been watching, she strained to hear what the commotion was down the hall.

"I said, put that gun down," Walter hollered again, louder this time.

"Will you shut up!" Roger yelled back, giving Walter a shove.

Finally grasping the situation, Lucille flipped a switch on the radio in front of her. "Emergency situation at City Hall. Requesting backup," she said, praying someone would answer.

"Lucille, what's goin' on down there?" the sheriff's voice sounded over the crackling radio. Impatiently he waited for a response. "Lucille?" he repeated. He waited several seconds, then tried again. "Lucille?"

Grinning, Roger picked up the small microphone. "Sorry. Lucille's really busy right now."

The sheriff pounded the dashboard with his fist, then spun his old Ford Bronco around, lights and sirens announcing his angered frustration as he sped toward City Hall.

* * *

Cleo pulled into the convenience store parking lot beside Kate's car. Like everyone else, she too had driven all over town. Terri was nowhere in sight. Deciding to see what these two teachers had come up with, she climbed out of her car and walked toward them.

"Look who's here," Doris said, nudging Kate.

Kate gazed solemnly at the principal. After speaking to her mother, Kate was in no mood to put up with this woman. Just as Cleo stepped in front of them, the sheriff roared past. The three women stared, transfixed by the flashing lights and eerie sound of the siren. "Oh, no," Kate murmured, fearing the worst.

"It could be something else," Doris said, still clinging to hope.

"It could be Terri," Cleo said, horrified. "Why did I ever give her that assignment?!"

Doris and Kate exchanged an incredulous look. Cleo had something to do with this?

* * *

"Edie, I'm sure that siren had nothing to do with Karen," Adele tried to soothe her daughter. Still seated in a nearby chair, Edie leaned onto her mother's hospital bed, sobbing into the bedspread. Adele stroked the back of her daughter's head. They had all heard the siren as it had screamed through the town. Brett was now down at the nurses' station, trying to find someone who knew what was going on.

Ten minutes later, he limped back into Adele's room. Edie lifted her head, her beautiful brown eyes still spilling tears.

"We're not sure what that was all about. It was the sheriff's outfit we heard. There's some kind of disturbance taking place at City Hall."

"Roger," Edie guessed.

Brett's eyes confirmed her fears.

CHAPTER 28

Shivering, Karen moved closer to the fire. She glanced at Sabrina and Bev. These two girls had managed to drink most of the wine in the bottle. They were now singing a silly song at the top of their voices. Bev's cure for depression had certainly worked for those two, but Karen had handed her cup of wine back to Bev. It wasn't an answer—at least, not for her. She had decided that no matter what her mother did, she had her own life to lead. One that didn't include being a drunk.

"You're not sing—ging," Bev slurred.

"I'm not in the mood to sing," Karen replied.

"What are you in the mode . . . mood to do?" Sabrina jabbered, giggling at herself.

"I'll tell you what I'm not in the mood for," Karen snapped, tiring of this. "I'm not in the mood to watch you two get plastered!"

Nearby, Terri shivered and silently agreed.

"Killjoy," Bev said, accused. "You're ruining our potty . . . party." She and Sabrina laughed again.

"I'm going home," Karen said, standing.

"Oh?" Bev said, amused. "You know how to fine . . . find your way out?"

Frowning, Karen realized Bev had a point. She could wander for days in this forest and never find her way back to the Jeep, especially in the dark.

Bev gave an exaggerated sigh. "I'll tick you . . . take you when we're all ready to go."

Karen knew her friend was in no shape to take them anywhere. The way things were looking, they were stuck here for the night. Her grandmother would be flipping out about now. Not only would Edie be coming home drunk, but Karen wasn't coming home at all. She glared up at the star-filled sky. "Was all of this really necessary?" she loudly complained, convinced no one really listened anyway.

Ignoring her, Bev and Sabrina began another series of silly camp songs. Still hidden in the bushes, Terri tried to look on the bright side—at least it would scare off the wild animals.

Infuriated, Karen stood up and began throwing pine cones and kicking rocks to release the anger she felt while Bev and Sabrina giggled at her. Finally calming down, she resigned herself to the fact that she would be spending the night in the forest and began looking around for more firewood. Keeping that fire going was important now; it was their only source of heat.

"Look, Karen thinks she's Paul Bunyan," Bev giggled as Karen began organizing a pile of wood scraps.

"All bunion? My mother has one of those on her big toe. She complains about it all the time," Sabrina contributed, drinking the last of the wine in her cup. She'd lost count of how many cups she'd had. This was the most fun she'd had in a very long time.

"Bunyan—B-u-n-y-a-n—that's what I said. What you meant was bunion—b-u-n-i-o-n."

"Oh, I get it. You know, you are a good speller—you should be a teacher," Sabrina gushed.

"Do you think so?" Bev asked, pleased by this compliment.

Sabrina frowned. "But only weird people like my sister become teachers."

"Your sister is not weird," Bev said in Kate's behalf. "She's snoopy and gives bad advice, but she's not weird. I'll tell you who's weird."

"Who?" Sabrina asked.

"Terri Jeppson," Bev sputtered, laughing. "She's as strange as they come."

Terri silently glowered through the brush at Bev.

"You know what—she was following us all over town today," Bev said, gesturing wildly with her hands.

"That's right. I forgot. Why did she do that?" Sabrina asked.

Bev stood up, staggering slightly as she prepared to perform for her new friend. She held out one hand, then pretended to write in it with another. "She was writing down everything we did. Remember . . . at the arcade . . . she's the one who was sitting behind us." Bev sat down next to Sabrina, laughing. "That's why we said what we did about getting drunk and having a good time with the boys."

Both girls laughed until their sides ached. Karen rolled her eyes as she moved back to the fire and added some of the wood she had gathered. She then tried a different direction, hoping to find enough wood to last until morning.

"Hey, we did get drunk," Sabrina said. "Now, where are the boys?"

Again, the two girls giggled, unaware of the sophomore girl who had started to cry softly behind them.

"This was all just a joke to them," Terri silently moaned. She was in more trouble than she'd ever been in her entire life, and for what? Enraged, she pulled out the little notebook and threw it as far as she could away from her. She was in the same predicament as Karen. She'd never find her way out of here by herself. Bev wasn't in any kind of shape to lead them out tonight. She was stuck.

"What are you doing here?" a voice asked sharply.

Startled, Terri jumped, then stared up at Karen.

Thoroughly disgusted, Karen pulled the younger girl to her feet. Her expression softened when she saw Terri's tears. "What are you doing here?" she repeated. "How did you get here?"

Terri stared down at her feet. How could she answer? Ashamed, she avoided Karen's searching gaze.

"Well?"

"I hid in the back of the Jeep," Terri finally stammered. "I'm sorry."

"You must be about half-frozen," Karen said, pushing the fifteen-year-old toward the fire. "C'mon, like it or not, we're all here for the night."

Bev's eyes grew huge when Karen returned with Terri. "Is that who I think it is?" she asked.

Karen nodded.

"Who is it?" Sabrina asked.

"Our good friend Terri," Bev chortled. "Pull up some needle pines," she invited. "It was too dark for you to see to write anymore anyway." She belched loudly, then giggled again.

"That was disgusting," Sabrina informed Bev.

"Thank you," Bev replied. "I'll tell you what's really disgusting," she added, pointing to Terri. "Her."

"Bev, that's enough," Karen warned, as she forced Terri to sit next to the fire.

"Where's your notebook, pretty girl?" Bev asked.

"What notebook?" Terri answered.

Bev glared at the younger girl. "I think this scrawny thing followed us up here to spy on us."

"Really?" Sabrina asked, her eyes widening.

"Really," Bev assured. "Let's see what she wrote," she said, suddenly jumping to her feet. She unsteadily approached Terri. "Give it up, I want that notebook," she demanded.

"I don't have it," Terri said, fearing the dark look in Bev's eyes.

"Bev, leave her alone," Karen advised.

Bev glared at Karen. "You know what, you're no fun."

Karen returned the glare. "Getting drunk is not my idea of fun."

"Well it should be. It runs in your family," Bev countered, still glaring.

Taking a deep breath, Karen reminded herself that Bev didn't really know what she was saying. The insult still cut deep. She walked away for a minute to get a handle on her emotions.

"As for you, you little pipsqueak," Bev exclaimed, "hand over the notebook."

"I don't have it," Terri said, backing away.

She wasn't quick enough. Bev knocked her to the ground, then after throwing off the blanket, began searching through Terri's jacket.

"Hey," Terri protested. "I told you I don't have it."

"Then what do you call this?" Bev triumphantly asked, pulling out a slip of paper.

"It's a grocery list," Terri said, trying to breathe. It wasn't easy with Bev sitting on top of her. "Leave me alone."

"I will not. Sabrina, come help me." Bev continued to search, unzipping Terri's jacket. "Sabrina?"

"She passed out a few minutes ago," Karen said, walking back to the fire. "And what do you think you're doing?"

"Helping Terri find her notebook," Bev said, grinning up at Karen. Just then, Terri rolled, sending Bev into the pile of wood Karen had gathered. "Why you little—" Bev started to say.

"Bev, cool it," Karen warned her. "Leave her alone. She's cold and scared, and the last thing she needs is you mauling her around."

"What do you call this?" Bev asked, slowly pulling herself out of the wood pile. A scrape on her nose had started to bleed.

"I'd say you brought it on yourself," Karen retorted. Reaching into her coat pocket, she pulled out some tissue. "Here, wipe at your nose. It's bleeding."

"I'm bleeding?" Bev asked, giving Terri a dirty look.

"Relax, it's just a scrape," Karen answered, picking up the blanket Terri had wrapped around herself. She shook out several pine needles, then handed it back to the frightened sophomore.

Bev stood, dusted herself off, and fell down again. Feeling like a nursemaid, Karen helped Bev move closer to the fire. "We'll leave in a few minutes," Bev assured Karen. "Soon as my head quits spinning." Fifteen minutes later, she was sound asleep.

"These two are real party animals," Karen grumbled, making sure Bev and Sabrina were close enough to the fire to stay warm, but far enough away to keep from getting burned.

"They're lucky to have you for a friend," Terri commented.

Surprised by the compliment, Karen glanced back at the younger girl.

"I mean it. I saw most of what happened tonight. Bev acted like a real jerk . . . and not just to me. And you're still making sure she's all right."

"She's my friend," Karen stated, sitting down next to the fire. "She's been there for me enough times."

"How long has she been drinking?"

Shrugging, Karen glanced at Terri. "Is this for your notebook?"

Terri shook her head. "No. That notebook was a bad idea."

"Yes, it was," Karen agreed. "Why were you following us around?"

Sighing, Terri decided she might as well confess. "Cleo asked me to find out who was writing the editorials for the paper."

Karen stared at Terri. "You're kidding?"

"I wish I was. I wish I'd told her no." Terri began to cry again. "My mother is probably so upset right now."

"I don't think she's the only one," Karen replied, thinking of her grandmother, Bev's parents, and Sabrina's, not to mention Kate.

"What can we do?"

"Nothing till morning. There's no way I'm going to try to find my way out of here in the dark. It was scary enough getting here . . . and Bev was sober then."

"Would you mind if I prayed?" Terri asked, sniffing.

"Suit yourself," Karen responded, surprised. Terri really thought a prayer would help? This was one deluded girl. After tonight, she knew prayers weren't answered.

"Would you join me?"

That was where Karen drew the line. Everything she had ever believed in had turned out to be a lie, prayer included.

"Karen?"

"You go ahead," Karen said. Unlike Edie, she wasn't a hypocrite.

* * *

"It'll be a miracle if we ever find Beyer again," Sheriff Latimer exclaimed. He still couldn't believe Walter had let that man escape. When he had arrived at City Hall, he had found Walter and Lucille tied up and gagged on the floor of the main office. Beyer had disappeared with Walter's gun and several rounds of ammunition.

"We could bring in those dogs from the Pocatello department. They could get here in less than two hours," Walter suggested, eager to prove himself after his embarrassing blunder.

"I've already made arrangements for them to arrive first thing in the morning to track down our missing girls. We're wondering if they headed up one of these canyons somewhere. This late, it would be like looking for a needle in a haystack."

"We're giving up the search tonight?" Walter asked.

"No, several men are still out looking right now. Most are volunteers. We've asked everyone to keep in close contact, especially since this Beyer character is on the loose."

"What about Roger's ex-wife?"

"She's stayin' at the hospital with her mama. It'll be easier to keep an eye on her that way. I've got one man stationed near the hospital to keep track of things there," the sheriff explained.

"What about Adele's house?"

The sheriff gave the deputy a pained look. "Do I have 'stupid' written all over my face?" he asked, irritated.

"No, sir."

"We've brought in the state and county police on this one. We have a man keeping an eye on that house even as we speak. Beyer hasn't shown up there. No tellin' where that man will head. If he was smart, he'd hightail it out of the state."

"How?" Walter asked.

Sheriff Latimer gave Walter a long, hard stare. "Beyer seems to be quite adept at making the most out of *any* opportunity." Turning, he reached for the radio, anxious to see if anyone had spotted Beyer or the girls.

* * *

"Okay, let's not panic," Mike tried to say as calmly as he could. "We'll find them. I know the forests around here very well."

"He does," Greg Erickson echoed, trying to ease his wife's heart.

"That's the only place we haven't looked. That has to be where they're at," Mike added.

"What about that crazy man who escaped from jail?" Sue asked worriedly.

"The police are looking for him," Mike replied.

"Do you think he did anything to those girls?" Sue pressed.

Mike glanced at Kate. It was a possibility that couldn't be ruled out. But it wouldn't do to panic everyone, especially if the girls were all right.

"This is my fault. I never should've sent Sabrina with Bev and Karen," Kate moaned, sinking down on the couch.

Sue glanced at Mike, then at her oldest daughter, someone who had been looking extremely pale all evening. Moving away from Greg, Sue sat next to Kate on the couch. "Kate, it's not your fault . . . no one's blaming you for this. I thought the same thing you did— that it would help cheer Sabrina up." She reached for a hug, drawing Kate against her. "We'll find those girls. It'll be okay. It has to be!"

* * *

"What a night this has been," Margo Jeppson wailed. Doris did her best to comfort the woman, but was convinced it was an impossible task. "First my daughter disappears. Then an armed killer is on the loose—"

"I don't think this man has ever killed anyone," Doris interjected. "I can't get hold of my husband . . ."

All but rolling her eyes, Doris wondered how she was going to get this woman to pull herself together. She reminded herself that Margo did have a reason to be distraught. She would be too if her daughter was missing and an armed man was on the loose. Suddenly, Doris felt close to tears herself. Especially when she thought about Bev and Karen, not to mention Kate's little sister, Sabrina. Here it was, nearly midnight, and still there had been no sign of those four girls.

Earlier, Doris had called her husband, telling him that she might not be coming home tonight. She had explained the situation, adding that if anything changed, she would let him know.

"How am I going to get though this?" Margo sobbed, wiping her nose on Doris' shoulder.

Doris flinched, but continued to hold the woman. "This should be Cleo's job," she thought to herself. "Cleo's the one who sent Terri off on this adventure."

Earlier that evening Cleo had confessed to everything, looking to Kate and Doris for sympathy. "I didn't ask her to go out at night . . . to follow those girls around like that," Cleo had said in her defense.

"No, you asked her to bring you the name of the person responsible for the editorials!" Doris had exclaimed. "You didn't tell her how . . . you just told her to do it! Knowing Terri as we do, did it ever occur to you that you were placing her in a precarious situation?!"

"I never dreamed she'd do anything like this," Cleo had stammered.

"We won't get anywhere pointing fingers at each other," Kate had said, glancing at both women.

Kate's right, Doris thought. *This mess is bad enough. I won't add to it by saying things I'll regret later.* Tightening her grip on Margo, she spoke soothingly until the younger woman began to calm down.

* * *

Mike jumped to his feet at the sound of the recently fixed doorbell. He didn't expect to see his home teachers standing at the front door. Kate was equally surprised by their appearance.

"We came as soon as we heard," George Rogers said, nervously exchanging glances with his partner, Ryan Shaft. "Is there anything we can do?"

"Come in," Mike invited, stepping to the side.

The two home teachers entered the already crowded living room and nodded as introductions were quickly made between them and Kate's parents.

"I hear everyone is gathering at City Hall," Ryan said. "George and I thought we'd head over, unless there's something else you'd like us to do."

Mike glanced at his wife, then at his mother-in-law. "Well, we were thinking of giving these two a priesthood blessing, to ease their minds. Then Kate's father and I were heading over to City Hall ourselves."

"Could we help?" George offered. "I happen to have some consecrated oil in my pocket," he said pulling out his set of keys. Attached to his key chain was a small vial.

"Sure," Greg replied. Moving to the chair they had set in the middle of the living room, they began with Sue.

CHAPTER 29

Outside City Hall, Mike ran into his co-worker, Brett Randall. According to Brett, the police wanted all available forest personnel to gather at that location. Hurrying inside, they caught each other up-to-date on what they'd last heard about the missing girls. They made their way into the small auditorium, grateful so many residents had gathered to help.

Sheriff Latimer was another who was extremely grateful for the support they had received from the community. Those who had already been out looking were starting to come in, exhausted, cold, and in need of nourishment. Several women from around the town had made up sandwiches, coffee, and hot chocolate, and were now in the auditorium serving these items. It seemed like this entire valley was pulling together, anxious to help in any way they could during this emergency.

In a far corner of the room, James Henderson paced back and forth like a caged animal. He had been out driving around the county for hours and had finally come in to see if anyone else had had better luck. The sheriff watched him for several seconds, renewing his earlier commitment to do whatever it took to find those four girls. Sheriff Latimer and his wife had raised five beautiful daughters. Two were married, two were off to college, one was still home, the same age as James' daughter. He could only imagine what James and the other parents were going through. Clearing his throat, the sheriff began trying to bring order to this assembly of determined individuals.

* * *

Roger Beyer cautiously made his way along the narrow canyon road. He kept the deputy's gun in his hand, its familiar shape giving him a sense of security. He had taken a man's jacket from the car he had stolen earlier, stuffing its pockets with ammunition. The car he had *borrowed* from the theater parking lot in Blaketown had just run out of gas. That was his luck lately. Nothing ever seemed to work out according to plan. Which is why he had come home to Blaketown. California had become too uncomfortable. Bills had piled up. The rent on his small apartment was four months overdue. The police were constantly on his case, convinced he was part of a drug ring, which he wasn't. He did have some standards; dealing drugs was beneath him.

Nothing more than a two-bit hustler, Roger went from job to job, taking advantage of whatever opportunities came his way. He had managed to make a fairly decent living for a while, hocking stolen goods he had swiped from the places he worked. Items that usually weren't missed until he had moved on or was fired for some other company infringement. His hot temper was usually the culprit; he didn't appreciate anyone telling him what to do.

He had been between jobs when his mother called with the news that Edie was out of prison. Unable to resist the temptation to see his ex-wife again, Roger had headed to Blaketown. He wanted to see Edie beaten, humbled, submissive, ready for him to take over her life again. There had been several other women in his life, but Edie always haunted his dreams.

As he trudged along the darkened road, Roger's frown deepened. Edie had changed all right, and in his opinion, it wasn't for the better. She was acting like she was something more than what he knew her to be. It infuriated him to see her look at him condescendingly, as she had done tonight. He hadn't seen respect or fear in her eyes. Instead, he had seen self-righteousness, anger, and an inner pride that refused to be silenced.

He took satisfaction in knowing he had managed to hurt someone Edie cared about. That was one way he could make her suffer. Roger grinned, wondering if Edie had found her mother yet. If he was really lucky, maybe that old battle-ax was dead. Adele Hadley had been a thorn in his side for much too long. Always letting him know he wasn't good enough for her daughter. Always complaining that he wasn't treating Edie right. Tonight he had shown Adele what he thought of her objections. There were other scores to settle, but they would have to wait for another time. Presently, he needed to get as far away from this town as possible. Then later, when things had quieted down, he would sneak back into town and make certain Edie would never forget him. Grinning at the thought, he picked up his pace, ducking behind a tall bush when a pair of headlights approached.

It would be daylight soon; the darkness was lifting. He had no idea what time it was. Time didn't really matter if he could just find a way out of this place. He walked another three miles, then tiring, wandered down into a campground. A nearby restroom was open and he walked in to use the public facilities. The water had been turned on in anticipation of the approaching tourist season. Roger ran the water in the sink, splashing its coldness on his face, then drank until he was satisfied.

Exploring the campground, he looked for anything he could use. He found a thin, dusty rope someone had left behind and attached it to one of his belt loops. Next, he came across a rusty pocketknife that must've been under the snow all winter. It wasn't much good, but he slipped it into his pocket. He started searching the individual campsites and came up with a soggy matchbook, a half-eaten candy bar, and a discarded pack of cigarettes. The pack was nearly half full.

"Roger, things are looking up," he said, pleased by that find. He tried a couple of the matches, but they were too wet to ignite. Snorting his disgust, he stuffed the matches and cigarettes into the pocket of his jeans, and ate the candy bar. It was time to get moving, something he would have to do to stay ahead of the lawmen he knew would be out looking for him. Most of them weren't as gullible as Walter. Walter was young and inexperienced. Roger had taken full advantage of that, realizing it might be his only chance to escape. Now, he had to keep this lucky trend going. He was a great believer in luck. It went one way or another. Currently, the tide was turning in his favor. That had to be a good sign.

As he made his way back toward the campground turnoff, he spied something that convinced him things were going his way. A deserted vehicle. He hurried forward, making certain no one was around. The dark-colored Jeep Cherokee was locked. Wishing he had the bag of tools he'd left at his mother's place, he looked around for a rock. He found one about the size of his fist and smashed one of the back windows. Reaching inside, he unlocked the door and climbed into the vehicle. He pulled himself over the front seat and examined the steering wheel. No keys in sight. Not a problem. He'd just hot-wire the thing—a talent he had acquired in California.

A few minutes later, the engine purred contentedly. Roger glanced at the gas gauge, an option he didn't have earlier. Earlier, he'd had to hurry. Now, he had time to make certain things were under control. He had half a tank of gas. That should get him to Pocatello. From there, he'd work something else out. He searched the glove box and found an owner's manual, the registration, and some receipts.

"Well, well, well," Roger gloated, "James Henderson. The car man himself. I'm mighty obliged to you sir," he laughed. He reached under the seat, and pulled out a wallet. It contained a twenty-dollar bill and some loose change, which he quickly pocketed. Roger then studied Bev Henderson's driver's license. Bev had driven this up here? Roger smiled. This *was* his lucky day. He knew his daughter, Karen, ran around with this girl. He wondered if the two of them were nearby. This opportunity might grant him some added leverage, not to mention a chance to make things mighty uncomfortable for Edie. Grinning, he shut off the engine and climbed out of the car. As the sky continued to lighten, making it easier to see, he spotted a thin wisp of smoke rising above a cluster of trees not too far from here. He set the pistol inside of a jacket pocket, zipping it for safe-keeping, then began to walk in the direction of the smoke.

* * *

Karen moaned. She had been having another nightmare, one where she had helplessly watched as her mother staggered from bar to bar. Twisting on the hard ground, she moaned again, then woke up. She blinked, trying to clear her head.

"Morning, princess," a deep voice called out to her.

Startled, Karen quickly sat up, staring at her father. "What are you doing here?" she hissed, glancing at the other girls. Everyone else was still asleep. She hadn't seen this man in nearly two years, but knew exactly who he was.

"Looking for you," Roger replied, grinning. He lit one of his cigarettes from the smoldering fire and stuck it in his mouth, inhaling deeply. He blew out a puff of smoke and smiled at his daughter. "I found Bev's outfit and figured you'd be with her."

"Did Mom send you to find me?" Karen sullenly asked. She'd had no idea this man was back in Blaketown. Would her life always take these strange twists?

Roger laughed. "Little girl, your mama has no idea where you are. I intend to keep it that way."

Karen glared at her father, wondering what he was up to. "What do you want?"

"You," he said, still grinning.

There had been a time in her life when she would've given anything to hear him say that. Now, she sensed it wasn't a good thing. "I don't know what's going on here, but—"

"It's best you don't. Now, grab your stuff and let's go." Roger stood. He reached for her arm and pulled her to her feet.

"Karen?" Terri sleepily asked. "Who's that man?"

"You go on back to sleep," Roger encouraged. "I'm her father. I'm taking her home."

"Home?" Terri repeated. Suddenly, her eyes widened. She sat up. "Can I come with you? I need to get home, too."

"I've only got room for Karen," Roger impatiently said, tapping the ashes from his cigarette onto the ground. His luck couldn't change, not now.

"But my mom will be so worried," Terri continued, brushing the pine needles from her clothes.

"You can ride home with these other girls," Roger replied.

"Terri, for once in your life, don't argue," Karen pleaded, seeing the anger in her father's expression.

Bev sat up, holding her head. "Oh, man," she groaned. "Could you all just keep it down?" She opened her eyes, then gaped at Karen and her father.

"Let's get out of here," Roger said, pushing his daughter ahead of him.

Focusing on Karen and the man who was shoving her around, Bev continued to stare. "Where are you taking her?" she demanded, trying to stand.

"None of your business," Roger responded. "I'm her father," he said, tightly gripping Karen's arm. "She's coming with me."

Bev glanced at Karen, seeing the fear in her friend's face. "Let her go," she said, remembering what Karen had said yesterday about her father. This wasn't a man to be trusted.

"It's okay, Bev," Karen lied, anxious to get her father away from these other girls before someone got hurt. "I'll go with him."

"What is going on?" Sabrina groaned. Her head felt like it was going to explode and everyone was yelling around her.

Deciding to ignore the other girls, Roger continued to push Karen away from the fire. "Let's get out of here," he commanded, shoving her out of sight.

"Karen?" Bev called out, certain her friend was in trouble. She tried to think, but her head pounded, reminding her of the *fun* she had had the night before. "Listen you guys, we can't let him take her like this. Something's wrong."

"Isn't he Karen's father?" Terri asked, still upset that he wouldn't take her along, too.

"He is . . . but in name only," Bev replied, rubbing her aching head. "He abandoned Karen years ago. He's never wanted anything to do with her."

"Then why does he want her now?" Terri asked, starting to pick up on Bev's concern.

"I'm not sure," Bev replied, "but I don't like it. C'mon, we need to follow them. I think Karen needs our help." She glanced around. The sun was starting to peek over the mountains. It wouldn't be too difficult to find her way around now. Reaching over, she shook Sabrina. "Hey, wake up!"

"I'm awake," Sabrina mumbled. "Don't yell."

"Let's go. We're getting out of here," Bev said.

"What about the fire?" Terri asked. It was still smoldering. She had always been taught at girls' camp that all campfires had to be properly extinguished before leaving the area.

"It's in a pit. It'll die out on its own," Bev said, heading the direction Karen and her father had left. "Are you coming or what?"

Terri nodded, glancing back at Sabrina who was still on the ground, groaning. "Sabrina, we're leaving."

"I heard," Sabrina snapped. She had never felt this rotten in her life. Shakily standing, she suddenly bolted into the brush, losing the contents of her stomach. "Wait up," she hollered a few minutes later, white as a sheet. Staggering forward, she broke through the brush behind Terri.

* * *

Greg Erickson teamed up with George and Ryan, the two home teachers, and headed off to search up a canyon behind George's ranch. Mike and Brett took James Henderson with them, going in the opposite direction to check out some of the local campgrounds. They drove around for a couple of hours, then stopped by a campground that Brett had recently inspected for the coming tourist season. As they drove near the restrooms, James spied his Jeep and let out a surprised yell. Stopping the Blazer, Mike, Brett, and James hurried out to investigate.

Alarmed, James pointed out the broken window. Who had broken that window and why? Wires had been pulled out underneath the steering column. He stared at his daughter's empty wallet. Where was she? What had happened? Mike hurried back to his Blazer to radio in what they had discovered.

"James," Mike called out a few minutes later, walking back to the Jeep. "The state police are on their way here to check things out. They said not to touch anything; they'll dust it for fingerprints."

James nodded. He had guessed that much. His stomach twisted again. Bev had to be okay. He wouldn't let himself believe otherwise.

Brett walked back up from the restroom. "Someone's been in there recently," he informed the other two men.

"What did you find?" Mike asked.

"The first thing I noticed were the tracks. There are boot prints all over this area." He paused. "Roger was wearing cowboys boots."

Mike glanced down at the ground, seeing that was true. He turned to Brett. "Did you find anything in the restroom?"

"Someone left the water running. I was through this area yesterday afternoon before I picked up Edie. Everything was shut off tight then. So sometime between then and this morning, someone was in there."

"The men's side?" Mike guessed.

Brett nodded.

"Now what?" James asked, anxious to head into the forest to start searching.

"Mike, look over there," Brett exclaimed, pointing to the thin column of grey smoke rising above the forest.

"A fire?" James asked.

Mike nodded. "I think we'd better take a look," he said. "James, use my radio to contact the police. Tell them we found a fire up here."

"You two are going over there?" James asked.

"Yes," Mike replied, motioning to Brett.

"But didn't the police say to stay put . . . ?" James started to protest.

"We know this area well. We'll be careful. If those girls are here, we need to find them before Roger does."

"I'm coming with you," James said stubbornly.

"We need you to stay here and make radio contact. And just so you know, there's a handgun in the glove box of my Blazer. Hopefully you won't need it, but Roger is armed and considered dangerous." Moving to the Blazer, Mike grabbed a rifle out of the back. "We'll take this tranquilizer gun. That should take care of him if we come across the guy."

"Good luck," James said, reaching to shake Mike's hand.

"We'll probably need it," Mike replied. Turning, he led Brett into the forest.

* * *

"That idiot is going the wrong way," Bev said through clenched teeth. Each step she took seemed to make the pounding in her head worse. "He's going to get us all lost!"

Terri gaped at Bev. "You don't know where we are?"

"I do! That's the problem. He doesn't. He's dragging Karen out into the middle of this forest! This is as far as I've ever explored." Bev glanced around. This area was already starting to look unfamiliar. She was well aware of how easy it was to get turned around out here.

"Could we mark our trail?" Sabrina asked. "Then we could find our way back."

"Good idea," Bev replied. "What can we use?"

The three girls looked around at the bushes and pine trees.

"I don't suppose anyone has a pocket knife?" Terri asked.

Bev carefully shook her head. Sudden movement was extremely painful.

"No," Sabrina responded.

"Well, whatever we do, we need to hurry or we'll lose them," Bev reminded them.

"Hey, wait, here's a nail file," Sabrina said, pulling it out of her coat pocket. She handed it to Terri.

"This isn't very sharp," Terri observed, "but it'll have to do." The other two watched as she half-cut, half-tore a piece of the thin blanket she had kept wrapped around herself. She then tied it to a tree. "There, we should be able to find that. I'll keep ripping off pieces as we go to mark our trail."

"Good plan," Bev said, surprised. Terri was more resourceful than she had ever thought possible. Deciding not to dwell on that, Bev led the way as they tried to pick up the trail Karen and her father were following. Momentarily stumped, she stopped until she saw a bent twig, then hurried forward, the other girls following behind.

* * *

"I can't believe this is taking so long," Roger panted. He didn't remember walking this far from the Jeep. Coughing, he threw what was left of his cigarette into a small creek. He then turned and looked at his daughter. This girl was the spitting image of her mother. Curious, he wondered if Karen had inherited anything from him.

"Are you sure you know where you're going?" Karen asked.

"She's got her mother's disposition too," Roger thought to himself. He itched to strike his daughter, but managed to contain his anger. Not yet. Not until they were out of this forest. Then he'd make sure this smart aleck knew who was in charge. "Don't *you* know your way out of here?" he countered.

Karen shook her head. "Bev led us to that grove. I have no idea how to find our way out."

Roger angrily swore. His luck had changed again, and not for the better. "Keep moving," he grunted, shoving his daughter forward.

They had to come to that campground sooner or later. He hoped sooner. He was running out of time.

* * *

Startled by a car driving by, Sue opened her eyes. She and Kate had fallen asleep on the couch, waiting for news. Now extremely stiff, she slowly stood, trying to stretch out the kinks.

"Ooooh," Kate groaned. "What time is it?"

Sue glanced at her watch. "It's nearly seven."

"When did we fall asleep?"

"I'm not sure. The last time I looked at my watch it was around four." She moved toward the kitchen to check out the answering machine, hoping someone had called while they were sleeping. Disappointed that they hadn't, she glanced back at Kate. "Still no word."

"Mike said he'd try to let us know if he heard or found anything." Rising, Kate began to stretch. Turning extremely pale, she suddenly bolted for the bathroom.

"Kate, what's wrong?" Sue asked, following her oldest daughter.

Kate's retching answered that question.

* * *

Doris refilled Margo's glass with apple juice. Earlier, Terri's mother had insisted she wanted to fast for her daughter's safe return. That was before she had nearly passed out.

"I did have a few episodes of low blood sugar during my last pregnancy," Margo had haltingly explained.

Taking matters into her own hands—again—Doris had quickly fixed Margo and her noisy younger children some breakfast, whipping together scrambled eggs, toast, and juice. Doris refrained from eating, choosing to participate in the stake-sponsored fast their town had been holding since late last night. Her stomach growled in protest as she watched Margo and her family eat. "It'll be all right," she silently assured herself. "This too will pass."

* * *

"Mommy?"

Gina Henderson glanced up from where she had been crying.

"Why are you so sad?" three-year-old Jake asked. His brother stood beside him, waiting for an answer.

"Because your sister is still missing," Gina replied.

"But we prayed she'd be all right," Drake pointed out.

"Yes we did," Gina agreed.

"Then we shouldn't cry," Jake said.

"Sometimes mommies aren't as strong as little boys," Gina said, pulling her sons against her. Holding them close, she continued to cry.

* * *

"I'm fine, Edie," Adele insisted as her daughter nervously fussed over her. Today the bruise on her face looked worse; the brilliant purple color descended from her forehead to her cheek on the right side.

"I want to make sure you're comfortable," Edie returned, setting the pillow she had fluffed up behind her mother's head.

"You've been a wonderful nurse, but you need to start taking care of yourself," Adele softly chided. "You haven't eaten a thing all morning."

"I can't, Mom," Edie said, trying not to cry. She'd already given herself a stress headache. She prayed fervently that Brett would find her daughter.

"Why don't you go home and get some rest?"

"I'm not leaving you alone," Edie argued, sitting down in a chair beside the hospital bed. "Besides, the police said they'd rather have us here together where they can protect us."

"I know," Adele sighed. She reached for her daughter's hand, giving it a squeeze. "I keep feeling like it will all work out."

"I hope you're right," Edie responded.

"Edie, why don't you pray with me, now?"

Edie gazed at her mother. "I'm not sure I can."

"We'll do it together," Adele invited. Closing her eyes, she began to offer one of the most beautiful prayers Edie had ever heard.

CHAPTER 30

"Where did they go?" Bev asked, panicking. She waited until the other girls had caught up with her.

"I'm glad you stopped. I need a break," Sabrina gasped.

Terri nodded, breathing fast and hard. They had kept up a brisk pace, trying to stay with Karen and her father. Terri had barely enough time to wrap a few trees with bits and pieces of the blanket along the way.

"I don't know which way they went from here," Bev said, whirling around. Thick trees hemmed them in on all sides. "This was really stupid! We should've gone back to the Jeep. We could've rounded up some help. Now we don't know where we are, and we've lost them!"

A gunshot shattered the air and they heard Karen scream.

"NO!" Bev cried out, running in that direction.

* * *

"You didn't have to shoot it," Karen muttered, looking away from the dead snake. She wiggled out of the heavy coat Bev had loaned her. The way they had kept moving, she was overheated.

"Listen, little girl," Roger snarled, "I've had it up to here with your mouth." He held one hand near the top of his head. "That could've been a rattler."

Karen glowered at her father. "It wasn't. It was a little water snake. I didn't even see it until you shot it." For a minute, she had thought he was shooting at her.

Roger stuck the gun back in his jacket pocket, zipped it, and grabbed hold of Karen, shaking her. "I tried to save your life, do you understand?" He flung her back, watching as she fell into a tree. She cried out as a rough branch grazed her arm. "There, now see what you made me do?!" he angrily sputtered. He pulled her to her feet, glancing at her arm. "That isn't so bad," he grumbled. "Quit your whining." Picking up her coat, he threw it at her. He didn't want to leave any trace of them behind. "C'mon, let's go," he said, waiting for her to move in front of him.

Angrily wiping at the hot tears sliding down her face, Karen walked in the direction her father had pointed.

* * *

"Bev?" Terri called out. "BEV?!"

"Not so loud," Sabrina begged, rubbing at her head. Whoever said getting drunk was fun was a liar. This was awful. Something she was determined to never try again.

"Down here," came a plaintive cry.

Terri walked over to a nearby tree and looked down. This area was very deceptive. It had stretched out flat for miles, but just beyond this grove of trees was a sharp incline. One Bev had plummeted down in her haste to save Karen. "Are you all right?" Terri asked, carefully making her way down to where Bev lay in a tumbled heap.

"Do I look okay?" Bev retorted. She tried to move, then grimaced in pain. "This is all we need right now!" As she had fallen, she had plowed into a fallen tree, one leg wedging underneath it at a painful angle.

"Is she hurt?" Sabrina called down. She wasn't sure she could make it down this hill. It seemed extremely steep.

"Yes," Terri replied. "Grab what's left of that blanket and bring it down, I think we're going to need it."

Sabrina quickly found the blanket and then cautiously slid down to the other two girls. She glanced at Bev's leg. "That looks broken," she said, remembering a similar incident at girls' camp two years ago. A girl had fallen on their hike, breaking one leg.

"You're a doctor!?" Bev snapped, her face ashen. All she could think of was Karen. What had happened to Karen? Tears began racing down her face.

Kneeling beside Bev, Sabrina took off her coat, placing it over the injured girl. It wouldn't be good to have her go into shock. Sabrina struggled to remember the first-aid training she had received every summer at girls' camp. What was she supposed to do after treating the patient for shock? She glanced around, looking for Terri.

"Let's see if we can pull her out from under that tree," Terri said, stepping out of a group of trees with two good-sized branches. She set them on the ground and moved to Bev's side.

Sabrina nodded and knelt down by Bev's other side. On the count of three, they gently drew Bev out from under the fallen tree. Bev gasped sharply, then lay still.

"She's unconscious," Sabrina exclaimed.

"Now what?" Terri asked, starting to panic. That wasn't supposed to happen.

Checking Bev's pulse, Sabrina relaxed. "I think it was the pain," she commented, checking Bev's pupils. They looked normal. She checked both of Bev's ears, but there was no sign of fluid.

"What are you doing?" Terri asked.

"Checking her vital signs," Sabrina responded. "I think she's in shock, but we'll keep her warm. She should be okay."

"I brought these. I thought maybe we could splint her leg," Terri said, reaching for the branches.

"You went to girls' camp, too?" Sabrina guessed, smiling at the other girl.

Terri stared, then forced a smile. "You're LDS?"

Sabrina slowly nodded, realizing she hadn't been setting much of an example.

"Kate's in my ward," Terri commented.

Blinking, Sabrina thought of her older sister. She wondered how Kate would handle this situation. One girl wounded. Another one probably dead. Sabrina closed her eyes. This couldn't be happening. "Let's get that leg immobilized," she said finally, gesturing to the branches.

* * *

"Feeling any better?" Sue asked, sitting down beside Kate at the kitchen table.

"I think the nausea is starting to let up," Kate replied, taking another sip of the herbal tea her mother had made. "I hope I don't have the flu."

"It's probably all of the commotion going on," Sue said, running a hand through her hair. "Why haven't they found those girls yet?"

"I wish I knew, Mom," Kate tearfully responded. "Maybe we should go out looking for them."

Sue shook her head. "Not a good idea, considering the shape you're in this morning."

"I'm feeling better."

Glancing at her daughter's pallid face, Sue didn't buy that story at all. "Besides, we promised your father and your husband we would stay put. Neither of us know this area very well. We'd probably end up lost, and that's not going to help anybody." She forced a smile. "We can do something, though, we can keep praying for the safe return of those girls."

Kate slowly nodded, reluctantly admitting there was nothing else they could do at this point.

* * *

"They found this where?" Edie asked, staring at the small notebook the police officer had handed her.

"James Henderson said Brett Randall found it where the girls must've camped last night. They said for you to read it, that it would explain a great deal. After you've finished, I'll take it to Terri Jeppson's mother."

"Don't forget about Kate Jeffries and her mother," Edie reminded the officer.

"We'll make sure everyone hears what we've found," he replied.

Edie glanced at her mother, then at the notebook in her hand. She opened it and began to read it aloud, so her mother could hear what it had to say. Several minutes later, Edie handed it back to the officer. He nodded politely and left the room.

"Karen thought I was drinking again," Edie said, stunned by this news. She closed her eyes, leaning against the wall. "I can't imagine what was going through her mind, especially after our talk. I promised her I would never drink again. If she thought I was— No wonder she disappeared last night. She's probably out to show me just how she feels."

Adele frowned. "It says right in that notebook Karen was the only one who wouldn't drink."

Opening her eyes, Edie sadly gazed at her mother. "That's the last thing it says. What happened next? Where are they? Why didn't they come home?"

Unable to answer, Adele looked away. It cut through her to see the terror in her daughter's eyes.

* * *

Margo glanced around the crowded living room. Doris was still here. In addition, Cleo Partridge and Gina Henderson as well as Kate Jeffries and her mother had been summoned to the Jeppson residence by Sheriff Latimer, who was still trying to put the pieces of this puzzle together.

Clearing his throat, the sheriff began. "Miss Partridge, if I understand this right, you asked Terri to find out who had been writing these editorials?"

Cleo glanced at Doris, then at Margo, and then finally at the sheriff. "Yes," she said, clasping her hands together. "Those editorials were becoming a nuisance. But I didn't mean for Terri to—"

"And according to you, Margo," he interrupted, unwilling to hear any more excuses (he'd heard too many already from a certain young deputy), "your daughter last called around six o'clock last night."

Margo nodded. She watched as the officer skimmed through Terri's notebook. She still couldn't believe her daughter had been spying on those girls, and on Doris and Kate as well.

"Now, according to this little book, after these young ladies saw Karen's mother go into the bar, Karen was very upset and they all headed over to Bev's house." He glanced at Gina for confirmation.

"Yes," Gina replied. "They took some of Bev's coats, flashlights, maybe some matches."

"According to this book, they also took a bottle of wine."

Gina turned a deep shade of crimson. She had suspected Bev had a problem, but had never been able to convince James. She wondered if he would listen now.

Sue glanced nervously at Kate. Wine? What had those girls done? How far had they gone to cheer Karen up?

"Then, they loaded in the Jeep and headed up the canyon, where everyone but Karen proceeded to get drunk," Sheriff Latimer stated.

Sue's eyes widened. "Sabrina got drunk?"

The sheriff glanced at the notebook and nodded. "Yes ma'am, according to this, she did. It sounds like those young ladies had themselves a little party up the canyon."

Margo cleared her throat quite loudly.

"We all know Terri didn't get drunk," the sheriff quickly amended, scratching his balding head. "That daughter of yours is quite a reporter," he added, smiling at Margo. "This book proves that Roger Beyer had nothing to do with their disappearance. At least, until we lost track of where he went last night."

Margo gripped the arm of the couch for support.

"We have no way of knowing what time Terri made that final entry. It must've been quite dark—her handwriting gets harder and harder to read," the sheriff continued.

"You said they found the Jeep," Doris said, hoping to pry more information out of this man. She knew how worried all of these women had been.

"Yes, we did find the Jeep," the sheriff verified. He didn't want to reveal what had turned up in that vehicle: Roger Beyer's fingerprints. There was no need to panic these parents further until it was absolutely necessary. "We've got some well-trained dogs up there right now, sniffing out a trail," he said, encouragingly. "We'll find those girls."

"Do you think they just got lost?" Margo asked, clinging to that possibility.

"Could be," he replied. "Hopefully we'll find out soon."

* * *

"Smart girls," Mike said, collecting another piece of blanket from a tree. He handed it to Brett. He could hear the dogs braying behind him. From the sound of things, they had picked up this trail, too. A few minutes later, the dogs appeared. They barked at Mike and Brett, sniffed at both men, then took off running again. Mike and Brett tried to follow, using the frenzied barking as a guide. The pieces of blanket were becoming rare. It was easier to keep track of the dogs. Behind Mike and Brett ran the dogs' trainer, and two winded state troopers. Everyone had the same thought, the same prayer in their hearts. Hurrying on, they hoped to find the girls before Roger Beyer did. Mike and Brett both prayed that the sharp sound they had heard earlier wasn't what they feared. Running forward, they raced against time and a growing sense of futility.

* * *

"Mom?" Bev called out as the image of her mother blended with a disturbing likeness of Gina.

"Not quite," Sabrina replied. She moved away from the makeshift stretcher that she and Terri were trying to construct out of tree branches, the remains of the blanket, and Terri's jacket. They had decided to leave Sabrina's coat in place as a cover for Bev to keep her warm. Sabrina smiled reassuringly at Bev. "How are you feeling?"

Bev winced, then glared up at Sabrina.

Sabrina patted Bev's shoulder sympathetically. "Hang in there. We're going to get you out of here." She and Terri had decided their best bet was to carry Bev out the way they had come. If they could manage to get Bev back up to the top of this incline, they would follow the blanket pieces Terri had tied along their trail. Terri had her day permit and could drive Bev's Jeep when they reached the campground. Once they were in Blaketown, they would send someone up after Karen and her father.

Sabrina had tried very hard not to think about Karen the past hour. They had all heard the shot and Karen's scream. Since then, there had been nothing. Sabrina's eyes filled with tears. She hadn't known Karen very long, but had already come to think of her as a friend. She didn't want to think about her being hurt. Another troubling thought plagued her. What if that horrible man came back this way? They had to hurry and get out of here. She moved back to the stretcher and worked with Terri to finish attaching the blanket and jacket securely to the sturdy branches they had broken off a nearby tree.

* * *

"I'm tired. I've got to stop," Karen panted.

For once, Roger agreed with her. He had been on the run most of the night. Exhausted, he motioned to a large rock and had her climb on top of it where he could keep an eye on her. He settled back against a tree, telling himself he would just rest for a couple of minutes. Ten minutes later, he couldn't keep his eyes open. Karen watched as he dozed lightly, then fell into a deep sleep. She waited several minutes to make sure before quietly crawling down from the rock. Slipping past her father, she noiselessly crept several yards, then broke into a run, hoping she was heading back the way they had come.

CHAPTER 31

Bev gripped the side of the stretcher to keep from screaming. It was killing her, getting up this hill. She knew these two girls were doing the best they could, but right now, she wished she had another bottle of wine. Then she wouldn't care how much this hurt. She wouldn't care that her best friend was probably dead.

She moaned, thinking of Karen. Guilt consumed her. If she hadn't dragged Karen up here, none of this would've happened. Unwanted tears burned from her eyes, forcing their release.

Out of breath, Terri stopped and looked at Sabrina. This was much harder than they had anticipated. Terri's gaze shifted to Bev. Bev's tears tugged at her heart. Trying to block out what she was feeling, she gripped her end of the stretcher and began making her way back up the hill.

* * *

Karen's side ached. She stopped running and leaned against a tree for support. Gasping for air, she almost didn't hear the growl behind her. Slowly she turned around, staring at the large mountain lion. It roared its displeasure at her again, creeping closer. Paralyzed with fear, Karen began to earnestly pray for help. If there was a God, she hoped he was listening now.

* * *

Another shot rang out. Sabrina nearly dropped the stretcher. They had almost made it to the top of the hill. To drop it now would've been disastrous. As it was, it caused Bev excruciating pain.

Bev shouted an obscenity, glaring up at Sabrina. Then she glared past Sabrina's shoulder. "What did he do? Miss her the first time?" She began to laugh hysterically.

Sabrina exchanged a worried glance with Terri. Quickly, they finished climbing the hill, setting the stretcher down when they reached the top.

"Bev, settle down," Sabrina said, trying to calm her friend. "We can't do anything to help Karen right now. But we can help you."

"No. Leave me," Bev suddenly said, her eyes filling with tears again. "This is all my fault. Just leave me. I don't care if he finds me. I don't care if I die!"

Terri knelt down beside the stretcher and grabbed Bev's arm. "Well I care," she said firmly. "I care very much and we're all going to get out of here, okay?!"

"Karen won't," Bev argued. "She won't ever get out of here."

"Maybe," Terri muttered. She stood, gesturing for Sabrina to pick up her end of the stretcher. She picked up the other end and the two girls began toting their reluctant patient back the way they had come.

* * *

Mike and Brett had stopped for several seconds, trying to catch their breath. They were both in excellent shape, but were no match for the dogs. When the second shot rang out, there was little doubt in their minds what they had heard. Grim-faced, they pushed themselves forward, fearing what they would find.

* * *

"That's twice now I've saved your scrawny hide," Roger said gruffly, glowering at his daughter. He had missed hitting the mountain lion, but the shot had scared it off. "Just where did you think you were going?"

Karen slid down the tree into a sitting position and began to cry.

"You are just like your mother, do you know that!" Roger said, exasperated. That's what Edie had always done; she had always burst into tears over the silliest things.

"I am nothing like my mother!" Karen said, the anger triggered by that comparison pushing away the fear.

"And what makes you such an expert?" Roger shot back.

"I will never become a drunken lush like she is!"

Roger grinned. This was interesting! Karen hated her mother? Even detested the woman who was trying so hard to give her a good life? Maybe Edie was already being punished, having to live in the same house with this ungrateful brat. Maybe the best way he could hurt Edie was to send this creature back home to Blaketown.

"I saw her go into a bar last night, after she promised she wouldn't drink anymore!" Karen continued, no longer able to keep it all inside.

Rubbing at the brown stubble on his chin, Roger laughed. "I saw your mama last night in that very bar," he said, deciding to enjoy this opportunity. "She made a real fool out of herself."

"I'm sure she did," Karen said, standing. "Let's go," she said, unwilling to hear anymore.

"She got herself all liquored up, then went around the room, begging drinks off every man in that place."

"I don't want to hear this!" Karen exclaimed, putting her hands over her ears.

Roger grabbed her, pulling her hands away, forcing her to listen. "You have a right to know what kind of sleaze is raising you," he said, loving the look of disgust on Karen's face. "Your mother is nothing more than a lying tramp. She went around that room, offering herself to anyone who'd pay her a little attention. It made me sick," he lied, relishing Karen's horrified expression. "That's why I came looking for you. I thought maybe you deserved better than that. I guess I was wrong." Releasing her, he began to walk away.

"No, wait," Karen cried out, following him. "I didn't know . . . you didn't explain." She tripped over a branch, picked herself up, and ran after her father.

* * *

Bev had finally calmed down. She was staring now, up at the trees as they moved along, strangely quiet.

"Are you still with us?" Sabrina finally asked, worried.

Refusing to answer, Bev continued to stare up toward the sky.

Terri turned around, motioning for Sabrina to stop. Both girls gently set the stretcher down. "Bev," Terri tried, lightly shaking the older girl's shoulder. Bev wouldn't look at her. Shaking her head, Terri moved away from the stretcher. She stared at Bev, then at Sabrina. "I think we should pray," she said, near tears.

Sabrina didn't argue. She walked over to Terri and knelt down beside her, waiting for the other girl to say something.

"You want me to say it?" Terri asked.

Sabrina nodded. She didn't exactly feel comfortable talking to her Father in Heaven just yet. Not after last night.

"Okay," Terri agreed. Closing her eyes, she began to pray for Bev, themselves, and Karen. Then, thinking of what their parents must be going through, she asked for a special blessing to be on all of them. When she finished, she kept her eyes closed, continuing to silently beg for strength. Fear threatened to paralyze her.

"What's that sound?" Sabrina asked, nudging Terri.

"What?" Terri responded, opening her eyes.

"Listen. What is that?"

Terri quickly stood. "It sounds like dogs . . . or wolves. Dogs wouldn't be in the forest, but wolves would be." She hurried back to the stretcher. Bev was still staring upward, blocking out everything around her. "C'mon, Sabrina. We've got to get her out of here."

"How? We'll never outrun them," Sabrina replied. She looked around for something she could use as a weapon. Finding a large stick, she stood, prepared to fight whatever was coming their way. She flinched when the first dog broke through the trees, howling his excitement. She stared, certain this was a hound dog of some kind. He was followed by four others.

"Don't let them come over here," Terri said, prepared to throw herself across Bev to protect the injured young woman. "Are they wild?"

Sabrina nervously gulped. She didn't dare put down the stick in her hand, but could see that as long as she held it, the dogs weren't going to get close enough for her to tell. Then she noticed something. As they jumped, yelped and pawed at the ground, she could see that they were all wearing collars. Relaxing, she dropped the stick. A yellow Labrador retriever walked up to her and sniffed her hand. When he excitedly started barking, a startled Sabrina nearly fell to the ground.

Terri ran up behind Sabrina, determined to keep the dogs from attacking the younger girl. She stared at the dogs as most of them wagged their tails. "Where did they come from?" she asked, deciding they weren't a threat.

Sabrina shook her head, slowly standing. "I don't know, but they seem glad to see us."

"Who is making all of that noise?" Bev asked, snapping out of the shocked trance she had fallen into.

"A pack of dogs," Sabrina said, reaching to pet the yellow Labrador.

"Dogs?" Bev asked, straining to see. Her eyes widened when two men burst through the trees.

"Mike?" Sabrina exclaimed, stunned.

Waving to her, Mike bent over and grabbed his knees, trying to catch his breath. As he straightened, Sabrina snapped out of her astonished state and nearly knocked him over with a fierce embrace.

* * *

Mike thoroughly examined the stretcher Sabrina and Terri had made. It seemed sound enough. He turned, grinning at the girls. "I'm amazed with you young women. You've done remarkably well. I think we can use this to get Bev out of here."

"You can't bring in a helicopter?" Sabrina wistfully asked.

"Take a look around, baby sister. What do you think?" Mike replied, glancing at the thick trees that surrounded them. Unfortunately, as tired as they all were, the only way out of here was to walk. He had already radioed James back at the Blazer, instructing him to contact Blaketown with the news that three of the girls had been found. It would take a while for them to come down, but they would eventually make it back to town.

"Is my daughter all right?" James had asked, concerned.

"It looks like her leg is broken, but otherwise, she's fine," Mike had answered. "Sabrina and Terri are okay, too."

"What about Karen?" James had asked, releasing the button on the radio microphone.

Mike had hated to answer that question. They still were missing details. He knew what these girls suspected, but no one was sure what had happened. He didn't want word to reach Edie until they were certain. "Karen is still missing. We'll send these three out and keep tracking her," he had finally responded.

"Mike, why don't you head back with these girls," Brett now suggested.

Standing, Mike shook his head. Who knew how many more miles they would have to go to find Karen and her father? Brett's normal limp was becoming more pronounced. Of the two, Mike was in better shape to continue.

"We'll need one of you to help us find our way out of here after we find that other girl," one of the state patrolmen commented.

Brett nodded. "I'll stay with you."

"Brett, I'll stay," Mike argued.

Brett gazed intently at Mike. "I promised Edie I would find her daughter. I mean to keep that promise." A lump formed in Brett's throat. He didn't want to be the one to tell Edie that Karen was dead. But after two gunshots, and the state of mind Roger had been in, it didn't give them much hope of finding her alive.

When he saw how much this meant to his friend, Mike clapped Brett on the shoulder, then handed him the tranquilizer gun. "Keep this with you," he said. "Our prayers will be with you."

Nodding, Brett slid the strap across his shoulders and moved away from Bev's stretcher.

* * *

Several minutes later, Brett wondered if he was going to survive this forced hike. He tried to ignore the pain radiating from his shorter leg as he limped after the dogs. Behind him followed their trainer and a state trooper. The other state trooper had gone back with Mike, helping him carry Bev's stretcher. Brett pictured Roger's belligerent face, the pain that man had caused Edie, and the anger kept him moving forward.

The dogs had immediately picked up Karen's scent again, after letting them sniff a blouse she had worn the day before all of this craziness had started. They were now somewhere ahead, barking up a storm. Brett increased his pace, wondering if they were onto something. Dread and hopeful anticipation clashed within him.

Suddenly breaking into a clearing, Brett stopped, glancing around. The other men followed his example. The dogs barked again, on the other side of the clearing. Hurrying forward, Brett quickly crossed the small meadow, pointing out a deer that was as startled to see them as they were to see it. It quickly bounded away to safety as the three men ran in the opposite direction.

Brett ducked under a low-hanging branch, then straightened. They were entering another thicket. One he hadn't seen before. He adjusted the rifle on his back, and cautiously made his way forward. He didn't want to repeat the mistake Bev had made earlier when she had plunged down that steep slope. He forced his way through the thick grove of trees, coming out near a shallow creek. Walking up to the now silent dogs, he understood why they had stopped. The trail had been lost in the water. Roger Beyer had outsmarted them again.

Brett wasn't one to show a lot of emotion, but tears pricked his eyes as he realized what this meant. He impatiently waited for the other men, anxious to learn if there was another alternative.

"Sorry," the trainer quietly said. "All we can do is let them sniff things out on both sides of the creek for a while. Who knows how long they walked down or upstream."

The yellow Labrador began growling, staring into the forest on the other side of the creek. Oblivious to the dog's reaction, the state trooper kicked at a rock to show his disgust over this setback. It ricocheted off a nearby tree and splashed into the creek.

"What was that?" a loud voice asked.

The three men looked at each other as the dogs began to bark again.

"I don't know," a younger, definitely female voice replied. "But listen to those dogs."

"I hear them," the man replied. "Stay behind me. Maybe we're closer to the campground than I think."

The state trooper hid behind a tree, motioning for the others to do the same.

Brett nearly fell over backward when Karen moved into sight, walking down to the creek. Edie's daughter was all right. Everything would be okay.

"See, here's that stream we had to wade through earlier today," Karen said, glancing back at her father.

"And there are those noisy mutts. I wonder what they're doing out here?" Roger asked, nervously glancing around. He waited for several seconds, but didn't see any sign of their master.

"Maybe someone's up here hunting," Karen suggested.

"Could be," Roger said. "Hunting what, though, that's my question." He stared uneasily into the trees.

"I don't know about you, but I'm dying for a drink." Karen knelt down by the creek and cupped her hand, holding it near a rock in the middle of the flowing water. Her grandmother had once told her that water flowing over a rock was purer than what lay in the bottom of a stream. She hoped that was true. She didn't want to get ill from drinking this.

Brett couldn't believe what he was seeing. Karen was having a companionable conversation with her biological father.

Roger moved into plain sight, kneeling down at the creek. When he stuck both hands in the water, the state trooper jumped out, aiming his pistol at Roger.

"You're under arrest," the officer barked, throwing his handcuffs to Brett as Roger slowly rose to his feet.

"Karen, cross the creek and come over here," Brett said, smiling warmly.

Startled, Karen glared at Brett, then slipped an arm around her father. "Leave us alone!" she exclaimed. She had spent the past hour getting acquainted with a man she had never known. She had begun to trust him and believed she had finally discovered a parent who cared about her. "Dad, what's going on?"

Taking advantage of the situation, Roger grabbed his daughter, holding her in front of him. Retrieving the gun from his jacket pocket, he held it to her head. He had no desire to return to jail, and he knew California would love to get hold of him. No doubt there were a few warrants out for his arrest in that state, not to mention the charges he was adding up here in Idaho. "Drop your gun," Roger said to the cop.

Believing there was no choice, the officer obediently set his gun on the ground.

Stunned, betrayed, and heartbroken, Karen slumped against her father. It had all been a lie, again.

Infuriated, Brett ducked behind a tree.

"Where did he go?" Roger asked, recognizing Brett as the man who had been dating his ex-wife. The jerk who had hit him in the bar last night. "Get Hop-Along back out here!" he demanded, still holding the gun against his daughter's head.

"Brett," the officer hollered over his shoulder. "You'd best do as he says."

Ignoring all of them, Brett knelt down behind the tree, taking careful aim with the rifle in his hand. He shut one eye and looked through the scope, zeroing in on his target. He waited until Roger moved the gun away from Karen's head to point it at the state trooper. Then, without warning, Brett pulled the trigger, sending a powerful tranquilizer into Roger Beyer's hip.

Roger yelped, dropping Karen and the gun. Cursing, he pulled out the empty syringe, but the damage was done. It immediately started taking effect, his right leg collapsing underneath him.

Brett set down the rifle and ran to the creek. Wading across, he gently pulled Karen to her feet and led the sobbing girl away from her father.

CHAPTER 32

Sue hung up the phone, then reached for Greg. Unable to speak for several seconds, she clung to her husband and cried as everyone who had gathered at Kate's house feared the worst. Finally, Sue drew back, wiping at her face. "They found her!" she said hoarsely. "Sabrina's all right. Mike will bring her here as soon as he can." Silently expressing gratitude to her Father in Heaven, Sue accepted joyful hugs from Kate, Doris, and Kate's home teachers. A few minutes later as everyone continued to visit quietly, Kate headed back to the bathroom. Her stomach had been a queasy mess today. Entering the small room, she lost the little bit of lunch she had been able to keep down earlier.

* * *

On the way back to the campground, Bev silently cried, mourning the loss of her best friend. Terri finally reached to hold Bev's hand, trying to comfort her. That compassionate gesture became a lifeline for Bev. The sixteen-year-old clung to Terri's hand as they made their way down the rough trail.

An ambulance was waiting at the campground when they had finally made it out of the forest. James Henderson eagerly approached the stretcher, leaning down to give his daughter a tender kiss. Bev desperately needed his assurance that everything would be all right but once James saw that she was in pain, he turned from her, insisting that she be taken immediately to the hospital.

Sabrina and Terri tiredly climbed into the back of the ambulance with Bev and an EMT.

James hollered to his daughter that he would meet her at the hospital. "I'm proud of you, girl. You're a trooper. A real trooper!" He didn't see his daughter's tears when the ambulance door was closed.

At the hospital, four anxious parents, as well as Kate, Doris, and Cleo, were pacing the floor outside the emergency room when the three girls were brought in. First, Terri and Sabrina were gently helped down out of the ambulance by the EMTs. Then Bev's gurney was rolled through the ER doors, and the two girls numbly followed their friend into the hospital. Gina Henderson, who had been among the parents waiting, quickly hurried after her stepdaughter's gurney, distressed by Bev's pale color.

Wordlessly, Sabrina hurried to her parents, wanting nothing more than for them to make what had happened go away. She knew it was impossible, but for now, she absorbed the loving concern that surrounded her as her family welcomed her back.

"Terri!" Margo Jeppson exclaimed, nearly squeezing the air out of her daughter.

"I'm sorry, Mom," Terri said, her voice muffled against her mother.

"I'm just glad you're okay," Margo murmured. She pulled Terri back to look her over. "Are you all right?"

"Yes," Terri answered, knowing the past twenty-four hours had shaped her into a different person. She had discovered a hidden strength, an inner peace she had never felt before. The testimony she had always believed had become very real. It burned within, revealing a powerful truth that would change the rest of her life. She was a child of God. He had helped her. Smiling at her mother, Terri wondered where this new awareness would take her.

Cleo stepped forward. "Terri . . . I . . . I can't tell you how sorry I am . . . about all of this."

"It wasn't your fault," Terri replied, glancing at the principal. "I should've said, 'No.'" She gave Cleo a discerning look. "Next time, I will."

Doris couldn't stop herself from grinning.

* * *

In the emergency room, as a nurse began cutting away Bev's pant leg, Gina tearfully smiled down at her stepdaughter. Sensing something was very wrong, she frowned. "Bev, what is it?"

Bev burst into tears again. "It's Karen," she sobbed. "They can't find her. Her father took her. He shot her. We heard the gun. He shot her. It's my fault. I took her up there. It's my fault."

Gina's mothering instinct overrode any past feelings of resentment or inadequacy. Leaning over the examination table, she gathered Bev into an intense embrace, ignoring Mabel's protests. Gina held Bev tightly, this troubled young woman who needed a mother. It was time she knew she had one. Time for Gina to step out of her husband's shadow before they lost their daughter forever.

CHAPTER 33

"Mom, there's something else I have to tell you," Sabrina said quietly. After hearing what Karen and Bev had been through, she was so grateful for the mother she had been blessed with. A mother who cared enough to set rules, who had always set a wonderful example. Sabrina ached inside, knowing how disappointed her mother would be to hear what she had to say about last night.

Sue smoothed Sabrina's hair back over her shoulder. Both were still in the emergency room, waiting for someone to give them permission to leave. Mike, Kate and Greg were out pacing in the hall. "Let's hear it," Sue replied, certain she already knew what her daughter was about to say.

"I really messed up," Sabrina tearfully confessed. "Bev brought a bottle of wine up with us last night. We didn't know she had until we were there . . . in that thicket. We'd all been talking about how rotten our lives were . . . but that's no excuse. I should've known better. Mom, I got drunk last night."

Sue allowed her daughter to sob for several minutes as she quietly waited, her arm around Sabrina's shoulders. Then, sensing this emotional storm was passing, she calmly discussed what would need to take place now. Sabrina needed to tell her father, someone who didn't know yet, and later, when they returned home to Bozeman, Sue would encourage her to meet with their branch president. Sabrina agreed to do both, promising her mother that she would never drink again.

"I hope not," Sue replied, smiling warmly at her youngest daughter. "Sometimes we all make mistakes. If you've learned from this one, we'll count our blessings."

"I've learned," Sabrina responded. "I've learned that it doesn't matter how strong you think you are, you can't ever let your guard down, not even once."

Sue tearfully nodded. She gave Sabrina another loving squeeze, then brought up another item that needed to be settled. "There is one other thing you need to do."

"What?"

"I want you to make up with Kate. She loves you so much! Your sister has worried herself sick over this. She hasn't been able to keep anything down all day."

As if on cue, Kate walked into the emergency room. "A nurse just came down and said we can take Sabrina home now."

Sabrina glanced at her mother, then at her sister. Their mother was right. Kate looked terrible. Slipping down off the examining table, Sabrina surprised her older sister, embracing her for the first time in nearly two years.

* * *

Edie anxiously paced the floor in her mother's hospital room. Karen had been found. She was all right. Brett was bringing her down from the forest. Edie knew Roger had been involved with her daughter's disappearance, but didn't know any of the details yet. Earlier, she had walked down the hall to see Bev, but by then, Karen's friend had fallen asleep. The pain pills had done an efficient job of helping the young woman relax. Bev's leg had been fractured in two places. It was now encased in a fluorescent pink cast, something the sixteen-year-old would wear for several weeks.

As Edie continued to pace back and forth, Adele spoke to her daughter firmly. "Come sit down and try to relax. You're making me nervous."

"I can't sit," Edie said, staring out the window again. Suddenly, she heard a familiar sound, a limping shuffle that told her the man she was growing to love was finally here. When he poked his head inside of the door, Edie flew across the room and into his arms. "Where is she?"

"In the emergency room," Brett replied, self-conscious about his dirty attire. He hadn't taken the time to change, instead bringing Karen straight to the hospital.

"Is she okay?" Edie asked, pulling back.

"She will be. She's asking for her mother."

Edie bit her bottom lip, tears appearing once again.

"I told her everything. Roger had filled her head with all kinds of lies, but I set her straight."

"And Roger—where is he now?"

Brett grinned. "Sleeping off a little something I took great delight in giving him." Unable to resist, he leaned forward bestowing a light kiss on Edie's soft cheek. "Your daughter awaits, ma'am," he said, his blue eyes twinkling.

Surprised by this gesture, Edie gazed at him. Then, she pulled him close for a lengthy kiss, one befitting a hero.

* * *

When Bev woke up, she had two surprises waiting for her. One was a giant stuffed bear her father had brought in to set in the corner of her hospital room. The other was a friend she thought she'd never see again in this world. "Karen?!" Bev cried out, reaching for the other girl.

Grinning, Karen sat down on the bed and returned Bev's intense hug. Both girls laughed and cried as they quickly caught each other up-to-date.

"So that's why your mom went into the bar?" Bev asked a few minutes later.

Karen nodded. "That creep, Roger," she fumed, determined to never call him "Dad" again, "told Mom if she didn't meet him there, he'd do something to me."

"She was trying to protect you," Bev contemplated.

"Yeah," Karen replied thickly, her heart still tender from the emotional roller-coaster she'd recently escaped.

"You know what I think?" Bev sighed.

"What?"

"We both have some pretty wonderful mothers."

Karen stared at her friend, surprised.

Outside in the hall, Edie and Gina tearfully smiled at each other, overhearing Bev's comment.

"In fact, that might make a wonderful editorial," Bev continued, snapping her fingers.

"Now what?" Karen asked, confused.

"Mothers—the real story."

"You can't be serious?"

"I am. I think it's high time we made some of these kids realize how important mothers are to our society."

Karen smiled in agreement. "But, after all of this, do you really think we'll still have a high school paper?"

"Doris was in here earlier. She said Cleo has enjoyed a healthy portion of humble pie the past couple of days. Our paper is one of the surest bets going in this town. She'll never shut it down."

Karen breathed a sigh of relief.

"Also, as managing editor, I'm assigning Terri to come up with a new column."

"Oh?" Karen asked, lifting an eyebrow.

Bev nodded. "I'll let her decide what she wants to do with it."

Rising, Karen walked over to examine Bev's IV.

"What are you doing?"

"Checking out what kind of drugs they're giving you in here," she teased, ducking when Bev threw a pillow at her. Laughing, Karen set the pillow on the end of the hospital bed and stepped out of the room. She walked over to her mother and slipped an arm around her waist. "Let's go home," she suggested.

Edie nodded in agreement. Arm in arm, the two of them walked down the hall.

EPILOGUE

June

Moving another box out of the way, Sabrina sat down on the couch beside Mike. Everyone was exhausted after this move.

Sabrina still couldn't believe everything that had happened the past few weeks. After talking things over, the Ericksons had decided that they liked what they had seen in this small Idaho town. Her dad had been toying with the idea of opening his own computer store for quite some time. He had pointed out that Blaketown needed just such a store, something to help it stay current with the computer age. Sue had been thrilled, certain this was the only way she would get to see much of her grandchildren, if that time ever came.

Sabrina had decided that Blaketown might be an all right place to finish high school, now that she had made some good friends. Things hadn't been so bad when she had returned to Bozeman; she probably could've made new friends there. But there was now a bond between herself, Karen, Terri, and Bev—something that seemed inclined to continue. They had kept in touch through phone calls and letters the past month while the Ericksons were getting ready to move. Bev was in counseling to wean herself away from alcohol. Karen suspected there would be a wedding in her family in the not-too-distant future, one that would supply her with a wonderful stepfather.

But Terri was the real surprise. She had changed so much it was almost scary. The time they had spent together in the forest had transformed her into a girl most people now admired. She still had her moments, but overall she was more mature, confident, and fun to be around.

Sabrina had also heard a couple of times from Marsha, who was still feeling like an outsider in her new location. Sabrina prayed that would change. She had recently sent Marsha a letter, informing her that Tracie was no longer a problem. Now that she was pregnant, Tracie's attention had been diverted from making others' lives miserable; she had made her own that way.

When her family had made the final decision to move, Sabrina's parents had been given permission to call Tyler to tell him the news. He had been shocked, but then agreed that if this move would benefit the entire family, it would be a good thing. As he pointed out, he would be heading back to college anyway when he came home from his mission.

Mike and Kate had been ecstatic, doing everything in their power to make this a smooth transition. They had located the perfect house not far from their duplex, an older brick home that had recently been remodeled inside. Sue, Greg, and Sabrina had loved it, proclaiming it "home."

Now they were finally here to stay. Everything had been unloaded from the moving van into their new house; they just had to unpack all of the boxes. At the moment, everyone was taking a lunch break, everyone but Kate. Still suffering from what Sabrina had decided must be a vicious flu bug, Kate had been throwing up throughout most of the day. As a result, their mother had gone to the local drugstore for something she thought would alleviate the problem. She was now back in the master bedroom with Kate.

"Is Kate feeling any better yet?" Greg asked, stepping back inside the house. He had elected to eat his hamburger and fries outside, enjoying the warm summer day.

"I don't know," Mike said, reaching for another fry. They had ordered lunch from the local drive-in, knowing everyone was too tired to worry about fixing meals. "I hope so. They've sure been back there a long time though," he added, glancing over his shoulder.

A few minutes later, Sue and Kate both appeared, each woman beaming with delight.

"Well, Dr. Erickson, your patient seems to be doing better," Mike observed.

"She is," Sue said, barely able to contain her excitement.

"What's wrong with her?" Sabrina asked, glancing at her mother and sister.

"Nothing eight more months won't cure," Kate bubbled, grinning at Mike.

"What?!" Mike and Greg exclaimed together. Dumbfounded by this news, they both stared.

"What?" Sabrina asked, not understanding.

"I'm gonna be a daddy?" Mike stammered.

"'Fraid so, Mikey. We just ran a test," Kate replied. Everyone watched in excited amusement as Mike ran across the cluttered room to whirl his wife around.

"I'm gonna be an aunt?" Sabrina excitedly asked.

When Mike released her, Kate smiled at her younger sister. "Yes, Breeny," she said softly.

Elated, Sabrina jumped up to give her sister a hug. "I can hardly wait to teach her all I know," she teased, drawing back to grin at Kate.

"Promise?" Kate asked.

Sabrina nodded. She would start by making sure her niece knew how wonderful Kate really was.

"Hey, what do you mean, 'her'?" Mike asked, indignantly. "That's my son you're talking about!"

"My grandson," Greg echoed, giving his oldest daughter a hug.

"You'd better have twins, dear, one of each," Sue suggested.

"Don't even think about wishing that on me," Kate replied. She then had an uncomfortable thought. Twins did run in their family. Aunt Paige had had twins. Paige's daughter, Tami, had had twins. Feeling slightly unwell, Kate sank down on the couch as everyone else began to laugh.

"It's a good thing we moved here," Sue continued. "You might need an extra hand." Patting Kate's shoulder, she grinned. Twins. Wouldn't that be something?

About the Author

A former resident of Ashton, Idaho, Cheri J. Crane graduated from Ricks College with plans to teach high school English, French, and drama. Instead of completing her degree at Brigham Young University, she married a sharp-looking returned missionary named Kennon. They made their home in Bennington, Idaho, where they now live with their three sons—Kris, Derek, and Devin.

Cheri enjoys numerous hobbies that include cooking, gardening, composing music, and participating in sports. She has spent most of her married life serving in the Primary and in the Young Women. She currently serves as a Primary teacher in her ward, working with the "pre-Beehives," as she calls them.

Cheri is the author of three best-selling young adult novels— *Kate's Turn, Kate's Return,* and *Forever Kate,* as well as a fourth novel, *The Fine Print.*